I0762024

ERA OF EVIL

SPENSER WARREN

First published in Chicago, IL, United States in 2019 by Pulse Pounding Publications

Library of Congress Control Number: 2019905598

ISBN: 978-1-7329901-6-6 (paperback)
ISBN: 978-1-7329901-7-3 (hardcover)
ISBN: 978-1-7329901-5-9 (ebook)

Cover design by: Matt Davies
Formatted by: Vellum

Version1

Will a hit man meet his end? Discover how to read your next Cal Boyle thriller — FREE!

Find out how to get your FREE copy of the Callahan Boyle prequel novella, *Marked for Murder*!

Read until the end to discover how to get your free copy of *Marked for Murder*, a book available only to my readers. *Marked for Murder* is an action-packed thriller that showcases one of Cal's first kills as a hit man in the Chicago mafia. I'm confident you'll love every page.

What happens when Cal kills the wrong man? From ferocious fist fights to careening car crashes, read as Cal navigates a burgeoning drug war between the Chicago mafia and a rival gang, whose leader is hellbent on ensuring Cal never sees another day. Will Cal find a way to take down his never-ending list of enemies?

Stay tuned for your exclusive offer to receive your FREE copy of Marked for Murder. Not only will you get your hands on a great read, you'll also be among the first to be notified of new releases by signing up for my "hit list." I'll keep the emails fast, friendly, and fun, and you can unsubscribe at any time.

Until then, I hope you enjoy *Era of Evil.*

For Nannie. Your consistent happiness and true-to-self nature inspires me.

1

Callahan Boyle slowed his jog along Pacific Beach in America's Finest City. He never imagined he'd be living in San Diego at any point in his life, yet here he was. With both Christmas and his thirtieth birthday approaching, he wasn't sure if he should be grateful he was avoiding another Chicago winter or relieved that he had Uncle Judd as the only family member he could turn to following his escape from the mob. Either way, his mood couldn't be described as merry or happy.

The gentle waves of the Pacific Ocean crashed against the sand. Families in wetsuits were laughing and enjoying the high-fifty-degree weather, glad they were able to surf and paddleboard so close to the holidays if they were locals, or excited to avoid the snow and icy roads of their less temperate homes if they were visiting.

Cal sighed as he spotted a group of college girls in jean shorts and bikini tops walking from the beach toward him. Even though the weather wasn't frigid, Cal couldn't understand how the young women were comfortable in the tiny clothing. He would normally wear a winter coat and perhaps long johns underneath his jeans at this time of year. Despite being away from Chicago's hellish winters, Cal was still clothed in one of his uncle's blue multicolored drug rugs and a pair of tan cargo pants.

One of the girls, a blonde with windswept wet hair and a seashell necklace, smiled at him. Normally, Cal would've smiled back. He was an attractive man and stood a tall six feet three inches, with brown hair and calming but fierce brown eyes. His only blemish was a scar just below his right ear from where his drunken father slashed him in a fit of rage when Cal was just a boy. But this time Cal had no desire to flirt with the girl, attractive as she was. He felt dead inside and was still awash in grief at the loss of Maria.

Cal wasn't the romantic type, and it had been a year into their relationship before he told Maria he loved her, but he realized now that she was his one true love. She was passionate, she was comforting, she was independent, but most importantly, she was patient. Despite Cal's mountain of faults, she'd stuck with him until the end. The end that was brought about when he was unable to save her.

He couldn't believe he put down Vinnie's gun after he thought he'd finally vanquished his adoptive father, mafia boss Alfredo Petrocelli. Had he done exactly what he'd been trained to do as a hit man—not put the gun down until he knew his foe was eliminated—he and Maria would still be together, and Alfredo would be dead. He'd likely be on the run, but he'd have his love by his side.

Cal wondered what else he could've done, what other avenues he could've pursued to ensure Maria lived that night, but he'd already exhausted all of the possibilities. The only thing he could've done differently was to leave the mob way before the Caruso business started, way before he met her.

Maria had been one of the reasons—perhaps the biggest reason aside from discovering the truth about his mother's death—that Cal chose to leave the mafia in the first place. Yes, he realized his desire to stop killing for pay, but he never would've found the courage to ask Alfredo to leave when he did had it not been for her.

Cal's heart remained stricken with grief, and his burden didn't feel any lighter as he looked out onto the beach. The morning clouds had yet to part, meaning the typical Southern California sunshine had yet to appear over the sand. Cal noticed the group of girls had stopped their approach. A beer-bellied man around Cal's height in a white tank top and open red button-down shirt was talking to them. He was paying particular attention to the blonde who had smiled at Cal. Cal could tell from the furrowing of their brows and wideness of their eyes that they weren't pleased the man was talking to them. The two girls flanking the blonde seemed unsure if they should make a run for it or stay and support their friend.

Cal stepped forward, his eyes trained on the uneasy young women. He hoped their gazes would meet, and they would see in his eyes that he sensed their pain and was ready to help. One of them, a black girl in an orange bikini top and faded denim shorts, looked at Cal with hesitation and turned toward her friend, who seemed on the verge of exasperation talking to the man. Even from a hundred feet away, Cal could decipher from the man's slurred speech that he was drunk. It wasn't even ten in the morning.

"Hold on, pretty little lady, I'm just trying to talk to you," the man shouted.

The girls darted toward Cal. The man stumbled after them. Now that the man was drawing closer, Cal realized the drunken beachgoer had a striking resemblance to Alfredo Petrocelli.

"Get back here, ma'am."

The girls broke into a full-on sprint. The drunk continued his pursuit and wheezed as his feet swept through the sand in an effort to catch up. He reached out and caught the blonde's right arm. She pumped her legs, struggling to escape his grip, but the man had both hands around her wrist and his feet set in the sand. There was little stopping him.

The girl screamed as her friends kept running, scampering past Cal. His eyes hardened as he turned back to look at them. They were too scared to ask for help. Cal knew he had to act fast. But what approach would he take? He'd promised Maria to continue down the path of good, leaving his previously violent instincts off the table. He could shout at the man to stop, hoping that, when combined with the girl's screams, it would motivate the other beachgoers into action.

It was the drunk's striking resemblance to Alfredo that caused his blood to boil and his mind-set to default to violence. He saw the same brown hair with gray streaks, the same bulging arms and shoulders, and the same devilish smile with wide white teeth that Alfredo had. Cal felt a rage build from his feet, through his legs, into his chest, and radiate into his arms. The tension escalated to a boiling point at the top of his head.

Almost as if he were on autopilot, Cal's protector instincts kicked into gear. He was off, racing toward the girl, ready to save her. There was no time for words, no time for diplomacy. Cal was determined to beat the shit out of the drunken man, to have at him as if he were pummeling Alfredo.

As Cal charged and his eyes met the drunk's, he noticed the morning boozer refused to loosen his grip on the girl. Cal had covered the distance between them rapidly, the pile of sand he ran through not even fazing him. His fist was raised, ready to strike. A blend of confusion and terror was written on the blonde girl's face. He just hoped her reflexes were quicker than that of the drunken man.

"Duck!"

In a flash, the girl dived for the sand below, the drunken man loosened his grip, and Cal's fist collided with the left side of his jaw. He was down on the ground in an instant and Cal was on top of him.

Cal's fist slammed into the man's head again. This time the man cried out in pain, and Cal heard the crunching of bone beneath his punches. Seeing Alfredo's face beneath him, Cal showed no mercy. His knuckle-clenched hands flew back and forth across his victim's face. The other beachgoers ran over to watch. Out of the corner of his eye, Cal saw the girl stand from the sand and collect herself, a smile shining across her face.

Cal grabbed the man by his shirt collar and looked into his slits for eyes, which became smaller by the second as his cheeks swelled.

"You thought you could get away with it? You thought you could take Maria from me and not expect to face me? Well, you were wrong."

Cal stopped his punches and realized every set of eyes on the beach was glued to him. The drunk slipped from Cal's grip, and his head collapsed into the sand. Cal knew he had to get out of there before the cops found out what happened. He'd done his part in saving the girl, but he couldn't take the fall for beating up the bad guy. One major slipup and he knew he would be in serious trouble.

Cal rose to his feet, brushed off the sand from his pants, and smiled at the girl. She winked at him, perhaps ready to resume what Cal had thought of as her attempt to flirt with him earlier. Cal could only nod, running off in the direction in which he'd come, ignoring the cries—some of support—of the beachgoers behind him.

Cal kept running as fast as he could through the sand and up to the rock leading to the beach's parking lot. He was ready to do whatever it took to get off of the beach without facing prosecution. He took one last look over his shoulder and saw that the commotion had stopped. He turned to face the other direction, but before he saw what it was, he knew he had hit something hard.

He'd struck the muscled pectorals of a San Diego police officer.

2

From the moment his wife, Susan, had told him he'd become a father, Alfredo Petrocelli had a lot of inklings about what being a dad would be like. Not once did he ever envision the scene before him—the marked gravestones of his two children. Luca had been dead for years, during which time Alfredo had grown used to the gentle ache of his youngest son's absence from his life. Yet it was the loss of his oldest son, Vinnie, whose death occurred just three months ago, that wrenched at him the most.

He remembered his smiling boys, how happy they were in their early years. The gently falling snow and mass of cold mush piled gently beside his boots reminded Alfredo of the fateful family ski trip nearly twenty years ago to Breckenridge, a vacation the family planned to never forget. Little did he know that the trip would be embedded in his memory for all the wrong reasons.

Alfredo shivered into the warmth of his coat at the recollection of the horrible accident leading to his youngest son's death. He stiffened his neck to combat the movement of the icy wind whipping at his face. The only warmth his sons felt now was whatever cushioning surrounded their dead bodies in the finely adorned caskets buried beneath the icy ground.

The wind passed, and Alfredo's cheeks turned a shade less rosy as he chose to focus on happier times. He remembered two years before Luca's death when an eight-year-old Vinnie gently guided his younger brother with a confident hand on his back as Luca rode his little bicycle without training wheels through the quiet streets of their Evanston neighborhood. Seeing Luca's slightly fearful yet joyous smile and hearing Vinnie's innocent laughs warmed Alfredo's wounded heart.

It was commonplace for most siblings to fight and vie for attention to the exclusion of loving relations. Alfredo and his oldest brother fought all the time as kids, always arguing over which toy belonged to whom, but that wasn't the case with his two boys. He and his wife, Susan, raised two gentle boys who got along with all the other children in the neighborhood, despite the family's mafia ties.

Alfredo scanned his brain for more happy memories, hoping to recall the fond games of catch he played with both of his children, or the time he encouraged the two of them to start their own lemonade stand and get their entrepreneurial feet wet before moving into the family business when they got older. Perhaps it was the harsh temperatures chilling his brain and slowing its function, or maybe his age was catching up to him, but he failed to recall any such memories. Sure, he'd played catch once or twice with Vinnie when he played for his middle school baseball team and had shot some HORSE before Vinnie tried out for the high school basketball team, but Alfredo was disappointed to remember those few memories as the extent of his early bonding experiences with his sons.

The time period had been a crucial one in his mafia career, a time where his father, Louie, then boss of the Chicago mafia, had agreed to let the family expand its fledgling drug empire into more neighborhoods. As new underboss of the family, it was Alfredo's job to lead the capos in securing new territories, distribution, and warehousing of drugs the mafia wanted to flood the market with. It was a significant expansion, and something Alfredo felt only he could do. The cash flow from the new drug markets would more than set him and his family up for life, even if the family cashed out after a few years.

Even if he had felt only he was capable of achieving the mafia's drug aims, Alfredo felt a pang of guilt that he'd been so focused on money and growing his power within the mafia as opposed to being present with his children. He felt the family ski trip was his first step in the direction of committing to be the father he always wanted to be, more loving than his own father. Yet after Luca's death, Alfredo went back to being Mr. Businessman.

The mob boss wondered what he could've done differently if he had the chance. If he'd spent more time with his children in their formative years, would Luca or Vinnie still be alive?

Alfredo stood at the graves, just one tiny plot of the larger section of Andersonville's Rosehill Cemetery in which the Petrocelli family and close friends had been laid to rest. Alfredo's good buddy Frankie Ramone had been buried a few yards away at the same time Vinnie went into the ground. To the south, Al Meransky's wife and young children buried the former North Side capo at Graceland Cemetery.

Alfredo grit his teeth and held his jaw firm as he thought of the great source of his frustration, the very reason he was standing above his oldest son's grave: Callahan Boyle.

It was a few years after Luca's death when Alfredo and Susan decided to take in the young boy, who was fast friends with Vinnie from their time playing at the South Side drug warehouse Alfredo oversaw. Alfredo was hesitant to do it at first, as the boy still had a loving mother after his father's accidental murder at Alfredo's behest. But seeing the void in his wife's heart, and after witnessing the power of the young boy in pushing another youngster over the warehouse catwalk railing to his death, Alfredo knew he wouldn't regret the decision to have Cal's mother killed in a car accident.

Cal grew up as a nice boy and successful athlete, much like Vinnie had been as a youngster. But Alfredo's earlier suspicion of Cal's violent nature was proven correct when Cal grew to become the most dangerous hit man of not only the Chicago mafia, but of any American mafia to boot. What a great decision it had been. So many of Alfredo's enemies were vanquished as a result of Cal's efforts. He had no idea that one day the decision would prove detrimental to his own family and that he'd lose his only living son and heir because of it. For the first time in nearly fifty years, a member of the Petrocelli family wasn't available to succeed the existing boss of the Chicago mafia.

As he looked upon his children's graves one final time before turning toward the running car waiting to take him to his latest doctor's appointment following his near murder at Cal's hand, Alfredo wondered if he'd been too kind to the boy. If he'd reserved more of his love for Vinnie, which admittedly had been hard for him given the high expectations he had for his son, maybe he wouldn't feel so shitty about his failings as a father.

He shouldn't have given the boy so much confidence. He

should have only used him as a tool for killing, as he ultimately realized too late. He could've kept the boy in Vinnie's life by letting them play as friends and could've let him live with his mother, only plucking him away and into the mafia when the time was right. Alfredo felt the anger well up inside of him at the thought of Cal getting the best of him.

Looking back, Alfredo concluded that Cal ultimately had done more harm than good. He wasn't even the bastard responsible for the death of Alfredo's most dangerous enemy to date, former Chicago mayor Ross Caruso. Instead, he'd lain waste to not only Alfredo's only living son but also his North Side capo, Al Meransky, and countless other men. The mafia power structure that Alfredo had worked so hard to build and maintain over his last five years as boss was crumbling beneath him.

Ignoring the call of his driver, Alfredo walked back to the graves of his children and placed a large paw on each of their tombstones. He couldn't let Cal Boyle get the better of his family or the Chicago mafia any longer. He was tired of answering police questions and waiting for them to see if they could find Cal, wherever he was hiding. He was tired of the doctor's appointments to examine his chest and lungs, thanks to the collapsed lung and subsequent thoracostomy from Cal's gunshot to the chest. He was tired of searching far and wide for respectable leaders to fill the void left by Vinnie, Meransky, and Frankie Ramone. He was going to take his power back. He was going to get his revenge.

Alfredo shed one more tear at the thought of his sons no longer being there. Most importantly, he didn't want Vinnie's death to be in vain. Alfredo bowed his head and exhaled, letting the frustration out of his body in his long release of breath.

"Sons, I swear to you that I will kill Callahan Boyle. I was foolish to think he could replace you, Luca, my sweet, sweet boy. Vin, I regret any point in your life where you thought I loved Cal more than you. I never did."

Alfredo looked up at the white expanse of snow blanketing the cemetery grounds and huddled for warmth beneath his coat. As cold as he was, he had to finish telling his sons his plans. Even if they would never hear him, he had to make sure their spirits knew how he felt.

"By the time I visit you again, once the grounds have thawed and the spring flowers bloom, Cal Boyle will be buried in his own grave. And I'll be the one that put him there."

Alfredo bowed toward the ground again, tapped the top of each of his son's graves, said a little prayer to himself, and made the slow walk back to the car. Alfredo had wanted many men dead in his lifetime, but he knew now that he'd never wanted anyone to die as much as Callahan Boyle.

3

Ignoring the repeated vibrations of the cell phone on her desk, Chicago police detective Brittany Wilson glanced at the application on her computer screen. It was the moment of truth. In just a few moments, she'd finally submit her application for the job she'd dreamed of holding since entering her criminal justice program in college—her application to become an FBI special agent.

There was nothing more she wanted in life than this. From harrowing patrol assignments in Austin as a rookie police officer under the guidance of the world's most perverted field training officer, to getting shot at on the way to a domestic violence call in West Garfield Park, to watching as her first partner was stabbed to death in front of her eyes by a junkie informant turned traitor in Logan Square, all of those tough moments as a Chicago police officer were worth it. The late nights, the sacrifices to earn her first promotion to detective at the young age of twenty-six, everything had prepared her for this next big step in her career—getting into the FBI.

Brittany moved her mouse over the "Submit" button, her

heart drumming faster than the grand finale of a fireworks show. Her desk vibrated again, three hurried drones of interruption shifting her focus away from the screen. She darted her eyes to her phone and saw that she'd missed several text messages from the man who'd requested her assistance on what could turn out to be the biggest case of her career, Lieutenant Mick Fisher. Fisher and the detectives assigned to what was being called the Chicago Warehouse Murders case had struggled to gain much traction in the three months since the killings.

The application would have to wait. Brittany stood from her desk, locked her computer screen, and headed for the hallway, avoiding the gazes of her surely jealous fellow officers in the Organized Crime Bureau, wondering how she got the Detectives Bureau to pull her in for one of the most critical cases in the current dossier of the Chicago Police Department.

She smiled, knowing that they were just jealous of her success. Her tenacity had served her well, and at the age of twenty-eight, Brittany could have any career path she wanted in the Chicago PD, though her sights were set much higher.

Brittany finally arrived outside the small office where Lieutenant Fisher sat. The man was in his midfifties, with thinning black hair, slicked back with far too much gel, adding as much to the volume of his hair as to its stickiness. His head was buried in his large left hand, and a loud exhale hung in the air, filling the silence of the room. Brittany wasn't sure if she should knock or sit down straight away, seeing as she was already late.

Fisher eventually looked up, gazed around his cluttered office, and beckoned Brittany inside. The entire perimeter of the office was covered in a combination of bookshelves and stacks of files, papers desperately trying to burst out of crumpled manila folders. Her new boss's desk was covered with books, more case files, and family portraits. Brittany was surprised the two chairs opposite the desk had little more than a winter coat slumped lazily across the backs of both of them.

Brittany entered the room, looked around, then settled her gaze on Mick Fisher. She wanted to take a seat but didn't want to get on the man's bad side by casually strolling in uninvited.

"Sit down, Wilson," Fisher finally summoned as he leaned back in his chair.

Brittany did as commanded, careful to smooth her skirt as she sat in the chair closest to the hallway. There was the tiniest smidgen of room for her to rest her foolscap pad of paper in case she needed to make detailed notes. She was sure the man they called Lieutenant Lunatic for his occasional outbursts at his subordinates would throw a lot at her in their meeting.

"Let's get started, shall we? Since you're already late." Fisher looked at Brittany with an expression bordering on teasing and disdain before glancing down at a stack of papers on his desk. "It's good to have you on the team for this one, Detective. Lieutenant Hollins at the Organized Crime Bureau really raved about you. Says your work in getting the mother of those two boys that were killed to speak out against the Kush Street Gang got them two solid convictions of guys that should've been off the street years ago."

Brittany batted her eyelids and found herself blushing, an orange-red tinge brightening the cheeks of her rich sepia skin. "Well, thank you, sir. It was tough work, but I've found that always being willing to offer a listening ear really gets people to trust you."

Fisher nodded, seemingly impressed. "Yes, that does seem to do the trick. Say, Wilson, I also heard from Lieutenant Hollins that you've got a vacation coming up. Not exactly the best time to be taking off, Christmas or not. This case is getting colder than my ass after standing outside for ten minutes scraping all the ice off of my car."

Brittany gulped, unsure why Fisher was calling her out for the vacation she'd more than earned. She couldn't remember the last day she'd taken off the job, with all the cases she'd helped her team clear over the past six months. Rest and relaxation were foreign concepts to her. Brittany's thoughts returned to the unsubmitted FBI application awaiting her at her computer, and she felt like giving in.

"I can postpone it if I really need to, sir. There's nothing more I want than to help you find the man who committed all of these murders, especially if it ties to some of those bigger cases . . ."

"Relax." The lieutenant smiled, his yellowed teeth shocking between flaky, chapped rose lips. "Everyone needs a little R & R every now and then. But after this meeting, and taking a little time off, I expect you to know this case backward and forward. Understood?"

Feeling her confidence growing, Brittany straightened up in her chair, accidentally knocking the coat to the floor. A slight worry filled her mind before she could shake the thought away and focus on Fisher.

"Absolutely. They don't call me the best detective in my bureau for nothing."

Fisher smiled and put on a smudgy pair of wire-rim glasses. "That's what I like to hear. If you can help us crack this case, Wilson, you'll really be going places."

"Should we start there, then?" Brittany asked, clicking her pen and setting her pad of paper on the desk in front of her, doing her best to take control of the conversation. "What's happened so far, and what's your team discovered?"

The lieutenant looked around, found a stack of papers on the far corner of his desk, and offered it to Brittany. She accepted, trying to keep the entire mass of papers in the haphazard order they were in, setting them down on the open seat beside her.

"That's everything right there. We've been on this case three months, Detective. Almost three months to the day since the Chicago Warehouse Murders took place. All we've got to show for it is a murder weapon, a bunch of dead bodies, and some flaky witnesses. Got no real leads on a suspect."

Britany reviewed the first piece of paper in the stack and saw the image of a Beretta M9, tagged as evidence.

"I'd say that's a start, at least. Is the Beretta the murder weapon?"

"Yeah, it is," Fisher said. "Found it lying in the warehouse on the night of the murders. Used to gun down about a dozen men inside and outside the facility. They were mobsters. We spoke with Alfredo Petrocelli, the known boss of the Chicago mafia, a month after the events happened. He was there that night, shot in the chest. It was a miracle he survived."

Brittany was surprised she hadn't heard these details about the case. "Mobsters? Was this some kind of gang war? Surely the Organized Crime Bureau would've heard about it."

"No, this wasn't some turf war. This was an intra-mafia battle. Petrocelli's kid, Vinnie, was one of the victims. The way old Alfredo told the story is that his son and some of his mafia buddies liked this low-level soldier's girlfriend. They took her to this warehouse to have some fun with her. Alfredo got wind of it and showed up with a cop friend of his, who was one of the bodies we found, to stop Vinnie before this soldier came to blow them all away. Obviously, given that we're investigating this case, that didn't happen."

"So this guy shows up to the warehouse. He was able to take out almost a dozen guys, including a Chicago cop?"

Fisher leaned back in his chair and removed his glasses. "Right on. Don't lose too much sleep over the guy, though. Captain Joe Blutarski was a crooked son of a bitch—probably on the mafia payroll for all we know. We asked Alfredo who the shooter was, but the boss says he'd never seen him before. I don't buy that for a second, but that's what he told our guys. He gave us an idea of what he looked like, though. Tall guy, brown hair, brown eyes, had some stubble. Not much other than that."

Something wasn't adding up to Brittany. Why would the Chicago PD go to such lengths to investigate a series of murders due to some inner mafia turmoil? Murder was murder, but it didn't seem to make sense for Fisher's team, and not her own, to be on this case.

"No offense, sir, but why do we care if this guy killed a bunch of his fellow mafiosos?"

"Great question. We care because of what our firearms examination unit was able to uncover. They compared the rounds found at the scene, both shell casings and in some of the victims, with the barrel of the Beretta. They then compared the same grooves in the barrel of the Beretta with bullet markings found in other crime scenes, including other crimes with mafia ties. Three guys were killed at the Petrocelli place in Evanston that night, including a high-ranking mafia member. A few weeks before, Mayor Caruso is murdered in what some believe was a revenge killing by the mafia. While we don't think this renegade soldier killed the mayor, we know that this Beretta was used at both of those crime scenes.

"This isn't just an intra-mafia dispute we're interested in solving, Wilson. This is something bigger. Whoever killed all these mobsters just to get his girlfriend back probably killed a hell of a lot of other people too. That type of person is dangerous. Not the kind of guy we want roaming the streets of Chicago."

Brittany nodded, realizing the gravity of the situation. So many questions were churning in her mind. She had a hard time believing Fisher's unit had stopped there. They had a weapon, they had a reason to believe the crimes were committed by the same person, they had a high-profile witness, but why didn't they have any leads?

"So let's get back to this guy," Brittany said. "Alfredo Petrocelli only provided a physical description? He'd never seen him before?"

Fisher cleared his throat and put the glasses back on. He looked out of the window of his office, blinds covered in dust preventing either of them from seeing much of the chilly December morning.

"That's all he gave us. Like I said, I think it's bullshit. But the guy clearly wasn't a fan of the Petrocellis if he laid waste to Vinnie and his buddies and almost took Alfredo out to boot."

"He said nothing about distinguishing features? There could be tens of thousands of men in the greater Chicagoland area fitting that description."

Fisher scratched behind his ear. "There might have been one distinguishing feature, something about a scar. It's not top of mind right now, but it oughta be in the case file."

"What about the girlfriend?" Brittany asked. "Did she take off with the alleged killer?"

The lieutenant sighed and pointed to the stack of papers next to Brittany. "That's the sad part. She got out of the warehouse, but we later found her deceased in a parking lot a mile or so away. We're not sure how she got there, but she suffered multiple gunshot wounds to her back."

Brittany wasn't fazed by the revelation. As a rookie patrol officer, she remembered vividly clasping her hand over her mouth when she heard that an entire family—a young mother and two young girls—had been the victims of a murder-suicide. Given all she'd seen in over six years on the force, nothing could trigger her so easily anymore.

"I see. So it's possible he could've killed her?"

"It's possible, I suppose, but I doubt it," Fisher said. "There was blood at the scene that makes us suspect there was another person there. Maybe a struggle between our killer and another person."

Brittany jotted this down on her pad. She had many more questions but figured she'd have a long night ahead of her going through the case notes.

"What about the other crimes? Did anyone see a man fitting the description Alfredo Petrocelli provided?"

Fisher let out a quick laugh before shifting forward in his seat, a measure of severity forcing his face still. "We might have an idea, but the witnesses we questioned at the Caruso murder scene and the Petrocelli Evanston residence scene have conveniently gone missing."

"Foul play?"

"Tough to say. But it's awfully suspicious that we had no problem questioning them before we got to Alfredo Petrocelli. Since then we haven't been able to reach them."

Brittany knew that was where she needed to start. She

wrote the words "find witnesses" in big block lettering at the top of her paper. Until she found them and got them to talk, she was afraid there wasn't much she could do, unless the suspect magically fell into their lap.

"Is there anything else, sir? I want to get a head start on reviewing these files so I can give you some recommendations when I come back."

"That's the important stuff, Wilson. If you can pull off your usual magic and find these witnesses, or even get Petrocelli to talk, we'll be in business."

Brittany smiled and stood from her chair, thanking Lieutenant Fisher and collecting her massive copy of the case file. As much as she needed some time off for Christmas, her heart thumped at the prospect of taking on and solving this case. If she did, there would be nothing stopping her from realizing her dream.

FBI, here we come.

4

Cal figured that one day he'd end up in the slammer. When he first started working for the mob, it was an understood part of the job—the chance for arrest was always high. Now that he was no longer bound by the law of omertà, he was more willing to open up to the police about what happened. He wanted to explain to the officers that he was in the right. He was only protecting the women from a creepy old man who got his jollies from making them uncomfortable.

Throughout the booking process, his arresting officer was having none of it. The drunken man Cal had pummeled was arrested for assault and battery himself after more police arrived and discussed the incident with the girls and other witnesses.

Cal was frustrated with himself for acting in the manner he did. He didn't have an alternate ID in San Diego, so he was booked under his own name. If the Chicago PD had him on their radar at all, they'd eventually discover he'd been arrested and would be swooping in on him as soon as they could.

He was pleasantly surprised after his swift hearing at the district court that his handcuffs were removed upon being placed in the small holding cell at the San Diego Police Department's Northern Division, especially given his assault on the drunken man. If he was indeed wanted elsewhere, he suspected much worse would've been said or done to him.

Cal sat on the small bed in his cell and leaned back against the wall, reflecting on the crime that put him here and all of the other crimes he'd committed over the years.

The thought of all the killings he'd committed under Alfredo Petrocelli's watch made him sick. Serving multiple life sentences wouldn't have been enough to make up for the lives of the people he killed, even if some of them were scumbags more evil than him. Part of him wanted to confess, to admit to the officer that he was much more than he was suspected of being, but he couldn't find the nerve to do it.

He closed his eyes for what seemed like hours but in reality was only minutes. When his eyes reopened, he saw his arresting officer, a tall man with bulging pectorals and biceps rippling beneath his police uniform. His black pants didn't have a hint of a wrinkle. His mocha skin shined even in the dim light of the jail. Cal realized, based on the man's physique, just how he was knocked off of his feet after running into him as he attempted to escape the beach.

Behind the officer was Cal's uncle, Judd Russell. Uncle Judd was his mother's older brother, who fled town after her funeral. Ever since Cal left Chicago for the safety of his uncle's home in San Diego, Judd was constantly apologizing for leaving Cal behind to stay with the Petrocellis. Cal assured him it was nothing to worry about and that he wasn't psychologically damaged from growing up with the mafia family instead of his uncle. That didn't stop Judd from being overly concerned about Cal's well-being.

Judd was dressed in what many outside of California would consider a flamboyant fashion but was just another day in the Judd Russell wardrobe experience. He was wearing a partially unbuttoned paisley blue short-sleeved shirt, purple khaki shorts, and matching flip-flops. In his hand, Judd carried a straw hat to round out the look. While his gray hair and goatee signified his age, his dress displayed the goofy youthfulness that those closest to him loved about him.

"Here he is, sir," the officer said, turning toward Uncle Judd. "Just make sure you sign him out at the desk now that bail has been taken care of."

Uncle Judd could only nod as the officer unlocked Cal's cell and watched closely as Cal followed Uncle Judd down the hallway and out to the desk. The attending officer gave Cal his cell phone, wallet, and keys, and Cal signed for everything before following Uncle Judd to the car. His uncle hadn't said anything yet, but Cal knew he would pipe up sooner or later.

They both sat in the front seat of a spotless gold 1967 Chevy Camaro. Judd looked in the rearview mirror and took a comb from his shirt's breast pocket. Cal expected his uncle to fix his hair into place, but instead Uncle Judd took the comb to his salt-and-pepper chest hair, which was threatening to spill down the front of his shirt.

"There, that's better."

Uncle Judd started the car and reversed out of the parking space. They'd left the parking lot and were driving down Eastgate Mall before either of them spoke again.

"You wanna tell me why you beat up that old man?"

Cal sighed. As much as he'd come to love and respect his

uncle in the near-three months they'd spent together, he was far too old for a lecture. He knew what he'd done, and while he had his regrets, he wasn't going to admit as much to his uncle.

"To be fair, he wasn't that old. There was a young girl that needed my help, so I helped her. Isn't that a good thing?"

Uncle Judd laughed and put the straw hat back on his head. He looked completely ridiculous. "Is that what you think is good? Beating a man to a pulp?"

"Probably not. But it seemed like a good idea at the time."

Judd shook his head and remained silent as they turned onto the 805, heading for home. Cal didn't want to think about his actions anymore. He just wanted to sit outside and feel the gentle ocean breeze from his uncle's backyard.

"You've got to be more careful, Cal," his uncle continued. "You're safe here right now for a reason. If you pull more shit like you did today, it's only a matter of time before the cops knock on my door looking for you. I don't agree with the choices you made in your past, but I feel awful about leaving you in Chicago with those mafia monsters to begin with."

Here we go again with the apologies.

"I thought we agreed to move forward, Cal. You were going to start getting out there and making a new life for yourself. But instead you do nothing but mope around all day. I lost someone I loved once too. It's heartbreaking. At some point, though, the rubber meets the road and you have to move on."

Cal looked out of the passenger window and rolled his eyes, but he knew his uncle was right. He'd harbored the guilt he felt over Maria's death for a long time. Without his girlfriend's love, Cal felt empty and emotionless the entire time he'd been staying with his uncle. He knew he needed to move forward, but could he?

It would take time for the sense of grief he felt to go away. After all, he was solely responsible for protecting Maria, and he had failed. It didn't help matters that beating up the drunk renewed a feeling he'd only vaguely acknowledged over the last few months: his desire to go after Alfredo.

Hearing the drunk's face crack beneath his fist made him feel good in the moment. It made him feel like he was making Alfredo pay for what he did to Maria. But how could he move forward now, as his uncle had said, when this desire was building stronger and stronger in his mind? Cal didn't see a way past it. He knew he couldn't tell Uncle Judd how he felt. It would only disappoint him.

Still, he realized the need to acknowledge his uncle's concerns. He turned toward Judd, and their eyes met. A deep sense of concern was apparent in Judd's expression. Cal was ready to speak when suddenly a loud smack shook their small car and pushed them toward the curb.

"What the hell was that?"

Cal turned back toward the rear window, wondering what it was that hit them with such force. The Camaro may have been old, but it was a solidly built car. Whatever hit them must have been packing some serious size.

Sure enough, Cal saw a Ford F-350 with a large grille guard back away from the vehicle and speed off to the left. Cal couldn't get a great look at the driver, and there was no way to assess the damage to the car until he stepped outside, but based on the head-ringing impact of the hit and shooting pain he felt in his back, he knew it had to be substantial.

He saw a man in the passenger side of the vehicle as it sped past. The man was bald and had a sneering expression through his jet-black goatee. Cal didn't like the look of him. It was almost as if the accident was intentional. Cal turned to Uncle Judd, who looked as rattled as Cal had ever seen him. Judd shifted the Camaro to neutral, released the clutch, and put on the brake.

A few cars honked at the stopped Camaro, which had one of its wheels on the curb from the force of the impact. Cal wanted to tell them off, but his more immediate concern was for Uncle Judd.

"Are you alright?" Cal placed his hand on his uncle's shoulder, concerned that he'd suffered a much worse fate than the sharp pains Cal felt in his own body.

"Yeah, yeah, I'll be fine. I guess we'll have to deal with the cops yet again, won't we? How are you holding up?"

"I've suffered worse. Remember how many times I've been shot?"

While his uncle took out his cell phone and called the police, Cal wondered if the accident was a result of a random driver who wasn't paying attention or if it had been the calculated effort of a professional toughie. Was someone trying to send a message?

Was it a friend of the drunken man Cal attacked earlier in the day? Or was it someone connected with the mafia? Had Cal been found?

Either way, Cal knew he couldn't remain passive. He had to find a way to put the pressure on Alfredo. He needed to configure a plan to get his revenge.

5

After the events of the day, Brittany Wilson needed a drink. But first she needed to make a phone call. Anytime Brittany had a major case to think through, she called her former boyfriend, and current San Diego police officer, Drew Mendelson, to review her theories.

She wasn't sure if their conversations ever made a lick of difference in her ability to solve crimes, but she liked to think of her calls with her ex as a positive force. As the old saying went, "If it ain't broke, don't fix it." In a way she missed their old conversations, before the collegial phone banter. She missed him.

Brittany poured herself a glass of merlot for instant consumption as soon as she got off the phone and walked across the wood floor of her kitchen to the carpeted living room before crashing on her black leather sectional sofa. It was way more furniture than she needed as a single woman, but it was great for entertaining.

She pulled out her cell phone from the pocket of her sweats and put the phone to her ear after dialing Drew's number. If he was still on duty, she knew he'd chew her out. But she couldn't help but call him now. She needed to find a lead in this case, and only Drew could test her harebrained theories.

"Well, hello, miss," a silky smooth voice said. She loved the way his sultry tone moved throughout her eardrums. It was just like the way his body felt when it moved against hers.

"I thought I told you no more calling when I'm on duty."

Drew's warning triggered Brittany back to reality and away from her bedroom fantasies.

"I know, I'm sorry. It's just I really think I've got a big one this time, the biggest case of my career. It's make or break, Drew. You're the only one I can talk with about this outside of the Chicago PD."

Drew chuckled. "Oh really? There's no new beau in your life?"

Brittany smiled into the phone. She wished she'd grabbed her glass of merlot from the kitchen so she could loosen up a bit. She wanted to let her flirtatious side run wild.

"No, there's no one in my life. I'm perpetually single. I basically have been since you left me for paradise."

"C'mon, Britt. You're telling me there's been nobody? And let's not confuse who left who here."

It was true: Brittany had been the one to dump Drew. When she began pushing for a promotion to detective, Brittany didn't have time for distractions. Her relationship with Drew, a fellow patrol officer, had to end. Drew eventually transferred to the police force in his father's hometown of Carlsbad before joining the San Diego police force last year. Brittany had been with men since the breakup, but those were one-night stands, nothing more serious than a dinner or cocktail date and a tumble or two between the sheets.

"Let's get back on subject," Brittany continued. "All I've got in this case is a vague description of a potential suspect from a corrupt mafia boss, a murder weapon connected to multiple crimes, and some witnesses no one's been able to talk to since the mafia boss was interviewed. I know I need to find these witnesses, but I'm not sure where to start."

Brittany gave Drew the overview of the case once he asked her to backtrack. Drew clicked his teeth. It was a habit Brittany couldn't stand when they were dating, and she found it even more annoying now. When Drew didn't say anything, Brittany felt compelled to continue.

"There's no way Alfredo Petrocelli can't know the identity of this soldier if Vinnie Petrocelli targeted the guy's girlfriend for his game of fun. Furthermore, he had to have known who else was involved at the Caruso murder scene, since there's the weapon connection, so I figure it's gotta be someone close to him. Someone he could be trying to protect. I know Vinnie died in that warehouse shoot-out but—"

"Whoa, whoa, whoa, take it easy. Listen to you, Britt. There's a whole lot of theories there. You don't know if Alfredo knew anything about Mayor Caruso's murder. What happened to your investigative instincts? Trusting only facts?"

"Damn it, I guess you're right. Sometimes I just have to go with my instincts long enough until I find the facts."

"That's just the thing," Drew said. "What makes you think this soldier was close to Petrocelli? There's a chain of command in the mafia for a reason. Alfredo staying out of the fray gives him plausible deniability when the police question him. He really may not know who this guy is."

Brittany was feeling irritated that Drew wasn't following her logic. "Well, is it merely coincidental that the three men in the mafia power structure who might know are all dead? Underboss Vinnie Petrocelli is dead, capos Al Meransky and Frankie Ramone are dead. The detectives that have worked this case also talked to the consigliera, and she's dumber than a box of rocks. She knows nothing."

Drew coughed. *This is when he usually starts getting impatient.*

"Look, Britt, like I said, I'm on duty. Unless you have something legitimate you want to bring to me, I'm afraid I won't be of much use to you anymore. You're the hotshot detective, not me. I really gotta get goin'."

"Are you saying you don't want to talk to me anymore? I couldn't care less if you were a cop in Shitsville, I'd still want to talk to you. I need you, Drew. You've been a help on more cases than you realize."

"I appreciate that. These are probably things your superior wouldn't want me to hear, however. It's probably in our best interest if you work these things out on your own. You're a smart girl, you'll figure it out."

Brittany felt a gentle tear roll down her cheek. It was exactly how it felt when she broke up with Drew. He tried to justify her rejection by indicating she was too good for him anyway. It was all so familiar.

"I'm sorry, Britt. I didn't mean to make you so upset."

Her sniffling on the phone must have been a giveaway.

"It's alright, I'll live. I guess this is goodbye, then."

"Wait a second," Drew said. "I really do have to go, but there's something I should tell you about a man we booked today for a battery charge. Seems like an interesting character."

Brittany raised her brow and prepared her stuck-up attitude. *Flirtatious Brittany has left the building.*

"Why in God's name would I care about that?"

"Because the guy was from Chicago. I have no idea if he's tied to your case or not, but he was a bit of a shady-looking guy. He nearly beat this drunken man to a pulp. He saved some young girl from this creep, but it didn't justify his extreme use of force."

It was time for Brittany to play tough now. "And? The fact that he's from Chicago could be a complete coincidence. What did this guy look like?"

Drew let out a deep exhale. "Yeah, it could, I'll admit. He was tall, about my height, fairly muscular. Brown hair, brown eyes."

Hmm, Brittany thought. She remembered from her conversation with Mick Fisher that the man Alfredo Petrocelli had described as the warehouse gunman had brown hair and brown eyes and was about Drew's height, six feet four. She'd also taken the time to review the official description from the case files, keeping in mind Fisher had mentioned something about a scar as a distinguishing feature. Brittany had discovered that the alleged warehouse gunman had a long scar below his right ear.

"Were there any distinguishing marks on the man? Tattoos, scars, that sort of thing?"

"Come to think of it, he did have an interesting scar on the side of his face near his ear. It was like someone had knifed him or something."

Brittany raced to her laptop in her bedroom and opened it. She knew Drew didn't have much time, so she had to be quick with her next line of questioning.

"That's interesting. Do you remember his name?"

"Yeah, hold on. I've got it here."

She heard Drew shuffle through some paperwork for a few seconds before coming back on the line. "The name is Boyle, Callahan Boyle. Has an address in Hyde Park. You want it?"

"Yes, I absolutely want it."

Brittany furiously typed the name and address into an open Word document and hoped her computer didn't have a random crash, as it so often did.

"Is he still there?"

"Nope. Someone signed him out on bail. You want that name?"

She jotted that name down as well. Judd Russell. Neither name rang a bell, and they could prove to lead her nowhere, but she had little else to go on until she talked to either Alfredo Petrocelli or dug up the witnesses to the related crimes.

"Thanks, Drew. This could be nothing, but I really appreciate your help. I've gotta run now. Bye."

Just like that Brittany had turned the tables by ending the call with her hurried ex. A quick Google search of both names linked to an obituary that was listed in the *Chicago Sun-Times*'s online edition seventeen years ago. The obituary in question belonged to a Mary Boyle. Listed as her only surviving relatives were three individuals: a sister, Rosalie Wilcox, and two men—a brother named Judd Russell, of San Diego, and a son named Callahan Boyle. Interestingly enough, her husband, Tom Boyle, had passed away shortly before her own death.

What happened with Boyle after that point? Did he live with his uncle Judd? Was Aunt Rosalie involved?

A quick search for Callahan Boyle confirmed the address that Drew had given her in Hyde Park. Brittany could look there if she wanted, but there was little point until she had more evidence. Boyle was in San Diego anyway. If she wanted immediate answers, that was where she needed to be.

During her search, Brittany also discovered multiple articles from Cal's days as a football player for his Evanston high school. Apparently, Cal had been a fine football player back in the day, and some of the online articles had pictures of him as a young man. Brittany made a note to print these and add them to her own file she was building on the case.

Still, there wasn't anything she could find that proved a connection between Cal and Alfredo Petrocelli. And she was curious what happened to Cal after his parents passed. From the football articles, she saw he was living in Evanston, but with whom? She doubted it was his uncle, since he was supposedly a San Diego resident when his sister passed away.

In an ideal world she'd have more answers than questions, but Boyle was the first worthwhile lead anyone had. To get the rest of the information she needed, she was going to have to pull some strings.

She knew one thing for sure: she was going to find the answers before everyone else and prove that she had what it took to become an FBI agent. She was going to prove too good to ignore.

But first she was going to San Diego. Her vacation was about to get hot.

6

Alfredo Petrocelli sat in his favorite chair in his favorite room of the old family house in Evanston that the Petrocellis had lived in for decades. Sure, Alfredo loved his penthouse apartment in the city, but he hadn't been there in months. Going back reminded him too much of Vinnie, who lived in a unit a few floors down. He entrusted Melissa Ranieri, his niece and consigliera, and the two newly appointed capos—Fernando "Flesh" Moran on the North Side, and Dominic "Death" Masucci on the South Side—to keep business running while he mourned. A new underboss to succeed Vinnie had yet to be named.

Alfredo's entire mafia operation was in shambles, and it was all Callahan Boyle's fault. Cal was directly responsible for the deaths of both Vinnie and Al Meransky. He killed Meransky in the very chair Alfredo was sitting in.

Yes, Vinnie had killed Frankie Ramone, Alfredo's long-time friend and South Side capo, but it was all due to Cal bumbling the Ross Caruso hit beyond measure. The hit was so poorly executed that Alfredo had some doubt over who actually committed the killing, despite all the evidence pointing to one person.

The mob boss let his mind wander to think of that person, that miserable youth named Tony Fregosi, when his niece, Melissa, entered the room, rolling in a cart with a kettle of hot tea, two cups, and saucers.

"My dearest uncle, how are you feeling today? Aunt Susan made some tea for us. She thinks it'll make you feel better."

Alfredo waved off his niece as she rolled the cart to the edge of the desk. He preferred the taste of his trusty brandy over bitter tea. Melissa raised her brow, took one of the tea saucers, and poured a small amount of brandy into the cup before sliding it to Alfredo.

"You don't need to wait on me hand and fucking foot. Don't you know who you are?"

"I'm your niece, sir. I love—"

"Save it," Alfredo said. "You're the consigliera of the Chicago mafia. Hell, you've been acting boss while I've been in and out of doctor's appointments the last few months. Don't let me or anyone else push you around. You got it?"

Melissa nodded and sat in one of the empty wooden chairs across from Alfredo's desk. The original straight-backed cushioned chairs had been fumigated after Meransky's blood splattered over them. Alfredo only kept his chair and had it refurbished because he loved it so much.

"Now, what is it you wanted to speak to me about? Surely you didn't stop by just to bring me tea."

The consigliera cleared her throat and crossed her legs. Any man would've killed to get the view Alfredo had of her from across the desk. Her legs were strong and golden, and her ample breasts were pressed tightly against her black sweater. Her normally bleached blonde hair more closely resembled the white of the snow that was piled on the ground outside.

"Well, I think we need to discuss just how well our new capos are doing and whether it makes sense to replace Vinnie as underboss. You have to understand that Flesh and Death were pretty low-level for guys that made it all the way to capo, even if Dominic was Frankie's top lieutenant on the South Side."

Alfredo took a swig of brandy, largely unconcerned with what Melissa had to say. As hard as he worked to preserve the power he had built up over the decades, he found himself suddenly unwilling to keep the throne of power as mob boss. Killing Ross Caruso and preserving his place as the mafia's chieftain seemed so important three months ago. Even though the former mayor was dead, it couldn't make up for the loss of Vinnie. All other mafia business seemed pointless to him.

"Look, Alfredo, I know losing Vinnie has hurt you. It's hurt me too," Melissa said after Alfredo shrugged off her concerns. "But think of all that you've accomplished for us, all that we've accomplished for Chicago. The Petrocellis have been the heads of the Chicago mafia for over three decades. No other mafia leaders across the country can claim that. We've created jobs, we've given people things that they otherwise would have no means of acquiring, whether it be sex, drugs, short-term winnings, good jobs at fair wages. You've led that. And we have to make sure we protect it."

Alfredo leaned back in his chair. It was true that he'd built a great mafia empire and that the mafia was an institution in Chicago as much as the Willis Tower or Wrigley Field. He had wanted to keep the strength of the mafia intact more than anything. He'd ruled his criminal organization with an iron fist, but given Vinnie's death, he saw a need to serve as more of a trusting leader. The future of the Chicago mafia would be something that the new leadership all built together.

"Melissa, what I have to say may not make a lot of sense given my behavior over the last several years, but it has to be said. I may not be as old as my father was when he passed the leadership reins to me after his unfortunate death, but like then, this is an important period of transition.

"I can't be as forceful or overbearing as I have been. I need to learn to trust you more, to trust these new leaders, both Moran and Masucci. I haven't known them as long as our good friend Frankie, but just like I came to trust Meransky after Henry Liotta moved on as North Side capo, I'll eventually learn to trust these men. The three of you are just as important to our success as I am. Understood?"

Melissa nodded and folded her hands into her lap. "So you're saying we're not going to replace Vinnie?"

Alfredo rose from the desk, still wearing a blue bathrobe over his white-and-blue-striped pajamas and brown slippers, and strode to the window to look out into the garden behind the study.

"That's right, dear. We're not replacing Vinnie. No one can replace Vinnie. It's up to the three of you to lead us forward. I'm still in charge of course, but in these last three months since Vinnie's death there's only been one thing on my mind."

Melissa swallowed so loudly that Alfredo could hear it from his corner of the room. "And what is that?"

Alfredo spun on his heel and turned toward her. A smile slowly crept its way up his face.

"All of my remaining energy will be spent tracking down

the man that killed my boy, the man that caused us so much devastation—Cal. It's his time to go."

Melissa put her hand just above her heart and rolled her eyes. "Oh my. Are you sure you're up for doing this? How are we going to get him? We don't even know where he is."

Alfredo nodded and turned back toward the window. Melting snow was falling in heaps off of the branches of the two large pine trees in the backyard. He wasn't concerned with finding Cal; he knew he would get ahold of him eventually. No one could hide from the mafia for too long.

"Melissa, do you remember that ambitious young man named Tony Fregosi? The driver?"

Melissa nodded. "The one who killed Caruso, right?"

Alfredo smiled devilishly as he glanced out the window.

"Yeah, sure. Cal made sure the kid hightailed it out of town after helping him get out of jail. Fortunately, the police bungled that shit so badly, thanks to old Joe Blutarski, that there hasn't been much tying us to that killing other than hearsay from some nosy detectives. But the kid is still out there. He can still hurt us."

"Okay, what does this have to do with Cal?"

"Many things, Melissa. Cal had a special bond with that boy. Why else do you think he'd go so far out of his way to help him? If something terrible happened to this Tony Fregosi, I bet Cal would come out of his hiding place."

Melissa stood and walked to the window, her high heels clomping against the cherry-stained hardwood floor. She stood next to her uncle and joined him in watching the trees.

"I see now," she said. "But we don't know where the boy is either. I'm sure he has family in the area. Maybe we can pressure them?"

"Precisely, my dear. Just like with Cal, we need to get

Tony to come out of his hiding place before we waste him. What I propose may sound harsh, but there's nothing more important to me than making sure Cal joins Vinnie six feet under."

Melissa turned to look at Alfredo. There was a mix of curiosity and concern on her face. "Go on."

"We kidnapped Maria to get Cal to come to us when we last tried to take him out. I know all about Tony Fregosi's family situation. Consider it one last contribution from our dearly departed friend Joe Blutarski. I understand Tony has two young sisters that he cares deeply about."

"No," Melissa urged. "Are you suggesting we do with them what we did with Maria?"

"I am. That's the best way to lure the boy in: by kidnapping one or both sisters. The hope is that Cal will follow. Consider this our highest priority."

Melissa shook her head. Alfredo could tell she was uncomfortable with his proposal.

"Who do you want on this one, sir?"

Alfredo smiled. "No one too important. Just a few people for protection if things get rough."

"Protection? What do you mean?"

"The protection is for me. I'm going to be the one to grab the girls. Just like I'll be the one that ends Cal."

7

Under normal circumstances, Uncle Judd was an exceptional chef. He could whip up anything, from a soufflé to a crème brûlée, and it would taste as exquisite as a similar dish found at any restaurant in the country. Since the hit-and-run accident from the previous afternoon left his uncle woozy, it was Cal's turn to make lunch. The result was less than exceptional.

"Dang nabit, Cal, didn't you ever learn how to make a half-decent sandwich living with those goombahs?"

Cal shrugged and took another bite from his cold panini. The chicken on the sandwich was still cold, and the Swiss cheese hadn't melted all the way through. Even using a panini press, Cal couldn't prepare a sandwich that passed muster.

"I think a slightly cold panini is the least of our worries right now. I have a bad feeling about the passenger of that Ford. The way he glared back at us made me think they didn't hit us by accident."

Uncle Judd set down his sandwich and pulled a pickle

from the jar on the table in front of him. After taking a crunchy bite, he spoke.

"You're telling me. No local would dare pull a hit-and-run on me like that."

Uncle Judd considered himself a sort of local celebrity in the Hillcrest neighborhood of San Diego. Though it was known as the city's gay neighborhood, Cal was pretty sure his uncle wasn't gay. Yet Judd had long been an LGBT activist since moving to California. Judd had told Cal that he felt his life's work was to be an activist, to give a voice to those without one. In addition to supporting the queer community, Judd had run for political office, only to come up short to a man with bigger pockets. Cal was sure he'd have been a Vietnam war protester had he been old enough to be draft eligible at the time.

"This whole thing has me thinking, though," Uncle Judd continued. "Between your ill-fated arrest and this accident, I'm wondering if we're in more trouble than I originally thought. I knew I was taking a big risk in keeping you here after you told me about your past. It was a risk I was willing to take because you're my sister's boy and I love you. Do you have any idea what this could mean?"

Cal finished his sandwich and took a long gulp from his glass of Judd's freshly brewed iced tea. While he figured the hit-and-run hadn't been an accident, he had no idea if the driver was a lone ranger or had been working for someone.

"It's hard to say. The mafia is more than just New York and Chicago, you know. If Alfredo found out where I was and he wanted me dead, it could happen soon enough."

"If he was involved, you'd think they would've done a better job, right?" Uncle Judd asked, flashing a smile at Cal. "But we could be jumping to conclusions. It may have been nothing."

"Perhaps. The mafia does want me dead, though. Alfredo said as much when he called me that night, just after Maria died in my arms."

Cal felt a gentle tear roll down his cheek at the memory of losing his girlfriend. Time hadn't made her loss any easier on him.

"Just when I thought I was free from them forever, I knew after that call I wouldn't be," Cal said. "If we don't want to be sitting ducks waiting for him to take us out, I need to do something about this."

Uncle Judd shook his head and stood up from his seat. He walked over to the refrigerator, grabbed the pitcher of iced tea, and brought it over to refill each of their glasses. "You can't say that. Things have been fine for three months. Don't you think if he wanted to get you that he'd have been after you by now? It could've been a coincidence after all."

While his uncle's question was a valid one, Cal didn't want to end up like one of his countless victims. He needed to go on the offensive. Only he wasn't sure how much he should share that sentiment with his uncle. He wondered if he'd regret bringing it up.

"Trust me, if that was one of Alfredo's guys or someone helping him, they'll keep coming back until they finish the job. There were many times I failed, and yet I stuck around until I got my target."

Cal saw Uncle Judd cringe as he spoke about his past. Uncle Judd was a pacifist and more of a "love, not war" type. Cal needed him to see the gravity of the situation.

Uncle Judd sighed and sat back down. "Look, I know you want to be on the attack, but maybe we should wait it out. We don't know anything about these guys yet. Don't do anything stupid until we find out."

"How do you propose we do that? One of the reasons I

let that guy have it at the beach was because he looked like Alfredo. I wanted to hurt that man like I want to hurt Alfredo. At some point I need to make him pay for what he's done."

Judd shook his head and slapped his knee. "Geez, Louise. You haven't changed a bit. Still hell-bent on violence just like you were in the mafia days, I'll bet."

A knock sounded against the door, sending the room into silence. Cal wanted to explain that he wasn't after revenge just for revenge's sake. He needed to go after Alfredo in order to keep both of them alive.

Another knock at the door. The jarring chime of the doorbell immediately followed.

"I wonder who that could be," Uncle Judd said. "You stay here in case it's an unsavory character."

Cal raised his brow. "What are you going to do to them, old man?"

"Funny." Uncle Judd rolled up the sleeves of his orange dress shirt and jokingly flexed his bronzed arms.

Uncle Judd walked from the eat-in kitchen, turned the corner, and headed for the hallway. Cal heard the light patter of his flip-flops against the faux-hardwood floor. The former hit man had no idea who was there, but whoever it was probably had no business showing up.

BRITTANY WILSON TOOK a deep breath as she finished ringing the doorbell of Judd Russell's Hillcrest home. It wasn't anything spectacular from the outside. Two large hedge bushes stood tall in front of the white-wood-sided house with a dark roof. There was an outdoor eating area off to the left of the house and several plants dotting the front lawn.

Brittany scanned the notes her ex, Drew, had given her again, making sure she had the correct address. There was nothing worse than being unprepared. Ever since Brittany touched down in San Diego earlier that morning, she'd been rehearsing exactly what she was going to say. She knew she couldn't threaten Callahan Boyle or Judd Russell with an arrest—she didn't have any evidence that Boyle had anything to do with her investigation. Still, she had a hunch, and she knew she had to follow it.

The first thing she needed to do was to figure out if Boyle was even the right man. He could always deny he was involved or even that he knew Alfredo Petrocelli, but if Brittany could make it clear early on that she wanted to take Alfredo and the mafia down, just maybe she'd get a reaction out of him. She imagined that if Callahan was the one who shot Alfredo, killed everyone in the warehouse, and potentially his kidnapped girlfriend to boot, that there had to be a reason why. If Brittany had to guess based on what little she knew, she figured Boyle wasn't the biggest fan of Alfredo Petrocelli.

Brittany nearly gasped when the front door opened to an older gentleman in an unbuttoned orange dress shirt with the sleeves rolled up. He wore white khaki shorts and brown flip-flops. Even with the gray hair and beard, the man was quintessential California.

"Hello there. Can I help you?"

Brittany looked closely at the man, though she wasn't sure why. Part of her felt nosy. She hoped she could see past him and into the house beyond, aiming for a glimpse of Callahan Boyle. It was then that she was confused, uncertain as to how to introduce herself. If she announced that she was a Chicago police detective, that would likely send both men running for the hills. But then again, if Callahan

Boyle was her suspect, she'd likely find out from that action.

Another part of her wanted to try a different tactic. She thought back to the still-unfinished FBI special agent application on her desktop computer at the station. Pretending to be someone she wasn't would potentially scare Boyle and his uncle Judd even more but would make her more plausible as someone who wanted to take down the mafia, perhaps for a much larger federal crime.

"I'm Special Agent Brittany Wilson of the FBI. I'm here—"

"You're what?"

She was prepared for the less-than-thrilled reaction.

"Listen, I'm with the FBI, but I'm not here to arrest anyone. I just want to put a few pieces of the puzzle together."

The man across from her raised his brow. "What puzzle?"

"A puzzle involving a man named Alfredo Petrocelli. My unit and I are working to put him away for a host of crimes. I understand there's a man staying with you, sir, named Callahan Boyle, and that he may be able to shed light on the situation. Can I ask your name, sir? Are you Judd Russell?"

The man in front of her looked like he'd seen a ghost. He slowly backed into the hall, leaving just enough room for Brittany to make her approach inside. This was turning out better than she expected.

"May I come in? It'll only take a minute. Nothing bad is going to happen here."

The man she assumed was Judd Russell stood frozen in front of her. He seemed unsure of what to do. Callahan Boyle had to be inside the house. She had a feeling her hunch was spot-on.

"There's no one here with those names. Unless you have a warrant for my arrest, you have no right to enter my abode. Good day."

In a flash the man slammed the door in her face.

8

Cal heard the racing footsteps of Uncle Judd move from the front entryway into the kitchen and out to the tiny back porch. Cal was surprised his uncle could move that fast given both his age and the recent car accident.

"What's going on?"

Uncle Judd's breathing was coming in shallow, ragged bursts. Cal stood from his chair and rushed over to his uncle. He didn't want the man to have a heart attack. Cal patted his uncle on the back, feeling slight discomfort at the compassionate gesture. He wasn't exactly Mr. Affectionate, despite how much he cared for Uncle Judd.

"Who was it? Is it the police?"

Judd shook his head furiously, his mane of salt-and-pepper hair flying about like a flag on a gusty day.

"No. It's worse. The FBI."

It was Cal's turn to be shocked. His heart was racing faster than any time he'd killed someone, more rapidly than any time he'd made love to Maria. How had they found him? Had they connected him to a murder? Another crime? He figured he'd be caught eventually, but not this fast.

"How many of them are there? Did they try to come in?"

Uncle Judd was bent at the waist, still working to catch his breath. Cal stood over him, anxious with anticipation. He was doing a much better job of hiding it.

"Just one. She said she's not here to make an arrest. Tells me she just wants to clear up a few things about Alfredo. Some crimes he may be involved in. I told her if she doesn't have a warrant that she should get lost."

"How did she find us?"

"I had no desire to ask. You wanna see if she's still out there?"

Cal didn't. The last thing he needed was to talk to an FBI agent. That would do them more harm than good. If he was going to be a prisoner eventually, he wanted to maintain his freedom for as long as possible.

"What do you think we do?" Cal asked. "Stay here and hope she leaves, or find a way to sneak out for a while? You're sure there's no one else?"

Uncle Judd stood at his full height, his breathing now under control.

"I'm thinking it's just her, but she could be tricking us. I say we run for it. Where do you think she'd be? Front or back?"

Cal wondered how to play this, even though he didn't like the idea of evading the FBI agent. The former hit man didn't want the agent to get the idea he was guilty of anything. Cal and Judd could exit one way and have a 50 percent chance of successfully escaping or getting caught. If they split up, at least one of them would make it if the agent was the only one at the house, but how could they be sure of that?

"I say she won't go around back. You could see her make a move through the yard from there, unless she hopes to jump us from the side of the house. But if she did that, she might not get either one of us."

"Perhaps she's not as clever as you," Uncle Judd said. "Not all FBI agents are regular Clarice Starlings."

"I'll take the front. She's more likely to be out there anyway, and I don't want her to cause you any trouble."

Uncle Judd waved off Cal's concern. "Nonsense. I can deal with her. She's not even sure you're here. If you think she'll stay out front, let me go out there, and you can get away out back. Go to Butch's Diner and get a coffee. If I can get her to skedaddle, I'll meet you there."

Cal was hesitant. He didn't want his uncle mixed up in his problems with the law. It was his fault the FBI had shown up on Judd's doorstep, and he was determined to fix it. Even then he agreed with his uncle's broader point. They needed to keep the FBI guessing.

If they knew Cal was here, the agent could send more of her men after him in order to find a way to build whatever case they were shaping against him. That was the last thing he wanted. Then there was no way he'd ever get back at Alfredo. He couldn't imagine that was the outcome Alfredo would want either.

"Alright, I'll head out back. Count to thirty. Will that give you enough time to go out the front door?"

Judd looked at Cal like he was crazy. "I'm not a spring chicken like you, Cal. How about a fifty count?"

So it was settled. Cal walked to the back door and began his count to fifty. Once he got to fifty, he and Judd would open their respective doors, check their surroundings, and make a break for it. Cal hoped the agent had gone home. If she was persistent like he was back in his hit man days, though, he knew she'd be waiting.

Cal's count reached fifty, and he opened the back door. He heard the sound of Uncle Judd pushing the front door open. Cal stepped out, looked in the backyard, and saw nothing. Confident he could escape, he gently closed the back door and walked to the small fence separating Judd's house from the neighbor. He looked both ways and, seeing nothing, hopped over the fence, and walked toward Robinson Avenue.

A commotion from the front of the house caught his attention.

"Ah!"

Less worried about being caught now, Cal ran toward the home's entrance, concerned something had happened to Uncle Judd. A lithe-looking figure turned toward him from the entanglement of bushes along the side of the house. A woman with rich sepia skin and long dark hair held in a ponytail spun toward him. She wore a blue blazer over a purple button-up and matching blue slacks. She had what appeared to be an FBI badge in her hand and set her fierce brown eyes on Cal.

Cal felt himself attracted to the young agent. She was a very beautiful woman. The spell was broken when Cal heard a groan from Uncle Judd and he moved past the agent toward his uncle. It appeared that Judd had slipped on something wet.

"I twisted my damned ankle."

Cal squatted by his uncle to examine his injury and shot a piercing glare at the agent, who stood with a hand on her hip.

"Did you do this?" Cal asked. The venom in his voice could cut through ice.

"Of course not," the agent said. "I'm afraid your uncle left the hose on and may have had a few sticky beverages out here recently."

Judd looked up at the woman and then at Cal. Cal figured the agent was full of shit, but there was no argument from Judd. In Cal's concern over his uncle's fate, he realized they both had failed to escape. Anything could happen to them now.

"How'd you know he was my uncle? Who are you?"

"I'm Special Agent Brittany Wilson of the FBI." Both of Brittany's eyes were locked on Cal. "Don't worry. Like I told your uncle, I'm not here to arrest you. In fact, I'm supposed to be on vacation."

Cal had a frown frozen on his face as he looked at her. He didn't trust this woman, or any law enforcement official for that matter. Still, he knew he couldn't get up and run away, especially with Uncle Judd having a bum ankle.

"I'll keep this short because I've never met you, Mr. Boyle, and I have nothing on you. But I've done some digging into the affairs of a man named Alfredo Petrocelli. I understand you are well acquainted."

Brittany's eyes shone bright above a devious smile. Cal knew better than to say anything. Alfredo had trained him and Vinnie in such measures when they were young men. Never speak against the mafia. Never break the law of omertà.

"I'm sorry, I've never heard of this man you speak of. If you want to come here to my uncle's house and disturb our afternoon without any sort of warrant, I'd be more than happy to report this to the nearest field office."

Cal was surprised that his threat didn't even cause a flinch.

"Fine, report me. We both know you won't do such a

thing, since a trip to any FBI field office would be dangerous for you. I'm far more interested in Alfredo Petrocelli's money-laundering activities as suspected boss of the Chicago Outfit, but you do fit the description of a wanted man Alfredo described to the police recently. Tall, brown hair, brown eyes, scar below your right ear. It may be a coincidence, it may not. I know you have a Chicago address, I know you went to school in Evanston. I know your mom died when you were twelve years old. There's an awful lot I know about you, Callahan."

Cal felt a strange trembling sensation in his chest. It was the quaking of fear, something he hadn't truly felt in years, even after having the deck stacked against him at the warehouse against Alfredo, Vinnie, and all of the mafia soldiers on hand that stood between him and Maria.

He was surprised the agent knew so much about him. Sure, anyone with Google could have discovered his mother's obituary and seen a connection between him and Uncle Judd. He imagined some of his old sports articles from his high school football days had made their way online, but how would she have found his address? How would she have known to look for him in the first place? Had she really talked to Alfredo and found a connection?

"I still don't know what you're talking about," Cal lied. "What does this have to do with me? Why accuse me of doing something that this Alfredo says I did?"

Uncle Judd nodded at Cal, seemingly pleased with how Cal was approaching the agent. While Judd hadn't had as much experience with the darker sides of life, he knew how to talk his way out of anything. Cal had already seen it twice when Judd had been pulled over for speeding.

"I'll admit I had some help. An old colleague of mine picked you up yesterday and took you to the police station."

Son of a bitch. That explains it.

"Look, I really don't have any information to make a case, but I believe you know Alfredo Petrocelli, Mr. Boyle. While the Chicago police are very interested in catching someone who blew away a bunch of mafia guys at a warehouse a few months back, I'm very interested in bringing down the Chicago mafia for all sorts of federal crimes. Men like Alfredo Petrocelli don't deserve to stay in power for too long. Wouldn't you agree?"

Cal looked back at her and wondered what exactly the FBI had been doing to investigate the various crime scenes.

"Like I said, I don't know Alfredo Petrocelli. But suppose I did? Why would I give a shit if he or the Chicago mafia were still in business?"

Cal saw the gears turning in the agent's head. He was positive she didn't know Alfredo had adopted him; otherwise, she would've explained the connection up front. She was still missing a lot of the pieces of the puzzle, and he wasn't going to give them to her.

"I don't know everything I need to know yet, but believe me, I'll find out. I may have had a lucky break, but it didn't take too long to find the two of you. I will find out how you're connected to Alfredo, Mr. Boyle. When I do, you better hope you were right, because if there's any connection at all, you'll be taken in for questioning and considered a prime suspect. Is that clear?"

Cal shrugged his shoulders. He couldn't care less what the woman had to say. Even if the FBI found a connection between him and Alfredo, he doubted they could prove anything, unless Alfredo was willing to testify against the former hit man.

"But I'm going to give you one chance, Callahan. One chance before I leave here to help me out. I want to bring down the mafia as much as I'm sure you do in your lying heart. You claim you don't know Alfredo Petrocelli, but I have a feeling you do. If you really hate him, you'll help me bring him down. I'll make sure nothing points to you if that's the case."

Cal didn't believe Special Agent Wilson for one second. "Why should I trust you? Look what happened to my uncle. Are you telling me he fell on his own doing?"

Brittany shook her head and rocked her weight on her heels. Cal took notice of the umber-colored, high-heeled shoes on her feet. They made her taller and seem much more powerful. Cal felt himself lusting after her despite her unwanted appearance.

"Locking away one guy for a few murders might make the headlines of a few local papers, but taking down the entire Chicago mafia power structure thanks to help from an inside man? That's the stuff careers, and even television shows, are made of, my friend. That's what I'm after. That's why you can trust me."

The agent crossed her arms and tapped her foot as she looked at Cal. Her facial expression was cemented in a *Hurry, I don't have all day* look. As convincing as Cal was sure she thought she was, he had to pass on her offer. He couldn't trust her. She was in the FBI. Besides, Cal had to go after Alfredo on his own.

9

Spending his afternoons lounging on the beach with a cold drink and a good book was nothing new for retired hit man Joey Bartellini. He never grew tired of the habit. That was part of why he'd moved to Southern California in the first place after his days as a hit man were done.

Following his enjoyable afternoon soaking up the sun and lusting after young women in bikinis, Joey headed to his favorite eatery in Pacific Beach, the PB Seafood Cantina. It was a place where people from every walk of life would come to eat, from elderly retired couples, to college kids, to bursting families, where the parents struggled to keep their children from running around the restaurant's small interior eating space into the more expansive seating area outside. At the late-afternoon hour, Joey was alone in the restaurant, enjoying a nice tuna salad sandwich with homemade chips and a pickle. It was basic, but it was tasty.

For the most part the retired hit man liked basic. After spending over twenty years as the Chicago Outfit's top hit man, simple beach living was enough to churn Joey Bartellini's gears. He'd started off by living near LA doing some part-time work for the LA mob to ease into his retirement. When the pace of life reminded him more of his hectic day-to-day back in Chicago than the peaceful, easy feeling he desired, he pulled the plug on further mafia gigs and moved to San Diego. It was great for him. He hadn't killed anyone in over five years, which was the longest he'd gone between killings since murdering his first man at twenty-one.

The restaurant was across the street from a CVS. Joey glanced up occasionally to see various sick people stumble toward the pharmacy, awaiting their prescription order. He didn't understand how pharmacists found the energy to deal with people with so many illnesses. In Joey's past, if you were deemed at all useless, as he felt those people needing the prescriptions were, you were put out to pasture.

He took one last bite of his sandwich and asked the waitress for a refill of his coffee. Joey glanced out of the window once again and was shocked at what he saw. A fit-looking young man of around thirty was helping an older gentleman, probably close to Joey's own age of sixty-five, into the pharmacy. It looked like the older man had ice taped around his right ankle.

Joey looked down to his refilled coffee and back out the window. He thought the younger man looked familiar but wrote off the resemblance. When he saw the man look back in his direction and through the restaurant window, he was sure his eyes hadn't deceived him.

Feeling spotted, Bartellini leaned back in the booth and out of sight. One of the first rules he'd learned as a hit man was to never let your target know of your presence. While he was no longer a killer and wasn't after the fit man, he still didn't like that he may have been seen. In fact, it worried him.

He paused for another minute and downed some more of his coffee before calling over the waitress to get the check. He had no idea why he was in such a hurry. A sense of adventure he hadn't felt in years was bubbling up inside of him.

The person he thought he'd seen was none other than the man who took his place as the chief hit man for the Chicago mafia, Callahan Boyle. From the little he'd heard from his friend and former boss, Alfredo Petrocelli, Cal had done an exemplary job ridding the mob of its enemies. Joey still followed the news, however, and saw a recent story where several mob soldiers were gunned down in a Chicago warehouse. In the same story, he'd read that Alfredo himself had nearly been taken out. What was even worse was hearing that Alfredo's son, Vinnie, had also been killed.

Which was why, in such chaos, Bartellini was surprised to see Boyle in San Diego. Wasn't Alfredo sending him after whatever men were responsible for the deaths of so many of his mob associates, and more importantly, his own son?

It struck Bartellini as odd, and he contemplated approaching Cal to find out exactly what had occurred. What he ultimately decided, as he thanked the waitress and paid his bill, was to pass on the opportunity. He was retired, and it was no longer his job to explore occasional curiosities. Instead, as a courtesy he decided to place a call to his old friend Alfredo. If Boyle had been involved in the deaths, he imagined Alfredo would be very interested in knowing where Cal was.

Bartellini walked away from the restaurant and out of sight of the CVS. He pulled out his cell phone and struggled to scroll through his long list of contacts until he found Alfredo's number. He shuddered as he saw Vinnie Petrocelli's name in his list of contacts beneath. He dialed Alfredo and waited.

"Joey Bartellini," came a voice from the other end. "It's been a long time, my friend."

Alfredo seemed in a cheery mood for someone who'd recently suffered a devastating injury and the loss of a son. Joey had several questions he wanted to ask his old friend but knew they'd have to wait. He wanted to get straight to the point of his call.

"Good to finally talk to you, Don Alfredo. I'd love to catch up, but I've got something you might want to know."

Joey heard Alfredo sigh over the phone. His mood had gone from chipper to exasperated in seconds.

"What might that be?"

"I saw a certain someone today. Someone I never thought I'd see again, considering I swore off returning to Chicago after I retired."

Alfredo's voice seemed to return to his more-enthusiastic tone.

"Whoever it is, this better be good."

"I have a feeling you'll be pleased. The person I saw was my successor and your adopted son, Callahan Boyle."

Bartellini heard a loud bang over the phone. He wondered if he scared his old friend right out of his seat.

"Are you sure, Joey? You're sure it was Cal?"

"Certain as death and taxes. He might have gotten a glimpse of me, but I hid just in time to cause some doubt."

"That's tremendous news, Joey, tremendous. You still in San Diego?"

"Sure am. Spotted Cal in the Pacific Beach neighborhood." Joey paused, the sense of adventure he felt earlier bubbling up to the surface. He couldn't ignore it anymore.

"Say, you need any help with this? I may be retired, but I'm still down here. I can work some connections if you need."

Alfredo pounded his fist on a surface. It was a habit Joey had seen in the past whenever Alfredo got really excited or really upset. He hoped it was the former and not the latter.

"Don't worry about a thing. Just call me back if you spot him. I meant it when I told you to enjoy your retirement all those years ago. I'm not going to go back on my word now. Besides, this is the greatest news I've heard in months. You've done the right thing in calling me. We'll have to catch up some other time. Goodbye now."

Joey put the phone back in his pocket and headed for home. That longtime itch to kill someone that he thought he'd suppressed upon his retirement was making its way to the surface of his brain.

He hoped today wasn't the last time he heard from Alfredo.

10

Alfredo Petrocelli hadn't been this excited in years. Getting the call from Joey Bartellini telling him exactly where Cal was made him grin from ear to ear. He pictured the mischievous smiles of the Grinch and the meddling hotel clerk played by Tim Curry from *Home Alone* 2.

"What are you so damned happy about?"

Alfredo turned to his wife. Susan was rarely allowed in the study that served as his office for all of his strategic planning activities. Like everything in their lives over the past several months, this was a true exception.

Alfredo looked upon his wife, her beauty transformative even at sixty years of age. Her beauty radiated just as brightly as it had when they were high school sweethearts. Her hair, while colored a dark almond these days, flowed smoothly around her porcelain-white face. Her cheekbones had just the right amount of plump above her pointed jaw. Yet with all of the sadness of losing another son, their last living child, Alfredo knew it had been a struggle for her to keep her composure. He was hoping this piece of news would change that.

"Honey, I've got some news."

Susan Petrocelli crossed her legs and folded her arms, her expression sour. "What news?"

"It's the answer to our prayers. I just got off the phone with Joey Bartellini. Remember old Joey?"

His wife nodded.

"I thought you would. He ran into someone out in San Diego, someone we—"

"Enough with the suspense," Susan said. "Who did he see?"

Alfredo cleared his throat and drummed his fingers against the top of the cherry-oak desk. "He saw Cal, Susan."

Susan kept her face frozen in place. Alfredo had no idea what his wife was thinking. Even through thirty-plus years of marriage, Alfredo didn't know all of her tells. She was very good at not revealing what she was thinking sometimes, especially when she'd been depressed.

"Isn't that good news? Now we know where he's been hiding. We can go after Cal, honey. We can make him pay for what he did to our boy."

Alfredo was ready to keep rambling, and he normally would've, had anyone else graced him with their presence. But this was his wife he was talking to. He'd seen the devastation on her face after Vinnie's death and its continued existence over the past few months. What she had expressed outwardly Alfredo felt inside.

"I don't know what to feel anymore, Alfredo. I still can't believe Cal killed poor Vinnie. Murdering him isn't going to bring our son back."

"That's true," Alfredo began. "But imagine how good it will feel for both of us to know that our son's killer isn't out there, free to roam the streets. Cal could still do a lot of damage to us and our family with what he knows. I usually don't share this part of my life with you because I know you don't want to hear it. But I think something needs to be done."

Susan shook her head and uncrossed her legs. "Alfredo, why are you asking for my opinion? You're going to make your own decisions. You've been doing that your entire life, even when your father was in charge. I can't help but feel this is a mistake. Cal was a part of our family once too. I hate him with every ounce of my being for what he did to our son. But there's another person we need to think about here —you. You've kept this all bottled up for way too long. I know what Vinnie meant to you. Don't let your hatred for Cal get in the way of feeling what you need to feel for Vinnie."

Alfredo didn't like where his wife was going with this. Her behavior was too rational, too calculated. It was just like her to think about others and to suggest he keep the foot off the gas for revenge. Alfredo didn't care what Susan's reaction to the news was. She was right; he was going to go after Cal anyway.

"I appreciate your concern, dear, I really do. But I'll be fine. Vinnie would want this, I know he would. He would want me to make sure Cal was taken care of and then to carry on with my life. That's the only way I can carry on. Put Cal in the ground and get things back to normal with the rest of the mafia."

Susan looked at Alfredo with concern. Alfredo knew he hadn't been the best husband over the past three months. From dealing with his own wounds, to answering police questions, to selecting new leaders for the mafia to replace those killed, Alfredo had largely ignored his wife's own pain and suffering. He realized now that this was the first real conversation they'd had since Vinnie's funeral, which Alfredo could barely remember, from being hopped up on so much pain medication.

"I know how important your precious mafia is to you, Alfredo. It's in your blood. But my blood has been carved out of my body and poured over the floors of this house ten times over. I couldn't give less of a shit about your business getting back to normal. If we have to sell this goddamned house, the penthouse downtown, and live on the fucking streets, that's what I'll do. I've already lost everything important to me. I don't want to lose you too."

Susan got up from her chair and marched from the room, leaving Alfredo speechless. Maybe it had been a bad idea to share Bartellini's news with her. He thought it would make her feel better. He thought sharing it with her would make him feel better. He still didn't know how to react.

I don't want to lose you too.

He wondered why she thought she was losing him. Had he been that distant from her?

The point was moot. If it hadn't been a good idea to share the news of Cal's presence in San Diego, he knew it wouldn't be a good idea to tell her about his kidnapping plans for Tony Fregosi's younger sisters. He'd already sent men to locate the Fregosi house and perform surveillance. He knew the girls only had their father at home to protect them. While Mr. Fregosi had reduced his hours at his second job since Tony's disappearance, he was away from home a lot. Someone had to pay the bills.

Alfredo knew it was only a matter of time before he'd be able to pounce and grab one or both of the girls. That would get Tony Fregosi to come running, and maybe Cal too.

Alfredo turned to his phone and decided to place a

phone call. While he'd love the kidnapping to bring Fregosi and Boyle to him, he knew he had plenty of resources at his disposal to ensure Cal was taken out, especially now that he knew where his adopted son was. If Cal was killed soon, maybe it would ease his wife's mind and get things back to normal. It was always good to have a backup plan.

Alfredo placed a call to none other than the boss of the smaller LA mob, Giovanni Lucerno. Lucerno had been in power in Southern California for nearly thirty years, coinciding with the time Alfredo's father, Louie Petrocelli, served as the boss of the Chicago mafia. Lucerno had given hints to the Commission of his intention to retire over the years, but no one was ready to take over. His flunkies had more concern over hot women and catching the next big surf than expanding their criminal empire. Alfredo had no such problems in Chicago.

"Who da fuck is dis?"

One of Lucerno's lackeys answered the call. Lucerno was a boss who didn't talk to you unless you were real fucking important. Alfredo was sure it was due to laziness more than anything else.

"Tell Mr. Lucerno there's a slice of deep-dish pizza waiting for him."

The lackey grumbled something on the phone and transferred the call to Lucerno. His old friend and fellow boss would likely be sitting in the darkest room of his house, an old walk-in closet he'd turned into a private reading room. The only things in there were a small desk and several bookshelves. No light or windows to be found.

"You better have a big slice of pepperoni for me, my old friend," Lucerno said upon answering.

Alfredo let out a laugh. "I sure do. But first I've gotta ask you to make a delivery."

“What on earth could I possibly do for you, my friend? You know you were a lifesaver for me a few years ago when you let Bartellini go to move out here. He really took care of some tricky business for us.”

“I’m glad to hear it. Speaking of old Joey, he just called me. Says one of my prime enemies is down in San Diego. I was hoping maybe you could send some of your guys after him.”

“My guys? Why don’t you have Joey do it himself? He’s getting up there in age, but he’s not ancient like me.”

That was true. Joey was in his midsixties, and Alfredo a few years younger. Giovanni Lucerno was pushing ninety but still sharp.

“Joey’s a last resort. I want him to enjoy his retirement. He deserved it after putting up with the likes of me and my old man for all those years. I need some strong young guys. Guys who can deal with someone a little younger.”

“Younger? Who are you after? Does this have something to do with all that warehouse trouble? Heard a lot of your guys got whacked.”

“The man’s name is Cal Boyle. He took Joey’s position after he retired. He killed my son, Gio. You can understand what I expect to be delivered.”

Giovanni didn’t speak for a few moments. Alfredo felt a well of anger boiling inside. Why wasn’t the old man talking?

“I see. And you don’t want to do it yourself?”

“I’d love to do it myself. But I’m not well enough to travel right now. I’d love to get Cal to come back to Chicago, where I can do some damage to him. I’m working on a way to get him back here. But since he’s in your neighborhood, I thought I’d give you guys the first opportunity.”

“I see. I bet this is real hard on Susan.”

Alfredo nodded and looked at the brandy atop his desk. He was tempted to drink it while he chatted with the slow-and-smooth-talking boss from LA, but he held off.

"Yes, it's very tough on her. She's not sure I should go through with taking him out. Maybe if you guys get it done, it'll be for the best."

Alfredo wasn't sure he believed the last part. He fantasized about putting his gun to Cal's temple and blowing his brains out himself. Part of him hoped Lucerno's men would succeed, even though he ultimately wanted his crack.

"Alright, Alfredo. I hear you. I've got a few guys that can get it done. You just tell me where he's hanging out and I'll send my best."

Alfredo told Lucerno what Joey had told him, that Cal was seen in San Diego's Pacific Beach neighborhood.

"Lots of traffic there. We'll have to be stealthy, then. Should be no problem for Marco. He's the guy I'm trying to get to take over for me. Big guy, real tough. He'll give you your revenge."

11

The events of the last few days caused Cal and Uncle Judd to hunker down inside the house. Until now, Cal's time in San Diego had been very peaceful. He felt little fear that the mafia or authorities would catch up with him, though he knew in the deep recesses of his mind that they eventually would. Between the hit-and-run with the large pickup truck and visit from Special Agent Brittany Wilson of the FBI, Cal had every reason to believe his luck was changing for the worse.

"Is your ankle getting any better yet? If I have to keep cooking, I'm sure we'll be able to add our intestinal lining to the things that ail us."

Cal's joke was met with a smile from Uncle Judd. Cal really wasn't a bad cook and had prepared many delicious meals for Maria when they were together. Though, in Uncle Judd's mind, Cal's cooking left a little something to be desired, especially after the cold paninis the other day. Judd had made less sarcastic comments about Cal's cooking after dinner the previous night and breakfast that morning.

"I'll live, that's for sure, as long as no one keeps coming

after us. I just hate being off my feet for so long. I haven't been to my yoga class in three days."

Uncle Judd spouted off some ingredients for a soup that he'd been craving for Cal to pick up from the nearest market. His car still hadn't been repaired from the accident, so Cal drove a rental to Whole Foods to pick up the groceries.

On the way to the store, Cal noticed a silver Lexus RX tailing him down Robinson Avenue. Whoever was driving wasn't as obvious as the driver of the truck that rear-ended them the day before, as they were following at a much greater distance. Yet each time Cal changed lanes, the Lexus did so as well. Even when Cal made a turn down Fifth Avenue, and later onto Washington Street, to throw them off, they found a way to catch up.

Not wanting to be too paranoid, Cal pulled into the Whole Foods. Whoever was tailing him was unlikely to pull off anything stupid in public. If the men were somehow working for Alfredo, he was sure they were only there to scare him and potentially bring him back to Chicago with them, not to kill him.

Cal turned off the ignition and exited the car. He stopped and turned to the rear of the parking lot, where the Lexus had parked. From his vantage point, it appeared as if two men were sitting in the front seats. They were looking at something across the street, their attention elsewhere. Cal knew better. They were just pretending to look away. If they knew him like Cal usually knew his targets, they should've been smarter about their behavior.

Cal entered the store, expecting that the men would follow. He knew to stay in view of other shoppers at all times. If he was anywhere too isolated for too long, they might take a shot at him.

He anchored himself near the produce section after grabbing a shopping basket. Most of the ingredients for Uncle Judd's soup were there anyway. After only five minutes of selecting ingredients and adding them to his basket, he saw two men enter the store who resembled the men following him. Both wore dark sunglasses and had overly bronzed skin.

One man wore a red short-sleeve button-up that was untucked over a pair of khakis. His dark hair was spiked, and the tips were dyed blond. It was quite the bizarre look and not the sort you would want to sport if you wished to remain inconspicuous. The other man blended in, with the typical San Diego surfer bro look. He wore a white tank top that showed off his bulging shoulders and biceps, a pair of khaki shorts, and flip-flops. The look on his face was anything but chill and more like that of a man ready to kill.

Cal glanced in their direction and noticed them still scanning the store. He wondered if they were going to come after him directly once they spotted him or if they would split up and search for him. If they split up, he'd have a harder time keeping tabs on the man he wasn't engaged with, so he made it easy for them to find him. He moved away from the lettuce and greens section and into the middle of the produce area by the potatoes.

Spiky Hair spotted Cal and moved quickly toward him. There was no question the men were in pursuit now. The man in the tank top followed behind, and Cal swore he heard him mutter something under his breath about the other man moving too fast.

Cal pretended to pick out some sweet potatoes as he contemplated his next move. He didn't have a gun or a knife to defend himself. He would have to improvise a suitable way to fend off his pursuers, who were both likely to be carrying.

He was still hopeful they wouldn't try to kill him on the spot, but he imagined they'd like to rough him up a bit in the store before taking him somewhere more suitable for punishment. He faced the potatoes and kept up his facade of looking for the perfect one. Cal felt the sense that Spiky Hair was reaching for him. Based on how fast the men were walking and how long Cal had his back turned, it made sense that he was close. Just when Cal felt a hand trying to grab hold of his shirt, he spun around in a 180-degree angle to his left and sent a sharp right hook into Spiky Hair's nose.

The man cursed and reached for his bleeding face, while Tank Top prepared his next move by reaching toward the waistband of his shorts. Cal didn't care to find out what sort of weapon Tank Top was concealing and used the only feasible item he could to fend the man off—an overly ripe tomato from his shopping basket. He grabbed it and threw it as hard as he could at Tank Top's face. The tomato hit him flush in the forehead, bursting upon impact. Tank Top cursed, wiping the tomato juice off of his face, giving Cal time to run toward the back of the store.

Spiky Hair was hot on his heels. Cal ran down the crowded aisle to the back of the store, weaving his way around a mother with two young children. He pushed through a line of people at the meat counter and nearly tripped over a wet floor sign just past the seafood area. Cal wasn't quite sure where he was running, just that he needed to keep going.

Shouts and high-pitched cries echoed behind him. He didn't know what the commotion was, but he realized that if he looked back, it would only slow him down. The ringing of a bullet just past his ear told him all he needed to know. He was being shot at.

Cal turned right into the baking aisle. He glanced over his shoulder as he made his way to the halfway point. Spiky Hair was in hot pursuit, with a suppressed pistol held high in his hand. The former hit man ducked behind the other patron of the aisle to avoid the line of fire. The thought of Tank Top barely crossed Cal's mind when he felt a sharp thud at the side of his head. He looked down and saw he'd been hit with a five-pound bag of flour. It wasn't enough to do any damage but distracted him long enough for Spiky Hair to complete the trap and Tank Top to pull out a switchblade.

Cal knew he was in a tough spot between knife bearer and gunman. Spiky Hair had lowered his weapon and was ready to fire. Customers were still screaming, and little kids were crying. The store manager was warning customers over the intercom that they should leave their items behind and make their way toward the exits.

Cal saw little chance of surviving this. He was cornered with no way out. The only thing that crossed his mind was that his eye felt like sand had been blown in it. It must have been the flour.

The flour! That's it!

Seeing the shortest window of opportunity, Cal picked up the bag that had fallen at his feet, did his best to rip open a big enough hole in the bag, and dove to the floor, aiming the bag upward at Spiky Hair as he did so. A gunshot rang out just as he hit the floor. He was sure he'd timed it just right to avoid the bullet and for the flour to cloud the vision of Spiky Hair. By the time he looked up, not only had Spiky Hair's face been covered in the white powdery substance, but Tank Top had fallen to the ground behind him, the unintended victim of Spiky Hair's gunshot.

With only one man to beat, Cal sprung into action. Spiky Hair recovered and pointed the gun at him. Cal contemplated reaching for Tank Top's knife, but he had no idea where it landed. His next tactic was more crazy than stupid. He would roll.

Spiky Hair fired. Cal rolled quickly to his left, narrowly avoiding the shot. With nowhere left to move, he did the next best thing and picked up the nearest cans of food he could find and chucked them at the gunman. Firing the cans in rapid succession did the trick and caused Spiky Hair to drop his weapon.

Before his pursuer could reach for the gun, Cal got to his feet and jumped him. He knew he'd have quite the fight on his hands. Cal got in a quick right hook before being elbowed hard in the stomach. The blow sent him backward just enough for Spiky Hair to recover and fire a hard left-right to Cal's temple.

Spiky Hair charged as Cal careened into the shelves, extending a right hook that Cal was just able to dodge. Cal used what little momentum he had to charge back and grab the man around the waist. He used every muscle in his body to drive the muscular Spiky Hair into the shelves across the aisle. While the blow would've done damage to a normal human being's back, Cal understood that this was no ordinary human being.

Cal's opponent recovered and raked him across the face, his sharp nails digging into Cal's flesh. The temporary blindness from the scratching allowed the man to pick up his gun. Cal kicked at his opponent's hand, which sent the gun hurtling across the aisle.

Cal tried to catch his breath, knowing the man was

unlikely to retrieve his weapon, when Spiky Hair charged once again. Cal sidestepped at the last second, and the man ran into a stray shopping cart. The foray gave Cal the one opportunity he needed to take him out. Tank Top's knife was still on the ground next to his dead body. Cal knew he would have to grab the knife fast before Spiky Hair recovered.

Cal raced for the knife and heard a loud grunting sound emanate from Spiky Hair as he charged again. Cal had the knife and held it to the side of his body, not wanting Spiky Hair to know he had it. He was only inches away when Cal turned and stuck the blade deep into the muscular man's stomach.

The goon cried out in pain and slowly sank to his knees. Cal felt the all-too-familiar rage course throughout his body as he dug the blade deeper into his opponent, driving him into the linoleum floor.

"Who the fuck sent you?"

"Fuck off." For someone whose entire lower half was covered in blood, Spiky Hair was pretty confident.

Cal pressed harder. He had to know who had been after him.

"Did Alfredo send you? Huh?"

Cal waited and watched as the man's eyes fluttered and the pool of blood across his abdomen grew ever larger. Cal wouldn't get a response. He could hear the wail of police sirens coming from outside.

Time to go.

12

Brittany Wilson was used to being rejected. Having Callahan Boyle and Judd Russell turn her away after her visit to Russell's home wasn't a surprise. What was surprising was the look she saw on Callahan Boyle's face when she insisted he had to know Alfredo Petrocelli. She just knew he was doing his best to keep his poker face on, to remain stoic in the face of questioning. It was a look Brittany had seen before. Most of the time, when she had seen that expression on the faces of those she interrogated, it turned out they were more guilty than they wanted her to believe.

The Chicago PD detective paced across her hotel room just north of the Gaslamp Quarter. In one hand she held a stack of articles she'd printed from the hotel's business center downstairs, featuring Callahan Boyle's name or pieces of news surrounding his high school football team. In the other hand she held her cell phone. She wondered if she should make the call to the man she'd spent the last hour researching.

While reading the articles on Boyle and his football

team online, she came across a consistent name in each of the pieces—Evanston Township High School football coach Doug Nelson. Coach Nelson was quite an interesting character, with colorful quotes that often had "[expletive]" used in place of his actual language in the articles. Brittany imagined him as the perfect role model for a group of impressionable young men.

She soon went down the rabbit hole of digging up more info on the coach. Several recent articles had appeared in the *Daily Herald* indicating that Coach Nelson had recently retired from his post due to battling prostate cancer. The online comments balanced a measure of sadness and reverence for the impressive coaching career that Mr. Nelson had. Brittany wondered if, given the news of the coach's illness, she should bother reaching out to him.

Though she was sure Coach Nelson had coached thousands of young men over his thirty-plus-year career at Evanston Township High School, she hoped that the name Callahan Boyle would stick out to him. Callahan had been in enough articles that Brittany figured he had to be pretty good, though there was no mention of him playing football after high school, and she really had no idea what he did for a living.

She held the phone tighter and pivoted her feet, walking away from the hotel room door and toward the window, which gave the viewer a peek of a small sliver of ocean if they looked hard enough. Brittany knew that if she was going to have any chance of tying Callahan Boyle to Alfredo Petrocelli, she had to know more about Boyle. Coach Nelson was her only shot at that, the only person aside from Judd Russell that she knew would have some insight into his past.

Her heart pounding, Brittany unlocked her phone screen and tossed the stack of articles on the bed. She had to get over the trepidation of bothering a man battling cancer. She knew she couldn't call as a member of law enforcement, so she had another trick up her sleeve, an alter ego she would use just for this purpose.

Brittany placed the phone to her ear after dialing the number she had for Coach Nelson. She waited for what seemed like a whole minute for the ringback tone to end before finally a blaring cacophony of sounds was audible.

"Turn that shit down, Delia! I'm on the phone," said a man who was presumably Coach Nelson. It only took him three words for the expletives to enter the conversation. "Hello, this is Doug."

"Hi, Doug," Brittany began, relieved she had indeed reached the coach. "My name is Heather Jones, and I'm a reporter with the *Daily Herald*. We're running a new Throwback Thursday feature in our sports section, and we're really interested in running a story on your 2004 conference championship team."

Coach Nelson coughed into the phone, not bothering to turn away from the mouthpiece. Brittany removed the phone from her ear, waited for the coughing fit to subside, and then resumed listening.

"I'm sorry, but did you say the '04 team? That was twelve years ago, miss. We've had a lot better teams since then. Why the hell would you wanna talk about that team?"

"Ah, of course you've coached many great teams over the years," Brittany said, having fun with the Heather Jones character. "Can you tell me what made that team special?"

Brittany figured she'd open the questioning with a few bullshit questions just to get the coach talking and in a good mood. She didn't want to bring up Callahan Boyle straight away.

"Well, let me think," Coach Nelson started. "Wait a

minute, I just did an interview with you guys a few weeks ago. Why are you calling me again?"

"Yes, that's right. I think I speak for everyone at the *Herald* when I say that we were deeply saddened to hear of your cancer diagnosis, and we're all wishing you the best. As I said earlier, this is just a blast-from-the-past-type feature, a little snippet from a bygone era."

Coach Nelson huffed and smacked his lips over the phone. A chorus of voices rang out, the volume increasing as each second passed.

"Goddamn it, Delia, turn that crap off!"

Brittany removed the phone from her ear again, wondering if she'd even get to ask Coach Nelson about Callahan Boyle.

"Sorry about that," Coach Nelson said. The noises stopped, but Brittany thought she heard a female voice yelling back at the coach. "My doctor says I need to start meditating to control my stress, says it will reduce the activity in my amygdala. Let's hope the activity in my prostate gets reduced also."

Coach Nelson laughed for a few seconds. Brittany wondered if he would answer her softball questions or whether she needed to keep pressing. She had no idea how long he would stay on the phone.

"Coach Nelson, do you have anything specific you'd like to share from that championship season?"

"Yeah, I suppose I can think of something. We had a good team that year. One of the best defenses in the state of Illinois. I'm sure you remember Franklin Tubbs. He was a great defensive end. It's a shame what happened to him before he could make the pros, rest in peace."

Brittany nodded, not entirely certain as to whom Coach

Nelson was speaking about. She hadn't recalled the name Franklin Tubbs in any of the articles she read.

"I wanted to talk more about the offense. In particular, your tight end that year, Callahan Boyle."

"Boyle? You're calling to talk about Boyle?" Coach Nelson seemed infuriatingly perplexed. "Don't get me wrong, the kid was a hell of a ball player, but he wasn't anything special. We had a lot of talented kids that year. You had Demetrius Williams at running back, Quinn Tittle at receiver, and 'Slingin Sammy' Sampson at quarterback. Sammy's with the Raiders now, you know?"

Brittany wasn't a big-time sports fan, but at least she'd known that much. "Yes, you're right. But as good as Tittle was, I seem to remember Boyle was Sampson's favorite target out there."

The Chicago PD detective wasn't certain if that was true, but it sounded good. She hoped Nelson wouldn't question it.

"Well, Boyle was a big son of a bitch for a seventeen-year-old kid. Made it easy for Sammy to rack up all those TDs. But Boyle was slower than shit. Couldn't run much either, at least compared to Tittle. I never had a white guy on the team that could run. Ha ha."

"Be that as it may," Brittany continued, "I remember that Boyle lost his parents a few years before playing for you. What type of impact did that have on his play on the field?"

"It had no impact as far as I'm concerned. Not too many kids had a support system like Cal had."

"What do you mean by that?"

"What do I mean? Hell, lady, I'm waiting for you to ask me a good question. After his parents were killed, Cal was taken in by one of the best families you could be taken in by."

"Could you refresh my memory on that one? I guess I didn't know his personal story as much as I thought."

"Ha! I stumped the reporter for once. That'll be one for the record books. Why, it's the Petrocelli family, of course. Alfredo and Susan adopted Cal after his parents died. Vinnie was Cal's best friend at the school. They were like true biological brothers. It's a shame what happened to Vinnie, though. I had no idea he'd be caught up in violence like that."

Bingo. Brittany had the connection she sought. So Callahan Boyle was adopted by the Petrocellis after all. Which meant that Alfredo had lied to the police when questioned about the renegade soldier's identity. Based on the description and the connection, Brittany now knew it was highly likely that Cal was the one who killed Vinnie Petrocelli and the soldiers at the warehouse that fateful night three months ago. But why?

"Is there anything else you're gonna ask me?" Coach Nelson fumed. It didn't seem like he wanted to continue the interview much longer.

"Oh no," Brittany said, eager to get off the phone. "I'll have one of my colleagues follow up in a few days. You've been more than helpful, Coach."

"It's about time," Coach Nelson said. "I think I'm done talking to the press for a while."

Brittany wanted to say something but was met with silence. Coach Nelson had disconnected the call. She smiled, knowing she'd gotten more information than she expected. She'd make one more play on Boyle before leaving San Diego but had more than enough to hit the ground running on the case when she returned from her "vacation." She'd be sure to pay Alfredo Petrocelli a visit to ask him about his relationship with the man Coach Nelson called "Cal."

If she could dig up one or both of the witnesses who had been missing since the police talked to Alfredo, she knew she'd have enough to get her arrest, and one more accolade in her FBI application.

Pretty soon she wouldn't have to pretend to be an FBI special agent. She'd be one for real.

13

The sound of gunfire reverberated sooner than Cal could react to it. Thankfully, his latest pursuer misfired. Cal thought about hitting the ground to avoid further gunfire but knew he'd be an easy target if he stayed down.

Instead, he raced away from the green apartment building where the shots were coming from. Screams echoed from the front of the grocery store at the sound of additional shots. Cal didn't care about the commotion elsewhere; he just knew he needed to get out of this new gunman's line of fire. A tree branch exploded behind him and two bullets peppered near his feet as he ran toward the sidewalk, away from the store.

He became entangled in bushes separating the parking lot from the sidewalk, making it difficult to run as fast as he wanted. Two more gunshots zipped overhead, forcing him to finally duck. Only after he hit the mulch did Cal realize these shots were coming toward the parking lot, not toward the street.

Cal stayed down in the bushes, wondering what was

going on. Twigs poked at his arms and legs. He turned his head to examine the chaos and felt a sharp stick poke at his eye. He cursed at the pain and then cursed at himself for being in this situation. The wail of police sirens grew closer, giving him hope that the shooters would lay off. Bullets continued to pepper the area.

A third gun emitted a torrent of ammunition seconds after the two gunmen stopped to reload. This gun sounded more like a pistol than the rifles the other two were using. Cal noticed that one of the rifles resumed shooting, but the second one hadn't. He looked between the bushes toward the green apartment building and saw a figure standing behind the rifle on the upper floor. The other gunman was down.

Who is the third shooter?

Cal heard the return fire of the rifle but noticed it was no longer aimed at him in the bushes. He rolled to his side and prepared to make his escape, hoping the presence of the other shooter would provide cover.

Cal exited the bushes and was shocked to see the person returning the rifleman's fire. Brittany Wilson stood behind a tree, quickly turning when she thought the rifleman was reloading to get a shot off. After a series of two quick fires, Cal noticed the rifleman had stopped. The police had to have arrived by now. He was likely making his own escape.

Brittany turned to Cal once the shooting stopped and smiled at him. She had saved his life. But why? And where had she come from?

"What the hell was that?"

"C'mon. We don't have time to chat now. The last thing either of us need is for the police to find us and ask questions. Let's get out of here."

Brittany started running down Seventh Avenue. Cal felt

compelled to follow her, even though he'd hoped not to see her again after she left Uncle Judd's house a few days prior. Behind, he heard the police entering the Whole Foods and doing their best to close off the perimeter.

With his head still pounding from Spiky Hair's punch, Cal struggled to keep up with the FBI agent. She must've been a track star in a past life. Her legs churned higher and faster than an elevated train. She ran to the intersection of Seventh and Robinson and turned onto Robinson, her legs still pumping like pistons.

Cal considered himself in decent shape but found himself winded by the time they stopped halfway up the street next to a parked Ford Taurus. He blamed the multiple near-death experiences of the afternoon.

He wanted to thank Brittany for what she had done but found it hard to speak as he caught his breath. His wooziness was only exacerbated by the running. He found himself leaning against the Taurus for support. Brittany just laughed at him.

"A lack of words from Mr. Boyle? Not so surprising from what I've heard about you."

Cal's voice struggled to break free from the confines of his throat. The expressions he struggled to share weren't ones of gratitude.

"What have you heard about me?"

Brittany laughed again and crossed her arms while shifting her weight onto her right leg. She looked much more like an agent on vacation, in a pair of denim shorts and a bejeweled orange strapless top that showed off her toned middle. Cal thought the outfit was more reminiscent of an exotic belly dancer than a law enforcement official, and a fine one at that.

Her dark hair was straightened and danced upon her

shoulders, which like the rest of her body were a rich brown. Her gun, a Glock 17, was tucked neatly in the back of her shorts. "Sometimes it's amazing what people will say when you tell them you're a sports reporter reminiscing about the good old days with a high school football coach."

Did she call Coach Nelson? Despite all the touchdowns Cal had scored for him, it would be just like the old coach to rat him out. He probably told Brittany all she needed to know that would connect him to Alfredo.

"All of a sudden the FBI's case against the mafia is looking pretty good. And if my colleagues at the Chicago Police Department were to find out about this—well, you'd be a very interesting suspect. Alfredo Petrocelli was nearly killed; his son, Vinnie, and many mafia soldiers were actually killed. Were you not happy that the Petrocellis took you in as a young boy? But fear not: this suggests Alfredo lied to the police and indeed knew who the soldier was that shot him. With some revised testimony, we can take both of you —but primarily you—down for a long time."

Brittany's smile was basking in confidence. Cal knew she had him and he would be hauled away and charged for a whole host of murders any day. He had known this day was coming, but not this fast.

"I just wanted to thank you for saving my life back there. I have no idea who those guys were, but it's pretty obvious they wanted to kill me. I couldn't have gotten out of there without your help, so thank you."

"The pleasure was all mine, Mr. Boyle, but you can call me Brittany. Now that I've saved your life, I think you owe me a little something, don't you think?"

Cal let out a breath of annoyance. "What would that be?"

He didn't need to ask. He already knew.

"Like I said before, I don't want to just take down the small fish, I want the big kahuna. Thanks to your football coach, I know you were adopted by Alfredo Petrocelli and were close with Vinnie Petrocelli growing up. I'm sure I can get the adoption papers with a court order, but I'm hoping your admission of the facts will make that unnecessary. You can help me bring the entire Chicago mafia down, Mr. Boyle. Think of it this way: Alfredo and all the other dirty criminals can be in jail with your help. You'd do some good for the city—hell, even the country. And this case would be the biggest of my career and get me my next promotion before I turn thirty. It's a win-win."

Agent Wilson's smugness sent Cal's heart into a thumping pattern of fury. He hated not having the upper hand. The worst part was that he found himself getting turned on by the blend of confidence and beauty that the supposedly vacationing agent was displaying. To Cal, she seemed just as crooked as any cop the mafia had on its payroll.

Still, Cal couldn't admit to anything, even if every word Wilson said was true. If he was going down, he was ready to go down with a fight.

"I'm not sure what the Bureau is investigating the mafia for," Cal said. "Even if you think I may know something about their activities, you have no proof of that or any proof that I was involved in the deaths of Vinnie Petrocelli or those mobsters. So, why should I help you? You may have saved my life, but I don't trust you one bit. As soon as you have what you need to put Alfredo in the slammer, you'll find a way to stick me in there with him."

Brittany shook her head. "As I've said before, that's not true, Mr. Boyle. I really need your help. Forget my own ambitions for a second and think of the good you'll be doing for anyone victimized by the Chicago mafia. Justice will be served. I'll do my best to keep your nose out of it to take down Alfredo. Though, if you really were the murderer at the warehouse that night, it'll be a tough sell."

"I wasn't the murderer." Cal knew it sounded like he was being overly defensive, but he wasn't concerned. "And I don't care what you have against me, I'm not going to help you. If you want to build a case against me and arrest me, then so be it. I'm standing right here."

Cal had issued the ultimate challenge move, and she knew it.

Brittany remained standing, with her arms crossed, and tapped her foot. "Have it your way, then. I tried to help you. Now I'm going to come after you just like the others. It won't take any time at all for me to build my case. I'm good at it. In fact, I'm the best."

Cal looked at her and back toward Robinson Avenue. He wished he could hitch a ride to Uncle Judd's and escape the glare of the special agent.

"Very well, then. Let's see what you can do."

Cal walked back toward Robinson, one part pissed off and one part worried that he really would spend eternity in the slammer before he could fully become the man he promised Maria he would be. Would working with Agent Wilson help him become that man? He didn't think so.

What he needed to do was get back to Chicago on his own terms. He needed to end the threats on his life and kill Alfredo once and for all.

14

Alfredo Petrocelli couldn't remember the last time he'd been asked to perform such "grunt work." Of all the dirty jobs a soldier might be asked to do in the mafia, kidnapping another human being was one of the most unusual.

It wasn't like killing, which, as gruesome as it was, was still an act even the softest of mob associates could get behind. That was easy enough and was something he'd done about a hundred times, more or less. Bribery, extortion, robbery, assault, battery, hustling prostitutes, gambling—they all seemed petty. Yet the act of taking someone against their will and keeping them prisoner didn't feel right to him, but it had to be done.

Of course, no one ordered Alfredo to kidnap Tony Fregosi's younger sisters—he decided to engage in the act himself. The fact that the girls were so young—the oldest being fifteen, and the youngest twelve—upset him even more. He wished there was another option to pluck away Tony Fregosi and bring in Cal, but he had no knowledge of the boy's whereabouts, and getting someone to find him could take months. After Giovanni Lucerno's LA thugs' attempt to assassinate Cal failed miserably, Alfredo knew he had to move forward with his plan.

His driver, a young Italian fresh off the boat from Sicily, parked across the street from the Fregosi house in the South Side neighborhood of Bridgeport, just south of I-55. The driver and the other men in the vehicle had scouted the house over the past two days, trying to get a sense of the girls' routine. His men had done their work well, under the orders of capo "Death" Masucci. Two days wasn't enough time to discover much, especially since both days were over the weekend, but the initial surveillance revealed the girls liked to go to a friend's house down the street. The men had seemed shocked when Masucci told them Alfredo wanted to execute the kidnapping himself that Monday.

They'd been waiting for about ten minutes when the man in the passenger seat pointed to two young girls walking in their direction from the sidewalk across the street.

"Is that them?" Alfredo asked.

"Yes, my don, it's them," said the man in the passenger seat. "We've seen them walking back from a neighbor's house each day around this time. Yesterday the girls crossed the street right in front of us and went to this old bag's house. Looks like they aren't doing that today."

Alfredo nodded and watched the two girls. The man next to him, a portly youngster in his early twenties, began spouting off the background information on the two girls. The oldest, Alexa, was rather tall for her age, with long brown hair and olive skin. She wore a big black parka over her black jeans. For a family that was allegedly poor, the coat looked surprisingly new. Maybe big brother had bought it for her with one of his last mafia paychecks.

The youngest, Tina, held her big sister's hand and looked microscopic compared to her sibling. The young girl was bundled to the nines, with a white hat, pink scarf, and a much-older-looking, drab-gray coat.

The girls stopped in front of the Fregosi house. It was a tiny, sore-looking house constructed of faded gray brick. A dirty bay window gave Alfredo and his crew a small peek into the home, only a sliver of room visible past the mostly drawn velvet curtain. The house was set off from the sidewalk, the basement of the home disappearing from view below the gated sidewalk.

The sisters broke hands and separated, Alexa choosing to enter the house, while Tina marched on. This presented an interesting challenge.

Which girl to go after?

The car had plenty of room for the two girls, but grabbing both in different locations would present too great of a challenge. It was easy to smuggle one person away if no one was paying attention, but two girls in two different locations would be tough.

"What should we do, boss?" the man in the passenger seat asked. He was obviously as perplexed as Alfredo was.

Alfredo wanted both girls. That would definitely get the Fregosi boy to come out of his hiding place. If he only grabbed one, there was always a chance that the girl he kidnapped wasn't the most loved sister, and the boy could stay away. Alfredo hoped he'd come back regardless of which one they took.

By the time he opened his mouth to speak, Alexa Fregosi had unlocked the door and entered the house. Alfredo recalled the impressive height of the girl for a fifteen-year-old and decided she was likely a feisty one. Not that he or any of the other men in the car couldn't overpower her, but he didn't want to take a chance. Just like any desperate predator, he chose the weakest of his prey.

"Let's take the younger girl," Alfredo said. "I'll get out there and follow her."

The driver turned around, his face awake in shock. "Yeh swur, boz? We take care of 'er, make swur you no get caught in zis."

Alfredo had difficulty understanding the driver's broken English. Recalling the mention of the old lady across the street, he had a plan for getting the girl into the car with little fanfare.

"I appreciate your concern, but I hardly know you numbskulls, and there's a chance you could fuck it up. I wanted this girl taken, so I'm going to take her. Just be ready when I get her in the car."

Each of the men looked at each other and then back at Alfredo before nodding. He could tell they were nervous, thinking the old man wouldn't be able to get the job done. They had no idea of Alfredo's true strengths, things that he did long before he became boss.

Alfredo exited the vehicle and shivered against the bitter evening chill. The neighborhood's streetlights had just started to come on, but Alfredo was thankful he had a somewhat decent cover of darkness as he strolled across the street and to the opposite sidewalk.

Tina Fregosi had walked several houses ahead, and Alfredo had a difficult time keeping up with the young girl. He wanted to catch her before she got too far, and he knew if she went for one of the other houses, she would be lost to them.

"Excuse me! Excuse me, young lady!"

The girl stopped walking and turned around, her face fogged by the icy breath escaping from her lungs. There seemed to be no fear on her face. Alfredo credited his smiling face and rosy cheeks for keeping the girl's nerves at bay.

"I'm looking for one of your neighbors' houses. I have a friend from church, and his mother lives in this neighborhood. She's very ill. I have hot food in my car that I want to take to her. Do you know which house she lives in?"

The girl's eyes lit up. "Are you looking for Mrs. Rittenhouse? She lives across the street. Her family moved away, though, so I don't know how you'd know her son from church."

Alfredo swallowed as he thought of what to say next. It'd be an easy enough explanation if he told the girl he knew her family before they left the area and they asked him to check up on the old bag.

"Yes, you're right. But her son and I still chat from time to time, and he said he's been thinking about Mama Rittenhouse. He wanted me to bring a few home-cooked meals to her to keep her warm through this cold winter."

The girl smiled and nodded. That's when Alfredo knew it was time to make his move.

"Say, you like Mrs. Rittenhouse, don't you?"

The girl nodded again.

"Why don't I fetch my meals out of the car and you can show me exactly where Mrs. Rittenhouse lives? Perhaps you can even give them to her, say they're from you and that you were thinking about her. Do you think she would like that?"

Tina Fregosi beamed and took a step closer to Alfredo. "Yeah, she loves it when I bring food to her. I'm sure she'd even give me some money. We could really use this money, sir, so I'd love it if I could take your food and give it to her."

This was working much better than Alfredo thought. He did a quick scan of the street, up and down both sidewalks.

The only thing he was worried about was if anyone was watching him and the girl from inside their house. He hoped his ear muffs and scarf would mask his features enough so he wouldn't be easy to identify.

"Come this way, then. I'll get them out of my trunk."

"Okay."

The girl skipped behind Alfredo as he walked across the street and toward the car. He knew exactly what to do. He would open the trunk, pretend to look for the food, and then throw the girl in. His men would take care of the rest.

Alfredo got to the trunk, opened it, and looked back to the girl. Though she'd seemed happy before, a curious expression replaced the glee that had shone in her eyes across the street. Had she seen something she shouldn't have?

"Alright, I've got some nice warm soup in here for Mrs. Rittenhouse. Won't she love it?"

When the girl didn't answer, Alfredo knew something was up. The young, portly man had exited the rear of the vehicle and stalked toward the girl.

Tina Fregosi screamed and started for her house across the street. Alfredo grabbed her before she could run off and lifted her high in the air, trying to force her into the trunk. The girl didn't weigh much, but his side screamed in pain as he lifted her. Portly Man ran over and pulled a damp cloth out of his pocket.

"Turn her here, turn her here," the man whispered.

Alfredo shifted her head toward the young man and removed his hand just as Portly Man placed the cloth over her mouth.

Tina Fregosi gagged and eventually her kicks stopped. She fell down into the carpet of the trunk, seemingly unconscious. Alfredo wanted to kill the young man for his initial incompetence, but they both ran around and entered the car before any neighbors caught wind of what happened.

The car sped off from the curb and raced into the night. Alfredo gave the directions for the safe house, resisted the urge to put a bullet in the brain of the young man next to him, and sighed. He'd gotten the first Christmas present he wanted; he only hoped the next ones would follow.

15

Cal's head was still ringing from the attempts on his life the day before. When Uncle Judd heard what happened, he immediately checked them into a hotel in Mission Bay until things died down a bit. He didn't want the police coming around his house to ask questions any more than Cal did.

"I'm sick of sitting around in this dumpy hotel room," Cal said.

Watching television and wasting away on crappy room service food was wearing on him. He tried to stay active by going down to the hotel gym or walking along the small beach behind the hotel, but he found there was little he could do to distract himself from the thoughts swimming in his head.

"Well, what else do you suppose we do?" Uncle Judd asked. "If we go back to the house, we know the cops will want to talk about you carving the guts of that guy at Whole Foods. Regardless of your innocence, they might do the same amount of digging as that FBI gal."

Cal sighed and his temple throbbed as he thought of

Special Agent Brittany Wilson. Her recent appearance in his life frustrated him beyond measure. On the one hand, she wanted to bring down the mafia, which Cal could get behind. On the other hand, she wanted his help to do it, and Cal was certain he would only serve so much of a purpose before he'd end up in the slammer and see his freedom disappear. Further complicating matters was his realization that Brittany was smoking hot. She created a lust inside of him that he hadn't felt since Maria.

"I can't keep sitting around here," Cal said. "I know I've hinted at it, but this time I've got to do something about it. I need to get back to Chicago and put some fear into Alfredo."

Cal sat up on the bed he was lounging on. Uncle Judd, his ankle feeling much better after a few days, and no longer needing crutches, walked over from the desk chair he'd been sitting in. Clasped in his hand was a mostly finished White Russian. Judd had been quite the regular at the hotel bar over the past few days, and taking drinks back to the room was something they let him get away with. Judd set the drink down on the nightstand and grabbed Cal by the shoulders.

"Hey now. I get that you're mad and you wanna go kill that a-hole who pretended to be your father all these years. I understand how you feel. But think about all that's happened over the last few days. First, that crazy FBI lady shows up on our doorstep and causes me to sprain my ankle, then you nearly get killed going grocery shopping."

Cal took a deep breath and shook his uncle's hands away. He'd only lived with Judd for three months, but in that time he knew when Judd was cueing up an important point. Whatever he had to say, Cal wasn't sure he wanted to hear it.

"What are you getting at?"

Uncle Judd sighed. He glanced at the remnants of his

White Russian, picked up the beverage, and offered it to Cal. Cal looked at the glass and scrunched up his face. Judd thrust the glass out further, until it was only inches from Cal's hand.

"C'mon, take it."

Cal reluctantly grabbed the drink from his uncle and gulped down the rest of the creamy and chocolatey liquid. Cal wasn't a big fan of Kahlúa but had to admit it tasted good combined with the vodka and cream. He looked back at his uncle.

"I think instead of going to Chicago, you need to think about leaving the country," his uncle said. "Maybe to Mexico. I know a guy that can fix you up with a good ID."

"Mexico? Are you kidding me? No, I can't keep hiding from these problems. You've said it yourself, I can't keep moping here in San Diego. In order for me to move on, I have to take Alfredo out. Then it ends, I promise you that."

"Are you sure revenge is the best idea? Maybe you should worry about saving your ass and getting out of Dodge."

Cal stood from the bed just inches from Judd's face. He felt an anger inside like he hadn't felt toward his uncle before. He remembered pummeling the drunk man at the beach and felt the sudden urge to do it again, almost forgetting it was Uncle Judd standing in front of him.

"I'll deal with the consequences of my actions. If I spend the rest of my life in jail but end Alfredo's life in the process, I'll be happier for it."

Uncle Judd opened his mouth to argue when a knock echoed throughout the room from the door.

"Who is that?"

Uncle Judd's whisper was barely audible. The last time

someone called on them at home it had ended in disaster. It could been housekeeping, but Cal had his suspicions.

"Don't move."

Cal stepped past his uncle and crept to the door as another knock rang out. Uncle Judd looked at him with curiosity. Cal got to the door and glanced through the peephole, seeing who he expected to see. He waved to his uncle to hide behind the wall separating the beds from the hallway leading to the door. Judd shrugged and gave a *Who is it?* look, but Cal didn't respond.

Once Judd was safely behind the wall, Cal reached for the lock, unlatched it, and unbolted the chain. He pulled the door handle toward him and stepped behind the closing door. Agent Wilson walked into the room with a confused look on her face. By the time the door closed and she turned to face Cal, he had her pinned against the opposite wall.

"What the hell are you doing here?"

Cal had his forearm against Brittany's throat and kept his legs tight against hers, preventing her from getting any extension to kick him. His left hand held her right arm to her side. Cal was surprised she didn't scream.

"Cal, Cal, Cal, what are you doing?" Uncle Judd came running from behind the corner, waving his hands in the air to stop Cal. "Assaulting a federal agent is the last thing we need to worry about."

"Don't worry, nothing will happen to Agent Wilson. I just want to know why she's here."

Cal grit his teeth and snarled at Brittany, but the young agent wasn't fazed. Despite his anger, Cal was both impressed by her actions and slightly aroused.

"I'm not here looking for trouble, Mr. Boyle."

"Let me guess: you're here to ask me to help you crack the case."

Brittany rolled her eyes. "I'm not here for that either. You may want to help me, though, after what I'm about to share with you."

It was Cal's turn to roll his eyes. "There's nothing you could say that would convince me to help you."

There was no sarcasm, no overarching confidence written on Agent Wilson's face. Apparently, whatever she had to say was grave in nature.

"I received some news from my boss today. He said that the sister of the boy wanted for Mayor Caruso's murder was kidnapped."

Cal gasped at the mention of Tony and the suggestion something had happened to his sister. He knew right away that Alfredo was behind it.

"I figured you might know who I was talking about," Brittany said. There was no joyous flash of teeth this time. "As much as my boss would like to find you, the boy, and bring down the mafia, we're dealing with a missing child here. Finding her and bringing her back safe has to be my top priority."

Her soft-brown eyes turned to Cal in a pleading fashion. As much as he wanted to look away, he couldn't shift his gaze. He wanted to do anything possible to help Brittany in that moment, but he wasn't sure if he could. He felt compelled to rescue the girl and support Tony. The boy was probably all alone and very scared. Cal wanted to make it right with them, but he still wasn't sure if he could trust Brittany.

"I'm asking for your help this time, Mr. Boyle. Not to help me but to help this girl. The information I've gathered thus far suggests that you know the ins and outs of the mafia. If they were involved in her disappearance, you're the only hope we have of getting her back."

Cal exhaled and looked at Uncle Judd, whose sympathetic eyes went soft in support. Cal knew what the right thing to do was, but he had a nagging sense that Brittany still wanted him more than she wanted to help the girl.

"Who says I can't go back to Chicago and find the girl myself?"

Brittany tried to ease out from beneath Cal's forearm. He wasn't having it.

"I used to feel that way, you know. Like I didn't need anyone else's help. I know I look like a supertough FBI agent, but I have my moments of doubt. I've already told you several times, Cal, that I'll do all I can to make sure you're kept out of this for as long as possible, though I can't say the same for my fellow agents or the Chicago PD. If we work together, I'm certain we'll find the girl. Maybe we can bring in Alfredo too."

Cal chuckled. "Save it for the judge, Agent Wilson. Alfredo doesn't deserve to sit behind bars. He deserves worse. I'm not going to play your little games. No matter how much you ask me."

Uncle Judd cleared his throat, and both Cal and Brittany turned to him. "Think of her, Cal."

Cal raised his brow, not entirely certain whom his uncle was talking about. It took him a moment, but eventually he knew. Uncle Judd was avoiding the name for Cal's benefit. He didn't want to give Brittany anything else to work with.

"Think of the man she'd want you to become, a force for good. I know I've told you to stay away from this agent as much as you've thought about staying away, but you can help find this missing girl. I know it."

Cal looked between Uncle Judd and Brittany, realizing his uncle was right. He could find a way to save her, and maybe he'd still be able to go after Alfredo in the process.

He'd break away for just long enough to make sure Alfredo was six feet under. He'd just have to hope he could find a way to either escape after it was over, or his punishers felt lenient.

"What do you say?" Brittany asked. "Want to accept some help for once? It took me a while, too, but I learned to like it."

Cal swore he saw a hint of a wink as Agent Wilson smiled back at him. He wondered if she had funny feelings in her stomach like he had for her. He shook the thought from his head and blamed the incident with Tank Top and Spiky Hair for his aching head's irrational thoughts.

"You're sure you think I should help?" Cal asked his uncle. He knew in his heart that he needed to make this choice but felt compelled to seek his uncle's support.

"I think finding the girl is the right thing to do. I'm not sure if I'd trust this young lady, but sometimes you've gotta do what's right even if it's not popular."

Cal nodded, sure he was making the right choice, despite the apprehension he felt in his chest.

"Alright, Agent Wilson. I'll help you. Let's go back to Chicago."

16

Alfredo Petrocelli brushed off his coat and stomped his black leather boots on the rug in front of the door before kicking them off. The gently falling snow from earlier in the afternoon had picked up in earnest over the last few hours, and Alfredo's driver was hesitant to drive the mob boss to the safe house where the Fregosi girl was being kept. Still, Alfredo urged the driver on, even as cars were swerving off roads, into sidewalks, and across lanes of traffic.

Alfredo guessed a good four inches had accumulated since he and the driver left the Petrocelli compound in Evanston an hour ago. It'd taken them twice as long to get to the house as usual, but Alfredo didn't mind. He needed to speak with the girl.

"Is she still in the basement?"

Alfredo looked at the two men flanking the door, both with quizzical expressions on their faces at Alfredo's disguise. He'd decided to use the Joe Lewis moniker again, seeing that it worked so well the last time he used it, when he confronted Mayor Caruso in his office at City Hall.

"Yes, sir," said the soldier to his left.

It was the same portly young man who had nearly cost them the entire operation. Alfredo was sure that the neighbor who'd seen the Tina Fregosi kidnapping take place and tipped off the police would remember the young man's short, round stature if she saw him in a lineup. Alfredo would deal with him later.

Despite the fact they'd been seen, the cops had no clue what car they had been driving, since the neighbor wasn't so good with details. Forty-eight hours after the kidnapping, they also had no clue of the girl's whereabouts. Alfredo could only hope word of the kidnapping had reached its intended audiences; otherwise, the whole effort would prove for naught.

"Good," Alfredo said, turning to the portly man. He pivoted to his right and looked over the other man flanking the door, tall and sporting a strong jaw with dark stubble. Alfredo was more familiar with this man, as he'd seen him guarding his penthouse a few times. He seemed strong and loyal. Alfredo didn't know much about him, but he already liked him.

He nodded to the man and spoke again. "Take me to her."

Alfredo followed the man through the near-empty living room, darkened from the curtains pulled tight against the windows. There weren't any couches or coffee tables in the room, only a card table and folding chairs, where the men on guard duty could sit around, play cards, and smoke cigars. A few discarded containers of dip were scattered on the table, along with some paper plates.

"Jesus Christ, clean this place up before I leave. This isn't a fucking bachelor pad. If we ever have to rent this place out, I don't want pizza stains all over the carpet."

The man with the strong jaw paused in front of him. "Yes, sir, we'll find a garbage bag."

"Good. Carry on."

The man resumed walking, and Alfredo followed him to the rear of the house, where they passed a small powder room that had been converted into a full bathroom. They stopped at the white wooden door leading to the basement. It was the only way in or out of the tiny space, as all the downstairs windows had been sealed and boarded up from the outside. As long as the girl didn't get past the door, she'd have no chance to escape.

Strong Jaw removed a key from his pocket and unlocked the padlock securing the door, then unlatched the old-fashioned lock above the door handle. Alfredo was pleased to see they were taking security very seriously. He hoped the other security measure downstairs was still intact.

Alfredo looked into the man's eyes as he readied his hand to open the door. Strong Jaw was smart and didn't say a word. Alfredo didn't want the girl to overhear anything in case she blabbed when he eventually decided to let her go. The mob boss nodded to the young associate and used the light from his cell phone to watch his footing as he descended the basement stairs.

The sound of sniffling could be heard from the minute Alfredo's feet touched the steps. His heart wrenched at the sound. As evil as many said he was, he still had a soul.

He recalled a memory of his youngest, Luca, crying in his room after an argument with another boy at school. The boy had punched him in the face, and Luca had been too young and scared to fight back. Over twenty years later, Alfredo still remembered how awful he felt as he tried to comfort his son.

Alfredo reached the bottom of the steps, and his woolen

socks dusted the top of the concrete basement floor. The door to the basement had closed, but the lock hadn't been set. The light from Alfredo's cell phone had gone off, leaving him unable to see the girl before him, enclosed by a brick wall on one side and a chain-link fence on the other three. It was her own little jail cell.

"Who—who are you?"

The young girl's question came out between muffled sniffles. Alfredo was sure the girl was wiping her eyes and snotty nose against her shirt. The cloth was likely the source of her muffled voice. Alfredo wasn't sure what his men had done to her—if they had given her food, or a box of Kleenex. He felt compelled to at least provide some comfort. No one so innocent should have to suffer like this, he thought.

"I'm afraid I can't tell you my name," Alfredo said. "I can only tell you I'm not here to hurt you."

The girl's sniffles turned into harsh, resounding cries. "I wanna go home!"

Tina Fregosi began full-on wailing. Alfredo felt his heart wrench again, and he reached out and touched the chain-link fence, as if the gesture would comfort the young girl. He really wasn't sure where she was positioned, which he knew could come back to bite him if he wasn't careful. The girl probably wasn't in a fighting mood yet, but he knew she would be after a few days. Humans couldn't help but utilize their instincts for survival. He stepped back from the fence, forgot any sympathetic thoughts he had for the girl, and straightened up.

"I'm sure you do want to go home, child. And I'd like to help you get there. But there's a few things I need you to tell me. Can you tell me what I need to know? I'm sure I can have these men that have been taking care of you give you a nice treat."

The young girl kept crying. Alfredo could almost feel her shakes as she wailed. He wanted to see where the girl was, but he didn't dare turn on the light of his cell phone. He'd just have to wait for his eyes to adjust to the darkness.

"Just take me home! Are you that old man who kidnapped me?"

Alfredo knew he could deny it. He was wearing the Joe Lewis disguise, complete with top hat, wig, and mustache, but he wasn't good at altering his voice. Yet he knew if he didn't deny it that it was another piece of evidence the girl could use against him if he let her go.

Now that he thought of it, he realized he shouldn't make any promises to the girl about letting her go. He was more likely to have her killed than not. After all, he couldn't take any chances of being connected to the kidnapping.

"My name is Joe Lewis," Alfredo said, artfully dodging the question. "I want to ask you a question about your brother, Tony. If you answer my questions, I promise I'll let you go. We'll see how soon we can get you home to your dad."

Alfredo knew it was a lie, but the girl couldn't see his expression, unless her eyes had adjusted really well to the lack of light in the basement. He had to know if the girl thought Tony would come back to find her. If she was confident he would, Alfredo figured he could expect the young boy any day now. Maybe she'd been in contact with her older brother.

"If you promise to let me out, I'll tell you. Just let me out."

The girl was still whining, but it was less pronounced. Alfredo felt slightly better about that.

He still couldn't shake the memories of his own children

in pain and how similar the girl sounded to them when they were her age.

"So, about your brother. I understand he's been away for a long time. Do you know why he ran away?"

Tina Fregosi kicked the chain-link fence in front of her. "He didn't run away. He went to live with one of his friends."

So that's what the old man told his girls. Of course, Alfredo knew better.

"Have you talked to your brother since he left? Has he told you when he's coming back?"

The girl sniffled some more and took her time in answering. Alfredo wondered if she'd answer at all. It wasn't like they'd built a great relationship to this point.

"No, but he's talked to my daddy. Maybe he knows when he's coming back."

"Ah," Alfredo said. This was what he had expected. *Time to turn up the pressure.* "Do you think your brother will come back home now? Now that you're no longer at home. Now that you've been taken away."

Alfredo refused to mention that the girl had been kidnapped. For all the girl knew, she'd been pushed in the trunk of his driver's car as part of an elaborate game. A little bit of nuthouse fun courtesy of Mrs. Rittenhouse.

"I know he'll come for me," the girl said. Her crying and sniffling had completely stopped. It was like his question about her brother had given her more confidence.

Alfredo felt the girl's presence directly beneath his feet. Her foot brushing against the bottom of the chain-link fence earlier had confirmed her position. He wanted to shine the light of his cell phone on her and face her just once, just to confirm she was telling the truth.

He bent down into a squat, his old knees creaking. He turned the light of his cell phone on and aimed it at the girl.

He expected her to shield her eyes. Instead, her face radiated fury.

It was only a blink of an eye, but that was all it took for the girl to force a wad of phlegm from the bottom of her lungs and through her mouth, a loogie of spit sailing right for Alfredo's face.

The mob boss's expression turned sour as he felt the girl's spit land atop his cheek. He took his scarf, wiped the mess away, and found himself moving from delighted to infuriated.

"You spoiled brat!" Alfredo rose to his feet and pointed his finger at the girl, keeping the light of his phone on so she could see the fury on his face. "You better respect me, you understand? Otherwise, you'll be dead if you pull another stunt like that!"

Alfredo turned for the stairs and marched up them two at a time, his legs feeling as spry as they had in his younger days. The girl started crying again, exactly the reaction he'd hoped for.

At least he'd discovered one thing: his plan was likely working. Now it was time for him to see if Cal and Tony took the bait.

17

Returning to Chicago felt strange at first for Cal. He felt like a soldier coming home from a long war, so changed by the battle fought far from the homeland that nothing seemed right to him upon venturing back. It was almost as if he'd never lived there. He was glad to be back in his hometown but wasn't thrilled to be dropped off at his old apartment by Agent Wilson after their charter flight had landed safely in a nearby suburban airfield.

Cal was thankful he'd paid six months' rent in advance, as the only signs that were stuck to his door were maintenance notices and a stray complaint from a new neighbor regarding an unpleasant odor. Uncertain if the mafia were watching his apartment, Cal told Uncle Judd to stand back while he opened the door and scoured each room with Agent Wilson's duty flashlight. He'd rather have had his old Beretta on hand as he searched his place, but he felt safe, thanks to the strength of the aluminum the flashlight was made of. It could serve as an effective weapon.

The thought of Brittany caused Cal's heart to race.

They'd been in increasingly close proximity over the last several hours, from the lengthy car ride to Las Vegas, where Brittany had secured the charter flight home, to the time spent sitting next to each other on the small plane. The flight was mostly silent, but Cal couldn't help but gaze upon Brittany's beauty as she slept next to him. At one moment, she rested her head on his shoulder, and Cal felt chills up his spine. It was how he used to feel with Maria.

On the other hand, Cal was sick of her and wished she'd never entered his life. He'd only agreed to help her because Tony's younger sister had been kidnapped, but he still wanted to go after Alfredo, and he was sure she'd stand in the way.

"Doesn't that smell better?" Uncle Judd asked, interrupting his thoughts. "I knew we'd get that awful stench out of here. Leave it to me to concoct a natural air freshener. Now, if only we could get that heat turned up a bit higher."

Cal laughed at his uncle and watched as he chopped some cucumbers and radishes for a salad. The gentle sound of simmering water could be heard from the stove that was hard-boiling the eggs for their salad.

"I'm sure it's been a while since you've had to deal with a real winter."

Uncle Judd nodded and moved to the stove to turn off the gas and allow the eggs to sit. Watching his uncle pad around in his shorts and tropical button-up in the chilly apartment while going about his business made Cal realize how different he was from him. Whereas Judd was easy-going and carefree, Cal was sitting in his chair, worried about his next steps.

"Sure is. What do you suppose we do? I guess we can't ditch that agent now that she knows where you live. We'd better hope she can uphold her promises about keeping you out of the slammer."

That much was true. The last thing Cal wanted was to be awoken from his slumber by a raiding army of Chicago police officers and FBI agents ready to haul him away for his crimes.

"She said she's going to talk to her boss and see if they have any more information on the girl's whereabouts. I think I'm gonna do some exploring on my own, though. I know all of the mafia's haunts and bet I can find her before they can."

"There's the Cal I know and love," Uncle Judd said. He threw the rest of the chopped veggies into the bowl of lettuce, poured his homemade balsamic vinaigrette over the salad, and tossed with tongs. "But like I said, I'm not sure how much good it'll do to seek revenge, as awful as Alfredo was. If you're insistent on doing it, though, at least tell me you've got a weapon."

Cal froze at the mention of the word "weapon." He'd emptied out his arsenal when he and Fonzie went to the warehouse to save Maria. He assumed all of the weapons they used that night were in police custody. He couldn't remember hiding anything else beneath the loose floorboard in his closet.

"Nope, I've got nothing. I could always go to some club the mafia runs protection for that's loosely guarded. I can still beat the shit out of anyone I need to, and I'll just take whatever weapon the poor soul has on him."

Uncle Judd scratched his goatee, the nails scraping against the combination of hair and skin in an irritating fashion, like rubbing sandpaper on your cheek.

"Isn't that dangerous? For them to be armed with guns to

kingdom come and you not to have anything other than your bare hands?"

Cal stood and joined his uncle in the kitchen. He clapped his hand across his back and smiled.

"Have I ever told you the story of the first time I killed a man with my bare hands? All I did was—"

Uncle Judd shook his head furiously and waved Cal off.

"No, no, no, I don't need to hear about that. Let's peel these eggs and eat this damn salad. I'm starving."

"Did you just say *damn*? I don't think I've heard you swear once since I've stayed with you."

Uncle Judd rolled his eyes and stuck out his tongue. "Fine. Darn."

They let the eggs cool under running water, cracked them, peeled the shells, and sliced them before mixing them in with the salad. They were both ravenously hungry.

"So, where do you think you'll go first, since you don't have a weapon? Where do you think they're keeping this girl?"

Cal chewed the first bite of his salad as he contemplated the question. Truth be told, the girl could be anywhere. He doubted she was at either Alfredo's penthouse or the Petrocelli compound back in Evanston, but the mafia had so many fronts and buildings associated with them that she could be anywhere in the city. Perhaps instead of focusing his search on the girl, he should aim his sights higher.

"I don't know if I should go looking for the girl first," Cal said. "Let Agent Wilson pull me in when she finds something good. I need to figure out where Alfredo is. It'll be a lot easier to find him than the girl."

Uncle Judd raised his bushy gray eyebrows at Cal's assertion. "How so? Don't tell me you're just gonna walk up to your old house and ask that wife of his where he's at or hope he shows up at the front door."

"Of course not. The place is probably armed to the teeth after what I did last time. I've got to start lower and work my way up. I'm just not sure where yet."

The ringing of Cal's apartment buzzer startled them. They looked at each other with shock, wondering who was calling for them. Could Agent Wilson have returned already?

"You think it's Brittany?" Cal asked.

"No, not this fast. Maybe it's the super."

Cal walked over to the intercom by the door, pushed the button, and spoke.

"Who is it?"

Cal held his breath as he waited for the person buzzing him to speak. It could've been someone from the mafia checking to see if he was back in town. He knew it was a foolish decision to answer.

"Cal, thank God it's you. Can you let me up?"

It was Cal's turn to raise his eyebrows. He looked back at Uncle Judd and then at the intercom, hoping his brain could make the connection between the voice that had spoken to him and the voice he thought he'd heard. There was no way he could've heard that voice. Was it possible he'd imagined it?

"Tony? Is that you?"

Cal waited for a response, his breath still stuck in his chest, and the gentle beat of his heart ratcheting up with each passing second.

"Yeah, Cal, it's me. Can you let me up? I really need your help."

He couldn't believe Tony was still alive. What was he

doing back in Chicago? Was he still being pursued by the police? So many questions raced through Cal's mind.

Cal pushed the button on the intercom to let the boy up.

"Is he the boy whose sister was kidnapped?" Uncle Judd asked in a whisper.

Cal nodded. He heard a set of racing steps reach the landing of his floor and stepped back, only to be tackled in a bear hug from his former driver. Cal was surprised by the boy's display of emotion. Somehow he found the energy to wrap his arms around the boy in a friendly embrace.

As they locked arms, Cal recalled the many misadventures they'd had over the past three months. Cal saved Tony's life first by gunning down Mayor Caruso's thugs in the back of O'Dooley's Pub after the former mayor was killed, then by neglecting Alfredo's order to kill him. Tony saved Cal's hide during his encounter with Caruso's goons outside of City Hall. They'd been through a lot. Despite it all, Tony had remained a true friend. He'd been far more faithful than Fonzie, the man Cal had thought was his best friend.

They broke the embrace and looked at each other. Tony nodded to Uncle Judd, who seemed to be watching the scene unfold behind them.

"Boy, am I glad to see you," Tony said. "Have you heard what happened to my sister? Those bastards took her."

Cal nodded and exhaled, acknowledging the pain that Tony inevitably suffered inside. He felt similarly about Maria. Someone you loved so deeply was gone, and there was no coming back. At least there was hope Tina Fregosi would return, whereas Maria never would.

"I heard, and I'm terribly sorry, Tony. How long have you been back here? I thought you were staying with your friend."

Tony filled Cal in on his travels over the last three months, first from staying with a friend in Indianapolis to hitchhiking across Indiana and Michigan, where he had heard the news of his sister's kidnapping. In return, Cal told Tony everything that happened since he left Chicago, including Alfredo and Vinnie asking Cal to kill a witness, to him finding out the witness was Maria, Maria being kidnapped and later shot after Cal thought he had Alfredo dead to rights, and then Fonzie turning on them all and preventing Maria from getting to the hospital in time before her death. Cal introduced Tony to Uncle Judd and explained he'd been staying with him in San Diego for the last three months.

"So we both just got back to Chicago?" Tony asked. "That's really weird."

"It's not weird, it was intentional," Cal said. "Alfredo kidnapped your sister because he wanted you to come back and have you taken out once and for all. He knew I'd return once I heard about what happened to her. It's also no secret I want to kill the bastard, so I was always going to make it back here sooner or later."

Tony nodded along with Cal and flashed a soft smile. "I'm glad you came back, Cal. I really need your help to find Tina. I know the police are looking for her, but we have to take action. I can't just let them take their sweet time with this. I know the sooner you find a kidnapping victim, the better chance they're still alive. You're going to help me find her, right?"

Killing Alfredo was still Cal's top priority, but he had made a promise to Brittany. He'd help her find Tina Fregosi. But now that Tony was back, he figured he could still help the special agent, but by doing things his own way.

"Of course I'll help you find her. But we have a lot of

work to do. The police don't know either one of us is back yet, and I'd like to keep it that way. We need to lay low while finding a way to push the envelope a bit. I've got to get my hands on some weapons."

While Cal was speaking, Uncle Judd had left the room. He returned, wheeling in an old, beat-up brown leather suitcase, the clasp's hinges taped shut with clear tape. Judd smiled as Cal and Tony watched him peel the tape off.

"Now, Cal, I asked you if you had any weapons," Uncle Judd said. He set the case down lengthwise, bent to one knee, and searched through the suitcase's contents, tossing a variety of shirts and pants on the floor behind him until he found what he was looking for.

"Aha, these should do the trick."

Uncle Judd stood with two of the smallest guns Cal had ever seen, one in each hand. Cal recognized them instantly as Beretta Picos. The gun had been his adoptive mother Susan's weapon of choice in case she needed to defend herself from the mafia's enemies. He had no idea why his peace-loving uncle had two of them.

"Where did you get those? I thought you didn't like guns?"

Uncle Judd laughed and presented a gun to both Cal and Tony.

"Not in the least. But a man's always gotta be prepared. Whose turn is it to swear now?"

18

"Oh my God, Alfredo!"

Alfredo Petrocelli felt like the king of the world again. For the first time since Vinnie's death, he was plunging deep into his wife, his thrusts sending the California king-sized headboard crashing into the wall. Even in his early sixties, Alfredo felt the sexual urge every now and then and appreciated the power his lust had over him. The minute he'd suggested sex to Susan, she almost jumped into bed. It made him happy to see her reaction to his overtures given his lack of vigor over the past three months.

"I don't know what's gotten into you, but I like it!"

Susan moaned as Alfredo kept thrusting into her missionary-style. The mob boss leaned down to kiss his wife, her beauty still shining even at her age. He felt himself nearing his release and grit his teeth as the explosive feeling of orgasm began in his loins.

Then the bedroom door opened.

"Aggh!"

"What the fuck?"

Alfredo pulled out of his wife just as his body began spasming. Susan Petrocelli's face was wrenched in horror as she fought to pull the covers over her naked body. The gesture had left her husband bare and exposed to whoever had intruded on their afternoon delight.

"Jesus, sir, I'm sorry about that. Should I come back?"

Alfredo was fuming. Not only had someone interrupted him as he was climaxing with his wife but now he had no choice but to bare all for this person. He'd teach this character a lesson.

Without looking, Alfredo grabbed the gun from his bedside table, turned around, and marched toward the intruder. Just as he stuck the gun in the man's chest he realized it was none other than his new South Side capo, Dominic "Death" Masucci.

"Haven't you heard of knocking? I ought to shoot you full of lead, you motherfucker."

The young capo froze, his eyes bugging out of his head. Alfredo could feel the electricity run through Masucci's body up to his temple, where his thinning black hair stood high and stiff from shock.

"I'm so sorry, sir. You're right, I should've knocked. I tried to reach you with some really important news, but I couldn't get ahold of you."

Alfredo growled at the man they called "Death" and jammed the gun further into his chest. The capo looked down at the weapon, his breath becoming more ragged. Alfredo enjoyed the power he held over someone so close to him in the mafia reporting chain, yet was sickened that Masucci wasn't fighting back.

"What could possibly be so important that it was worth interrupting what was going on back there?"

Alfredo looked behind him toward the bed, where

Susan had the blankets pulled up to her eyeballs. Alfredo soon realized his mistake of drawing out his wife's discomfort. He removed the gun from Masucci's chest, told him to turn around toward the door, and walked to the large walk-in closet where he and Susan kept their wardrobes.

After thirty seconds, Alfredo returned with two large robes draped over his arm. He allowed his wife to dress first before he slipped on his own ruby-red robe. He thought he heard a whimper from Death as he faced the door.

"Alright, Death. You can turn around. Don't worry, I'm not gonna shoot you."

Alfredo waited as his capo turned to face him. He feigned a sucker punch to the stomach but was pleased to see the capo didn't fall for it.

"Good man," Alfredo said. "If you're gonna work in this position for me, you can't always let me pull your chain, even when you deserve it. Now, what did you want?"

Masucci exhaled a sigh of relief. "I've had a guy watching the Fregosi place ever since . . ." Masucci glanced at Susan, who got up and tiptoed toward the master bathroom. Keeping his voice low, he continued. ". . . we nabbed that girl, just like you asked."

"And?"

"Well, the guy I've got there called me a few times before he finally reached me. Said that he saw Tony Fregosi. The boy's back in Chicago."

Alfredo wanted to throw his hands up in the air and shout in celebration. *The plan had worked!* His cautious side, one that had so often lived with disappointment, knew better.

"Are you sure he saw him?"

Masucci nodded. "Yes, I'm positive. He double-checked

the face with the photo of the boy that he had. Snuck a picture, too, with his phone. It's definitely him."

Alfredo's smile felt as wide as a smile could possibly get. He was ready to congratulate his capo for the discovery and completely forgive him for walking in during his bout of coitus with his wife.

"My guy followed Tony for a while, all the way to some guy's apartment. He kept waiting and thought of going home until he saw the boy and this big tall guy walk out. I'm not sure who he was."

Alfredo clutched at his heart, hoping it was his adopted son. He just had to be sure before he allowed his life force to dance with jubilation.

"Did your friend say what the guy looked like? What part of the city did the boy go?"

Masucci had a quizzical look on his face, as if doubting the question's importance.

"He just said he was a tall guy, brown hair, some stubble. Looked like an angry motherfucker. The apartment building was in Hyde Park."

Alfredo nearly fell to his knees with excitement at the news. So much so that Masucci reached out to Alfredo to hold him steady. He had confirmation that his plan had worked and that all the effort in kidnapping Tina Fregosi was worth it.

He nearly wept with joy knowing that Cal had come back. He could finally get revenge for poor Vinnie and put Cal where he belonged. He only wondered how fast he could move forward with his plan. Could he take out Cal and Tony in one fell swoop? The mob boss didn't have all the answers yet, but he at least knew he was ever closer to getting his revenge.

"Wow, Dom. That's the best possible news. Tell your guy to keep on it. Give him a nice cigar or two from me."

Masucci prepared to speak again, but Alfredo heard Susan returning from the bathroom, so he shoved his capo out of the room, clapping him on the back on the way out.

Alfredo turned toward his wife, who lifted a brow in his direction.

"What are you so excited about? A total stranger just saw me naked."

Alfredo moved toward his wife and took her in his arms, now savoring the post-lovemaking high that had been so rudely interrupted.

"Oh c'mon, honey. Dominic's sort of new around here, but he's not a stranger. Would you rather have had old Frankie see you naked?"

Susan pulled away from her husband at the mention of the former South Side capo.

"It's too soon to speak about poor Frankie. But yes, I would have. At least with Frankie I would've known he wasn't trying to ogle me. Who knows what that young guy will fantasize about after seeing this?"

Alfredo waved off his wife's concerns and sat her on the bed. He rubbed her leg gently beneath her matching red robe, ready to share the good news with her.

"Honey, you know what Dom told me just now?"

Susan stared at her husband with a pained look on her face. "I haven't a clue. Does it explain why you're so damned giddy after threatening to kill him?"

Alfredo chuckled. "Yes, darling. What he said is that the pipsqueak boy who killed Mayor Caruso and got away, thanks to Cal, is back. Not only can we finally finish him off but we can kill Cal too. He's back in Chicago."

Susan shook her head. "I don't understand."

Alfredo looked deep in his wife's eyes, his own still alight with excitement, while hers were clouded with doubt.

"This is great news, honey. We can finally let Vinnie rest in peace and put his death behind us. Cal will be gone forever once I'm through with him. We'll get to live a normal life again."

"I still don't get it. I don't think you do either. Life will never be normal without my son in it again. I still don't think going after Cal is a good idea, as much as I want him to pay for killing Vinnie."

Alfredo slapped his wife's thigh. "So you admit it: you want Cal gone just as much as I do. Don't you worry, honey, because as soon as I leave this room, preparations for his death shall begin."

19

Brittany Wilson was back in Mick Fisher's office only three hours after she'd landed at the Chicago Executive Airport. In that three-hour span, she had Cal and Uncle Judd dropped off at Cal's apartment, raced back to the office, and buried herself in every piece of documentation she could find pertaining to the warehouse murder cases, the murders at the Petrocelli compound in Evanston, Mayor Caruso's murder case, and now the kidnapping of Tina Fregosi. Other than the mafia and perhaps Callahan Boyle, there had to be some other connection.

She'd had a few brief chats with detectives on her team who had worked the cases before her arrival, their disapproval at a much younger and more junior detective being assigned their former case evident on their faces. In that brief period of time, she hadn't gleaned much. She hoped her meeting with Fisher would clarify things. Her same foolscap notepad rested on top of her right leg, which was crossed confidently over the left, its silky smoothness barely touched by her midthigh-length black skirt. Next to her on the floor in her backpack was a copy of the tiny case file that had been assembled for Tina Fregosi since her kidnapping, and whatever personal belongings she'd brought with her to San Diego. There was no time for returning home to unpack.

"Wilson, I'm glad you're finally back. A quality detective like you deserves her rest of course, but it's time to get down to business, especially with this Tina Fregosi kidnapping. Even though Christmas is coming up, I think it's going to be a real stretch for any of us to see much of our families on the twenty-fifth."

Brittany sighed at the mention of her family. Her family would be so proud of her, working her ass off through Christmas to bring an endangered girl home, to keep a heinous murderer off the streets, and destabilizing the corrupt power of an organized crime institution. Her Olympic gymnast sister, Victoria, certainly couldn't scoff at that. Her father would have to recognize the sacrifice she was making to save the lives of others, something Victoria wouldn't know anything about.

She let the thoughts of her family slip to the back of her mind as she focused on what her new boss had to say. Nothing could distract her now. She needed to home every bit of her attention on finding Tina Fregosi. Then she could worry about bringing down the mafia with Cal's help. Then she would be one step closer to the FBI. She wouldn't have to pretend to be a federal agent like she had in San Diego. She'd be one.

"I had a nice vacation, but I'm ready to do what I do best, and that's solve crimes. We're gonna find this girl, sir, I'm sure of it."

Mick Fisher eyed Brittany up and down, a worn pencil dangling from his mouth. Brittany wasn't sure if the lieutenant doubted her assertion or if he was thinking through the details of the case, determining the order of events from the evidence gleaned thus far and how to proceed.

Fisher removed the pencil from his mouth, tapped the eraser down on the desk, and rested it on his own notepad.

"Where'd you run off to? Nowhere too glamorous, I trust."

"Not too glamorous. There wasn't the time for that. I just went to San Diego."

"Ah. Know someone out there? Maybe an old friend or something?"

Brittany felt like raising her brow but knew she couldn't give away her feelings. Had her boss found out about her relationship with Drew and that she had pretended to be an FBI agent in front of Cal? If Mick knew about Cal, she figured their conversation would take on an entirely new tone.

"I'm just making some small talk with you, Wilson. I know you're all about the results, and I like that. But sometimes you've gotta learn to shoot the shit every once in a while. It makes you, I don't know, more . . . What's the word?"

Brittany searched the dictionary of her mind, unsure of what her boss was going for. After ten seconds she found a word.

"'Relatable'?"

Fisher picked the pencil up and slammed it down on the desk.

"That's it," he said, beaming with excitement. "'Relatable.' Anyway, I wanted us to talk about the Fregosi kidnapping and let you know what we've discovered while you were away."

Fisher opened the original Tina Fregosi case file on his desk in the only fraction of space available for use to spread the file's contents. Her boss prepared to speak again when Brittany's phone rang. The phone was the only item she'd managed to wedge onto the crowded desk. Fisher flashed cold eyes at her at the interruption.

"You gonna answer that?"

While her boss had spoken, Brittany had instinctively reached into her backpack, rummaging through its contents to find her phone. Even though she'd seen the vibrating phone go off in front of her, she still felt the need to search for it. She was startled when she felt another phone in her backpack. Her heart fluttered as she suddenly realized that she'd accidentally taken Cal's phone when they got off the plane, since he'd carelessly left it in his seat. She'd meant to give it back to him when she dropped him off but had forgotten.

Before she could react, her boss picked up the phone, rolling his eyes as he answered.

"Yeah, who is this?"

Brittany panicked inside, hoping that whoever had placed the call to Cal's phone wouldn't give away her method of interrogation, prompting an internal affairs investigation and dashing her future career ambitions. The young detective wasn't sure if she should force the phone from Fisher's hands or if she should play it cool and let him believe it was her phone. Despite her increased breathing and perspiring forehead, she figured that was the right choice.

"You're saying you know the whereabouts of Tina Fregosi? How did you get Detective Wilson's number?"

Brittany's heart hammered into her chest once more. That her boss had revealed her identity would leave her no choice but to backpedal and explain that the phone wasn't hers when the caller revealed they were calling Cal. The thought made her sweat even more, a chilly river coursing down her arms and back. Cal was her secret to solving the entire investigation and putting every piece of the puzzle together. He was the key to her getting out of the Chicago PD and into the FBI. She couldn't reveal her ace in the hole until she had full credit. She was starting to think she should rip the phone from her boss's hands.

Mick Fisher nodded along with the caller, but his eyes gave away his confusion. "How long has she been in this building? You're sure you saw her go in?"

Brittany sat upright in her seat, extremely nervous at the prospect of what the caller was saying. It struck her as odd that someone was calling Cal regarding the whereabouts of Tina Fregosi. Her hands raised up to her mouth, and she found herself chewing on her nails. It was a childish habit, she knew, but she couldn't force them away.

"Alright, whoever you are, thank you for this information. My team and I will follow up right away."

Her boss waited for a response, then shook his head and gave the phone back to Brittany. She timidly accepted it, taking the phone and dropping it in her bag like a hot potato.

"What was that about?" Brittany wiped her hands on her skirt and made an attempt to smooth her dark curly hair. She hadn't bothered with straightening it when they left San Diego.

"That was one of the strangest calls I've ever received in my entire career. The guy just went on and on and never shut up. I asked him questions and he didn't answer them directly. It was like it was prerecorded."

"What did he say?"

Her boss wrinkled his face and leaned back in his chair, joining Brittany in crossing her legs.

"He gave us a tip on where Tina Fregosi is. He claims she's in an old storefront in Fulton Market, thought it might be undergoing renovation. It's a construction nightmare over there in the West Loop."

"So what do we do? We're going to check it out, right?"

Brittany anxiously awaited her boss's decision. His scratching at the back of his head caused her to rub the back of her neck. Fisher kept scratching and it caused her to keep rubbing. She wasn't sure if this game of nervous cat and mouse would end.

"As much as I don't trust that call, it's been two days since the kidnapping, and this is the only lead we've got aside from a report from a neighbor. I say we check it out. First, I want to verify everything and find out if this caller is even real. Get Detective Jackson and round up a team. If this checks out, I want to move on this in two hours, you hear?"

Brittany shot out of her chair in excitement. She was more than ready to find the Fregosi girl and further strengthen her career prospects. She knew the man sitting before her would be beyond pleased if the news the caller provided was true.

"Absolutely, sir. I'll get a team and we'll be ready to move on the area. We'll study Fulton Market in and out and see if we can find out who might be holding her."

Fisher nodded before standing up. "Perhaps when you return, Wilson, we can discuss who this Cal is."

Halfway to the door, Brittany froze. The caller must have revealed what she'd hoped would've been kept secret. There was so much she wanted to say but knew she couldn't.

"Yes, sir, once we find the girl we can debrief."

Fisher looked down at his desk, his eyes dodging Brittany's in shame. "Let's hope this is real and we can get Tina back safe."

Brittany nodded and raced out the door. For the first time since she'd taken on the warehouse murder case and discovered Cal, she felt ill at ease about her plans and their course of action. Since the caller had identified Cal by name, she was more certain than ever that it could be a trap set by the mafia or someone else who wanted Cal dead. She had little choice but to go through with it now, or else admit to her boss what she'd been up to while on vacation.

Brittany walked past Detective Jackson's desk, the man ten years her senior busy on the phone. She'd speak with him later. For now she had to find a way to reach Cal. Only he could know what kind of mess they were walking into and whether they could make it out with the Fregosi girl's life intact.

20

"Who just called?"

Cal glanced at Tony as they walked out of the hotel they'd checked into as an extra precaution in case the mafia was on their tail. He realized as he and Tony were about to leave his apartment that he didn't have his phone on him. He hoped Brittany had found it when they got off the charter plane. He had no idea where it might be otherwise. A victim of the 21st century, Cal felt lost without his cell phone.

"It was Uncle Judd," Tony said. "Says that FBI agent called."

Cal rolled his eyes. *Time for this shit again.* "What did she want?"

"She said she needed to talk to you. Her team is moving on a location in Fulton Market, and she thinks it might be a setup."

Cal scanned his brain, trying to recall any mention made by the mafia leadership about a property in Fulton Market. He couldn't come up with anything, though he wouldn't be shocked if the mafia had bought some property in the booming section of the West Loop.

"Why does she think it's a setup? Did Uncle Judd give you any more than that?"

"No, that's all he said."

They stopped at a traffic light, waiting to cross the street. Cal had no destination in mind. He just wanted to keep moving. Anything was better than sitting around in a dumpy hotel room.

Cal knew he'd have to abandon his apartment if the mafia found out he was in town, so he'd been proactive in securing a place to stay in the event of an early evacuation. He'd have to remember to tell Uncle Judd of the accommodations the next time he spoke to him. His uncle was probably fine for now.

"I wish we knew what she meant by setup," Cal said. "I have no idea how I can be helpful to her in Fulton Market. Alfredo's got nothing over there as far as I know."

The signal indicated they could cross. Tony turned to Cal, a questioning look on his face as they walked.

"Why are you working with this agent anyway? Why help the law?"

Cal sighed. "Sometimes you're put in a bad position, Tony. I'm not sure how much she knows about my past, but she's a very smart woman. She probably has an idea of the type of work I did. She's got ambition, wants to bring the whole mafia down. I'm only helping her because we both want to find your sister."

And kill Alfredo.

To Cal's surprise, Tony broke out in a wide grin.

"If I didn't know any better, Cal, I'd say you liked her."

Cal formed his face into something resembling sour

grapes. "Absolutely not. If anything, I want to get rid of her, not keep her around."

Cal knew that was a lie too. Part of him couldn't stand the fact that Brittany Wilson had arrived in his life, but another part of him was glad she had. She gave him someone to find beautiful again, which had been so hard since Maria's death.

"So, are you gonna call her? I think we should at least see what she's up to."

Cal shook his head. He was going to do this on his own. His promise to help Brittany was one thing, but he'd also told himself he was going to find a moment to break away. It would take the FBI time to assemble their resources and travel to Fulton Market. Cal and Tony could get there on a quick trip down the Pink Line and be ready in an instant.

If it really was a setup, maybe Alfredo was there waiting. Cal would just have to outsmart the old man.

"Let's go ourselves," Cal told Tony. "I normally wouldn't throw caution to the wind like this when we don't know what we're getting into, but I killed so many of Alfredo's guys on the way out of town that I doubt he can set up anything too elaborate."

Tony didn't argue and followed Cal to the Harold Washington Library-State/Van Buren Pink Line stop. They rode the train to Morgan and walked to Fulton Market. There wasn't much activity on a cold Thursday before Christmas. While Fulton Market was an up-and-coming area, there was still a lot of construction to be done to make the place into something more than butcher shops, meatpacking plants, and a smattering of restaurants.

"Let's just keep walking," Cal said. "See if we see anything."

Tony's breath was heavy, and Cal wondered if the kid

was nervous at the prospect of them facing any action. The last time the kid had faced such a traumatic event, he'd killed Mayor Caruso and had nearly been killed himself.

"You alright, kid? That weapon you've got is a simple six-shooter. It'll serve you well if you're willing to use it."

Tony took a deep breath and nodded. "I know. I did a pretty good job the last time I shot a gun, didn't I? Even if I regret it."

They stopped alongside an old warehouse across from a wholesale meat shop on the corner of Sangamon and Fulton Market. It was time for Cal to have the conversation with Tony that he'd been avoiding ever since he helped the boy escape from the Cook County Correctional Center three months ago.

"Look, Tony, don't beat yourself up over that. I've made more than one kill in my life that I wish I could take back. I wish I could take it all back and never have been involved with the mafia in the first place. But that's something I'll always have to live with. I should've taken Caruso out, not you. It's my fault I didn't get him sooner."

Tony turned toward Cal, a tear of guilt streaming down his face. "How can you say that I shouldn't beat myself up over it? You just said you regret what you've done, too, and that it's something you'll always have to live with. I should be rotting in prison right now, Cal, and yet I'm out here free. Every night I pour sweat and shake thinking about what I've done. I killed another human being, and all for a more evil man than Caruso probably ever was. I don't want to have to do that again."

Cal blinked several times. He didn't know what to say to the boy, but the feeling of lead solidified in his heart, and a sense of helplessness filled his brain. If only he'd been able to quell the fire of ambition Tony had in rising up in the mafia, maybe the boy wouldn't be as devastated about his life decisions as he was, and Cal wouldn't have to struggle to dispense advice.

"I guess what I meant to say was that I'm fighting on a different path now. So are you. By finding your sister and bringing her home, you're making sure those mafia bastards don't lay waste to someone else's life."

A slow smile spread across Tony's face. He suddenly jumped and pointed to a building under renovation across the street.

"Cal, look!"

Cal spun around, reaching for the tiny gun in his reclaimed hip holster on pure instinct. A man wearing all black, from his stocking cap to his buckled leather boots, dashed into the building, closing a green metal door behind him.

"Do we follow him?" Tony asked.

Cal nodded, and they slowly crept toward the building, the silence from the closed-off street providing an eerie soundtrack to their movements. Cal scanned the tops of the buildings as they walked, searching for any sign of ambush from above. The sun poked its way through a wintry pillow of clouds and shone on the roof of the building to the immediate left of the one they were heading toward. Cal saw a glare out of the corner of his eye and knew they had company.

"Move, move!"

For the second time that week, Cal was faced with a sniper-style attack. Two quick shots rang out from above as he and Tony raced for cover behind a parked bulldozer in front of the building. Fortunately, the sniper's bullets hit nothing but the concrete of the street. Cal could see the shell casings as he looked behind him past the bulldozer.

"Holy shit," Tony said. The young man's breath was labored once again, and his hands gripped the bulldozer as tightly as a blood pressure cuff gripped one's arm at a doctor's visit. Unlike Cal, Tony wasn't holding his gun. Cal wondered if Tony would be able to fight back against whoever these men were.

"Are you alright? Can you do this with me?"

Tony turned to Cal and released his grip from the bulldozer. "Yeah, I can do it. That was just scary, that's all."

Cal looked above and saw nothing but the faded green awning of the building. It would be too tough for the sniper to shoot them from this angle. They may be safe for the time being, but Cal knew that wouldn't last long.

"I know it's scary, but the fact that there's someone shooting at us means we're getting close to something. Maybe your sister is here."

Tony reached for his gun and had it positioned perfectly in his hands, his left hand covering his right as he prepped his aim. The boy rose to his feet and stepped away from the bulldozer, his sudden bravery inspiring him to engage with the sniper. Before Cal could react, Tony fired.

"Tony, stop!"

Two more bullets blasted from the rooftop, and Tony was left with little choice but to jump back behind the bulldozer. Cal was ready to scold him for his foolishness when he saw two more men dressed in black rush in from across the street, headed straight for them with guns pointed.

Undeterred by the sniper, Tony rose again, ready to fire. Cal forced him down and took aim at the two men. The man immediately in front of him got a shot off first, hitting a boarded-up window behind Cal's head. Cal didn't miss, as his first of six bullets hit the man straight in the chest.

Two quick bullets made their way toward Cal right as

the first man went down. He felt one nick the sleeve of his coat. Before he could return fire, the man shouted in pain as Tony shot him in the left knee. Cal didn't hesitate to finish him off, shooting the man in the neck.

"Damnit, Cal. I had him!"

"Too bad. We needed to finish this quick so we can get inside. Let's see where that man ran off to."

Not knowing what would face them, Cal performed a quick scan of the street, then ran for the door. The ambush that they just faced may have been the easy part. He just hoped Alfredo was somewhere behind door number one, his life ready to be taken as Cal's prize.

21

The surveillance van carrying Brittany's team couldn't have arrived on the scene soon enough. Accessing Fulton Market from Halsted was nearly impossible due to the massive amount of construction vehicles and debris, even in winter. They'd gone around the construction by driving down Lake and turning on Morgan, before finally stopping in front of one of what had to be a dozen meat shops on Fulton Market, where the caller had told her boss that Tina Fregosi had been spotted entering an abandoned building facing south.

Mick Fisher called in some favors from City Hall, who found through the city's buildings and permits department that the building in question was owned by a bank. There was nothing indicating if the edifice had been sold to the bank or was up for resale. Brittany could see from the tiny passenger seat window that, much like many of the other businesses on Fulton Market, the building needed some refurbishing.

Without time to get a permit to enter the property or to properly validate the anonymous tip, Fisher had Brittany assemble a small team—enough people to fit in a van and with just enough weaponry to be dangerous if things went awry. Brittany had her marching orders, and she was determined to execute.

As soon as her team stopped, she saw a body clothed in black lying in the street. Just in front of him was a man with a gun extended. The driver of the van, a tech guy Brittany had rounded up who had been brought along more for his computer skills for last-minute research than his driving, began to panic.

"Shooter!"

Detective Bruce Jackson and the other two men Brittany had brought with her grabbed their weapons and were ready to bust out of the back of the van with guns blazing. Before the rear door could open a crack, the shooter in the street had been shot in the kneecap and finished off with a shot to the neck.

"He's down," Brittany said.

The men grumbled and kept the door closed. Jackson shuffled closer to the front seat so he could get a better look, given the lack of windows in the back.

"What've we got?"

Brittany looked to the street and just caught sight of two men running from behind a bulldozer into the building in question. She wouldn't bet her life on it, but she was sure she saw Cal.

She turned toward Detective Jackson and raised her voice so it could carry through the glass separating the front seat from the rear of the van. "Two Joes in black out in the street. Looks like the two guys that took care of them are heading into the building."

"Sounds like we have an insecure area and that the tip

may be legit," Jackson said. "We need to secure the perimeter and call for backup."

Brittany felt her pulse quicken and beads of sweat form on her forehead. Despite being a decade junior of Detective Jackson, Fisher had put her in charge. The success or failure of this mission was on her. She knew what would be on the line if she didn't execute.

"I don't like this one bit. We don't even know who these opposing forces are, or what could possibly be going on in that building. But if the girl is in there, she could be in trouble."

Her colleague nodded and started toward Russ and Ernie, explaining the plan. Still flustered, Brittany turned to the driver and shook him, wondering how he could be texting during such a tense situation.

"Patrick, you have to call for backup, understand? Call Fisher. He'll get a team out here."

Brittany unbuckled her seat belt and opened the door. Jackson, Russ, and Ernie were already outside, weapons at the ready. As soon as Ernie and Russ stepped around the van to cross the street, gunfire rang out.

"Ah! Fuck!"

A sniper positioned atop the building next door to their target fired at the group of detectives. Russ had been shot and was crawling on his belly to get back behind the surveillance van. The others had made it back just in time.

"Jesus Christ, it's a setup!"

Brittany turned to face a heated Detective Jackson. She was upset with herself that she hadn't said as much to her boss. She had a feeling that someone reporting a tip to Cal's phone had to have purposefully wanted him there. If Brittany's thinking was correct, the plan had worked. Worst of all, instead of calling Uncle Judd back to connect to her, Cal had raced into harm's way on his own, setting off a chain reaction that cornered her team in a dangerous death trap with an opportunistic sniper. She only hoped Russ wasn't seriously hurt.

"God damnit, this doesn't look good."

Brittany turned to look at Ernie, who'd managed to pull a now-unconscious Russ behind the van. The sniper had hit him twice. One wound on his right shoulder and the other at the back of his leg. Brittany hoped he would be alright.

Her first instinct was to return the sniper's fire. If Ernie was going to be dealing with Russ, the least she could do was try to take out the rest of the bad guys. Jackson had already beaten her to the punch and was firing at the marksman.

"Damn coward. Pretty sure he's hiding now. At least he isn't shooting at us anymore."

Brittany's mind was still racing. Chaos was unfolding all around her. She had to worry about a sniper, a severely wounded detective just feet away, and a screaming Patrick, who was taking cover in the van. Not to mention the slight possibility that Tina Fregosi was inside that building. Even though the entire foray appeared to be a setup, she had to at least see if the girl was there.

"Do we wait him out?"

Ernie's question surprised both Brittany and Jackson. He was putting pressure on both of Russ's wounds and only lifted one of his hands to check for a pulse. It was clear that Ernie wasn't going to be of much help if he was going to take care of Russ.

"Alright, wait it out," Jackson said. "If Patrick called for backup, we should have units here any minute. Let them get that sniper down and have them rush the building."

Brittany turned and glared at her fellow detective. Even

though this mission had already gone catastrophically wrong, she wanted some good to come from it. She had to find out if that girl was inside the building. None of them had any clue if or when backup would arrive. They could still find out if Tina Fregosi was really there before her kidnappers had time to react and potentially move her.

"No, we need to get in that building. I saw two guys running in there, and that girl might be in trouble."

Detective Jackson rolled his eyes, a ghostly white surrounded by his dark flesh.

"Detective Wilson, the whole thing was a trap. Don't you see that? God, sometimes I wonder why everyone thinks you're so damn bright."

Brittany was fuming. She opened the back door of the surveillance van, crouching to make sure she wasn't vulnerable to the sniper, walked back to Russ, and dragged his body to the back of the van.

"Hey! You could be hurting him."

"Patrick! Get over here and keep Detective Hunter alive until backup gets here. Call an ambulance while you're at it. What's the ETA?"

Brittany's yells at the young tech fell on deaf ears as more shots rang out. Two bullets peppered the surveillance van door that Brittany was only too lucky to use as a shield. She turned to her right and saw two more men clothed in black rushing at her. All this was doing was making her one very pissed-off woman.

Yelling, Brittany spun to her right and fired as quickly as she could at the approaching gunmen. She felt the same way she did when she first picked up a gun at age twenty, out on the range at her best friend's father's farm, hitting every target in sight.

"Die, motherfuckers!"

Brittany watched as the two men went down without much fanfare, both collapsing from gunshot wounds to the chest. Feeling the fire burning inside her still, she closed the surveillance van door and ran back behind the passenger side of the van.

"Jackson! Neussbaum! Go the front of that building. I'll cover you if that sniper shows his face again. I'm going to head around back. I know there's something inside there, and we have to find out what it is."

Both detectives snapped to attention. Yet it was Ernie who provided the dissent. "Wilson, I think Jackson is right. Why don't we wait until backup gets here? We need to secure the perimeter."

"Detective Neussbaum, Fisher left me in charge, and I'm giving out the orders. Understood?"

Both detectives nodded and did as she asked. They crouched and kept their guns pointed toward the sky, ready to fend off the sniper, but no shots ever came. Jackson and Neussbaum ran for the front door of the building and looked back at Brittany, waiting for further instructions. She reached into the pocket of her jacket and grabbed the small headset with a mouthpiece that would connect her with Detective Jackson.

"Hold. You're both right. Secure the perimeter until further assistance arrives. I'm going to secure the rear."

She could see Detective Jackson shake his head. "Secure the rear? You're the only one going back there. You could get roasted."

"Don't worry about me. I'll manage."

"Don't go in, Wilson. Don't go in."

Brittany took off the headset as she raced into the street, less cautious than she normally would be as she headed for the rear of the building. She kept her back to the wall as cover whenever she could, doing her best to get a sense of her surroundings before making her move.

She finally reached the rear door, felt for the handle, and found it was unlocked. She was proud of herself for forcing her fellow detectives to hold back until more help could arrive. That would still make her look sane in Fisher's book, despite what happened to Detective Hunter. What she was about to do next would make her look less sane.

She opened the door and entered the building, feeling calm and collected, just as she knew she would as an FBI special agent. The building was pitch-black and as cold as the chilliest winter day. She reached for the new flashlight she'd grabbed at the station. The light showed what she had both hoped and feared to see, all wrapped into one.

A girl was seated in a chair twenty yards in front of her. The flashlight picked up something else. The floor was soaked in blood.

22

Cal raced into the building and struggled to get his bearings. The entirety of the space was pitch-black, save for the soft-gray light that poured in from a few windows near the roof. The scant amount he could see suggested little more was present in the space than steel beams that went from floor to ceiling.

"This place is creepy, man," Tony said.

"Shh. We can't give ourselves away."

Cal whispered in the softest voice he could, yet he was sure whomever he and Tony had followed into the building was already aware of their presence. Cal didn't like the fact that he had no clue how many of Alfredo's henchmen he was up against, especially considering he only had four bullets left to work with in his small Beretta Pico. Tony had just four shots remaining as well. Uncle Judd hadn't given them extra ammo.

"What do we do?"

Cal turned to Tony and held his index finger firm against his lips. He wasn't sure if the boy could see him, but Cal knew he would lose his patience if he spoke aloud.

A faint light, soft and yellow like a bumblebee at the onset of springtime, blinked in the center of the massive building. Cal felt himself shivering, in part from the wintry chill that felt ten times more frigid inside, and also from the prospect of facing imminent danger. His hit man senses hadn't completely faded in his three months away from the mob. He turned toward Tony, ensuring his weapon was at the ready, and pointed in the direction of the light. He hoped the boy would follow his lead.

Slowly, the two of them crept toward the light. It seemed to get brighter and brighter as they approached. Cal thought he heard the soft rustling of feet to his right. He shook it off, convinced it was only the pitter-patter of Tony's shoes against the concrete floor.

Cal kept walking, the Beretta Pico held high in front of him. A whooshing sound and a gentle breeze came from the direction Tony was standing. Startled, Cal spun to face the intrusion. The only thing he saw was darkness. A hard object pounded against his head, leaving him no choice but to crumple to the ground.

When Cal came to, he realized he was being dragged against the cold concrete ground, his feet bumping into the steel beams as he moved. He turned his neck upward to get a sense of what was happening. An instant bout of nausea triggered in his stomach from the combination of pain and the speed at which he was dragged.

Two men conversed as they moved deeper into the building's recesses. One of the men had Cal by the ankle. Cal was sure the other was up ahead, as he couldn't see him from his field of vision. Even with pain radiating in his head, Cal felt he would have no problem using his other leg to kick one of the men off of him before springing to his feet to finish the other one off.

Thinking about executing the sudden movement made him realize how painful it felt for him to move even his fingers. Whether it was from damage to his nervous system, or the frigid temperature of the building, he wasn't certain.

The man dragging him stopped moving, and Cal kept his body frozen in place. At this point, he was left with two choices: fight back immediately despite the pain and hope like hell he wasn't facing any more men, or continue to play possum and fight back when the moment was right.

The thought of Tony and his younger sister made him choose the latter. While it appeared now that the whole operation Brittany had been called in for was simply a trap of some kind, Cal had come in the building with a purpose and intended to see it through. Not to mention he had no clue what happened to Tony during his brief bout of unconsciousness. If anything happened to him so close to his return, Cal really wouldn't be able to forgive himself.

Suddenly a whisper.

"What do we do with this one?"

"Same as we did with the other one. Load him in the car and take him to the boss. It's a good thing the old man didn't hit him from the roof. The boss still has a shot to nail him on his own that way."

Cal figured these punks were working for Alfredo. He couldn't let them just take him and Tony with them to visit the old man. He'd find a way to let them think they were getting away with it for as long as he could before making his move, even with his Beretta Pico confiscated. Then he'd get Tony out of there and they'd figure out what to do next.

Cal felt the man dragging him begin moving again. This time he was certain he was heading for the exits. A faint clack of a door handle clicking into place sounded a dozen yards ahead. Cal shifted his gaze to the left in search of the source of the noise and saw what looked like blood pooled on the floor.

His eyes ventured upward and he saw a faded wooden chair with what appeared to be a droopy-looking girl sitting in it. Only this girl wasn't held in place by any restraints, nor did she seem to be moving.

Strange, Cal thought.

Is that Tina Fregosi? Has she bled out?

Surely, Alfredo would've let the girl live a bit longer if it meant he got a shot at Cal. Killing her now seemed to defeat the purpose. Unless he was extremely confident his goons could take Cal and Tony back with them.

Cal felt himself shivering again, and not just from the cold. An involuntary chattering of teeth caused the man dragging him to let go and start walking toward Cal's face. Before Cal could plan his next move, the man's companion began shouting.

"Hey! What are you doing here?"

The man heading for Cal's head froze and turned back.

"This is Agent Brittany Wilson of the FBI. Put your hands up where I can see them! I have a few questions for you gentlemen after some of your colleagues shot at me and my team waiting outside. I said hands up!"

Damnit. Cal knew how far Brittany's speech would go with these soldiers—not very far. He pushed his weight off the floor and tried to rediscover his balance, the pain in his head nearly anchoring him back down the cold, dead ground.

"Fuck questions," one of the men said. "And fuck you."

Cal began charging toward the men. The sound of gunfire deafened him, just as he'd managed to tackle one of the gunmen to the ground. Cal couldn't tell if he'd taken the gunman down before he hit his target.

A return shot rang out, and Cal felt the weight of a body fall on his legs. He wanted to groan in pain, but the man he'd tackled gave him a hard uppercut to the jaw. Infuriated, Cal fired back with a shot of his own between the man's eyes. The shot was so powerful that the man's head sank down into the floor and remained still. Cal jumped off him and ran over to Brittany, praying she hadn't been hit by the gunman.

He nearly tripped over the body of the fallen man as he ran to her. He pushed his hands forward, trying to feel his way through the darkness, hoping to find her. He felt something slam into him that nearly caused him to fall back to the ground.

"Oh Jesus, I'm sorry."

Hearing Brittany's voice filled him with relief, but his heart was still racing. He was beyond pissed that Tony had been taken, but Brittany was alive and they'd taken care of the bad guys for now. He had no doubts that Alfredo wasn't hiding out in this building. His time would have to come later.

"Are you alright? Did they hurt you?"

Brittany shook her head. "No, I'm fine. Seems like all of these guys are shitty shots. We should get out of here, though."

Cal nodded, then remembered what he'd seen earlier from his position on the ground. Just behind them was the lifeless-looking girl in the wooden chair with the blood on the floor. Without thinking, Cal ran to the girl, and Brittany was hot on his heels. They weren't concerned that anyone else might be in the building. They were only concerned that they might have found Tina Fregosi and that she had been killed before they had a chance to save her.

As soon as Cal brushed back the stringy brown hair from the girl's face he realized they'd been duped. Sitting before them was a child-sized, scarecrow-like doll. The "blood" on the floor was actually a spilt can of red paint. Cal could even see the tiny can of paint hidden behind a beam close to the light source.

"Goddamn it."

Brittany looked at Cal and sighed. "You're telling me."

For a short time, both of them stood there, feeling foolish and ashamed. Cal knew Tony had been taken but couldn't make himself move in an effort to see if the car the men were referring to was outside. He felt defeated at the prospect of coming so close but ultimately failing at his mission. Not only was the girl not there but Alfredo was nowhere in sight.

"You should have fucking returned my call," Brittany said, her face resembling stone in the faint light of the building. "I could've told you about my team's plan so we weren't ambushed by some crazy sniper from the moment we arrived. You could've helped me instead of running in here on your own."

Brittany's words were so stinging that Cal felt like he'd been slapped in the face. He didn't have to stand for this. He'd agreed to help the agent but would do so on his terms. Plus he'd just saved her life. Where was the gratitude for that?

"First of all, I don't even have my phone to call you. Secondly, I know this area much better than you do. I knew I would find the building where they were keeping the girl, and I did."

"Oh wow. Do you see what the fuck is in front of us?

Some Raggedy Andy with a wig on and ketchup all over the floor!"

"It's paint."

"Whatever."

Both Cal and Brittany were breathing heavy and ready to keep screaming at each other. Sirens outside made Cal rethink his plan to yell at the agent.

"I imagine it won't look good when your team finds you inside this warehouse," Cal said. "C'mon, let's go."

23

Cal and Brittany ran through the back doors, the sound of police sirens growing louder every second. When they reached Wayman Street, they saw a man running toward Halsted. He was carrying a rifle. A sniper rifle.

"That's him!" Brittany said. "That's the fucking sniper that shot one of my men."

Before Cal could protest, Brittany started after him. Cal wanted to look inside the parked Dodge van behind the building, to see if Tony was being held inside, but he couldn't help but run after the FBI agent.

As he ran, he felt a feverish sense of guilt overcome him now that Tony had been taken too. Sweat began coating his body in a swampish sheen before cooling into an icy shiver.

Cal wasn't so sure Alfredo planned to keep Tony alive to entrap Cal into saving him the way he had by kidnapping Tina Fregosi. As the suspected murderer of former mayor Ross Caruso, Tony could still blab about his involvement with the mafia to the police and put a lot of people in jail for a long time, including Alfredo. Cal wouldn't be surprised if Tony was dead on arrival, wherever he was going.

And it was all his fault. He should have had the boy stay with Uncle Judd back at his apartment and let his jovial relative share some fun jokes with a boy who hadn't had any time for fun while running from the law. But Tony talked Cal into letting him tag along.

The man they were chasing was beyond fast. Despite Brittany's speed, she was having a hard time catching up to him. Cal wasn't in as nearly good of shape as he should have been, and the pain in his head prevented him from focusing on what was in front of him for too long, but he was able to keep a close enough distance behind Agent Wilson to stay dangerous.

"God, who is this guy? I used to run track. I should be running circles around him."

Cal didn't bother to respond. He was breathing too hard against the chill of the winter air to try and talk while he sprinted down the street. The sniper made a sharp left down Green Street, making an effort to run further from the oncoming police sirens. Cal wasn't sure how long the man would try to evade them. He hoped one of them would be able to catch up to him and get some answers. If they had any chance of saving Tony and getting a lead on the girl, they'd have no choice but to reach him.

For a moment, Cal was sure Brittany would be able to do it. She pumped her legs hard and fast until she was able to reach for the man with an extended right arm. The sniper felt her presence and made a sharp dash to the left, causing Brittany to lose her balance and tumble hard into the concrete.

The sniper kept running, getting ever closer to Kinzie

Street. Cal knew the area well and realized there were many directions the man could take if he didn't catch up to him.

"Keep going," Brittany yelled through gritted teeth.

Cal didn't waste any time in trying to help the fallen agent. Despite the tremendous pounding of his head and his thighs burning hotter than a furnace inside a foundry, Cal kept chasing the man. The sniper looked over his shoulder once, and Cal was sure it would prove to be his fatal mistake. Cal was too close now, and he wondered whether it would be best to reach for him, as Brittany had done, or dive on top of the man.

A silver Camaro screeched to a halt in front of him on Kinzie, just as the sniper ran through the intersection. A blue Dodge van, perhaps the same van that had been parked behind the dilapidated building they had just left, moved around the car and turned onto Green, beyond the Camaro. Cal tried his best to maneuver around the blockade and continue his pursuit, but the Camaro reversed and pulled forward each time Cal made a move. Still woozy from being hit over the head, Cal found he couldn't react fast enough.

The blue van stopped, and the sniper opened the side door, ready to make his escape. Cal caught a glimpse of the man's face and was surprised at what he saw. He thought he and Brittany had been chasing a man around their own age, young and extremely fast. Yet the man staring back at him was none other than the former top hit man of the Chicago mafia, Joey Bartellini.

The van sped off once Joey got inside, and the Camaro raced down Kinzie in the opposite direction. Brittany was running toward the Camaro with her gun extended, her breath as laborious as Cal's own. Eventually, she saw her effort was futile and stopped.

Brittany joined Cal in the middle of the intersection, appearing angry and breathless. They'd failed to catch up to the sniper, and now two members of the Fregosi family were in peril. But was the man Cal had seen really Joey Bartellini? He couldn't imagine the old man being able to run that fast, but perhaps retirement rejuvenated him.

Brittany collected herself, no longer bending at the waist. Cal could see that the anger on her face from earlier hadn't left. She looked like a woman who still had plenty to say.

"Goddamn it, Boyle. Look at what just happened. That sniper was the only lead we had at finding out who these people were that took the Fregosi girl. That may have been a setup back there, but these people know something. They just wanted to rub our noses in it first. Now how will we get to them?"

Cal wasn't going to let the agent lecture him. There was still hope for finding Tina Fregosi, and maybe Tony too. He just had to assess all his options. He couldn't act rashly next time like he had moments ago.

"Leave that to me. I know exactly who these people are."

Brittany put her hands on her hips and frowned. "How do you know who these people are? Is there something you'd like to tell me, Callahan?"

Though Cal figured Brittany already knew he was the adopted son of Alfredo Petrocelli, Cal hadn't revealed the nature of his involvement in the mafia with her. He never told her that he knew the exact order of their operations. The men that attacked her team and picked up the sniper were men he'd seen before, lowlife soldiers who worked for Frankie Ramone long before his death. Admitting as much would certainly make him a prime suspect in the other cases she was investigating. That was something he still wasn't willing to do.

"Absolutely not."

"Then what were you doing just now? Why interfere with my team and our investigation?"

"Because you asked me to," Cal snarled.

Brittany stuck her arms out further and walked closer to Cal, until she was inches away from his face. "I called Uncle Judd because I had your cell phone by accident and knew I couldn't reach you. Apparently, he was able to get ahold of you and tell you that my team and I were coming down here and that I'd appreciate your help if you covered for me. I didn't ask you to start blowing people away before I got here and had my team secure the scene. Now one of my men is hurt, and I'm going to have a hell of a lot to explain to my boss."

Brittany's eyes flared at him as she ended her rant. Cal felt a familiar locomotive of anger steaming through his body, doing its best to travel to the surface. He realized why she was angry. He'd definitely acted on impulse and went with Tony to the scene before he had all of the facts. He'd purposefully violated the agreement they had to work together to help the girl in order to do things his way.

As he looked into Brittany's eyes, Cal wondered if he'd ruined the best opportunity they'd have to find Tina Fregosi. While he knew the mafia inside and out, he had no clue what Alfredo had done to change his operations since Cal left town. He could've been hiding the girl anywhere, and Cal had no friends in the mafia left to bribe. He was as blind as the FBI or the Chicago PD were in this case.

Perhaps his desire for immediate revenge was driving him to make decisions he would regret. He already regretted his actions that led to Tony being taken and endangered again. What would Maria think if she'd seen Cal's behavior? He wasn't any closer to becoming the man she'd thought he was when she died in his arms, a man capable of delivering great good. So far, he was failing big-time.

"I don't care what you have to tell your boss," Cal replied. Though he realized he was in the wrong, he couldn't help but let the venom flow through his words. He had to get this off his chest. "We didn't just lose a chance to find Tina Fregosi back there, but we lost her brother. He came with me to help me find his sister, who he loves very much. I feel like complete shit right now."

Brittany removed her hands from her hips, and Cal felt the air calm around them. The tough nature they both possessed wasn't going to lead them anywhere productive. If they had any hope of finding Tina and Tony, they'd have to stop quarreling and work together.

"I know how that must feel, especially considering how much the police want her brother too. I can't imagine we have much time left to save him if those guys back there were with the mafia." Brittany paused, her eyebrows furrowed. "Look, Cal, I thought back in San Diego that we promised to work together as a team. You've got to let me and my team do what we do best when we have the opportunity. If you can't do that, I'll be left with little choice but to tell my boss what I know about you, and then we'll have less hope of saving the girl. I can play it that way if you want, but I won't."

Cal let out a breath, the fog from the cold shielding Brittany's face from his view. Her softening eyes were able to temper the flames of anger he felt in his body, until even his pounding head felt a calm euphoria. He appreciated her effort to reconcile them, but at the same time he didn't believe what she had to say, despite the feelings in his body.

"How do I know I can trust you? You've always talked a good game, and I can see you want to find this girl. But I've dealt with a lot of shady characters in my life and they always prove to have no one's intentions in mind but their own."

Brittany looked up at Cal, her soft features glowing even in the wintry grayness. He felt a feeling in his body he hadn't felt in a long time, not since he'd first started dating Maria.

"This is how you know you can trust me."

Brittany leaned in, her lips protruding upward in an effort to meet Cal's. On instinct, and completely forgetting Brittany's profession, Cal bent down to meet her. They kissed, and it was the sweetest kiss Cal had ever felt.

At that moment he felt his fears abandon him, and there was no one he'd rather trust.

24

Alfredo Petrocelli waited by the phone at the bedside table. For the first time since Vinnie's death, he went to his Gold Coast penthouse, no longer harboring the sinking feeling in the pit of his stomach that he would no longer be able to visit his son's condo a few floors down. Instead, Alfredo was excited at the prospect of finally catching his son's killer. If his trap worked as well as he'd hoped, Cal would be on his way to the safehouse where the Fregosi girl was being kept, safely in the custody of his low-level mafia soldiers.

Alfredo wanted him to feel beyond terrible for what he had done. Not only would Cal die at Alfredo's hand, but he would see the young girl he couldn't save die as well. Of course, Alfredo would make it appear as if the girl had been slain by none other than Cal himself. A murder-suicide. If the Fregosi boy was brought in along with Cal, it would turn out even better. All of Alfredo's problems would be solved, and he could focus on expanding his great mafia empire.

His niece and consigliera, Melissa Ranieri, knocked on the door and entered the bedroom carrying a thermos filled with coffee. The smell of the liquid wafted into Alfredo's nostrils and added to the pleasantness of the evening.

"Don Alfredo, I have some news regarding the events of this afternoon."

Alfredo couldn't help but rub the palms of his hands together as his niece sat on the bed next to him. He was hoping to hear from "Death" Masucci, as his men had been the ones to orchestrate the "kidnapping" at the old Fulton Market building, but the fact that he would receive his update from Melissa didn't upset him.

His niece didn't speak for a time, instead fixing her bleached blonde hair into a ponytail behind her head. Rather than donning one of her elegant dresses or short skirts, Melissa wore a gray athletic jumper and looked like she was about to go out for a run. Alfredo was ready for her to spit it out.

"Well, what happened?"

Melissa patted Alfredo's knee and turned to face her uncle. "There's some really good news, actually. Cal came to the building just like you'd hoped from your voice message. Tony Fregosi came with him. We now have two of the Fregosi children in our custody."

Alfredo's eyes gleamed with joy, and a speck of moisture formed around the edges. They'd finally found the boy who had been eluding them for three months. Alfredo would make sure the boy didn't last long. Once Melissa told him they had Cal as well, he would be sure Tony was the first to go. He'd keep Cal on edge for a while and then finish the deed.

"Great news, dear. What about Cal? Is he in our custody too?"

Melissa removed her hand from her uncle's leg. Her face grew tense.

"Well, that's part of the not-so-good news. Are you sure when you called Cal's cell phone that no one else heard what you said? Cal was at the scene today, but so was the Chicago PD. Cal and one of the detectives took down most of Dom's men and ran after our sniper, who fortunately got away."

Alfredo couldn't help but rise to his feet. Melissa sank down into the bed, her eyes fixating on the floor, before looking up at him. Alfredo saw the fear in his niece's eyes. For the first time in a long time, he wanted to play up to that fear. He had to show that he was firmly in charge of the mafia again, no longer bound by feelings of guilt or regret toward Vinnie's loss.

"So the reports from Giovanni Lucerno were true," Alfredo said. "Cal does have some chick cop working with him. It was a woman, right?"

Melissa nodded.

Alfredo walked to the bedside table and picked up an empty glass vase. Susan liked him to keep flowers in the penthouse during the rare occasions she would visit. Since neither of them had been there in months, the vase was purposefully empty; no smells of fragrance and life filled the room. Alfredo took the vase and looked at it, turning it over in his hands, inspecting it for smudged fingerprints. He walked toward the open door of the bedroom leading into the great room and chucked the vase outside.

The sound of breaking glass echoed throughout the home. Out of the corner of his eye, Alfredo saw his niece's face painted in shock.

"Jesus, what has gotten into you?"

Alfredo heard the tone of his niece's voice and was pleasantly surprised. Instead of a tone of anger or disapproval, it was one of excitement and affirmation. Alfredo turned to

Melissa and smiled, to the point where he was convinced it had to appear sadistic.

"I've got that fire in me again. I can't believe we couldn't corral Cal. It seems like he's always getting away. The LA mob couldn't stop him, Dom's guys couldn't take him out. I swore my trap was going to work."

Alfredo felt his voice rise and saw the look of concern return to his niece's face. He had every right to be furious, to hell with what Melissa thought. Even though the mafia now had Tony Fregosi in custody, Alfredo wouldn't rest until Cal joined him. Killing Callahan Boyle was the real prize. He couldn't rest—Vinnie couldn't rest—until Cal was six feet under.

"The trap did work," Melissa reassured him. "Cal and Tony both came back to Chicago, just like you hoped. You got Tony today, and it'll only be a matter of time before you find Cal. He can't be that hard to track down."

Alfredo nodded and walked toward the open door leading out to the great room, avoiding the shards of glass scattered upon the floor. Kidnapping the Fregosi girl may have brought Cal back, but now that Cal got away, he wasn't sure what his next move would be. Cal wouldn't be foolish enough to fall for the same trap twice, so he had to think deeper. He had to find a way to make it seem like he wanted Cal to find the girl's whereabouts. Now that the mafia had Tony Fregosi, too, he was sure that wouldn't be too difficult. He'd just have to figure out a way to send the message.

"Melissa, you said Cal can't be that hard to track down. I want you to think of every possible way we might find him. Have Fernando's guys go to his old apartment in Hyde Park, see if he's still shacking up there now that he's back. If he's not there, we need to search the usual hangouts."

"You want Flesh's guys to go after Cal?"

"Yes, damn it, I want Flesh's guys to go after Cal. Dom's men didn't do such a great job today, did they? Make the call as soon as you leave here. Think of where Cal liked to hang out. Now that that doofus Fonzie got blown away, or whatever the fuck happened to him, I'm not sure if Cal has any friends left to ask."

Melissa nodded. "Wait, I think I have a better idea. Just give me a minute."

She got up and walked out into the great room. Alfredo tapped his foot in irritation that his consigliera had abandoned him when he was in the middle of brainstorming his next plan.

A moment later Melissa returned, but this time a man walked in behind her. It was someone Alfredo hadn't seen in over five years, his former top hit man, Joey Bartellini.

"Joey! What the hell are you doing here?"

Bartellini walked up to Alfredo, wrapped him in a friendly embrace, and kissed his former boss on both cheeks before patting him on the shoulder. Alfredo didn't know what to say, he was so shocked at Joey's appearance.

"I talk to you for the first time in years a few days ago and now you're in my bedroom. How the hell did you get out here?"

Joey looked toward Melissa and nodded. "When a member of the family calls and says there's trouble, you've gotta listen."

Alfredo shook his head and smiled in disbelief. While part of him was glad to see his old friend Joey, he was also upset Melissa had gone behind his back and involved Bartellini without his knowledge. Even though Joey was good back in the day, Alfredo didn't want the old man to slip now that he was older and retired. Plus, Alfredo wasn't even sure he liked the guy anymore.

"Joey, I meant it when I said I wanted you to enjoy your retirement. But I'm glad Melissa called you." He shot daggers at his niece, letting her know where the decision stood among her choices as consigliera.

She slowly backed out of the room, and Alfredo waved her off before turning to the doors and closing them.

"Now, Joey, let's talk about why you're here and what I might need your help with, capisce?"

Joey sat down eagerly on the chaise longue at the side of Alfredo's king-sized bed. He certainly had no problem making himself feel at home. Alfredo turned to the bedside table, expecting a bottle of brandy to be waiting for him like it so often was in his study at the Evanston house. He waved off the thought of a drink as he looked at his former hit man and thought of how he could help take out his most recently departed top killer.

"Boss, before you say anything, I've gotta admit something to you. I've got the old fire in my belly. That fire of knowing I'm after somebody and with the right move that I can get 'em. I felt it when I was on the roof shooting those cops and trying to nail Cal and his buddy this afternoon."

Alfredo raised a brow. *Joey was the sniper?*

"I know, I wouldn't believe it either if I were you, my old ass climbing on that roof and then running like the wind when Cal and that detective chased after me. I don't know how I did it either to tell you the truth. Must be all those years of the California sunshine."

Joey smiled and patted his hand down on his knee. Alfredo nodded and was genuinely impressed with his friend. If the old man could scale a roof and run away from a man and woman over thirty years younger than him, that had to count for something. Besides, the man was a born hunter of human beings. If there was anyone in the city that could find Cal, it would be him.

"Joey, I want you to do something for me. You've mastered the art of being a hit man better than anyone I know, including Cal. Until that son of a bitch is dead, I want you to hunt him down night and day like a hawk. While I'd love to kill him myself, I'm giving you permission to kill if you see the opportunity. You got it?"

Joey's face lit up again. Like a child about to receive exactly what he'd asked Santa for on Christmas.

"You bet, sir. If there's one thing today showed me, it's that this old man's still got it."

25

Cal was two drinks into what he expected to be a long night at the bar. He'd gone to O'Dooley's Pub on Polk Street in the South Loop, the same bar at which Mayor Caruso was killed. He never expected to return to the bar but for some reason felt drawn to it, as if he knew he'd eventually be caught and held responsible for his crimes and wanted one last hurrah.

He shoved his finished pint of Guinness toward the bartender and beckoned the blonde woman with large breasts over to order another. Lusting after her was the furthest thing from his mind, despite the buzz he felt. If anything, he felt devastation. He wasn't any closer to finding Alfredo or Tina Fregosi than when he returned to Chicago earlier that day. On top of that, Tony was gone and possibly already dead.

Though his mind was filled with worry, Cal's body was tired. He couldn't do anything about the day's events now, instead shifting his focus to the atmosphere of the narrow bar surrounding him. Thankfully, no one there seemed to recognize him.

He decided he would worry about finding the three of them when he had a clearer head in the morning. It wasn't like he could go straight to Alfredo's penthouse or the family house in Evanston right now. Or could he? He was pretty sure if Alfredo or any of his men saw him he would be shot on sight, so Cal ruled that out. Still, Alfredo would be the easier of the three to find, as they had no realistic leads on the girl, and Tony could've been taken to any number of places.

Cal looked down the length of the bar and saw a midthirties couple deep in the throes of passion, if you counted sucking each other's faces as being deep in the throes of passion. The busty bartender caught him staring, gave him a wink, and set Cal's next pint of beer, a Heineken this time, down on the bar.

Watching the couple kiss made Cal think back to his own kiss with Brittany. Despite her berating him for his involvement in the operation that afternoon, Cal couldn't deny that he was glad Brittany made a move to kiss him. All the confusion he felt over wanting her despite his worry of her implicating him for his past crimes dissipated with her sweet and tender kiss. Cal wanted to keep kissing her; he even felt the lustful urge to bring her back to his place and kick out Uncle Judd for the night.

Uncle Judd!

Cal wondered how long it had been since he'd made contact with his uncle. Though Brittany had given him his cell phone back after their brief romantic rendezvous, he hadn't bothered to use it. Not even the occasional glance to see how the Bulls or Hawks were doing. Cal completely forgot to warn his uncle about the possibility of mafia soldiers coming to sweep his apartment.

Getting the hotel room at the Travelodge would go for

naught if his uncle wasn't around to rest peacefully in it. Cal thought about calling his uncle from the bar. That would've been the most immediate option. If his uncle answered the phone and sounded calm, Cal would figure he was safe and sound and that the apartment hadn't been searched. But if Uncle Judd was being held at gunpoint by a soldier with an itchy trigger finger, it would be just another trap set against Cal, just like the events at the Fulton Market building that afternoon.

Cal realized he couldn't make the call. He had to go back to his apartment. It would be risky, especially if there was a horde of men waiting for him. With only four bullets in the tiny Beretta Pico and no backup ammunition, the trip would be even riskier. It didn't matter, though. He had to go back.

Cal looked at the couple again, this time without their faces pressed together, chugged his Heineken, paid the bill, and left the pub.

Throughout the taxi ride back to his apartment, Cal couldn't help but worry that something had happened to Judd. Cal already felt terrible that Tony had been taken into mafia custody and that Tina Fregosi was still being held. If Uncle Judd had been taken in, too, he felt what was left of his cold heart would be ripped out of him.

Cal fidgeted with his phone, not texting or browsing the Web, instead shifting it back and forth with his hands. He wished he had a trusty apple that he could hold and peel with his jackknife. Only the jackknife was gone, discarded in the parking lot he'd left Maria's dead body and Fonzie's dying form in. It was probably in a police evidence bag now, with fingerprints that had no matching ID. Cal had to give himself credit that he hadn't been arrested and wasn't in any other trouble with the law outside of his run-in with the San Diego cop. If he stayed as close as he wanted to stay with Brittany, he knew that could change.

The driver dropped him off a block away, as Cal requested. Cal couldn't pay the fare soon enough. He walked to the end of the block and crossed the street to the park across from his building. He wanted to get a sense of whether anyone was outside waiting for him. No one was standing around the front of the building, and there weren't any strangers walking by.

Satisfied, he strolled across the street to the point where he'd started his journey and approached the rear of his apartment. No one was there either. He walked around the side of the building. Seeing no one hiding in the bushes, he entered the apartment from the front. He reached into his coat pocket, where he kept the Pico, and gripped the butt of the weapon tightly as he walked up to his top-floor unit.

He reached the door and saw that it was nudged open slightly. Something Uncle Judd wouldn't have done. He crept back against the wall and held his position while he pushed the door open with the barrel of the weapon. He waited to a thirty count, expecting a torrent of gunfire if he came into view. There was none.

Just to be safe, Cal took the most random thing he could —the boot on his right foot—and kicked it off toward the inside of the door. No shots rang out this time either. He was starting to think no one was inside. Cal edged closer to the door along the length of the wall, peeked around the corner, and entered.

The barrel of his gun was extended, and he moved swiftly through the living room, sweeping for any sign of intruders. While he didn't see or hear anyone, someone had definitely been inside. His dining room table and chairs had been tipped over, and cushions from his living room furniture were strewn about. The cabinets of his entertainment center were opened, and by the time he swept through the kitchen, bathroom, and master bedroom, Cal could see remnants of other personal items scattered all over the floor.

It only took Cal five minutes to determine no one was in the apartment. He walked back to the door, took a deep breath, and closed it. Now was the time to try the phone call.

He took his cell phone out of his pocket and called his uncle. Unlike some older adults with cell phones, Uncle Judd always made a point to answer. If he didn't manage to answer, it was because he was truly busy.

This time the phone didn't even ring once.

"Your call has been forwarded to an automatic voice message system—"

Cal clicked the phone off and put it back in his pocket. His worst fears had come true. Tony was gone, and now Uncle Judd was gone with him. If Cal had any doubts about trusting Brittany, even after their kiss, he'd have to completely abandon them now. They'd have to work together to find everyone important to him.

26

Brittany Wilson was shaking, and it wasn't from the six-degrees-below-zero temperatures whirling about outside just two days before Christmas. She'd been called in for an eight-o'clock briefing regarding her actions at the Fulton Market building. She'd never been requested for such a meeting before in her young career. Odds were that it wouldn't be good.

"Wilson, follow me to my office."

The command from Fisher startled her loose, and she jumped up from her cubicle chair. From the minute she received the call from her boss that he wanted to meet, she'd been on edge. She didn't even get to enjoy whatever feelings of bliss she'd felt after kissing Cal following the showdown yesterday.

She'd been so mad at him that he'd gone back against the agreement they made in San Diego to help each other, but she couldn't help but kiss him. He was dangerously handsome and it had felt so right at the time.

She'd felt butterflies in her stomach about Cal from the moment she first saw him. Until yesterday she'd kept her professional demeanor in check in not letting herself fall for him. But she had to keep Cal's waning trust. Despite his speech indicating he couldn't stand her, she knew what he really wanted. Based on Cal's reaction, she'd been right.

Brittany brushed those thoughts away, along with the crumbs from a blueberry muffin off of her tan slacks, as she walked to Mick Fisher's office. She noticed the mess of books and papers formerly scattered across his desk were stacked in four piles along the wall to the immediate right of the door. Brittany stared at the piles longer than she should have.

"Sit down, Wilson. I see you've noticed I decided to clean up a little."

Brittany felt her shoulders shrug but knew she had to remain strong in the face of her boss's criticism. She couldn't cower now when the chips were down, or she'd never be able to forgive herself. That was something weak women did, not strong women like her.

She sat in the seat furthest from the door and immediately crossed her legs. She set her posture as straight as she could and tucked her straightened black hair behind her ear, ready to present a composed version of herself.

"Speaking of cleaning, you've got an awful mess to clean up after what happened yesterday, so start sweeping," Fisher said.

"Excuse me, sir?"

"Talk. I want to know why you thought it was a good idea to go in that building after Lord knows who and leave your team behind."

Brittany was startled at the way her boss spoke to her. Even though Mick Fisher wasn't yelling at her, his hissing tone said it all.

"Let me explain. As I'm sure Detective Jackson told you,

we got to Fulton Market, and we saw two dead men in the road. There was a sniper on the roof across the street. As soon as we stepped out of the car to secure the area, we were ambushed by the sniper. I'm sorry about what happened to Detective Hunter, but let me assure you there was nothing more I could've done to prevent it. We were following orders, which were to secure the area and perform our initial investigation on the tip."

"Orders you directly violated, Wilson." Fisher stood up from his chair, shoved his gray jacket backward, and placed his hands on his hips. "Why did you go in that building before the area was secure? What compelled you to leave your post and enter that building?"

Brittany sighed and debated sharing the full story with her boss. Part of her knew she should tell the truth, but another part of her knew that her standing at the Chicago Police Department could be in jeopardy, which would cause her chances of joining the FBI to vanish. She might need to reveal even more of her methods if she spoke honestly.

"Right when we got there, I saw two men run inside the building. I'll admit I didn't know who they were, but I had a feeling it had something to do with the girl. I just desperately wanted to save her."

Fisher let out a chuckle. "You've always got to play the hero, don't you, Wilson? That's what Hollins said about you. Even when it's not smart and you don't have all the evidence to make the call. That's what's going on here."

Brittany flipped a strand of loose hair behind her ear and took a deep breath. Her boss had hit the nail on the head. She figured she would go with it and reaffirm her dedication to the case.

"Absolutely, sir. Ever since I joined the Chicago PD, I've always strived to be the best officer I could be. You know how many cases I've taken from completely cold to solved in my short time as a detective, sir? I just thought that there really was something there. That's why I rushed into that building."

Fisher shook his head and sat again. "I appreciate your dedication," he said in a much gentler voice. "But I've gotta wonder if you've used more of these unorthodox methods in past cases. Which brings me to my next question. The phone call from the anonymous tipper. It was directed to the cell phone of a gentleman named Cal. I want to know who this man is and his relevance to these cases. Now."

Brittany froze. Everything she'd done in the short time she'd been investigating the warehouse murder case had been what her boss would consider unorthodox. From going out to San Diego on a whim and pursuing an unknown lead, to saving that lead from a group of bad guys determined to kill him, to kissing that lead and loving every second of it, despite the fact he could be the very warehouse murderer she should be taking in was definitely outside the scope of any law enforcement agency's playbook.

At the end of the day, she wouldn't have changed anything she did, with the possible exception of rushing into the building yesterday and putting her team in danger. The only reason they faced peril was because Cal was already on the scene with guns blazing. But he had a connection to Alfredo Petrocelli. Brittany knew that with more time she could bring Petrocelli and the mafia down, thanks to Cal's help.

Should she give up that source just because her boss asked? Would she be able to be the hero and save so many from the mafia's evil if she spoke about Cal? Would she feel a sense of betrayal after their kiss yesterday, one of the finest of her life?

"Quit delaying. Answer."

Brittany uttered the first words she could think of. "Cal's the man I went to visit out in San Diego. I must have brought his phone back by mistake."

"You went on vacation just to see him? Who is he?"

"Forgive me, sir, but I don't think my personal life is any of your business."

Fisher rose to his feet again, this time pointing at her and raising his voice. "Do you realize the severity of this situation? I ought to have you suspended for what happened."

"Suspended?"

"Yes, damn it, suspended. Whoever this *man* was that you were visiting, he put the lives of a lot of people in danger with that fake tip, especially given that the girl wasn't even there. Whoever was calling your friend set us all up."

Brittany fought the urge to roll her eyes. "Okay, but at least it was only the bad guys that died out there. We can see if their bodies have anything useful on them and use that to find the girl. We still have more leads than—"

Her boss held up his hand, the palm facing her like a sudden stop sign that crept up on a driver too fast. "I take it you haven't heard what happened to Detective Hunter."

Brittany felt a lump catch in her throat. She had a feeling but was too afraid to ask.

"Well, before you ask, I'll tell you," Fisher said. "He died. Sniper got him in the neck."

Brittany placed her hand over her heart and felt a rush of tears form at the edges of her eyes. Brittany wasn't one for crying. She remembered losing her mother at fourteen years old and barely shedding a tear. Perhaps it was because her father and sister were so distraught that she felt the need to be the strong one. As the first tear formed, she wondered if she felt genuine sadness at the loss of her colleague, or if she was weeping for her own career, which was spiraling out of control before her.

"That's so terrible," she said between sniffles. "Russ was a really nice man."

Fisher nodded and grabbed two Kleenex from a box of tissues on the desk and handed them to her. Apparently the blame game was over and he was playing the empathy card. For now.

"Look, Brittany, don't completely beat yourself up over this. After all, I'm the one that told you to send a team out there without much more to go off of than a tip. You just took it too far by going into the building and leaving the team behind. I'm trying to warn you, that's all."

Brittany used the tissues to dot her eyes. Fisher didn't seem so angry with her now, but she still had to be cautious. She wanted to show the proper contrition for her actions, and she thought she knew the best way to do that.

"Sir, I'll tell you everything. I'm terribly sorry about what happened, and I'll play everything by the book from now on. I'll admit I've gone outside of the lines a bit, but I've discovered a lot of information that can help us."

Fisher had resumed sitting while she was wiping her tears, and crossed his legs and leaned back in his seat, intrigued.

"Go on."

"Cal, the man whose phone the gentleman called yesterday, is someone who might be of interest to our warehouse murder case."

Brittany proceeded to tell her boss of her time in San Diego. From calling her old boyfriend Drew, to showing up at Judd Russell's door, to questioning Cal about his ties to the mafia. When she mentioned she discovered that Cal had been adopted by Alfredo Petrocelli and had the physical characteristics of the man identified as the warehouse killer, and a potential suspect in numerous other cases, she saw her boss's eyes light up. She was getting somewhere again.

"I'm quite surprised, Wilson. Your methods are definitely unusual but appear effective nonetheless. What's this gentleman's last name?"

Brittany swallowed hard. "Boyle. Callahan Boyle."

Her boss reached for a notepad and scribbled the name in slanted cursive.

"Well, Wilson. You found the man. I want you to bring him in."

"Excuse me, sir?"

"From what you told me, Wilson, he sounds like he could be our man. I want you to find me some good hard evidence that points to him and bring him in. We need a witness testimony of someone who can identify him, anything like that."

Brittany stood, rattled but ready to present an agreeable image to her boss. "Are you sure? If I stay close to him, he might be able to give me more on Alfredo Petrocelli. I'm sure you'd be thrilled to put him away for a long time."

Fisher glared at her before looking down at the notepad again. "I don't give a shit about that, Wilson. There's a chance this guy could be one of the most dangerous men we've had on our streets, and we're this close to being able to make an arrest. You said he was adopted by Petrocelli. Get the adoption papers that prove that fact beyond the shadow of a doubt and get the old man to spill the beans. Cut him a deal if you have to. You've got him for abetting a fugitive. You might be able to get more than one man to trial for this."

Brittany nodded, swallowed, and walked toward the

door. Regardless of what path she took, she had a lot of work to do.

"Hey, Wilson," her boss said.

"Yes?"

"If you don't bring this Boyle character in, I will. I can't forget what happened yesterday. Consider this your makeup opportunity."

Brittany knew that if she didn't deliver she could kiss her career goodbye.

27

Cal woke up early and took a long, hot shower. After returning to his apartment the night before only to see it ransacked and with Uncle Judd nowhere to be found, Cal decided to return to the Travelodge, where he and Tony had booked a room the day before. Instead of hunkering down safely with Tony and Uncle Judd, Cal awoke alone, with both of his companions in whereabouts unknown.

Cal knew he needed to maintain his trust in Brittany. If anyone could help him find Tony and Uncle Judd, it was her. What a great thirtieth birthday present that would be.

The thought of another birthday was almost upsetting to Cal. What should be a celebration of life seemed meaningless without those he cared for around. He had no idea if their own lives may have been extinguished, much like a birthday candle being blown out.

His next move after the shower was to call Brittany. His heart pounded with anxiety as he thought of what to say. Would she be just as nervous as he was following their kiss?

Would she dismiss it and forget it happened? Or would she want to kiss him again?

Brittany agreed to meet Cal for coffee and a light breakfast at the Starbucks on Taylor and Bishop. Brittany wasn't overly hungry. She nibbled on a cake pop and slurped the occasional sip of a vanilla latte. Cal drank from a large cup of black coffee. He barely was able to eat half of his breakfast sandwich before his stomach felt upset. He wasn't sure if something was wrong with the food or if he was that upset that Uncle Judd and Tony were out of sight.

"Uncle Judd wasn't at your place when you went home last night?"

Cal shook his head. "I've tried calling him last night and this morning and haven't heard anything. It's not like him to not answer."

Brittany finished her cake pop and tossed the stick onto the table. "Yeah, but you think he would've called by now, right?"

Cal nodded. He didn't want to give any more evidence to support Brittany's theories, but he had to share his thoughts with her. If he confirmed a few things she'd discovered, knowing that she could eventually confirm them herself, it wouldn't bother him in the slightest if it meant Uncle Judd was safely returned.

"I think maybe Alfredo had something to do with it. Probably knew I'd go back to my place at some point. Only instead of grabbing me, they got Uncle Judd."

Brittany smiled, seemingly impressed with the revelation. "Admitting you know the guy now, huh? I didn't hear the call directly, but I have a feeling Alfredo was the one that called to tip us off to the possibility of Tina Fregosi being at Fulton Market. His men didn't get you yesterday, so he's gotta find a way to get to you somehow. Maybe taking Uncle Judd was it."

Cal sipped at his coffee, which was still piping hot. His tongue felt more raw than a child's rear after a parent's spanking.

"Tony's gone, too, so he's got that to hang over my head. I was hoping I could get your help in finding them."

Brittany smiled. "I'm glad you're starting to trust me."

Cal felt a sense of warmth spread throughout his chest that wasn't from the coffee.

Brittany took a deep breath and spoke again. "I don't exactly have a lot of leads. I'll reconvene with the team once I get back to the office, but we have no idea where that van went yesterday. You know these guys. Where do you think they would head?"

Cal sighed. He hoped Brittany would have more intel.

"That's tough to say. I doubt Alfredo has much experience with kidnapping." Cal knew that was a lie of course, but he couldn't admit what happened to Maria on the night she was murdered.

"He's got a lot of businesses all over the city that seem legitimate on the surface that might have a secret basement or back room where he could be keeping Tina. Maybe Tony and Uncle Judd too."

"Do you know of any specific examples? Maybe we start looking there."

Cal shook his head again. "That's not the route I'd like to go. Alfredo made that call with the intention of killing me. It was a perfectly placed trap that almost ended up destroying both of us. Who says we can't set a trap for him?"

Cal saw Brittany cringe. She took a long gulp from her latte, licked the foam from her lips, and set the cup down. Cal wondered if the lick was for his benefit.

"I don't think that's a good idea."

Cal laughed. Brittany, a hotshot FBI agent, not a fan of setting traps?

"Last time I checked, you worked for the FBI. You can't spare a few men to help out with this? It's not just Uncle Judd I'm worried about. We promised we'd work together to get Tina Fregosi back. The longer we wait, the more vulnerable she is. Maybe Alfredo lost his nerve and killed her. He hasn't gotten to me as fast as I'm sure he wanted to."

Brittany looked deep into Cal's eyes, as if searching for the answer to their problems. It had taken Cal so long to trust Brittany, almost until he had no other choice, that he felt a sudden realization that she may be the one rejecting Cal's call for help.

"Look, Cal, I still want us to work together to find this girl. Especially after what happened yesterday. But I've got to warn you about something. My boss wants me to come after you, even though I promised you I wouldn't. We lost an agent at Fulton Market yesterday, and he thinks I made a bad call racing into the building. He knows the call was meant for you. I can try to hold him off, but I can't use a bunch of Bureau resources to set a trap for Alfredo. Especially when we aren't sure if it will help us get the girl back."

Cal felt his eyes grow larger and the muscles in his neck quiver with tension. "You told your boss about me? What the hell, Brittany?"

Brittany held her hand up. "Cal, I told you I didn't want to say anything. I was left with no choice. My career is on the line here."

Cal chuckled. "Your career is on the line? My entire life is on the line if you do what your boss wants you to do, even though I'm much more innocent than you think I am."

Cal had to keep up the lie to save his own hide.

"A few other lives are on the line too," Cal added. "Think real hard before you come after me. Think about those lives that won't be saved without my help."

Brittany just stared at him. He couldn't believe this was happening. Was he wrong to trust her? Did their kiss not mean anything yesterday? He felt foolish for reveling in the kiss and thinking that their relationship would change. Of course it would remain adversarial. Such was the nature of a relationship between an FBI agent and a former mafia hit man.

"Cal, I'm not going to go after you. But I can't stall too long. We've gotta find the girl, and we've gotta do it fast. I can't use my team for what you had in mind, but I want to help you. It's just gonna have to be the two of us. Can you roll with that?"

Cal felt his spirits perk up slightly. She wasn't completely abandoning him and turning him in at the first possible opportunity. Cal cleared his throat. He wanted to make sure he could keep trusting her. He wanted to know if they were both on the same page.

"That kiss yesterday meant something to me. Did it mean anything to you? I need to know."

Cal thought he saw Brittany blush. It had to have meant something to her. He just hoped he wasn't wrong. His ears drummed as he waited for her response. Putting his emotions on the line wasn't easy for him.

"Of course it did. Who knows, once this is all over, maybe we can go on a proper date? One without overpriced coffee and stale cake pops."

Cal smiled. "I'm glad. I was afraid I was going crazy. I still think I can trust you. Let me tell you what I had in mind."

Cal told Brittany everything. It wasn't the most thought-out plan, and it would be hard to achieve with just the two of them, but it was something they could pull off that very day. If everything went according to plan, he'd force Alfredo to reveal where Tina, Tony, and Uncle Judd were, and he'd be a hero.

He just hoped he didn't become a martyr in the process.

28

The basement they were keeping Tina Fregosi in was pitch-black. Given that they fed her oatmeal, she was certain it was daybreak. Keeping her in the dark was starting to have its desired effect. Tina was beyond scared—scared that no one would find her.

She wasn't certain what day it was, but she'd counted how many times she'd gone to sleep since taken to this awful place. She refused to sleep the first night, her body unable to do anything more than kick and scream. She'd only slept after the bad guys drugged her to keep her quiet. She'd managed to fall asleep on her own the past three nights. She figured this was her fifth day away from home.

A loud bang echoed from up the stairs, and Tina inched closer to the wire-mesh cage. Instead of feeling fear and dread, she felt a twinge of excitement. Her only visitors thus far had been the evil men that fed her and took away the small bucket she used for relieving herself.

Would today be the day someone came to rescue her? Had her brother finally returned to save her? She sure hoped so.

Heavy footsteps clomped down the stairs, and Tina gripped the fence tighter, with just the faintest bit of hope that it wouldn't be any of the men in leather jackets coming to see her. A pair of legs reached the bottom of the stairs, and she was disappointed to see the older gentleman there again. Even in the faint light visible from the top of the stairs, Tina saw the sinister smile on the man's face. It creeped her out.

"How is little Miss Tina today?"

"Go away! I wanna go home!"

Tina knew she had to keep begging. She had to keep pleading. She knew the more annoying she got, the greater likelihood the men keeping her would let her go. She knew the men keeping her had to be low on the totem pole of whatever group of bad guys they worked for; otherwise, why would they be watching a twelve-year-old girl? Maybe she could get the old man to crack. She wasn't sure who he was, but she imagined he was the ring leader.

"Of course you'd like to go home. Let me tell you, Christmas is almost here, and I've got a big present for you. Do you want to see what Santa brought?"

Tina rolled her eyes. She knew from having two older siblings that Santa wasn't real. The corny interpretation by the old man didn't make her any more likely to believe in jolly Saint Nick.

"Just let me go. That would be the best present you could give me."

The older man frowned, took off his pork pie hat, and rested it on his slight belly. He scratched at his hair, which Tina could tell was a wig from the unnatural movement of the gray material.

"Someday I may grant your wish. But first I should probably tell you why you're here. What you being here means in the grand scheme of things. Perhaps it'll make sense, don't you think?"

Tina spat at the man again, just missing him. She didn't care about the consequences. She wanted him to lose control of his temper. Then maybe she could put her best idea of an escape attempt to use. She'd found a rusted nail in her small enclosed pen and had done her best to keep it hidden. She doubted the nail would do much damage, but maybe it would allow her to claw at the man's eyes and run out of his grip. It was the best option she had.

"You little shit!"

The old man moved toward the cage, furious. For a moment Tina thought the plan would work. A few more footsteps sounded from the stairs, stopping the man in his tracks.

"Should we bring down the present, sir?"

The old man grumbled and turned toward the stairs. "Not yet. Give me two minutes."

The man put his hat back on and turned back to Tina, pointing what she imagined to be the world's grubbiest finger at her.

"You listen to me. You're here for one reason and one reason only. I look at you and I see my six-year-old boy that died in a skiing accident. I see my much older boy, who was just brutally murdered. I'd never harm my kids, just like I won't harm you, unless you give me good reason to. I loved my kids, provided for them, made sure they had good lives, and now they're gone. Just like you're gone from your family."

Tina had no idea what the man was getting at. What did the deaths of his kids have to do with her? She felt herself retreating from the fence toward the brick wall behind her.

She felt a great sense of discomfort settle in the middle of her chest.

"And sometimes, Tina, you've got to get back at those that have caused your kids harm. That brings me to why you're here in this room. I knew that by you being here, your brother and a friend of his would come back for you. Your brother and his friend have done some very awful things, especially to my older son. But I knew with you in trouble, they would come back. It's time for them to pay for what they've done and for justice to be served."

Tina felt her heart beat faster. Had this man done something to Tony?

"What happened to my brother?"

The old man smiled and started laughing at her. "As I said, justice will be served, my dear. How fair is it for a parent to see both of their kids die so young? How fair is it that two degenerate bastards can bring down everything I've ever worked for by their evil deeds?"

The man turned back to the stairs and shouted, "Alright, bring down Santa's bag!"

More footsteps came down the stairs. Tina was starting to worry. What could this present be? The man hinted something about her brother. The way he spoke of justice meant that if her brother was here it wasn't under great circumstances. Still, she held out hope that maybe what the man said was a lie. She retreated further into her cell, not sure how close she wanted to be to the surprise.

"Oh, Tina, don't be shy. Don't you want to see your present?"

At last a balding man with a thick dark beard reached the bottom of the stairs and stood next to the old man, with a young man's body draped over his shoulder. He walked closer to the fence, and Tina watched as he leaned the young man up against it, his long mop of dark hair dangling through the openings.

"Go on, say hello to your new friend," the old man said.

Her heart was beating hard, and she was as scared as could be, but Tina somehow found the ability to inch closer to the fence. The young man didn't move. Tina had no idea if he was dead or alive.

"That's it, get closer," the old man said. "You know how I told you that I had a special present for you? Brush his hair away from his face and you'll see what I mean."

Compelled by the creepy man's voice, Tina pushed the boy's dark hair away and screamed at what she saw. Justice had been served alright. Her poor brother, who she hadn't seen in so long, looked almost nothing like himself. His face had been beaten and bruised. His eyes were so puffy and swollen that she wondered how he'd see out of them again.

"What did you do to him?"

It was a scream as much as it was a question.

Before she could move, the man holding Tony opened the padlock and sat him down inside. Tina could no longer think about an escape attempt. She could only sit in a heap on the cold cement floor, weeping for her beaten brother.

"Alfredo . . . Alfredo."

Tina turned toward her brother, sure she'd heard him speak. She had no idea where he found the strength to talk, how he could even make his lips move. She tilted her ear toward him and listened again.

"Petro . . . celli. Alfredo . . . Petrocelli."

Apparently, the old man heard Tony speak too. "What is it? What is he saying?"

Tina heard her brother clear his throat. She scooted closer to him so she could hear every word he said. She had an eerie feeling they would be his last. That was how battered his face looked.

"Alfredo Petrocelli . . . He's . . . the man . . . who kidnapped you. The boss . . . the boss . . . of the Chicago mafia."

Tony's words were much clearer and louder this time. He'd managed to find some strength inside him, some power to use his vocal cords to tell Tina the message she needed to hear.

"When you get out of here, Tina, tell the police everything. He ordered the death of Mayor Caruso too."

Tina looked at her brother, dried blood and a sheen of sweat coating his face and hair, then at the old man. Both times she'd seen him, she knew something had been off. The guy had to have been wearing a disguise.

If the man was fuming before when she spat at him, he was downright enraged this time. His shoulders moved up and down in anger. It seemed there would be no stopping him. Like a possessed wrestler trying to enter a steel cage, Alfredo nearly ripped open the door as he entered.

He headed straight for Tony, pulled his head back, and rocked him repeatedly in the face with hard right hooks. Tina's hands flew to her mouth in horror. The old man only got three shots in, but they'd been enough. Her brother fell back to the concrete floor, out cold.

Suddenly, Tina felt a rage boil up inside her. She'd been kidnapped, drugged, and left in a cold, dark basement for almost a week. She took the nail she'd found in her cell and was ready to put it to good use.

The old man turned toward her. She had the nail ready, diving forward with her tiny hand and striking the old man in the leg with it. Only the nail didn't take, instead bouncing off of the man and onto the floor.

She'd failed.

Alfredo's eyes gleamed with hatred. He rushed at her, grabbed her by the hair, and threw her against the brick wall. She felt her head hammer against it and a loud pounding of pain flood her brain. She didn't know if she would live or die.

"Damn, boss."

Tina only heard two more things before she lost consciousness. The first was the closing of the fence's door, and the second was a stern warning from Alfredo.

"Clean up that bitch's mess and tell Tony I'll be back. This will be his last Christmas."

Tina's head throbbed, and then she saw nothing but darkness.

29

Cal was beyond ready to see his adoptive father for the first time since he thought he'd killed him three months ago. If he'd been more careful, he would've killed Alfredo before the mob boss shot Maria. Maybe Cal and Maria would've been engaged by now had he not failed her.

Alfredo's desire for revenge had to be just as great as Cal's. The former hit man maintained hope that he could get his adoptive father to spill the beans regarding Tina and Tony Fregosi's whereabouts, while getting the chance to kill him in the process. Cal wasn't one to wait too long, and he knew the chances of getting brought in for a past crime grew stronger every day, making him less concerned about killing Alfredo in front of Brittany.

The first part of the trap was determining the place to attack. Cal wanted to pick somewhere he knew well enough that he could lure Alfredo to, while maintaining the ability to hold the upper hand. He didn't want to give Alfredo enough time to gather men and find a way to trap him instead. Several places ran through his mind before he settled on Rosehill Cemetery, in Andersonville, where Vinnie was buried.

Threatening to tamper with Vinnie's gravesite was a surefire way to piss Alfredo off and get him to fall for Cal's trap. Cal also knew that based on where the Petrocelli grave plots were located he'd have the opportunity to jump Alfredo and corner him out of view from anyone else visiting the cemetery in the frigid conditions. A hill with a large oak tree sloped down just past the gravesite Cal knew had been selected for Vinnie. Ironically, his own future gravesite was the closest to the slope of the hill, separated from Vinnie's current resting place by a matter of feet.

That was where the task of contacting Alfredo about Cal's whereabouts came into play. Cal thought about calling Alfredo directly, just as the mob boss tried to do by calling his cell phone when it was still in Brittany's hands, but that would probably raise too many alarms in Alfredo's mind. Instead, Brittany decided she would call from one of the few pay phones inside a hotel lobby not far from the Starbucks in which they ate breakfast. She called Alfredo's house phone, pretending to represent the cemetery staff.

"Oh, sir, someone's been messing around with your son's gravestone. Yes, dear, we sent someone out to get rid of him, but he keeps coming back. What does he look like? Oh, I'd say he's a tall gentleman, dear. Brown hair, brown eyes, kind of a mean glare."

Cal had to stifle a laugh outside the booth as he heard Brittany give her best *Mrs. Doubtfire* impersonation in providing Alfredo the description of the supposed events unfolding. Cal was sure it would set Alfredo off. The only disadvantage of their plan was they had to haul ass from downtown to Andersonville. They had no clue how fast Alfredo would arrive.

Brittany and Cal found a Lyft driver who was able to get them to the cemetery in twenty minutes flat. Cal knew Alfredo could've easily gotten there just as fast if he was coming from the family compound in Evanston, but he had to hope the mob boss wasn't already there. Even if he was, he would be in reaction mode, and perhaps Cal could sneak up on him.

Alas, Alfredo hadn't arrived by the time Cal and Brittany trudged up the frozen ground toward the Petrocelli gravesite. Despite being in better shape than Cal, Brittany panted for breath, steam escaping from her mouth faster than prisoners during a jailbreak.

"So, this is where Vinnie is buried? You still want to tell me you had nothing to do with that?"

Cal thought he saw Brittany wink. He couldn't help but let out a chuckle, despite wanting to maintain a sense of innocence regarding the whole ordeal. Sometimes he wondered why Brittany and her boss were so concerned about him anyway, since he was done with the hit man life. Other than Alfredo, he had no desire to kill anyone.

"I had nothing to do with it," Cal lied as he took his position behind the oak tree just past Vinnie's gravestone. "Maybe throw some snow on the grave so Alfredo really thinks someone's been messing with it. We don't want him to think something's up."

Brittany huffed, trudged toward Vinnie's tombstone, and bunched up a large pile of snow in the center of the tombstone's face. "Is this good? Should I give it a few kicks?"

"Sure, the bastard wasn't the nicest brother anyway. Knock the damn thing over for all I care."

"Hey, that's not very nice. What happened to respecting the dead and allowing them to rest in peace?"

"Fuck that."

A strong gust of wind sounded, nearly sending Brittany sliding down the small hill. Cal thought he heard the crunching of boots in the distance, running toward them. He wondered if Alfredo was finally on the way.

"Hide! I think I heard something."

Brittany cocked her head, holding on to Vinnie's tombstone for support. "You think so? I didn't hear anything."

"Just get in position!"

Cal whispered as loud as he could and did his best to restrain himself from yelling as Brittany scampered behind a taller gravestone to the right of the Petrocelli plot. It was a good distance away; having lots of money afforded the Petrocellis the ability to be relatively reclusive in death.

They waited for several minutes, wondering what the source of the crunching noise was just moments before. Cal looked over his shoulder to where Brittany was hiding, her standard-issue Glock 17 held high in her hand. They looked at each other and then out into the distance. Nothing but more graves and trees were visible. Cal wondered how long they'd wait. What if Alfredo never showed up?

"Cal, did you hear that? Did yo—?"

An explosion of gunfire cascaded down onto the tall gravestone that Brittany was leaning behind. The agent turned completely away from Cal and hit the cold ground as bullet after bullet sprayed toward her.

So much for their trap being effective. Now he and Brittany were the ones who were cornered.

There was a break in the gunfire for a moment, and Cal heard the rustling of boots moving across the frigid blades of grass. He peeked from behind the oak tree and had his

Beretta Pico pointed in the direction of the shooter. He thought he saw a man in a black trench coat duck behind the tree but couldn't be sure, as the man was completely covered before Cal could decide to fire.

Cal looked back to Brittany and shifted his head toward the tree, alerting her to the man's presence. Brittany nodded, peering around the tombstone, before shots rang out again. Cal kept his eyes peeled on the tree, waiting for an opening. He had no idea if Alfredo was the shooter or not, but he was ready to fire if he had an open shot. Brittany returned fire, sending the sounds of gunfire ricocheting off the trees.

Cal shifted his gaze to the rest of the cemetery grounds. A car pulled up along the road closest to the Petrocelli burial site. He scanned the car, wondering who dared get out with the smattering of gunfire between Brittany and the man behind the tree. A tall figure with a fedora stepped out of the back seat and slowly walked in Cal's direction. The man was heading straight for Vinnie Petrocelli's grave.

It took Cal a moment to register just who he was looking at. Once the visitor was fifty yards away, almost in line with the man firing at Brittany, Cal realized he was looking at Alfredo Petrocelli.

Cal had his Beretta Pico ready and planned to fire at any moment. There was nothing more in the world he wanted than to kill Alfredo Petrocelli, yet he knew he couldn't kill him straight away. He needed to keep him alive long enough to find out what happened to the Fregosi children. Cal had to resist the impulse to fire.

He couldn't anyway. Almost as if he'd been deaf to the state of affairs surrounding him since departing the safety of the vehicle, Alfredo finally jumped behind the nearest gravestone he could. Unlike the one Brittany was perched behind, it was a normal-sized headstone. A good portion of Alfredo's body was visible if Cal decided to shoot.

The gunfire had slowed between Brittany and the gunman behind the tree, prompting Cal to look over to the tall gravestone to see how Brittany was holding up. She was reloading, taking more bullets from her coat pocket and emptying them into the chamber. Cal nodded toward the grave where Alfredo was hiding, hoping Brittany would realize what his intentions were.

Brittany nodded, turned away from Cal, and readied for a counterattack against the man behind the tree. Cal caught a glimpse of him and thought he saw flowing gray hair beneath his black stocking cap. The same gray hair he saw after leaving the scene at Fulton Market. Joey Bartellini's hair.

Cal watched as Brittany fired two more rounds in the direction of the tree before bolting for a shorter but thicker tombstone to her right. Bartellini came further out from the tree and fired, sending two bullets toward the thick concrete structure before he was forced to reload. Brittany returned fire, and the two seemed like they would be locked in a never-ending shootout, with neither of them managing to hit anything.

Cal realized Brittany and Bartellini's battle was the perfect cover for him to make his move. He extended his Beretta and crouched low to the ground, skirting the perimeter of the area to avoid attracting attention from Bartellini. He wanted Alfredo all to himself. If he had it his way, he was going to get him.

After an initial crawl, Cal began jogging toward Alfredo, ducking behind tombstones as he went. Alfredo was still crouched behind the same tombstone, facing the opposite direction.

Cal crept closer and extended his gun. His core reverberated in excitement at the prospect of finally ending Alfredo's life.

Suddenly, Alfredo leapt up from the ground and turned toward Cal, his hand reaching for the inside of his peacoat.

"At last, Cal, we meet again."

30

Cal's index finger dusted the trigger, ready to fire the instant Alfredo pulled out his gun from his coat. The sense of calm he felt earlier had completely vanished. All of the feelings of hatred he felt for his adoptive father came rushing back. His lungs filled with hot air that he wanted to unleash in the form of a roaring yell, voicing the agony Alfredo caused him when he fired the fatal round into Maria's back. His soul felt disgusted at allowing Alfredo to manipulate him into living a life where he killed countless others in order to make a living.

Because of the evil of the man standing before him, Cal had lost the love of his life, and his best friend had gone astray. Not to mention the fates of his uncle and young friend Tony were hanging in the balance. It was this thought that forced Cal to avoid firing. He had to find out where Tony and Tina Fregosi were. He had to fulfill the promise he made to Maria as she died in his arms on that fateful night three months prior. He had to use his talents to live a life of good.

"Relax," Alfredo said, his hand moving from the inside of his peacoat back to the cold, bitter air.

Without a glove, Cal saw just how dry and red Alfredo's hand was, as if the fury of the cold winds was marking Alfredo for the hardened man he was.

"Why don't you put that gun down, Cal? Let's fight each other like gentlemen."

Cal scoffed. "Gentlemen? You're nothing of the sort. You know we both want to kill each other. So why should I put my gun down and trust you to fight fairly?"

Alfredo smiled. Cal knew he wanted to break out into laughter but respected the older man for restraining himself. Being surrounded by the dead, including his own son, may have forced Alfredo to consider himself a little smaller in the grand scheme of the world. Perhaps he also didn't want to alert the attention of Joey Bartellini, who was still dueling with Brittany, both of them maneuvering for a better position. Cal was sure Bartellini knew that he and Alfredo were facing off. Cal was confident he wouldn't interfere unless Alfredo's life was in danger.

"I suppose you know me too well," Alfredo said in response. "You bet I want to kill you. You're directly responsible for where my son resides just thirty yards behind you. There's nothing more I'd like than to have you join him."

Cal's face was as hard as the stone that surrounded their feet. "I saw that sad excuse of a plot you reserved for me next to Vinnie. I'd rather be buried alive than wind up there."

Alfredo shook his head. "What makes you think I'd bury your ass there? As far as I'm concerned, the chances of you having your entire body intact for a nice Christian burial are slim. When I'm through with you, you'll be in more pieces than a broken window."

Both men stared at each other for a period of time, the faint sound of growling freezing their icy breaths. Cal held his gun steady, not pointing it directly at Alfredo, but more than ready to raise it to fire. But he had to find out about the Fregosis. He just couldn't escape the pure hatred he felt for Alfredo to do so.

A loud crash sounded in the distance. On instinct, Cal looked toward where he last saw Brittany, hoping she was still holding her own against the former hit man. The slight dart of his eyes was the opening Alfredo needed. The mob boss dashed his hand inside his coat pocket and pulled out his weapon. Cal recovered just in time, his peripheral vision locked on Alfredo.

Cal raised his gun and shot Alfredo in the shoulder, sending the mob boss's gun to the ground. Cal charged now, realizing his opportunity. The mafia chieftain screamed and fell to his knees. Anger and fury fueled every step Cal took as he marched toward Alfredo. He soon reached him and sent his fist flying at Alfredo's nose.

Blood spurted in the air, a portion coating Cal's hand as he continued his assault with two more punches. He wanted to keep going, driving his fists into Alfredo's flesh until he'd beaten him to a pulp. But he had to focus on the task at hand. He raised his Beretta Pico and held the weapon against Alfredo's temple. It was time to talk.

"Where are they?"

Alfredo raised his hands in the air. Cal swore he saw tears joining the blood slowly streaking out of Alfredo's busted nose. Was the big man capable of being this vulnerable? Cal didn't think so, and he didn't trust Alfredo for a second.

"Quit trying to bide time. Tell me where those kids are."

"What kids?" Alfredo sniffled.

"You know damn well what kids I'm talking about. The Fregosis. Tina's the little girl that you tried to tip me off about, only you didn't know an FBI agent had my phone, did you?"

Alfredo leaned into the shoulder of his coat, doing his best to wipe his nose against it. It would need a trip to the dry cleaner's.

"Wow, Cal. I never figured you for one to turn into a narc. Just what have you told them about me? Surely I'm not going down unless you are."

Cal thrust the gun tighter against Alfredo's temple. "It's not going to come to that. I'm not going to have to give you or your precious mafia up, because you'll be dead as soon as I find those kids."

Alfredo laughed now, letting his abdomen bellow into a deep chorus of joy. Cal felt increasingly uncomfortable with the entire situation. He glanced down the hill and into the distance, where Brittany and Bartellini had been firing at each other. There were no new gunshots. That worried him a bit.

"You can't kill me. Without me, you have no chance in hell of finding those kids. You have no more leads into the mafia anymore. I'm all you've got. The police, the FBI, they don't know us either. We can move that girl all over town and no one will ever know."

Cal's shoulders heaved and his temple throbbed. He had the urge to pull the trigger right then, to send Alfredo to his death, joining the thousands of others lying in the cemetery. But he couldn't. He had to keep pressing. For the kids. He did the only sensible thing he could to show his anger without killing his adoptive father. He took the small gun, removed it from Alfredo's temple and shot him again in the shoulder, just above where he'd got him with his earlier shot.

"Ahh!"

Cal thrust the gun back in Alfredo's face. "Tell me where she is. I understand why you took Tony, but this girl is innocent in all of this. Where is she?"

Alfredo looked up at Cal like a kid who'd had all of his Christmas presents taken from him. Cal wasn't sure if he was going to cry or scream further in pain.

A volley of gunfire exploded around them, sending both men cowering for the ground. Cal didn't have to look up to see who it was. Joey Bartellini was coming after him now, trying to finish him off.

Cal grabbed his Pico and gripped it tight. He only had four bullets left. If Alfredo knew his weapons well, he'd know that Cal only had a limited arsenal from which to draw from, making his own weapon all the more effective.

Two more shots rang out. Cal fired at the first piece of flesh he could see, but Joey was able to duck behind a tree before Cal's shot connected. Cal readied to shoot again, before noticing Alfredo stirring out of the corner of his eye. Much to Cal's relief, he heard gunshots echo in Bartellini's direction. Brittany was still alive after all.

A new sound joined the chorus as police sirens wailed in the distance. Cal had no idea how soon the cops would arrive. He was determined to beat a confession out of Alfredo if it was the last thing he did.

Confident Bartellini was engaged with Brittany, Cal pointed his gun back at Alfredo. He rose to his feet and put the gun against Alfredo's temple again. This time he mustered a look of fear so intense that Alfredo had no choice but to quake beneath Cal's gaze.

"I've already shot you twice, Alfredo. I see no reason why

I shouldn't shoot you again, this time to kill. With the police on their way, I can't have you telling them that I was the one who shot you. Though I don't think that was a problem when they asked you who shot and killed all your men at the warehouse."

Alfredo shook his head. "Go ahead, Cal. Do what you have to do. I'll join my son in his final resting place with a clean conscience. But you, murdering me in cold daylight, are still the ruthless killer you hoped not to be when you asked out of the mafia. I guess some things never change."

Running footsteps and the sound of the sirens drawing closer shifted Cal's focus to the scene around him. Brittany was sprinting away from the cemetery, taking cover behind nearby gravestones in case Bartellini fired upon her. It took a second for Cal to realize what she was doing.

She was trying to escape, not wanting her FBI team to know she was a part of the events. *Damn it.*

With Brittany no longer around to provide a distraction, Bartellini began running toward him. Cal removed the gun from Alfredo's head and fired two quick rounds at the former hit man. He caught old Joey with the second shot, dusting his arm and causing him to drop his weapon. Joey raised his arm in the air in a fit of cursing and painful frustration.

Cal quickly turned the weapon to Alfredo again.

"You're right, Alfredo. I am still a killer. But I've only got one shot left, and Joey's dealing with some pain at the moment. You're the last man I have to kill, and then the killing stops. I'll be able to move on with my life and be a force for good, just like Maria wanted me to be. And it all starts now."

Cal cocked the hammer, the finality of what he was about to do registering in his victim's face. Alfredo shook his head violently and looked to where Joey Bartellini had stood. The former hit man was running in the same direction Brittany had disappeared, leaving his boss behind to face Cal's wrath as the police sirens drew closer.

"The girl and her brother are together, one happy family. Somewhere you spent a lot of time growing up but I'm sure would pain you to go back to. That's all I can say."

Cal looked at his adoptive father as if he were speaking in tongues. Perhaps he was. Cal wanted nothing more than to shoot Alfredo, but he wasn't completely sure what he was referring to. Was it worth letting him live so he could find out?

The sirens were too close now. Brittany had a large head start on him. He had to catch up and use whatever information Alfredo had given him to see if he could save the Fregosis. Alfredo had said that they were together, meaning Tony wasn't dead yet.

Against his better judgment, Cal brought the gun back to his side and took off running.

He'd been so close to killing Alfredo, but he felt he couldn't pull the trigger until all the lives Alfredo was attempting to ruin were safe.

31

Brittany Wilson had hardly escaped the Rosehill Cemetery when she saw the text she'd long awaited on her phone. Maxwell Huggins, the owner of O'Dooley's Pub and the man who'd been out of town for almost two months, was finally willing to speak with her.

Truth be told, Brittany had been lucky in reaching the man. Her fellow detectives hadn't been able to speak with him, one of few who had witnessed the events unfolding around former mayor Ross Caruso's murder, since they had interviewed Alfredo Petrocelli after the mob boss left the hospital two months ago.

Huggins claimed he'd been on vacation in Arizona, doing his best to both escape the winter and tend to his dying mother. He left a nephew and neighbor to run things at the pub while he was away. Brittany didn't exactly buy that, but she'd be sure to ask the man about it when they met.

The pub owner didn't want to meet Brittany in public for fear of the mafia recognizing him, but she was sure he'd be keen for a free meal. When she asked Huggins to meet her at the Firehouse Cafe just outside the cemetery, she was pleasantly surprised that he agreed, even if it was only for what he deemed "a little bit."

Brittany was seated at a table for two near a large stone fireplace by the time Huggins, a squat man with a curly black beard and matching hair serving as a crown circling his balding head, entered the restaurant. Huggins held a red stocking cap in his hand and looked around before his gaze settled on Brittany. His eyes darted from side to side as he trudged over to the table, perhaps because he had second thoughts about meeting with the detective. Brittany knew she needed to reassure him and keep him talking for just as long as it took.

"Mr. Huggins, thanks so much for meeting me today," Brittany said, extending her hand over the polished beechwood table.

The bar owner scratched his head, appearing hesitant. After a few seconds, he finally returned the gesture. He was avoiding eye contact and instead gazing off into the distance.

"Can I get you something to drink?"

Brittany looked up from her menu at the tall, big-bosomed waitress. A piece of gum was visible between her teeth.

"No, that's quite alright. But I'd like some chicken tenders and some onion rings if you've got 'em," Huggins said.

The waitress jotted down the order.

"For you, ma'am?"

Brittany pursed her lips, not having made a decision yet despite the fact she'd already been seated for the last ten minutes. Ultimately, her choice of meal didn't matter. It was Huggins she came for.

"I'll have the shepherd's pie. It sounds delicious."

"It is," the waitress said. "I'll put those orders in right away."

Satisfied they wouldn't be bothered again, Brittany cut right to the chase. "So, Mr. Huggins, can you tell me where you've been the last few months? My colleagues have been trying to contact you, and you've been radio silent until now. Why is that?"

Huggins grumbled something under his breath and looked down at his lap. Brittany wondered if he'd ever find the nerve to talk to her. He finally glanced up and flashed the world's smallest smile.

"Well, I was visiting my mother in Arizona, like I said. I normally don't go down there until after the first of the year, but she's not doing too well. If I didn't go down there now, I wasn't sure if I'd see her again."

Brittany placed her hand over her heart, feigning concern. "I'm very sorry to hear that. Did her care require you to be gone for two months?"

Huggins shrugged. "So what if it did? That's none of your concern."

It was time for Brittany to press harder. "Why do you keep looking around? No one here is going to come after you for talking to me."

The man across from her scratched his head yet again. The waitress arrived with a piping-hot basket of onion rings and told them she'd be back with the rest. Huggins suddenly leaned forward, the steam from the onion rings disappearing into his beard.

"Look, I probably shouldn't be saying this, but here goes. I really was down in Arizona visiting my mom. But I wasn't gonna stay for two months. I only stayed that long because someone told me to."

"Who would this someone be?"

The owner of O'Dooley's Pub looked over his shoulder, out toward the front door. He turned back to Brittany and started to speak again when the waitress returned with Huggins's chicken fingers and Brittany's shepherd's pie. While the food looked delicious, Brittany was starving for information, and only Maxwell Huggins could feed it to her.

"It was a woman. Her name was Melissa. I think her last name was Ranieri."

The name didn't ring a bell. "What did she want?"

Huggins was preoccupied with chewing a piece of his chicken tender. His mouth was formed in an O, and she heard faint blowing sounds. He reached for his water glass and took a long sip through the straw. The food must have been too hot.

Undeterred, Huggins grabbed an onion ring and broke it in half, taking the piece with a floppy fried onion hanging out of the batter and dropping the crunchy piece into the basket. He held it in his hand for a moment before continuing.

"She wanted me to extend my trip. She even gave me a few grand for it. The pub's been in rough shape lately, especially with the mayor being murdered there and all. I was glad to do it. I'm a businessman, ma'am. I needed the money."

That was the second time Brittany had been called "ma'am" that afternoon. She wasn't sure she liked it.

"So, why did you decide to talk to me now? If this Melissa woman bought you off?"

Huggins stuffed another chicken tender in his mouth, chewed for seemingly five minutes, took another swig of water, then looked at Brittany.

"It just didn't feel right. I saw a lot that day. I just needed to get it off my chest and tell someone. Momma wouldn't understand, and I'm going through a divorce. It's not like I could tell my wife about it."

"Go on," Brittany urged. "What did you see that day?"

Huggins recounted what he saw on the day of Ross Caruso's murder. He'd mentioned the mayor arriving at the pub with a few of his hired hands, two of which sat with him at the bar. The mayor eventually drifted outside due to a clogged toilet to relieve himself, only to be killed behind the bar minutes later. Huggins hadn't seen the incident but witnessed the sheer pandemonium when two more of Caruso's flunkies opened the rear door and were murdered in the entryway. The pub's patrons had spilled out into the street, screaming and running for their lives.

He shared what he saw in the alley behind the pub, witnessing a man fitting Cal's description—the same one Alfredo Petrocelli had originally given the police—killing the mayor's other hired hands after they shot at a boy who dove in front of a dumpster. The scene had been set for Brittany. Now she needed to be sure Huggins could confirm the killer's identity.

"Mr. Huggins, this man you saw—could you describe what he looked like more clearly?"

Huggins shook his head. "The man threatened me. Said he'd kill me if I told anyone anything."

"There's nothing he can do now," Brittany said. If that man had truly been Cal, she sure as hell hoped he didn't find his way to the cafe after escaping the cemetery.

"Like I said, he was a tall guy. Had a real mean glare on him, maybe a beard, maybe not. It wasn't as thick as mine, though, if he did have one." Huggins tugged at his curly beard, a stray hair falling into his nearly empty basket of onion rings.

"Did he have any distinguishing features?"

"Not that I recall."

Damn it. Brittany was ready to pull out the photos for a photo lineup, which she had already briefed Mr. Huggins about prior to his arrival at the restaurant. She wanted as vivid a picture of that day painted in his head as possible. She'd try one more question.

"Do you remember the murder weapon? The gun the man used?"

Huggins shook his head again, reached into his onion ring basket, and grabbed and bit into the very ring his stray hair had fallen onto.

"I can't say I do. I don't know too much about guns." Huggins took another bite of his onion ring, prompting Brittany to peer down at her barely touched shepherd's pie. After seeing her interviewee take the bite of the hairy onion ring, she realized she was no longer hungry.

"Actually," Huggins said, his face seeming more alive than it had at any point during their conversation, "it was a Beretta. My nephew, the one that's been running the pub since I've been gone, he's got one. Hell, come to think of it he may even have two."

Brittany beamed, unable to contain the smile on her face. She reached into her coat pocket and grabbed the envelope with the photos, prepared to proceed with the photo lineup. She knew the rules she needed to follow, and she adhered to them to the letter, just as she had with the man in Evanston, whom she'd also been able to dig up from the woodwork. She could only hope Huggins identified the same suspect.

When the owner of O'Dooley's Pub pointed at the photograph of Callahan Boyle, Brittany felt a mixture of elation and sadness. She truly hoped Cal had nothing to do with the crimes, but she knew that was unlikely the more she understood about the case. But she was even closer to her FBI dream. Fisher would be ecstatic at the news.

"Thank you for your time, Mr. Huggins. You've been more than helpful."

Maxwell Huggins nodded, stood, and brushed the crumbs of his fried food off of his jeans. He left a few dollar bills on the table for a tip, placed his stocking cap atop his head, and walked out the door.

Brittany had placed the phone call to her boss before Huggins walked out. Her plan was in motion, and she was ready to execute it. When Fisher answered, she said the words every detective relishes.

"Sir, I think we've got him."

32

"I had him, Vin. I could've killed him and ended this, but I let you down. I'm sorry."

Alfredo clutched a framed photograph of the Petrocelli family, with brothers Vinnie and Luca beaming between the protective half embraces of Alfredo and Susan. The photo had been their Christmas card one year. All Alfredo wanted this Christmas was to have both of his sons back, but that was a wish not even Santa could fulfill.

"One of these days I'm not gonna be here to keep fixing you up."

The mob boss gasped as he shifted back in one of three spare queen-sized beds his lifelong friend and retired mafia doctor, Edmund Parker, had in his home.

"I know, Doc. You almost didn't have to worry about it. That son of a bitch had me dead to rights."

Doc Parker, tall and thin with a wispy white mustache, walked around the foot of the bed, grabbed the photo from Alfredo's hands, and set it on the bedside table. Had it been anyone else, Alfredo would've cursed the man and put up his fists, even after suffering two shots to the shoulder thanks to Cal.

Doc Parker was someone everyone in the mafia liked. Even the occasional enemy of the mafia had found themselves under Doc Parker's care at some point. The doc always lent his precise hands in healing whomever needed it.

"Well, thankfully you're still alive and you didn't join Vinnie in that graveyard. I thought the old photo would calm you down a bit, not rile you up."

Alfredo tilted his head back, as if the doc were standing several feet above him and he couldn't see. "You're not riling me up. I loved that photo. Forgot I ever gave it to you. My God, we were much younger men back then."

"More foolish," Doc Parker offered.

"Hell, I'm still as foolish now as I ever was."

Alfredo turned to the photo and gazed into Vinnie's eyes again. Yes, he'd let his son down by not exacting his revenge on Cal in the cemetery, though he knew there was time for that. Cal and Alfredo were as connected as yin and yang. Whether Alfredo got out of the bed he was lying in in an hour or two days from now, he'd find Cal. Either that or Cal would find him. He wasn't quite sure which.

"Seeing my kids in that photo made me realize that I never put my kids first. It was always the mafia, this family empire that I built. Is that the pressure of the multigenerational family business? That you have to fight to keep it going and make it better and better than what it was when your father was running it?"

Alfredo waved his hand and felt like he was asking the question to no one. He knew Doc Parker was there. He could see him standing in front of him at the foot of the bed, listening as he ran his hand over his paper-thin mustache. The doctor adjusted his gold-rimmed glasses, pulling them closer to his forehead, then gestured back to the photograph.

"Alfredo, I know you loved those kids. You were doing your best for them in the only way you knew how."

But had he? Alfredo thought back to all the nights he'd spent out on the streets, away from home. He remembered his first big job for his father, where he'd served as a hit man of sorts while he and Susan were newlyweds, not even thinking of having kids yet. He recalled the time he oversaw the Chicago mafia's entry into the drug market while his children were young, supervising the mafia's distribution in various warehouses on the South and West Sides, like the one Vinnie had been murdered in.

Should he have done more to convince Vinnie not to enter the family business? Should he have allowed his son to pursue his dream of going to medical school, becoming someone admirable, like his friend Edmund Parker? Maybe if he'd been more present in the lives of his children, things would've turned out differently. He realized he had similar thoughts at the cemetery, the last time he reflected about his shortcomings as a father.

"It was all about the money, Edmund. I wanted to be rich, I wanted to be powerful. I put all of those material things before my duties as a father. I never wanted it to be that way, of course, but as much as we try to have it all sometimes, the reality is that you just can't."

Doc Parker nodded in agreement. "Yes, but you can't blame yourself for what happened in the past. You've got to find a way to move forward, as hard as it may be."

Alfredo felt an immense surge of pain in his shoulder as

he reflected further on his loss, causing him to wince. The gentle heartache he'd felt for months was taking on a new form in the radiating physical pain he felt in his shoulder.

Doc Parker reached into the front pocket of his flannel shirt, presumably for medication he no longer was allowed to prescribe.

"Leave it. You gave me enough of those damned things already."

Parker smiled at the raised tone of Alfredo's voice. Alfredo wondered if that was what everyone expected him to sound like and if that was why Edmund was so pleased. Why couldn't he have been more nurturing and supportive, like Susan? He always wanted to express his love to his children in that way but never could.

"It's hard to move forward when you know you've screwed up so much like I have. Even when I adopted Cal, I didn't do it out of love. I did it because I saw how powerful he could become under my guidance. I saw how he could enhance my power, my wealth. As much as I want a do-over, I know I'll never get that chance. That's what hurts."

Doc Parker sat at the foot of the bed. Alfredo imagined him patting his leg beneath the covers like Susan used to do on the rare occasion he'd been sick or injured during his early mafia career. Come to think of it, she rarely did that anymore, not even after his injuries at the warehouse. His regrets didn't stop at his relationships with his children.

"Well, you got a do-over today," Parker said, his hand nowhere near his body, as Alfredo had imagined. "Sounds like Boyle could've finished you off, and by all means maybe he would've. I guess the man upstairs was looking after you."

Alfredo let out a *pshh* sound and rolled his eyes. At his

age, he no longer believed in such nonsense. "If the man upstairs was really looking after me, he would've let me die so I could see Vinnie and Luca again, the hell with my earthly empire."

"See, maybe you have learned something," Parker said. "Why do you think he did it? I mean, why didn't Cal take you out when he had the opportunity? As much pain as he's caused you, you did kill his girlfriend after all."

Alfredo shook his head, the all-too-familiar anger rising from deep in his stomach to the top of his chest. His head throbbed in harmony with his shoulder. He felt like exploding. Seeing the gentleness in his friend's expression, and acknowledging his regret over the lack of affection he showed for his children during their youth, caused him to reconsider.

"It's because of the kids."

Why did Cal care so much about the damned Fregosi kids? Would the Cal that Alfredo knew, a man likely as hell-bent on revenge as he was, really forego that opportunity just to save Tony and Tina Fregosi?

"What kids?" Doc Parker seemed genuinely curious.

Alfredo sighed, not sure how much of his operational plan he wanted to reveal outside of his inner circle. Hell, there was no inner circle anymore. With Vinnie, Frankie Ramone, and Al Meransky now gone, his niece, Melissa, was the only person in the mafia he could completely trust. His two new capos were nothing of the sort.

He told Doc Parker everything. How he had some flunkies stake out the Fregosi girl, hoping her kidnapping would lure Tony Fregosi out of his hiding place and Cal along with it. How the plan was Alfredo's ultimate objective in getting his sweet revenge, a revenge that Vinnie's voice was still clamoring for.

"I guess the plan worked, didn't it? You got him here."

"Yeah, it worked alright. And I almost finished the job."

Alfredo paused, his gaze now turning to the small bedroom window to his left. A gentle snowfall had begun. He fought hard to cease the memories of his children playing in the snow outside of their Evanston home. Seeing the happy smiles on Vinnie's and Luca's faces as they threw snowballs at each other brought a tear to his eye.

He wiped away the moisture as quickly as it formed and cleared his throat. All of his reflection was causing him to think about his actions. Was kidnapping the kids the right idea?

"What was your real reaction, Doc, when I told you I kidnapped those kids?"

Doc Parker shrugged and exhaled. He stood from the bed and walked toward the door, jiggling the bottle of pills in his hand as he moved. After a long pause, he turned to face Alfredo. He was one of the few men not easily intimidated by the eldest Petrocelli.

"I don't think it was a good idea. I see what this desire for revenge is doing to you. It's killing you, eating you alive inside. You may have lived to see another day today, but what Cal did to Vinnie will linger within you until one of you is dead."

"What do you think I should do?"

Alfredo felt his anger bubbling up again, wondering why his longtime friend would question his decision-making.

"I think you know the right answer. You told me how you wished you'd been there for your kids instead of working so hard trying to maintain your father's empire. Your father was real proud of you, Alfredo. He always was. Give yourself a rest. Nothing's gonna bring Vinnie or Luca back this

Christmas. Go home, hug your wife, put Boyle out of mind for a while, and have some of your flunkies drop off those kids."

Alfredo looked at Edmund Parker quizzically. What he'd said sounded so philosophical, so wise. Alfredo wondered if the solution to his problems really was that simple. But he knew he couldn't just forget about Cal, and he certainly couldn't release the kids back to their father.

"That boy will talk the minute I set him free. Not to mention if the police get him, he'll rat me out for God knows what. He blabbed to the girl too."

Doc Parker tapped his foot on the ground and shook his head. "I never said this was easy, Alfredo, but it's right. Figure out the details later, I know you can."

Alfredo considered this. What the doc said made good sense. He still felt guilty about holding Tina Fregosi in the basement of the old house. He felt no remorse about the boy. That kid was a goner as far as he was concerned.

Feeling a renewed sense of energy at knowing what he needed to do, Alfredo sat up and rose from the bed, waving off the concerned expression on Doc Parker's face. He took one last look at the old family portrait, nodded, and headed for the door. By the time he patted Doc Parker on the shoulder and started for the stairs, the doc hardly had time to utter his ask.

"So what are you going to do?"

Alfredo turned back two steps from the top. "I'm gonna do what I should've done twenty-five years ago. I'm gonna be a good man for those kids."

Doc Parker smiled, and Alfredo bid him goodbye before finishing his trip down the steps.

He was going to be a good man for some kids alright. But

as much as he wanted to right wrongs and let the Fregosi girl go, he knew the only kids he could be a good man for were his own.

33

"You were so great out there," Cal said.

His breath was scalding hot inside the hotel shower. He could feel the heat of it as it blew on Brittany's neck beneath him, even with the steam from the shower and the piping-hot water.

"Yeah? Did you like that?"

"I fucking loved it."

Brittany turned her head to face Cal, and they locked lips as he continued to penetrate her. From the minute they escaped the confines of the cemetery, they didn't have to speak, didn't have to look at each other; they just knew. With their lives in danger yet again, coupled with a narrow escape from the police, Cal and Brittany went straight to the cheap hotel room Cal was staying in and into the shower.

Cal wasn't normally a fan of shower sex, but it had been over three months since he'd been with Maria. With Maria, the sex was the purest form of lovemaking. It was gentle yet erotic and intense at the same time. Being with her longer than any other lover in his life created a loving and sexy connection with his former girlfriend.

With Brittany, it was pure animal lust. Neither seemed to want anything more than to touch the other and get off. Cal's hands couldn't get enough of Brittany's womanly flesh and the scent of her freshly shampooed hair. They thrust together like wild animals until they both climaxed.

They shared an awkward laugh and soaped each other's bodies before drying off and returning to the room to place a room service order from the hotel's restaurant. In addition to the hotel's best champagne, which was barely superior to a bottle of the stuff most restaurants served on New Year's Eve, Cal ordered an overly cooked sirloin steak with mashed potatoes and green beans. Brittany selected the salmon with broccoli and wild rice. Her broccoli was al dente, and the salmon was cold by the time it arrived.

"You've heard nothing from Uncle Judd still?" Brittany asked between bites, sitting on the bed Cal originally planned to share with his uncle, while he sat on the bed that had been earmarked for Tony.

Cal gnawed on his gristly steak, trying to chew it as fast as he could so he could respond. He took a long gulp of champagne, wishing it were water as the bubbly concoction tickled his throat.

"Nothing. But I have a feeling if the mafia did something to him, they'd let me know. Like they did with the trap at Fulton Market."

Brittany nodded, and they finished the remainder of the meal in silence. Neither of them had spoken in depth about the crossfire at the cemetery that afternoon, other than Cal's comment in the shower. Cal watched Brittany as she ate, unsure if she enjoyed the sex as much as he did. He wondered if they'd traveled too far across the line this time. If it was anyone's problem, it was hers and not his.

"What was it like, seeing Alfredo? I thought I heard gunshots."

"I had to shoot him twice. If I hadn't, he would've shot me first."

Cal watched Brittany's face for any tells as he spoke. Though he trusted her more than he ever had, he didn't want to self-incriminate. He saw a look of panic before assuring her.

"Don't worry, he's not dead. I only shot him in the shoulder."

Brittany sighed in relief. "Maybe this isn't in my place to ask, but do you wish you would've killed him?"

Cal fought the urge to nod and reveal his deepest desires for revenge to Brittany. If he told her, she might put the pieces together and find a way to nail him. He couldn't have that, not as close as he'd been to finally killing Alfredo and getting the information out of him hinting at Tina Fregosi's whereabouts. The reminder prompted him to shift the conversation.

"He told me something interesting. A hint at where Tina Fregosi might be."

Brittany set her plate down in earnest on the bedside table. "Really? You got it out of him?"

Cal shrugged. "He could be lying, of course. It's not like he told me the exact location. Just something he hinted at."

"Where? Where was it?"

"He just said it's somewhere that would pain me to go back to."

Brittany turned her head to the side. She looked like she was thinking about something.

"Do you know where that would be? A place you grew up?"

Cal raised his gaze to meet hers. He looked deep into her

brown eyes and felt he could trust her now more than any other time since they'd first met. She was no longer the FBI agent who could bring his life down. He was no longer the hit man trying to keep his past a secret.

He wondered how long he could keep his secret from her. He wondered how long they could be affectionate and work together, with both of them having such conflicting goals. While they both wanted to bring Alfredo and the mafia down, there was nothing more Cal wanted than to see Alfredo dead, while he assumed Brittany would settle for a lifelong prison sentence.

"I have a hunch, but how often can you go after hunches?"

"I operate from hunches all the time," Brittany said, smiling. "That's how I've made my entire career. I guess I get lucky enough that my hunches turn into facts. Only you better be damned sure about this one. I'd rather not get shot at again by some crazy old mafia man."

Cal smiled too. Old Joey Bartellini was a tough character. The fact that Brittany escaped his pursuit unscathed was no small feat. Cal set his plate on top of Brittany's, adding her silverware to the top to make for an easier cleanup for the waitstaff.

"It might be my old home. Where I grew up with my parents before they were killed."

Brittany placed her hand over her heart before walking over and joining Cal on his bed. She put a hand on his back and rubbed it up and down in an effort to console him.

"Oh, Cal. I'm sorry."

"I'm surprised you don't know the exact location of where I grew up."

Brittany removed her hand and scratched her head. "C'mon, Cal, we've been through this. I'm just doing my job.

My job is to get Tina Fregosi back and help bring down the mafia. We're doing that together, right?"

"Yeah, I suppose we are. I'm not quite sure what other leads we have. Maybe we go first thing in the morning and check it out."

"Okay." Brittany flipped her hair behind her ear, sounding uncharacteristically uncertain. "I just want to make sure we're positive that this isn't a trap, that we know Tina Fregosi is actually in that house."

Cal drummed his fingers quietly on his thighs. "Either way, if she is there, Alfredo will have men protecting her. He's not going to give her up easily. Not until he gets me."

Cal saw the intensity in Brittany's eyes. He knew what she wanted to ask him, yet she didn't dare. Instead, she reached over him to the bedside table and grabbed a half-full bottle of water. She took a long swig from the bottle before setting it down.

"So your parents—what happened to them?"

Cal leaned back on his elbows on the bed, not wanting to talk about his parents, especially since he had a feeling she already knew what happened. Soon Brittany joined him and began tracing circles on his pecs.

"My father worked in a warehouse. Loading and unloading goods, I guess. One day my mom got a call that he'd been shot. Until a few months ago, I thought it had been an angry coworker. Turns out it was Alfredo."

"Oh God!" Brittany's involuntary gasp didn't stop Cal from telling his story. It was as if his brain was on autopilot, explaining just what an evil man Alfredo was and why all of the FBI's efforts should be spent on tracking him down, and why he was so justified in his pursuit of killing him.

"Yeah, he shot my father. But that wasn't the worst of it. He saw the power in me, saw what I could become. So he made sure I had no other choice but to live with him and Vinnie, who was my best friend at that age."

Cal paused, his heartbeat pounding faster in his chest. Brittany put her hand on his shoulder, the pain of concern plastered on her face.

"What was the worst of it?"

"He killed my mother. He set it up to look like a normal car accident, but he was the one who arranged it. Two mafia thugs ran through an intersection and T-boned her."

Brittany's hand went to her mouth. Cal thought he saw tears form in her eyes. This was how he knew he could trust her.

"That's terrible, Cal. To be orphaned like that, and yet he adopted you? When did you find out about what really happened?"

"Not long before I found out about my father, actually. It was this lowlife guy, some theater actor. Told me her death wasn't an accident."

Cal didn't worry about giving her clues on MacErlean. Fonzie had dumped the informant's body in the river along with any of the evidence that he was killed.

He turned to her and frowned. "My father was an abusive man. He hurt me and my mother in that house. That's why Alfredo put Tina there. He knows how it will make me feel to go back."

Brittany shook her head and reached for Cal's hand. Feeling a twinge of love in his heart, Cal met her hand with his. Having someone to comfort him, someone to connect with this deeply felt good again. Any painful memories of Maria's death that had filled his thoughts over the last three months vanished in that moment. Cal felt like a man again.

They looked into each other's eyes, and Cal's lips brushed against hers. They collapsed into the bed, Brittany's body writhing on top of his. His hands grabbed at her breasts once again, like they had in the shower, pawing at her like he'd never touch another woman again.

Soon their clothes were off and they were beneath the covers for another round of birthday sex. Cal was starting to think they were making a pretty good team.

34

The basement floor felt colder than it had at any point since she'd been kidnapped. Tina Fregosi wondered if the man called Alfredo had ordered his men to turn the heat off. She thought she heard the chattering of teeth and shivering of a body against the wall upstairs, but it may have been her imagination. It was still pitch-black down in the basement, and she felt like she'd never be able to escape.

She reached for the back of her head, still throbbing and sore after being shoved into the wall by the old man. She'd been out cold for a long time, long enough to receive stitches and a gauze bandage that was wrapped tightly around her head. The tightness of the bandage, or perhaps the force of her head crashing into the wall, had given her a massive headache. Her hair was matted with blood, and she wondered if she'd suffered brain damage as a result of the throw.

Yet if she thought she had it bad, a glance at her brother, Tony, told her she had plenty to be thankful for. Thanks to a thin sliver of moonlight that peered through a corner of the basement window, she saw her brother's face was even worse than before. His cheeks and eyes were so protruded, due to the beatings he'd sustained, that Tina wondered if he'd blow up like a balloon. Blood and dried tears caked his face, and his shaggy black hair was filled with hardening red liquid just as hers was.

Tina noticed that Tony was handcuffed to the chain-link fence that enclosed them on two sides. But only one of his hands and one of his feet kept Tony chained to the fence. Tina thought that was odd but didn't expect her brother to put up much of a fight if he tried to use either of his free appendages to fight off one of Alfredo's men.

Though Tina was free to move within the cell, she felt more hopeless and trapped than ever. Her one hope, her one saving grace, was the expectation that Tony would come back to Chicago to save her from this evil man. Now that her brother was trapped in the basement with her, what more could she do?

She looked past Tony to the far corner of the tiny space, seeing only a small dog bowl, where the bad guys poured water for her to drink, and an old mop bucket that was used for urination. She tried not to go so as to avoid the snarls and looks of disgust of the men sent to retrieve the bucket, but she couldn't help herself. The human body could only go so long without completing its essential functions.

Seeing her brother hanging limply by his handcuffs and worrying about spending the rest of her life in the cell brought a tear to Tina's eye. Soon a torrent of sadness washed down her face, and her gentle cries turned into sobs. There was no doubt one of the men would come rushing downstairs to shut her up, but she didn't care.

Tina cried. Her body shook as she moaned and wailed.

Life almost didn't seem worth living during times like this. She was a happy girl with a loving father, sister, and brother before Tony disappeared and their life wasn't the same. Why was she foolish enough to follow the old man to his car under the premise of taking home-cooked meals to Mrs. Rittenhouse? She'd been duped, as many young girls had been duped before her, and it may have cost her her freedom.

"Sis?"

Tina stopped crying at the faintest whisper of a word. She looked at her brother and saw no emotion on his face, and his eyes remained closed. Could it have been him speaking?

"Tina?"

It was.

"Tony! Oh my God, Tony!"

Tina crawled over to her brother and hugged him around the neck. She couldn't believe her brother was even alive, he looked so disfigured. She hugged him and held him tight until he whimpered for her to let go.

"Does it hurt?"

Tony groaned. "Of course it hurts. They pummeled my fucking face in."

"Tony!"

At twelve years old, Tina still wasn't okay with hearing foul language. Her brother's swearing made her feel uneasy, but she was glad he was functioning. She only hoped his swelling would slow and that his face would return to normal. She couldn't imagine seeing her brother's handsome features turning permanently grotesque.

"What's wrong, sis? Why are you crying?"

Tony's question was just as soft as the time he first uttered her name. Maybe her brother had screamed his lungs out before he'd been brought to the house, where they'd beaten him beyond recognition.

"I just hate this place. I wanna go home. I don't know if we'll ever get out of here."

Even with her brother's concern and attempt to comfort her, Tina felt her tears resume and her body begin to shake. The frigid conditions of the house and her sense of dread filled her with a chill that reminded her of the subzero temperatures of a typical Chicago winter.

"We'll get out of here, trust me. People out there are looking for us. Someone will find us."

"What if they never do?"

Tina began full-on sobbing. There was no other reaction she could muster. Even with her brother inches away from her, she felt isolated, unable to cope.

"Calm down. Those guys will come down here if you keep crying. Maybe they'll beat you like they beat me. You don't want that, do you?"

Even through puffy eyelids, Tina could tell her brother was serious. She straightened her posture and found what little strength she had within her to silence her cries. Her brother had said that people were looking for them, that someone would find them. Who could possibly be looking for them? Their dad? How would he know where they were?

Maybe, Tina thought, Tony had some friends on the outside. Friends who were involved with whatever Tony was running away from. Friends who could help them.

Even if Tony had friends looking for them, could she really count on them to save her? After all, there were a lot of bad dudes in the house making sure they were kept in the basement, and she was sure there would be plenty more if that was what the old man desired.

She remembered the threat the old man had issued just

before she lost consciousness. He threatened to kill Tony, to ensure that this would be his last Christmas. Though he could theoretically wait until just before the following Christmas to kill Tony, it didn't seem like the mafia boss wanted to keep her brother alive much longer. Tina's worries of never escaping shifted to a deeper fear: that she would be alone again because her brother would be killed.

Tina turned to her brother, her tears stopping. She would have to find a way to act like a big girl. Before she knew how to do that, the basement door kicked open, and two pairs of boots stomped down the stairs.

"What do I do?" Tina whispered to her brother. Maybe he could calm her steadily rising heartbeat and make sure she didn't cry again.

"Be quiet."

Tina leaned closer to him, not sure she heard him correctly. By the time she bent her ear close enough, she saw the ugly faces of two hulking men hovering over them from outside the fence. Tina couldn't help but recoil upon meeting their gaze, her legs kicking into autopilot as she scooted closer to the wall at the back of the cell.

One of the men, a balding guy with a goatee and scruffy facial hair along the sides of his face, gave her a look so terrifying that she nearly fell back on her butt from a squatting position. His gaze and the gaze of his partner, a burly man who wore sunglasses even in the dark basement and had a similar goatee and short hair, turned to Tony.

Tina saw from the looks in their eyes that they'd come to do something to him. Was now the time they would ensure he didn't see another Christmas? Tina felt her fear turning into a source of strength. She had to fight for her brother, since he was too weak to fight for himself.

"Leave him alone! You monsters have done enough."

The man with the sunglasses ignored her, unlocking the padlock that secured the entry to the cell. Once the gate opened, he held up a giant black club, extending it in front of him in Tina's direction. She'd learned her lesson from going after Alfredo with the nail and didn't want to be attacked with the club after sustaining a bloody head injury.

The man's accomplice entered the cell behind him, produced a tiny handcuff key from his pocket, and began undoing Tony's locks.

"Where are you taking him?"

After some maneuvering on the part of the scruffy man, Tony was free from his handcuffs, and the man picked him up like a rag doll. The usual spark that had always been present in Tony's eyes was nowhere to be found. Tina saw no sense of him fighting back. He was too beaten, too worn down.

"I asked you, where are you taking him?"

The scruffy man carried her brother in his arms like a groom carried his new bride over the threshold. He walked out of the cell and toward the steps. The man with the club and sunglasses glared at Tina, pounding the club in his hands for full effect.

Tina wanted to scream. It was her last chance of anyone hearing her in the neighborhood and stopping these awful men from taking her brother to be killed. Maybe she would be found that way.

Before her mouth could open, the man with the club walked over, pulled something out of his pocket, and stuffed it past her lips. It tasted like a dirty, disgusting sock. Tina wanted to spit it out, but the man held her jaw together so she was forced to cough and gag on the awful taste. He took duct tape out of his pocket and taped the sock to her mouth, then bound her wrists, giving her no other option but to keep it in place.

The man laughed and walked out of the cell, securing the padlock before he and the other man walked up the stairs, leaving her all alone in the basement once again.

"Let's take him to the spot. Do what should've been done a long time ago."

Tina shivered as she wondered what they meant. She willed herself to spit the sock out, to have it break free of the tape, but she realized it was no use. With her brother gone, she knew she'd die down there, hopeless, and far too young.

35

Cal awoke, his mind groggy and filled with cobwebs. He turned to the bedside table and saw the light of the hotel's alarm clock. It was 2:13 in the morning. How long had it been since he'd fallen asleep after the night's final lovemaking with Brittany? He couldn't remember but knew he'd had too much champagne, given the massive headache he'd experienced since waking.

He turned to his left, expecting to feel Brittany's warm body next to him. When he felt nothing but the lump of covers, he knew something was wrong. Cal was pretty sure Brittany enjoyed their rendezvous as much as he had, so why would she have gotten up in the middle of the night? Had she gone back home?

Cal rose, his torso lifting off of the stiff mattress. He saw Brittany sitting on the luggage rack against the wall, her cell phone pressed to her ear. She looked at him with surprise out of the corner of her eye. What was she discussing on the phone?

Brittany removed the phone from her ear and hung up, pressing the screen with her thumb. She stood from the luggage rack and smoothed her shirt over her panties. Not expecting to stay the night, Brittany hadn't brought any clothes to the hotel. That was just as well with Cal, as he got to enjoy the sight of her fit legs and her sexy leopard panties walking toward him.

As she neared the bed, Cal wondered whether it was worth asking Brittany who she was talking to. Though Cal had come to trust her, he wondered if she was talking to someone he'd rather she not engage with, especially someone from the FBI. He knew the more time he spent with her, the greater he was at risk, but he found himself caring less and less about that due to her immense beauty.

His suspicions caused his neck hair to stand up. If there was one thing he learned from his life as a hit man, it was to trust his instincts. He couldn't help but probe her.

"Who was that?"

Brittany crawled back into bed, lifting the covers so she could get comfortable before settling into the mattress and placing them back over her body.

"No one important. Let's try to get some sleep, okay? You wore me out tonight."

Brittany winked at Cal and turned to face the wall, cutting off the conversation. Cal wanted to tap her shoulder, to reengage her in the discussion, but he knew he couldn't blow up at her as he had in the past. He was turning over a new leaf, and part of that was keeping his emotions in check.

"I can't imagine someone calling you with something this important in the middle of the night. Is it a breakthrough in the case?"

Brittany sighed and tucked her pillow between her head and her right arm, trying to get comfortable. "No, it was nothing like that. All we have to go on is what Alfredo told you, I'm afraid. It was just my boss. He gets very demanding sometimes."

Cal watched as Brittany spoke, wondering what facial expression the wall across from her had a chance to witness. He could often tell whether someone was lying to his face or not. Given Brittany's position, he had no clue if she was speaking the truth.

He decided to question further.

"Have you told anyone else about what Alfredo said? Maybe you could get some help checking out the old house. Could keep me out of harm's way that way and let you and your team do the job."

Brittany rolled over onto her back and looked up at Cal, who was lying on his side, watching her. "No, I haven't told anyone anything, Cal. My boss is on my ass because he knows I've been with you. He thinks something is up. I told you, Cal, that I'd try to keep you out of it so we could find the girl and bring down Alfredo. That's still what I'm trying to do."

Cal's heart beat faster at the prospect of Brittany's boss knowing about their partnership. Was Brittany really planning on being true to her word about keeping him out of the spotlight so any of his past crimes wouldn't be suspected? Did Brittany have any real evidence that Cal had committed any crimes? He'd been a little more truthful with her than he'd liked while they ate room service, but he didn't think he'd mentioned anything too revealing.

Brittany rolled over again and faced the wall. Cal returned to lying on his back, staring at the popcorn ceiling, wondering just how many rough bumps there were, even in the darkness. He'd have to trust Brittany and assume she was telling the truth. Soon he could hear her shallow breathing, indicating she'd fallen asleep again.

Sleep was harder to come by for Cal. He tried doing everything he could to fall back asleep, from counting sheep, to reading a book on his phone, to performing a scan of his body and willing each limb to slowly fall asleep, hoping his brain would follow, but he couldn't. Part of him wondered if his hit man instincts were kicking in again, keeping him alive.

What if Brittany had called one of her fed buddies? What if they were on their way to take him in right now? Cal wondered what leverage Brittany would have over him and realized his thoughts were foolish. Yet his body had shifted into a seated position and he'd placed a foot into one of his boots beside the bed.

Cal kicked the shoe off and shook his head. It was only paranoia that was overwhelming him. He lay down again. This time his eyes felt a heaviness that preceded sleep. He was out within seconds.

A loud pounding on the hotel door awoke him. Cal wasn't sure how long he'd been out this time, but it felt like he'd slept forever. He looked back at the hotel clock again. It was after five o'clock. Only instead of the faint alarm clock light blinding him, the brightest light was that above the bedside table. He looked at the bed next to him and found it empty. Brittany was gone again.

A glance around the hotel room showed that everything Brittany had brought with her had disappeared. There was no sign of her in the room. Maybe she'd gone for an early coffee and forgot the hotel key. That was fairly likely. Still, Cal didn't want to leave it to chance.

He walked to the office chair across the room and reached into his coat for the tiny Beretta Pico, complete with one bullet, just in case. It would have to do.

More pounding at the door. Cal wondered why Brittany

was pounding so intently if she'd just been locked out of the room. Maybe it wasn't her after all. None of her stuff was in the room, so something else was going on.

Cal tiptoed closer to the door, holding the gun in front of him as he walked. If it was anyone from the mafia, he felt capable enough to hit someone with the one bullet he had left before taking care of anyone else by hand. He was in fighting shape and ready to run over anyone who got in his way.

Muffled voices sounded behind the door, and Cal realized it wasn't Brittany who was knocking. He readied his gun and pointed it at the tiny peephole before realizing just who he was dealing with. It wasn't anyone from the mafia that was coming to kill him. There were radios sounding. Police radios. Cal was being taken in.

He did what any sensible criminal would do and hid the gun in the nearest place he could think of. He lifted the toilet tank and put the gun in the water. Maybe whoever was coming to arrest him wouldn't look for it. He heard kicking at the door now, and it sounded like whoever was behind it wasn't taking no for an answer.

Cal stepped out of the bathroom, unlatched the deadbolt, and waited for the door to explode. If he wanted, he knew he could take out anyone who entered, but he was done playing those games. He was sure now that the call Brittany had made earlier in the night had been to someone in the FBI, giving them whatever evidence they needed to bring him in. But what was that evidence? How would they find the girl now that the police were there to stop him?

The door burst open, and two Chicago police officers raced into the room, rifles extended in front of them. One of them spotted Cal as soon as he turned, and yelled.

"Get down! Get down on the ground now!"

Cal put his hands behind his head and dropped to his knees. The officer charged toward him and waited for the other officer to clear the rest of the room. The first officer pushed Cal to the ground, bringing out a pair of handcuffs to arrest him as the other officer stood above him, pointing his rifle at Cal's head.

The cuffs dug into his skin like his jackknife had dug into the flesh of so many of his victims. He was undoubtedly being charged for some sort of murder, but he had no clue which one. The officer hoisted Cal to his feet, while the other stared into Cal's eyes like Saint Peter determining his soul's eternal fate.

Cal had known this day would come. A hit man's end usually came when they were either killed or arrested. Very few men got to walk away unscathed like he had. Even then, he'd lost the person he loved most in the world during the process. How he'd gotten away with so many murders without anything being remotely tied to him was amazing. Only no one would be able to help him out of jail this time. He was on his own.

"You're under arrest for the murder of Vinnie Petrocelli, Al Meransky . . ." The officer continued to read off all the names. They sounded like the soldiers Cal killed at the warehouse that night. "You have the right to remain silent. Anything you say can and will be used against you . . ."

Cal tuned out as the first officer read him his Miranda rights and the other officer led him out of the hotel room. Several more members of the Chicago PD filled the hallway as they escorted him to the elevator. He wondered how they managed to nail him for all the murders. Had Alfredo confessed Cal was there that night? Had another witness turned up? Did they tie his fingerprints on his discarded weapons to the prints from his battery crime in San Diego?

Regardless, Cal had been trained well by the mafia. He wouldn't talk until he needed to, which would likely be never. The only pain in his heart as the elevator descended was knowing how close they'd come to finding Tina Fregosi and how Brittany wouldn't know the first thing about getting her back.

36

Cal sat in the holding cell at the Cook County Department of Corrections. It was an awfully similar cell to the one he'd helped Tony Fregosi escape from three months ago. This time it was Cal's turn to be questioned about his involvement in a murder.

This wasn't the ideal way he wanted to spend Christmas Eve, but Brittany turning on him had put that out of his control. How could she pretend to be interested in recovering Tina Fregosi and bringing down the mafia, not to mention maintain a sexual interest in Cal, if she turned around and had Cal arrested before he could help her find the girl? Cal wondered how they'd find Tina now, given that he had no idea if Brittany planned to follow through with their plan to search his childhood home.

Even if a team of her FBI agents and Chicago police officers was able to search the house, how would they know it wasn't a trap? Alfredo loved to play games and would lose little sleep over massacring several federal agents and local pigs who could disrupt his mafia's power.

It was at times like this that Cal wished he had Uncle

Judd beside him. He still had no clue what happened to his uncle. He wasn't going to get any answers sitting in a jail cell. He had to get out, find out what happened to Judd, and help rescue the Fregosis. If Tony was still alive to be rescued.

Cal wasn't concerned with spending the rest of his life in jail or facing the consequences of his actions anymore. Those thoughts were behind him now. Cal knew that someday he'd be held responsible for the damage he'd done to so many lives. This was only the beginning of what he expected to be a long, drawn-out process.

A pounding on the door awoke Cal from his daydreaming. He didn't bother to glance at who entered. He knew it wasn't his state-appointed attorney. Even if one had showed, Cal wouldn't give the person much of a shot. He doubted any self-respecting state's attorney would want a supposed mafia hit man as their client.

"Mr. Callahan Boyle, is that correct?"

The officer walked into the cell and tossed a thick manila folder onto the table, before turning to the cell door and closing it behind him. There was a faint buzz in the air from the fluorescent light overhead. Cal's hands were cuffed behind him to the chair, making sure he was a good boy. Though the police had no way of proving just how dangerous Cal was, they weren't going to take a chance to find out.

"I'm just trying to be friendly with you. Why won't you tell me what your name is?"

The officer flashed a grin, pearly-white teeth shining bright against the contrast of his ochre skin tone. He was tall, maybe an inch shorter than Cal, and wore a sky-blue police uniform with pressed black slacks. The man's bald head reflected the dimming light above. He sat down across from Cal when the hit man didn't acknowledge him, frowned, and tapped his hands on the table.

"I guess you're not gonna talk to me, huh? Is that it?"

The officer looked around the small holding cell, gazing first at the white ceiling, with more than its fair share of obscure stains, to a chair lined up in the corner near the back wall, and finally back to the door. Only a tiny window at the top of the entry exposed the outside world to them.

Cal felt a sense of relaxation as the officer's eyes traveled the room. Cal was still determined not to talk, and his hope was that the officer was more relaxed than the typical cop. Suddenly, the cop turned toward Cal with both fists firmly rooted in the table and his head shaking like one of those corny sports bobbleheads. The veins in his temple threatened to burst open from the angry pressure.

"Goddamn it, you will answer me! I'm Detective Benson Forbes, and I don't have time to put up with lowlife trash like you. Now, tell me your name."

Cal looked up at the man. At first he'd been startled by the officer's sudden transformation from Zen-like police officer to enraged drill sergeant. After having the chance to pause, he returned the harsh gaze and snarled at Forbes. Cal wasn't intimidated by men like him; he'd dealt with far worse men in his life who yelled at him even more. His father and Alfredo immediately came to mind.

Forbes stood, seemingly unamused by Cal's reaction. His knuckles dug into the old wooden table like an anteater burying its nose in the ground for food. He started breathing heavily, huffing and puffing. Cal wondered if he'd realized the effect he was going for didn't intimidate him in the slightest.

"Alright, Boyle. I will assume, based on this case file I just set down, that you indeed are Callahan Boyle, the adopted son of noted mafia boss Alfredo Petrocelli. Is that correct?"

Cal looked at the impressive paper stack and then back at the officer. His eyes were as still as a statue. Forbes growled at him.

"Alright, I see my colleagues were right about you. Not going to talk until your attorney shows up, huh? Well, it doesn't matter if you stay quiet or not. We've got the court records. We saw Alfredo and Susan Petrocelli adopted you after your mother's death. Go right ahead and look, it's in the file."

Cal rolled his eyes. Even if he wanted to look, his hands were cuffed to the chair behind him. Forbes smiled, realizing his position of power.

"Oh, that's right, you can't."

After another snicker, the officer proceeded with the rest of his questions.

"I'm sure you know why you were brought in here, correct? You're believed to be a primary suspect in the murder of your own adopted brother, Vinnie Petrocelli. Must have wronged you quite a bit for you to kill him like that. You know what else? There were at least a dozen other guys killed that night, all with the same gun. Not just at the warehouse where Vinnie was killed either. You know anything about that?"

Cal didn't blink. He'd kill each and every one of those men again if he had to. They were all lowlifes, degenerates that needed to be stopped. They wanted to do harm to an innocent young woman like Maria. They all deserved what they had coming to them.

"We also discovered that this same Beretta that was found at the warehouse, used to kill those dozen individuals, was also used to murder two men at the scene of Mayor

Caruso's murder. We have a key witness who will testify he saw you there that day. I wonder just who else you've killed, Mr. Boyle."

Forbes's eyes grew wider as he continued his story, and yet Cal didn't budge. He knew what the officer was trying to do. He was trying to intimidate Cal with an overwhelming amount of evidence to get him to confess. Until he was put on trial and a verdict was given, Cal's mouth would remain shut. It had to be if he wanted to buy the time he'd need to think clearly to get out of jail and help save Tina and Tony.

Benson Forbes's face was shiny from the sheen of sweat and drew slightly closer to Cal's. Cal finally had to blink, his eyes incapable of holding their gaze forever. Forbes held strong for thirty seconds more, trying to see if Cal would blink again. Cal held his breath, hoping he could keep his composure before he said something he'd regret. Finally, Forbes drew away and removed his fists from the table, beginning to pace the room.

Cal wondered how much more he could take. The man was pretty good at his job, though Cal knew he'd never be able to make him crack. Not unless torture was brought into the game.

"Would you like to know just how we were able to arrest you? One of our best and brightest young detectives, an Officer Brittany Wilson, was able to put all the pieces together. Pieces none of our detectives were able to uncover in the three months since these murders took place. But I bet you know she's a smart cookie. I heard you had a thing for her."

Forbes chuckled and flashed his smile again. Cal felt the pressure building around him. He felt like cracking. Brittany had played him from the start, pretending to be an FBI agent when in reality she was a Chicago police detective, able to nail him for the state crime of murder. While he had a feeling she couldn't be trusted from the first time he laid eyes on her in San Diego, Cal's emotions had gotten the better of him.

He wondered if he should speak up now and get Forbes's mind off of the investigation. He had to get the police focused on the real item they should be concerned with. He had to get them focused on finding the Fregosis.

"You want me to talk?"

Forbes's pacing had taken him to the door, his back turned to Cal. As soon as Cal spoke, the officer pivoted on his feet and turned to Cal, his eyes alight with fire. He pointed a strong index finger at Cal and pumped it in the air a few times.

"By God, the man does have a pulse. Start talking."

"What you should be asking me is how I can help you get Tina Fregosi out of the mafia's clutches. I know where she is. I was trying to tell this FBI agent—er, detective—where she is. We would've found her had you and your squadron of pigs not brought me to this rotten jail cell."

The officer glared at him again. He was breathing heavy, and the sides of his head were pulsing even faster this time, if such a thing was possible.

"How dare you change the subject on me? But let's say you're onto something. How do you know where the girl is?"

"I can't tell you that. I just know that she's out there. If you'll listen to me, you can find her and save a life."

"I see what you're trying to do, Boyle. You're setting yourself up for a little plea deal. Well, guess what: that ain't gonna work on my watch. See my captain ain't making any deals with guys like you. We'll find Tina Fregosi on our own and her pipsqueak brother that killed the mayor too. Then we'll get Alfredo to fess up to exactly who you are, and you'll both rot in jail, right where you belong."

Forbes marched out of the room, opened the cell door, and slammed it shut. As much as Cal wanted to help the Fregosis now, there wasn't much he could do.

37

Alfredo Petrocelli smiled despite the whipping winds of the frigid air that lapped at his face like a dog seeing its owner for the first time after a long vacation. He was standing outside with Dominic "Death" Masucci, his South Side capo, in the middle of an abandoned lot that had once been home to a school on the West Side of the city. Two of Death's flunkies joined them, both smoking cigarettes and wearing brown stocking caps. Alfredo slowly pivoted in a circle, his feet brushing the light dusting of snow that had fallen overnight.

The sky was gray, and the air was on the verge of bone-chilling. Though they were miles away from Lake Michigan, Alfredo recalled the weather forecast from the morning as he sat at the kitchen table sipping his coffee while Susan changed his shoulder bandages. A lake effect breeze was meant to send the temperatures into the low single digits, setting the stage for an icy-cold Christmas in Chicago the next day.

As he stood waiting for the truck containing Tony

Fregosi, Alfredo recalled the words he'd said to his men in the basement of the old house. He'd truly meant it when he said it would be Tony Fregosi's last Christmas. Even after having the heart-to-heart with Doc Parker, Alfredo didn't want the boy to live another day. He was going to be the father he always planned to be—a good role model for his kids. He'd pay them back in their deaths by killing the Fregosi boy on the spot.

He smiled as he thought through the plan. The men driving the truck would dump the boy off, he'd get out, and Alfredo would put him out of his misery. It would be so simple, so unlike killing Callahan Boyle. That was just too complicated, too much emotion involved. Everything needed to be perfect for Alfredo to take his time and enjoy that kill.

"Sir, it's Melissa."

Alfredo turned behind him and saw Death marching toward him with his arm extended. The mob boss looked at Masucci's hand and saw his cell phone was held tightly between gloved fingers. That was funny; he hadn't heard it ring. Alfredo ripped the phone from the capo's grasp, looked at it, then asked who it was, not hearing what he had to say the first time.

"It's your niece, sir. She said an important call came through. She wouldn't tell me who it was."

Alfredo flared his nostrils and wedged the phone beneath his ear, taking care to walk away from Death and his cronies so they wouldn't overhear something important.

"Yeah?"

"Oh God, Alfredo. I don't know what's happened, but there's a ton of policemen here."

"At the Evanston house?"

"No. Well, yes. Aunt Susan said a couple of them stopped there and asked if you were home, but she was able to get rid of them. But I'm talking about the penthouse. There were four men here."

"Jesus Christ! Four men! Why did you let them in without a warrant? Can they hear you?"

"I didn't let them in. I swear I didn't. They just forced their way in here. I'm hiding in the bedroom closet with the door shut. It's pretty soundproof, right?"

"Where are those fuckfaces that I pay to guard the place?"

It sounded like Melissa was weeping. Alfredo wasn't sure if he should keep yelling or comfort his niece. He figured the police were so fed up with him that they forced their way inside, and there was nothing she could do.

"I don't know where they are!"

Melissa's outburst caused Alfredo to remove the phone from his ear. He winced, then brought the phone back to his ear to finish the conversation.

"Alright, just get them out of there and tell me what they want."

"I think they're gone. After the last one left, I deadbolted the front door and ran straight here. They wanted to talk to you about something. I think they wanted to ask you questions about Cal."

Shit. What did the police want to know about Cal? Why were they showing up at both of his residences to ask about him? Something major must have happened. Maybe they'd tied some of Cal's crimes to the mafia. Alfredo couldn't have that at all. Perhaps he'd need to be on the run just like Cal, just like Tony Fregosi.

"Did they say what kind of questions? Did you or Susan hear anything?"

Melissa sniffled. "No, they didn't say, but I think they know about you two. They said it's very important that they speak to you. Several cases are resting on you talking to them."

Melissa paused, and Alfredo heard her blow her nose into a tissue. "Is this the funeral?"

The Funeral. Alfredo's code word for the end of the mafia. It wasn't his code word per se, but a code word his grandfather had established in the seventies, when he first took over as the boss of the Chicago family. It was only to be used between the boss and the consigliera when the police or rival families threatened to shut down the entire enterprise. It wasn't that time yet, no matter how much of a mess the police were trying to uncover.

"No. Stay there and call Susan for me, will you? You need a united front while I figure out what to do next. It might be a while before I can come back home, you got it?"

"Yes. I'm worried about you, though. You'll be alright out there?"

Alfredo turned to the sky, his eyes tickled with cold as he glanced into the nonexistent sun.

"Of course I'll be alright. You've just gotta hold down the fort for a while until I call back."

Alfredo hung up and walked the phone back to Masucci. He pulled out his own phone and searched for the one phone number that could make this situation right.

As much as Alfredo wanted to be the man that killed Callahan Boyle, he knew that unless he got really lucky he wouldn't be. Though he'd killed many men, he wasn't a trained killer like Boyle and Joey Bartellini. Old Joey would have to find where Cal was now, but Alfredo had a pretty good idea.

Alfredo's former top hit man answered on the third ring.

"Boss, you've got a bead?"

"Yeah, I think so. Look, Joey, things are turning from bad to worse. The police showed up at my house and at the penthouse. Melissa said they were asking about Cal. Seems to me like something's amiss. What do you figure?"

"Ah. That's very interesting, boss. Could mean Boyle's been arrested and they want a piece of you too."

Alfredo fumed, his face contorting into a series of microexpressions before he found the effort to return to the phone call.

"Goddamn it. What do you think they found out?"

"It doesn't matter. This is good news, Alfredo. If Boyle's been arrested, that means he can't go anywhere. Maybe it's time someone paid him a visit."

Alfredo's face lit up. Old Joey was right. He knew he could trust his old friend with this phone call. While he wished he'd be the one to hunt down Cal, Alfredo knew it would be far too dangerous for him to risk his life entering the Cook County Department of Corrections to find him. Joey was a hired hand, skilled in working around the law to get the bad guys. If anyone could kill Cal in those conditions, it was Joey.

"I think you're right. Find out where he is and take care of it once and for all. Call me when it's done."

Joey chuckled before clearing his throat. "You got it, boss. After today Cal will be finished."

Alfredo hung up and put the phone in his pocket. The movement of Masucci and his men behind him told him something was happening. He pivoted once again toward the main entrance of the parking lot and saw the truck he'd been waiting for driving slowly toward him.

The smile that spread across Alfredo's face was the biggest smile he'd formed in a long time. Not only was Joey

Bartellini on his way to finally take care of Cal, but Tony Fregosi would soon be dumped out of the truck and finished for good.

Alfredo reached into his coat pocket, feeling the barrel of his gun. Tony Fregosi's last Christmas had already passed.

38

Driving with tinted windows and peering through swollen eyelids wasn't easy for Tony Fregosi, but he was the best damned driver the mafia ever employed, and he'd found a way to drive to the meeting place where Alfredo and his henchmen planned to kill him.

It was hard playing possum, pretending to be far more injured than he actually felt. While his face was bruised and swollen, his ribs constantly sore, and his muscles aching, Tony had a strength and resolve in him that was stronger than any kick or punch delivered by one of the mafia soldiers. Three months on the run and staying in dumpy motels after being booted from his friend Thomas's house did that to him. Leaving his sister behind crushed him, but he knew the only way to keep her out of Alfredo's clutches was to go through with his plan.

It wasn't easy at first. He was accompanied by two men, who both sat in the front of the truck cabin while he was spread across the back seat. The driver wore sunglasses despite the wintry gray and had close-cropped hair, while his partner resembled him nearly to the letter, with the exception of a goatee. Even through half-closed eyes, Tony saw they were tough and wouldn't be easy to take down.

He knew that if he could get his hands on a weapon of some kind, he'd be able to get the job done. Lucky for him, an old twenty-pound dumbbell was on the floor behind the driver's seat. The men had kicked and punched Tony to further weaken him before loading him in the truck but had foolishly not tied him down.

Tony waited until the men were engaged in conversation before making his move. He eyed the dumbbell, picked it up as quickly as he could muster, and bashed it on the back of the passenger's skull. The man shouted in agony, dazed but not down, and reached toward his waist.

Heart leaping in his chest, Tony was scared for what would happen next. He lifted the weight again and brought it toward the man, hitting him square in the forehead as the passenger turned around with his gun to finish Tony off. The man dropped his gun in the back seat, leaving it ready for the taking.

The driver began jerking the truck wildly from side to side, causing the other cars on the road to honk loudly. The man grunted and reached into his jacket for a weapon. The evil in his eyes told Tony everything he intended to do with him. Tony had no choice but to pick up the discarded gun.

Just as the driver had drawn his pistol, Tony did the first thing he could think of. He fired twice into the driver's side with the passenger's discarded weapon. Instantly, the truck veered to the left, heading for oncoming traffic. Tony knew he needed to take over the steering wheel, though he still had to worry about the dazed man in the passenger seat.

The passenger recovered, removed a hunting knife from his coat, and slashed it toward Tony. Tony moved his arm back in surprise and fell into the back seat, dropping the gun. The truck continued its path into oncoming traffic, with a horde of cars honking and swerving out of the truck's way.

The passenger didn't seem too concerned as he began climbing over the center console to get to the rear.

"I'm gonna get you, kid. You killed my friend!"

Tony was shaking at first, unsure of what to do. He then remembered the gun lying in the seat next to him. He reached for it, tightened his grip around the base, pointed, and fired just as the passenger slashed at him with the knife.

Tony couldn't watch as a large red dot formed in the center of the man's head. The man nearly fell on top of Tony in the back seat; Tony scampered away to avoid being crushed by the large mafia soldier.

A loud bang sounded, and Tony felt the truck shake. They had crashed into something. Tony held on for dear life to the closest sturdy object in the vehicle and gripped it for several seconds. Cars continued honking as Tony fought to catch his breath.

It was almost two full minutes before Tony could dare look out of the window to see what they'd hit. Thankfully, it was just a wire-mesh fence of an auto shop and not a moving vehicle. Still, a damaged truck would look suspicious to Alfredo and his goons as he drove it to the meeting place, if he could even drive it at all. Tony would worry about that later.

Eventually, Tony straightened himself, placed the bodies as neatly as he could in seats, backed away from the fence the truck had hit, and headed where the GPS told him to go. He'd heard the men mention something about a parking lot and that Tony would be killed there.

He drove as fast as he could, coming up with a game plan along the way. Though it was tough to see out of his puffy eyes, he managed to do a good job of judging the traffic and navigating to the spot.

As he drew closer, he debated why he was heading for the parking lot at all. He could've just as easily turned around to save his sister and break her free from Alfredo's clutches.

Yet hearing that Alfredo was going to be in the parking lot made his blood boil. Nothing would please him more than killing the mafia boss on the spot, much like he'd killed Mayor Caruso. Then he'd have one less person to run from.

Tony drove through the entrance gate of the parking lot and wondered how he'd execute his impromptu plan. The four men standing there were expecting him to be taken from the truck and the two dead men in the car to lead him out. Now that they were dead, he knew he would have to find a way to take them by surprise.

He drove around the outside of the lot until he found a good amount of room to back the truck up toward where the men were standing. He hoped they wouldn't rush to the truck and question his motives, so he backed the truck up as quickly as possible without making it seem like he intended to run the men over. Two young flunkies held their guns high before another man beckoned them to lower their weapons.

Tony saw from the rearview mirror that Alfredo was smiling, knowing Tony was to be delivered to him in the truck. He was probably the one readying to take Tony out.

Tony slowed down, hitting the brakes as he rehearsed the game plan in his head. As soon as he put the truck in park, he'd grab his newfound gun once again, climb over the dead driver in the passenger seat, open the door, and aim for Alfredo. The mob boss would be the only man Tony could reasonably hit from that position. He'd need to shoot from the driver's side or the small window in the rear of the truck to take aim at the other men.

Alfredo was the one he wanted, though. The man that caused him and his sister so much pain. He'd take out the bastard, then move on to the others before he regrouped.

At last, he grabbed the gun, and climbed over the fat driver's body, trying not to get blood all over his pants. He pulled the driver's hat that he'd confiscated low over his face and opened the door. He knew the second he stepped from the truck Alfredo and his men would recognize he wasn't one of Alfredo's soldiers, given his smaller build. He had to act fast.

Tony stepped out of the truck, knowing he had no time to waste. He aimed his gun and fired in the direction he thought Alfredo was in. He was ready to whoop for joy when he realized he hit his target, before realizing he'd shot a taller, balding man in the forehead, sending him to the ground instantly.

Alfredo started running as soon as the echo from the gunshot finished. Tony trained his weapon on the mafia boss. A figure filled Tony's vision the instant he pulled the trigger, falling to the ground with a crunch. One of the soldiers had taken the fall for Alfredo, absorbing a bullet to the chest to save the mafia boss.

Return fire sent Tony scrambling for the truck, his jaw clenching at killing two of the men but not assassinating the man who'd caused him so much pain. He wanted to scream in anger, to curse at the fallen mafia soldier for taking the bullet for one of the most evil men Tony had the misfortune of knowing.

Bullets peppered the truck as Tony hid behind the open passenger door. Tony noticed the echo of bullets getting closer. The other soldier was acting bold, perhaps thinking he could outmaneuver Tony, given his youth. A car started in the distance, and the sound of tires screeching filled Tony's ears. Alfredo was getting away.

Tony cursed again, stood, and fired from behind the passenger door. He saw the whites of the mafia soldier's eyes as he shot two more bullets in his direction. He didn't have time to see if he'd killed the man as he fell to the ground.

Tony jumped in the truck, slammed the door, climbed over the dead body again, and fired it up. He sped away from the scene, not worrying if the soldier was still alive and would continue shooting at the truck. He knew he could chase Alfredo and run the bastard off the road. Maybe that would make him feel good, but it would only be temporary.

The more permanent solution was to return to the house where they kept him and his sister. Saving her was far more important than taking out Alfredo, as much as he wanted to. Before he could save his sister, he had to regroup and find reinforcements. There was no one better to have on hand as a reinforcement than Cal.

He just hoped he could find him.

39

The questioning at the hands of Detective Forbes and his colleague, a fat redheaded woman named Detective Bassitt, unnerved Cal. Even with the help of his frail, state-appointed attorney, Cal felt like he didn't have a chance in ever escaping the Cook County Department of Corrections, or ever seeing the light of day again.

His attorney had argued that the photo used by the two witnesses to identify Cal in a photo lineup hadn't been taken with Cal's consent—rather, it had been sneakily taken by Brittany while they had the breakfast at Starbucks a few days ago—which left the state with a missing piece of the puzzle if the lineup was deemed invalid, but the district attorney assigned to the case quickly squashed that notion. The next argument centered around Brittany's decision to become sexually involved with Cal, but the full-busted DA laughed at that type of behavior being a crime.

On and on the questions went. Cal was grilled, drilled, and had his motives questioned ten times over. Eventually, the police and his attorney left, and Cal was told he'd be kept in custody until a hearing date could be set.

The questioning had only been a few hours ago, but Cal was furious. He sat in the cell, on top of a dirty pillow with God-knows-what smeared on the faded white pillowcase, chewing on the inside of his cheek, forcing the bite marks deeper and deeper to release the anger he felt inside.

Instead of sitting on his ass in a dark jail cell with his head dizzying from the thoughts of how he could possibly find Tina and Tony, Cal could've been active, running and tearing down doors to save the innocent children.

Cal thought back through various prison movies he'd seen. Would he have time to find an officer to get close to, discover a useful tool, and dig a big enough hole in the wall to escape, covering his tracks with a poster of a beautiful woman à la Andy Dufresne?

No, the hearing would be the day after Christmas. Cal would spend Christmas in jail and have a minimum of two nights in the slammer before the possibility of bail. Given the number of murders he was accused of, however, he doubted bail would be an option.

A clanking noise caused Cal to lift his head. A portly officer with a tumble of brown curly hair beneath his cap jingled his keys.

"What?"

Cal realized his utterance had been sharper than he intended. Alfredo's shouts and screams were so cemented in Cal's brain that he couldn't help but act in a similar manner sometimes.

"Jesus Christ, Boyle. No need to yell like that." The officer turned behind him and tilted his head to the left. "You've got a visitor."

He had a visitor? Cal couldn't think of anyone who

would want to visit him. Who would be there to help him in a time like this? Uncle Judd flashed in his mind, but he had no idea if Uncle Judd was alive. He hadn't been at the hotel and he wasn't at the apartment. Could Uncle Judd have returned?

"Hold your horses, Boyle. Don't try anything funny."

Cal watched as the officer inserted a bronze key into the lock of the jail cell. For a second, Cal debated barging from his seat and tackling the man in order to escape.

The key clicked in the lock and the door opened. Cal remained seated, not wanting to make the officer suspicious about his motives. Just as the officer prepared to enter the cell, Cal saw the man's face scrunch together and a faint exhale of a breath leave his mouth. His features slackened and his hands fell toward the ground, anchoring the rest of his body with them. Cal only realized what happened after the fat man collided with the ground. The person who had come to visit him wasn't going to behave and wait behind the visitor phone booths to talk to Cal. They were intending to make their presence felt right away.

The glistening of a knife blade with fresh blood falling from its edge alerted Cal to the shadowy presence in an ill-fitting police uniform standing just inside the open jail cell door. He hadn't gotten a close look at the man despite their multiple encounters in the past week. The person before him was a former mentor, a former friend. Now he was clearly visiting Cal to do one thing and one thing only. Take him out.

Joey Bartellini flashed a sinister smile at Cal and took a small step toward where Cal was seated. Since he was free to move within the cell, Cal couldn't give him a chance to take advantage. He leapt from the dirty pillow and ran toward Bartellini. The older gentleman took a sharp slash at Cal with his knife, causing Cal to veer to the left. Cal circled back before he hit the cell wall and kicked the knife out of Bartellini's hand with a sharp right sweep.

The sudden movement sent a blast of pain to his tight hamstrings. Cal knew he'd have to get back in the gym when all was said and done, if only he was able to escape Bartellini and this jail cell first. Despite being in his midsixties, Joey was one tough customer. He definitely hadn't let himself go in retirement.

Just as Cal regained his footing, the old man charged toward him again, landing a quick blow to Cal's side. Cal jammed his fist forward, connecting with the side of Bartellini's face. He thought he heard a crunch beneath his fingers and wondered if he'd really hurt the old man.

His hesitation gave Bartellini the momentum he needed to give Cal a hard uppercut to the jaw. Cal rubbed the area, the pain hot and sending a volley of fresh blood into his mouth. It almost felt like the old man had broken it. While Cal held his hand at his jaw, he saw old Joey bend to the floor to retrieve his knife.

Cal knew better than to stand still and tend to his wound, but he couldn't force himself to move. Bartellini picked up the knife and charged toward Cal. He couldn't uproot his feet from the ground. Cal knew he had to do something, but he couldn't fathom what.

Bartellini was inches away from him, a snarl on his face, sweat exuding above his brow beneath the policeman's cap. He had to have been as excited about this moment as Cal was when he was faced with the chance to kill Alfredo. That was when Cal's brain clicked into gear and he saw his opportunity. He couldn't back down now and be defeated. He had to rise to the occasion and take out old Joey.

Joey plunged the knife once again in his direction, but

Cal dodged to the right and pummeled the old hit man's side with repetitive blows. He felt something sharp crack over his back, leading to an involuntary cry of pain. He brought his hands up, trying to fight off Joey again. Another crack hit him in the back of the head and his lights were out.

40

When Brittany Wilson made the call to her boss to have Cal arrested, her heart crumbled like her sister's poorly made chocolate-chip cookies from her youth. Brittany really had grown fond of Cal over the last several days, and she was pretty sure it wasn't lust that drove the way she felt about him.

She knew she made the right call, but her heart didn't feel any less ache over it than it did when she called Mick Fisher at five that morning. She had to sneak out of the hotel room before anyone arrived. She'd made the call from her car, the confirmation that her interviews with Alfredo's elderly neighbor from Evanston and Mr. Huggins had been logged into evidence and that the photo lineups would likely be accepted giving her the confidence to finally turn Cal over to her boss.

Mick Fisher walked over to her desk with two cups of coffee in his hands. Judging from the amount of steam pouring over the tops of the cheap white Styrofoam, Brittany knew they were piping hot. Seeing her boss with a smile on his face made her realize she'd done the right thing for her career. She didn't want to have to live with the pressure of letting Cal remain free. The fact that he'd given her a small hint as to Tina Fregosi's whereabouts was an added bonus.

"Wilson, it's shaping up to be a great Christmas Eve, isn't it?"

Brittany took a cup from her boss's extended hand and carefully held it up to her lips. She blew on it several times, afraid to feel the scalding sensation from an overly hot cup of coffee. She nodded at Fisher, not wanting to delay her response any longer than necessary while summoning the courage to take a sip. At last she did and recoiled at both the bitterness and the steaming-hot sensation of the liquid against her tongue.

"Yeah, that's some hot coffee alright. Hotter than even I like it."

Fisher stood and smiled, proud as a father of a newborn. It wasn't typical for the lieutenant to wear a sweater to the office. Perhaps the fact that it was Christmas Eve, coupled with Cal's arrest, caused her boss to be more casual than usual. Brittany maintained her professional image, wearing a knee-length maroon skirt with a matching suit jacket over an olive-green blouse. It was her best attempt at Christmas colors.

"Thanks for the coffee. I assume you want to talk to me about Callahan Boyle."

Fisher chuckled and smiled. Brittany wasn't in the mood for games this morning. Her boss had nothing to hold over her head now that Cal was behind bars and the police were after Alfredo as an additional witness. It was time for her to focus on her next task—saving Tina Fregosi—before she could finally focus her efforts on her FBI application.

"I must say that whatever techniques you used to get

close to Boyle, that's impressive stuff. If we can get a hold of Petrocelli and have him confirm Cal was the guy who killed his son and all of those mafia soldiers at the warehouse that night, this guy's gonna have no chance of leaving jail."

Brittany looked up at her boss, expressionless. "He might be, sir. From the times I talked with Cal, he was very tight-lipped about everything, even regarding his relationship with Alfredo Petrocelli. But we know he was adopted by him, and as soon as we can get Alfredo to talk, I'm sure we can put the pieces together."

Fisher set his coffee down on Brittany's desk and flashed a thumbs-up. She could tell he was really loving the direction of the case, especially given the pressures he was facing from his own superiors. Brittany had a feeling that was why she'd been brought to the Detectives Bureau to deal with this string of cases in the first place.

"Say, Wilson," Fisher continued, "how would you feel about being our detective on the ground in questioning Petrocelli? I'd love to grill him myself, but I know I'll get my chance down the road. As soon as we find the bastard, how about you reel him in?"

Brittany tapped her fingers on the desk as if she were readying a memo. There was so much running through her head at the moment, from thoughts about Cal and the guilt she felt for purposefully misleading him, to the desire to solve these cases and advance her career, to frustration with Fisher that he'd put her in this position. Of course she wanted to go after Alfredo, but there were more important items to consider.

"Excuse me for saying so, sir, but I think chasing Alfredo right now would be shortsighted."

Fisher raised both brows and steeled his gaze. "Why?"

"Because there's a little girl out there that needs our help."

Fisher put his hands on his hips and looked at his feet. Brittany saw his boots were caked with dirt and salt. A combination of dirty snow and poorly maintained sidewalks in action.

"Don't you think I want to help this girl too? But if we nab Petrocelli, we've got ourselves a shot to clean up a whole host of murders, including the mayor's."

Brittany crossed her arms and leaned back in her chair. She knew it was going to be tough to convince her boss of what needed to be done. But she had to do it.

"I'm aware of that. But not only was I able to put Boyle behind bars like you wanted, but I was able to get him to tell me where Alfredo is keeping her."

Fisher removed his right hand from his hips and waved it in the air. "Wait a minute, Wilson. This is huge. Why didn't you mention this before?"

"I tried, sir, I—"

"When would Cal have seen Alfredo? If Boyle did what we think he did, why wouldn't he want Alfredo dead?"

"I'm not sure, sir," Brittany lied. She couldn't tell her boss about the shoot-out in the cemetery and that the only reason Cal was able to get the information was because he had Alfredo dead to rights.

"Cal and Alfredo could be in cahoots for all we know. Even if Vinnie was the one who kidnapped the girlfriend like Alfredo said, and Cal was the renegade soldier who killed all of those mafia guys to get her back, they could've been aligned the whole time."

Fisher didn't seem convinced. Brittany hoped he wouldn't try to poke more holes in her story.

"Are you suggesting we pursue this lead? Ahead of

tracking Petrocelli and getting him to give up the whereabouts of Tina Fregosi ourselves? Remember the last time we relied on a hunch? We were blindsided. We lost one of our best men."

Brittany opened her eyes wide, matching the earlier coldness of her boss. "We're wasting precious time. We haven't gotten to Alfredo yet despite hours of trying. We'll be extra prepared, have a team of our best to check it out."

Fisher put his hands back on his hips again and huffed, nodded his head, and stared at the popcorn ceiling and the painfully bright fluorescent lights of the station.

"You know what? You're right. My money is on Petrocelli getting out of Dodge anyway. You tell me where you think she's at and get a squad together. Fully loaded this time, no silly stuff."

Her boss picked up his still-steaming cup of coffee and walked away, before finally turning back.

"By God, Wilson, I hope you're right. I just wanna get this girl back to her family before Christmas."

Brittany blinked and watched as her boss walked away. Her FBI future, the exhilaration at bringing the mafia to its knees, could wait. Bringing Tina Fregosi back to her family was the biggest item on her Christmas list.

41

Sharp bumps repeatedly pounded Cal's side as he slid across a cold floor. He wasn't sliding by choice—he was being dragged like a heavy bag of garbage out to the dumpster. But where was he being taken? Angry voices shouted in the distance. Whoever was dragging Cal barked assurances that everything was fine and that he had "an unruly one" on his hands.

Cal wondered what the person dragging him meant by "an unruly one" until he remembered exactly where he was and what he'd been through over the last several hours. Benson Forbes, the fat redheaded officer with the annoying gum-chewing habit, the shit-stained pillow case, and Joey Bartellini—all of them played in his mind like a highlight reel. Cal may not have been in a jail cell any longer, but he was no more free than a ten-year-old waiting for the school bell to ring for the final time before summer.

The pain in Cal's head was excruciating, causing him to wonder just how hard he'd been hit. His brain rattled against his skull like dice at a high-stakes casino. His vision was fading in and out, but he saw lights and shapes walking in the hallway. Were the shapes more police officers? Why hadn't they recognized his captor, whom he now realized was Joey Bartellini, and stopped him?

Cal heard his captor grunt and open a wide set of double doors leading to another hallway. He still had no idea where they were headed, perhaps to a shower. The absence of sound was immediate to him as his body walloped over a ledge beneath the opened doors. Had there been more noises than those of the inmates and policemen in the holding cell area? The whole experience was so new to Cal that he couldn't keep his thoughts organized.

Another set of doors opened and shut just as Cal was dragged across the threshold. He felt dust bunnies crawling on his skin and clothes, like roadkill being eaten alive by flies and their maggot offspring.

Why was he so worried about the icky feelings he felt when he had much worse problems to deal with?

Cal's captor lifted him up and placed him against a thick metal object. It was too big to be a pole, he thought, but he had no idea what it could be. His vision became clearer as he saw Bartellini pull a set of handcuffs from his pocket. It was evident that Bartellini had taken Cal to some kind of janitor's closet or supply room. What looked like the spillover from a red bucket of paint was off to Cal's right, but it could just as easily have been blood. Perhaps other cops took disobedient prisoners back here to punish them, away from the cameras, to dish out real justice.

Cal felt the tight clasp of one of the cuffs around his wrist and winced at the sensation. He still hadn't gotten used to the stinging sensation of being handcuffed.

His gaze shifted to Bartellini. He saw the ugly slits of tense eyes and the brooding darkness of coffee-stained teeth. The retired hit man seemed to be enjoying the act of getting back into the killing game again. Feeling more conscious and helpless over his current predicament, Cal opened his mouth to protest. Bartellini kneed him in the groin.

Cal yelled in agony. The pain of the shot to the nether region cascaded to his stomach. He recalled the sensation of eating too much candy as a child and the stern warning that followed from his mother. He wanted to roll over and moan in pain, but in his upright position there was little he could do.

"I finally got it done," Bartellini said. "I've done something no one has been able to do—capture Callahan Boyle. Well, I guess the police did it first, but I was able to waltz in right under their own nose and kill two officers to boot. God, I missed that feeling."

Cal spit at Joey's feet. As much as he hated himself for his former profession as killer extraordinaire, he'd never enjoyed killing others as much as Bartellini just claimed.

"They'll catch you, you know? You'll be just like those other men in here, left to rot inside a jail cell."

"Is that so?"

Bartellini removed a large black club from his belt and bludgeoned Cal's side with it. It felt as if his ribs had cracked in half. His cry of pain was so loud that someone had to hear him.

"I'm actually doing you a favor, Cal. I'm saving you from that same fate. I couldn't care less if I spend the rest of my life here, seeing as I don't have much left to live. But once I take you down, I can live the rest of my life with pride knowing I got the job done."

Joey brought the club forward and struck again, sending another flood of pain to Cal's other side. He felt like passing out, like giving up. His arm dangled from whatever he was attached to. It could've been a giant boiler, a drum of soap, anything for all he knew. He just knew he couldn't take any more pain. He didn't know how much longer he could hang on.

"In fact," Joey continued, "let's make my future incarceration a lot easier for the courts. I want them to know exactly what crime I committed. It's funny, isn't it, Cal? We spend our entire careers as hit men trying not to get caught, but the minute we have our grandest kill in front of us, sometimes it pays to be public about it."

Bartellini paused and reached into his pocket to pull out a cell phone.

"In fact, I think I'll record your death for the boss right now, just so he knows there were no slipups."

Cal saw Bartellini raise the phone with one hand as he went for the hip holster with the dispatched officer's weapon with the other. It couldn't end this way for Cal, not like this.

He blinked hard, quickly thinking of what to do. Bartellini had the weapon in hand but was too focused on the cell phone, muttering his frustration as he tried to get the camera to work.

Cal looked behind him for the first time and saw his right hand cuffed to a long metal tube sitting in front of a glass window. Upon closer inspection, Cal realized it was a laundry machine. It was then that he saw that his left hand was free.

Bartellini had gotten lazy. While Cal's free hand wasn't his dominant one, it gave him something to work with. All he needed was an impromptu weapon. But what could he use? Death was drawing closer. He needed a distraction.

"Hey, Joey."

Bartellini looked up from his phone and frowned. “What?”

“You know the saying you can’t teach an old dog new tricks?”

Bartellini’s frown grew more intense, his gaze signaling displeasure. Cal’s mind, though screaming in pain, was working fast. He had a free hand and legs that felt like lead, but Bartellini was smartly too far away for Cal to do anything with his limbs. What else could he do?

That was when he saw it. He moved his left hand behind him, feeling for the handle that would open the machine. That would do the trick. He wouldn’t have much time, but he was confident he could take care of Joey with this one move, then find a way to escape before the real police discovered his whereabouts.

He just had to get Joey near him. It would be easier said than done.

“It doesn’t matter how old I am.” Joey’s frown left his face, but Cal could see the anger in his eyes. His plan was starting to work. Joey walked closer to Cal, until he was only inches away from his face, the officer’s gun pointed at Cal’s chest.

Cal knew he wouldn’t have much time. He’d seen Joey gaze toward his left arm and suspected Joey already knew he’d messed up. Maybe the old hit man was intentionally giving Cal a false sense of confidence, luring him into taking action, only to shoot him at close range. That was a risk Cal was going to have to take.

Bartellini raised his eyes to meet Cal’s gaze. “You’re not going to even reach half of my age.”

The retired hit man snickered, seemingly amused with himself. Cal held his gaze firm and swallowed for dramatic effect. If he showed Joey that he was even the slightest bit scared, maybe he could turn the tables and convince the old hit man that he really felt the end was near.

"You'll let me have my last words, right?" Cal had his hand on the handle of the machine. Now that Joey was close enough, he was sure he could return the favor and kick him in the groin just as Bartellini had done to Cal earlier.

Joey raised his brow, but the movement caused him to lower his weapon.

It was time to act.

Cal thrust his left leg into Joey's groin, sending the old hit man into a crouched position. Not hearing the clang of a gun against the ground, Cal knew he was in danger if Joey recovered. Cal kicked his leg out again, this time connecting with Joey's hand and causing the weapon to crash to the floor.

Cal opened the door to the laundry machine—he hadn't bothered to determine whether it was a washer or dryer—then quickly removed his hand. Joey moved to punch Cal in the face, but Cal ducked and grabbed ahold of Joey's police uniform and pulled him closer to him.

Using his free hand, Cal took Bartellini and slammed him into the machine, moving his own body out of the way in the process. The old man let out a loud groan, but Cal was right back to work. He shifted his body behind Joey, knocked off his police cap, grabbed his gray ponytail, and dragged his head closer to the open door.

With a swift motion, he slammed the door repeatedly into Bartellini's head with as much force and fury as he could muster. With each movement forward, Cal felt a wave of anger fleeing his body, wishing the person he was inflicting damage on was Alfredo rather than a man that used to be his mentor.

Cal slammed the door more times than he could count,

until at least two minutes passed. On the last thrust forward, he held the door firmly against old Joey's head. The next time he moved the door back in his direction, he noticed that the inside of the machine was painted in blood. Bartellini's body fell to the floor, and Cal felt his neck for a pulse with his free hand. The bastard was still alive.

Cal couldn't take any chances. He watched as Bartellini lay flat on his back, head oozing blood. Cal reached for and grabbed the discarded gun. The second he saw Joey Bartellini turn over and look into his eyes, Cal knew what he had to do.

"Guess I'll outlive you after all."

Cal aimed for Bartellini's head and pulled the trigger. He felt around for the key to the cuffs, unlocked them, then quickly pulled the uniform off of Joey. He hoped no blood had splattered on the uniform from the laundry machine beating or the shooting.

Once he was dressed in the officer's uniform, Cal tried to play it cool. He opened the same double doors he'd been dragged through and turned left. He couldn't take the right back to the cell area. Several shouts in that direction indicated the police officers and detainees realized something had gone wrong. No sirens sounded yet, but Cal knew if he didn't get out of there fast, there was a chance the place would be on lockdown and he'd have no chance of escaping, even in the officer's uniform.

He took the nearest exit he could find and walked through a section of gravel to a barbed-wire fence with a guard shack at the rear of the property, leading to a parking lot, where the staff likely parked.

"Have a good night."

Cal smiled and nodded at the elderly gentleman manning the shack and hoped his face resembled the slain officer enough to escape unscathed. His breath was labored and his heart pounded fast, but he made it across the road and to the parking lot. A car honked at him.

If it wasn't for a small inkling that he wanted to see who the driver was, he wouldn't have looked back. He would've used the pair of keys in the officer's pants to find a car to steal before making his next move. But after looking through the window and seeing the longish gray locks shaking back and forth with the movement of the man's head, he knew he'd made the right choice.

He walked to the passenger's side, smiled, and opened the door. He knew he'd been worried for nothing before.

It sure was good to see Uncle Judd again.

42

Brittany Wilson felt a trembling sensation in her heart. Even though her thoughts were dour, she forced a cheerful expression, not daring show to her Chicago PD colleagues how she felt inside. What they were about to do would be a make-or-break moment in her career, and she sure as hell hoped it wasn't a break moment. Compounding matters was the fact that the Chicago field office of the FBI had brought in a team to assist with their tactical operation.

Rescuing Tina Fregosi was the only thing on Brittany's mind. She prayed that Cal's suggestion that Alfredo was hiding her in the basement of Cal's childhood home was accurate. Thanks to some digging, Brittany discovered that the home had been sold to a real estate holding company shortly after Cal's parents died. While they couldn't confirm it was a mafia stronghold, the holding company owned a handful of other suspected mafia hangouts in the city.

Brittany shook in her coat, more so from the icy tingling of her nerves than due to the freezing temperatures. She stood beside her new boss and his youngest son, Max, who was on an unapproved observation of his father's work.

"This will be a piece of cake," Mick Fisher had told Brittany when she objected to her boss's version of "bring your kid to work" day. "There's nothing for the little guy to worry about."

Brittany doubted that. Even though they were standing beside Fisher's Ford Expedition across the street from the house, she had a bad feeling about this one.

Both the FBI and Chicago Police Department had assembled tactical SWAT teams decked in full gear for the operation. Her team had been tasked with staking out the front of the property, while five FBI special agents, the very team she hoped to be a part of someday soon, would cover the rear. A person from each team would meet in the middle and sweep the outside of the house before joining the rest of the force inside.

It seemed that ten people was the right number to enter the house with. Brittany thought it was unlikely for there to be much more opposition than that since the house was so tiny, but they had no idea just how many men the mafia might have inside. It could've been ten or a hundred for all she knew.

Her team was also able to pull an old blueprint of the house that had been filed with the city, though that was when the house was first built. If Alfredo Petrocelli and the Chicago mafia purchased the house after adopting Cal, he could've retrofitted it with all sorts of rooms and hiding places that would present unforeseen challenges.

"Operation Frog commence," said the voice of the lead FBI agent over the mic.

Brittany glanced between her boss and the five men

heading for the front of the house. Fisher's young son pulled at his father's pant leg and looked up at him with wide eyes.

Brittany wondered what the boy was thinking. Did he really want to be here for this? Or had Mick brought him along as a sad excuse for father-son bonding time? She couldn't think of an activity more dangerous, but it wasn't her child to worry about.

As the men drew closer, Brittany pulled up a pair of binoculars to her eyes. It wasn't that she needed them to see what was going on, but she felt more official with them in hand, since this was a rare occasion where she was an observer rather than getting in on the action.

The men had their weapons drawn and were ready to engage. She felt herself in the shoes of the men as they walked. She noticed her eyes moving to the windows and the roof of the home, her peripheral vision executing a quick scan of bushes, trees, the sides of the house, and neighboring homes for any hint of movement. Fortunately for the men and her rising heartbeat, there was none.

Fisher's boy tugged at his father's pant leg some more until he received a scolding gaze from his father.

"Not now, Max. We're moving in."

A man broke off from the pack and went to the right side of the house. Brittany assumed a member of the FBI team approaching from the rear would do the same. She adjusted her earpiece to ensure she heard every word.

"Perimeter is clear."

"Copy, we're clear," the Chicago PD leader responded.

Both units were close enough to the house that they could brush the ends of their rifles against the brick. Brittany held her breath, her heart thundering in anticipation of what would happen next.

"Proceed to entry point," said the FBI leader.

The members of the Chicago PD's task force headed for the door, ready to use any means necessary to enter after stating their business. The warrant was already in hand.

"Unit B, have you reached your destination?"

Unit B was the code name for the Chicago PD.

"Roger that."

"Initiate Operation Frog," the lead special agent said over the mic. Everything needed to go right here, or there would be hell to pay.

Brittany pressed her earpiece further into her ear, as if she wasn't picking up any sound from the earlier transmissions. She held it in place as she listened to the Chicago PD task force leader shout at the entryway.

There was a five-second pause, maybe longer. Brittany heard nothing from either team.

Time to go in.

She heard the thud of the entry ram colliding with the front door and knew the team was entering. She closed her eyes tightly, ever sensitive to abrupt sounds. The thud turned into a loud bang, and Brittany felt a huge wave of heat spread across the front of her body. She thought she was on fire, burning alive. A large hand pulled her to the ground, keeping her clear from a smoldering ball of flame. Piercing screams filled her ears. It was the most horrifying thing she ever experienced.

Whoever hadn't died immediately from the explosion screamed in agony, the charring smell of their burning flesh not as sickening as the sadistic motherfucker who planned the bombing, knowing the Chicago PD and FBI would be there. Had Cal done this? Did he set her up, knowing she would pursue the clue?

But he couldn't have, could he? From all his interactions with her, Brittany surmised he genuinely hated Alfredo and that he would do anything to get the girl back. So why would he mislead her? Perhaps the girl really was here or had been recently. There was no way to know now with the house waving back at her in a canvas of reds, oranges, and yellows.

Brittany finally looked up and saw that it was her boss's hand that had pulled her down, away from the bomb's devastation. He'd likely saved her life. A thud pounded in her heart and a stone fell into her stomach as she realized most of the team that had charged the building were gone for good.

She had to get up and race toward the men. There was a small chance some of the screaming ones were alive. She could help them.

"Max, get back here!"

Max Fisher was beating her to the punch. Brittany watched as Fisher's kid ran toward the house's smoking carcass. What was the boy doing? Was this mere curiosity, or had something else drawn his eye? Either way, it was beyond dangerous.

Another fireball and deafening explosion boomed from the house. It could've been another bomb or a gas line going poof. They weren't waiting to find out.

"Son!"

Her boss screamed, and both Brittany and Fisher were on their feet in an instant, running toward the house. Brittany didn't care that she was putting her own life at risk. They'd come to save one child, and they wouldn't lose another one on her watch.

The smoke from the second explosion was thick and blinding. Brittany had no problem clearing the initial fog of gray and gaining visibility of the home. Her boss, however, wasn't in top shape and struggled to keep moving as he choked his way forward. She hoped she didn't have to save his hide too.

Brittany squinted through her eyelids and held her breath, not wanting to risk eye damage or smoke inhalation. In the distance, just behind a charred fence pole that used to encase the back garden, Brittany thought she saw Max Fisher. Her heart leapt, and she was thankful the boy appeared alive.

Just when she turned to her boss, ready to shout that the boy survived the blast, a man scooped him up and started running toward an alley behind the property.

"Hey! Where are you going?"

Brittany pulled out her pistol and screamed, determined to stop whoever had grabbed the boy. Had he come from the house? Did he have anything to do with the explosion?

"I said get back here! Put him down or I'll shoot!"

The man who grabbed the boy maintained his back to her the entire time, until now. With the swiftness and grace of a figure skater, the captor spun around and fired in her direction.

Brittany felt something nick her hair as she fell to the ground. Her heart rate rose and her breath came in fast. It had been an incredibly close call. While some of her dark locks of hair were gone, she'd managed to avoid most of the bullet's damage. But the captor was getting away with the boy.

She tried to get to her feet and resume her chase, but she couldn't find the energy. The coughing and wheezing of her boss behind her, coupled with his occasional mumbles of his son's name, caused her heart to feel weary. She had failed yet again.

"Did you see him? Did you see my boy?"

Brittany looked up at her boss, a tear starting to form in the corner of her eye.

"Yes, I saw him. He's alive. Some guy got him."

Fisher stood there, soaking it all in. Whatever happened there, and whether it was indeed a trap or not, didn't matter now. There wasn't a kidnapped girl there they could save, and Brittany didn't have the answers she thought she had when Cal was jailed. There was so much left unsolved.

"Do you think it was the mafia? Do you think the same people that got the Fregosi girl have my boy?"

Brittany's mind was clouded, each thought another question failing to answer the one that had come before. She wasn't sure which way to turn, but now there was more at stake. Not only was a girl still missing, not only was her career on the line, but her boss's son had been taken. It didn't matter how foolish it had been for Mick to bring Max Fisher to the stakeout. She had to find a way to get him back too.

"It's possible, sir. I suggest we go after them."

Fisher nodded and scanned his surroundings. He hung his head in shame, knowing that dozens of lives had been lost and that his son's life was in imminent danger.

"Talk to Boyle. I want to know what the fuck is going on here. I sure as hell hope he hasn't been the one setting us up."

43

Alfredo put his cell phone down on the table and smiled at the latest update from his lone living capo, Fernando "Flesh" Moran. Moran had told him that the feds had indeed shown up at the old Boyle house, and the bombs detonated perfectly. The men stationed nearby didn't have to take out any of the feds or Chicago police officers, since the bombs had done their part. They'd even managed to kidnap another kid to boot, the son of Lieutenant Mick Fisher. He'd give Alfredo yet more leverage as he figured out what to do with the Fregosi girl.

They'd moved Tina Fregosi from Cal's childhood home to a new location, an empty storefront in the Edgewater neighborhood. White canvas sheets obstructed the view inside the shop from the gazes of passers-by on the street. The shop was as functional as Alfredo needed: it had a toilet and running water, an old refrigerator for storing the essentials, and a small closet, where they could keep the girl. The table Alfredo had set his phone on was next to the only other item of worth in the shop, a counter that had formerly housed a cash register.

Two of Moran's men walked into the shop carrying a bulky-looking thirty-inch television screen. The sight made Alfredo's blood temperature soar, and his head was filled with the rush of annoyance.

"What the hell are you doing with that thing? Get that outta here!"

One of the men, still wearing sunglasses despite the darkness of the retail shop, turned to Alfredo as if he were only taking a casual suggestion from an older brother. The other man, clean-shaven and without a stocking cap like his friend, cringed.

"We're gonna be bored as fuck watching this girl," said the scruffy sunglasses guy. "At least let us watch some TV for a bit."

Alfredo stewed as the men set the television on the counter. He walked toward the bearded punk and was ready to wail on him with a few hard rights before thinking better of it. He had bigger fish to fry, like figuring out what to do with Tina Fregosi.

The girl had become a burden he no longer wanted to carry. He had to kill her. No, he needed to kill her. He grabbed his phone and walked to the rear of the shop, toward the closet where the girl was being kept. Moran had two more punks that were in there with her. It seemed like all of the men that had been with her at the house—underlings of ousted capo "Death" Masucci—had vanished into thin air the moment he died. No matter. He didn't care who was around as long as he was there to strike fear into her eyes.

As soon as he stepped into the closet, Moran's men cleared out, and the girl cowered beneath Alfredo's gaze. Her bottom lip trembled, her eyes were stretched wide, and her tears morphed into a monsoon of sadness. Her eyelashes fluttered and her hands flailed about in her lap—Alfredo had no clue why she wasn't tied up—but it didn't matter. She was defeated, and Alfredo loved when his enemies were beyond hope.

"Why did you take me here? Why can't I just go home?"

The shrieking voice resounded in Alfredo's ears like a dying animal crying for salvation, or for the biggest predator in the herd to end it once and for all. That was exactly what Alfredo wanted to do. He was tired of keeping her around, and for what reason? So he could gain leverage on Cal? Cal was in jail, likely doomed by the far superior hit man of old, Joey Bartellini. As much as he wanted to be the one to kill his ungrateful adopted son, he was relieved to know his death was imminent at the hands of his old friend.

Was he still keeping her around so he could get back at her brother? The kid's eyes were swollen to such a degree that it was a miracle he was able to drive himself at all. He had a better chance of running into a telephone pole and ending his own life than what he'd managed to do up until that point, killing Masucci and one of his men before driving off. He'd find a way to kill himself. Alfredo had no use for the girl now.

Alfredo walked toward her, until her knees were nearly touching his feet as she sat in a cross-legged position on the cold gray floor. He realized he was being less than cautious, given only one measly leg was chained to the plastic white shelving that lined the inner wall, but he didn't give a damn. The venom he wanted to spew at the punk with the television was baring through his teeth, threatening to leave his mouth in the form of spit and land on the girl's forehead.

Would serve the little bitch right after what she did to me. A caged animal lashing out at its master.

"You think I'd let you go home?"

The girl's cries turned into high-pitched wails. Alfredo was eating it up.

Cry me a river, you spoiled brat.

"Quit your whining. I ought to kill you like I killed your brother."

It was a lie, but the remark caused the girl to scream at the top of her lungs. Alfredo grabbed the girl's hair and yanked it, wanting to drag her across the floor. She yelped further when her chain stopped her. The mob boss yanked harder, wanting to see if his brute strength could break the chain and free the girl.

"What did you do to Tony? What did you do?"

Her shrieks had no effect on Alfredo's conscience. Her crying was exactly what he'd forced himself to suppress as he recovered from his collapsed lung and relearned how to breathe, before returning home. The girl's tears were all he remembered feeling when he saw Vinnie's body lying at peace in his polished wooden casket. That moment made it real, when he knew his son wasn't coming back and he'd lost both of his boys before they reached the age of thirty, leaving him and Susan without both of the precious lives they'd brought into the world.

He yanked at Tina's hair harder. The unmistakable "Ow, stop!" cries of the girl only fueled him. Alfredo raised his other hand, ready to strike her across the face. He wanted her face to match that of her dipshit brother. The fact that Tony Fregosi was still alive hadn't bothered him much before, but it did now, especially after he told the brat he'd killed her brother.

"I'll teach you to spit at me," Alfredo growled.

His hand was leveling down toward the girl's face, his good shoulder swinging his arm into a swift forward motion. Something flashed in the corner of his eye, but he remained unfazed. It was only the sharp voice of Melissa that caused him to stop just short of striking the girl's face.

"What the hell are you doing, Alfredo?"

Alfredo dropped the girl's hair and straightened himself up, his right hand falling in line with his side, and his shoulders stiffening at his niece's presence. The two punks who'd brought in the TV flanked Melissa outside the closet door, and Alfredo suddenly felt like he'd been caught with his fly open. The fact she'd called him by name instead of "Uncle" made him realize the graveness of the situation.

"What am I doing? Uh, well—I'm doing nothing."

Alfredo felt the words struggle to break free, like his vocal cords were tied in knots. He knew he'd been caught trying to abuse the girl. The looks of shock on everyone's faces made him wonder if they were finally questioning what he was doing with her in the first place.

Melissa shook her head and crossed her arms. "Quit worrying about her and come out here. We've got bigger problems."

The two men behind Melissa walked away, allowing her to turn around and wait for Alfredo. They walked back into the main shop, the resounding cries of Tina Fregosi becoming increasingly softer behind them. The new television was on, and the former shop's cable must have still been connected, as the local news blared across the screen.

From the still shot, Alfredo could see the Cook County Department of Corrections building. He smiled, wondering if old Joey had finally taken out the bastard known as Callahan Boyle. But Melissa had said they had bigger problems. As if on cue, his stomach began doing somersaults.

A reporter came into view on the screen. The young woman began talking, saying something about a break-in at the prison and that multiple officers had been killed. They believed at least one prisoner had escaped in the riot.

Alfredo's heartbeat accelerated even faster. He placed his hand on Melissa's shoulder, trying to steady himself. He needed to sit down. This couldn't be happening yet again.

They flashed the mug shot on the screen of the suspected missing prisoner, and Alfredo's eyes closed. He shook his head in disbelief, refusing to acknowledge the news bulletin. All eyes were on him, he could feel it. Only once he heard that the television had been turned off did he dare open his eyes.

He looked up and saw the droopy nature of his niece's cheeks. Alfredo's heart beat in pain at the thought that Joey had failed to do the job. He knew Melissa was feeling just as awful about the outcome. Tina Fregosi was still crying in the closet, and he was suddenly glad he'd kept her alive. She'd have a part to play after all.

"Alright, that confirms it, then. We keep the girl, find a way to contact Cal. Let him know we'll kill the girl unless he comes to get her. No more games, no more traps. Now that Joey's gone, I want my shot at him. Tonight I'm going to kill Cal."

44

Cal's face lit up in surprise as they drove south from the Cook County Department of Corrections. Uncle Judd was back.

Where had he gone in the first place? Why did he make it seem like something had happened to him?

"I bet you've got a lot of questions for me," Uncle Judd began. "But first things first. You look like shit, and I'm sure every cop in this town will be looking for an escaped prisoner dressed as a police officer. Reach around to the back. I grabbed a change of clothes from your place before I left."

It didn't bother Cal one bit that he needed to get undressed in front of his uncle. He ripped off the powder-blue officer's shirt, stripped out of the black slacks, and threw the duty belt on the floor of the back seat. In place of the discarded uniform, he donned an outfit he hadn't worn in years: a brown turtleneck sweater with a black collar vest. He struggled into a pair of black jeans as they continued on California.

"Where are we going?" Cal asked. He knew the prison was less than ten minutes away from his childhood home, the place where he suspected Alfredo was keeping Tina Fregosi. Naturally, that would have been his first choice of a visiting place after getting out of jail, but he had no idea how his uncle had read his mind.

"Where do you think? Your apartment was raided. Plus there's probably hundreds of police that will recognize you if we go downtown once word gets out about your escape. Let's go somewhere they won't expect."

Cal turned to Judd, his eyebrows etched upward as if he were attending his first peep show. He was glad they were going to his childhood home, and he hoped that his hunch would turn out to be correct. He had no idea if Brittany and her team were on the scene, or if they'd taken any action in the hours since his arrest. Frankly, Cal didn't give a damn. While he never wanted to see that traitor of a woman again, he was still committed to saving Tina.

"What happened to you?" Cal asked. He had to know if his uncle had landed in any sort of trouble, or if he'd picked up some of Cal's hit man instincts for evasiveness in the brief amount of time they'd spent together.

"Well, that part's easy. I have an old lady friend that lives in Chinatown. Figured I'd pay her a visit."

Cal eyed his uncle and smiled. "No way. I didn't know you'd be shacking up with some lady the minute we got in town."

Uncle Judd laughed and tightened his grip on the steering wheel. "I'm no dummy. I expected your mob friends to send a party once they found out you were here. It was only a matter of when, not if. When Tony mentioned you didn't have your phone, I didn't feel like taking any chances. I got out of Dodge for a while, went back to the apartment this morning, and saw it was trashed. Heard on the news a big suspect was hauled into jail, so I figured I'd get a car and wait. I didn't even have to come in and visit before I saw you walking out."

"Were you surprised?"

"Surprised, no. You've always been the type who can weasel their way out of anything."

Cal laughed. They'd be at the house soon, and Cal would be able to see if he'd been right. He'd have the officer's weapon at the minimum, and he could figure out his action plan from there. It would be just like old times.

"So about this lady friend—"

A sudden honking noise and the screeching of tires alerted Cal that something was off. Uncle Judd swerved hard to the right, trying to avoid the large truck that had almost turned right into them off of Kedzie. Cal instinctively reached for the handle above the door and stiffened against the seat. Judd held the wheel steady, until the tires knocking into the sidewalk as the car accelerated into a patch of grass off the side of the road. Other cars blared their horns and continued driving past, not bothering to play witness to the accident. People had more important things to worry about, apparently.

The car came to a stop before colliding with the iron fence in front of them. Cal caught his breath and looked over at Uncle Judd. A gentle nod told him what he needed to know. His uncle was alright, but Cal could tell he was shaken up.

Cal turned in his seat and saw that the truck had come to a stop.

Why did they have the worst luck with car accidents?

Cal brushed himself off, unbuckled his seat belt, and opened the passenger door. Uncle Judd cried out for him to stop, but Cal wasn't in the mood for peaceful negotiation. He was pissed.

Did he have to worry about this person too? Had the mafia already discovered he'd escaped? Cal was halfway to the car when he realized he hadn't grabbed the gun from the duty belt in the back seat. He couldn't worry about that now.

He heard the door of the truck open and waited for the driver to come around from the front of the vehicle. His hands formed into fists, ready to fight. Anger throbbed through his veins. He just wanted to pummel someone. It didn't matter that he'd bashed Joey Bartellini's head in with the prison laundry machine door. He was still infuriated, ravenous for revenge.

When he saw the driver stumble around the front of the truck, he released his fists and raised his brow in confusion. The driver's face looked like he'd been stung by a swarm of wasps. Even through the disfigurement, Cal could tell that the face belonged to someone he knew. Someone he was beyond excited to see.

"I'm sorry, sir. I'm so sorry. I can't see real good right now and—"

The driver stopped as he looked up at Cal. Their eyes locked, and for the second time in three days, Tony Fregosi ran toward Cal to embrace him.

This time Cal gave in completely. He wrapped his muscular arms around Tony and squeezed his young friend tight. Two of the people he cared about most, first Uncle Judd and now Tony, had been brought back into his life. Joy spread throughout his chest, and it suddenly felt like there was hope again. They still had to find Tina, but at least everyone else was safe.

"What happened to your face?"

Cal turned and saw Uncle Judd, relieved that his uncle was able to make it out of the car without pain.

"C'mon, let's not get into—"

Cal was cut off.

"They beat the shit out of me," Tony started. "Two guys loaded me up in a truck to die. I managed to play possum and kill them. I drove to the spot they were gonna kill me at, and I saw Alfredo there. I tried to kill him, Cal, but I was only able to get some of his guys. He ran away before I could do anything. I figured I'd head back to where they were keeping Tina at some point, but I hoped I would find you first. I can't believe I did."

"Yeah, it's quite a coincidence. You're lucky I'm not planning on calling your insurance company."

Tony tried to smile, but Cal could tell it was difficult. Both cheeks and eyes were bruised and puffy. Tony's lips were pale in comparison to the size of the rest of his face. Cal wondered if he needed to see a doctor. That was when he thought of what Tony had said earlier. Uncle Judd beat him to it.

"Kid, you said you know where the mafia is keeping your sister."

"Yeah. They took me there too. After they grabbed me in Fulton Market."

Tony frowned and looked at Cal with a dose of concern, like he'd failed his friend for getting taken. Cal knew it was his own fault Tony had been seized. He felt as guilty as a father leaving his children home alone for the first time.

"Tony, are we close to where they were keeping your sister?" Cal asked.

"Yeah, it's not too much further."

"Down California, right? Then a left on Thirty-Ninth?"

"Yeah. There's one more turn after that."

"Jesus," Cal said. He'd been right all along. They'd kept Tina Fregosi at his childhood home. But why? Was it another way for Alfredo to get back at him? Was there another trap coming?

The three of them stood in the grass for a minute, looking at each other. Cars continued to honk at the scene as they passed by, though Tony had at least pulled the truck onto the sidewalk so it wasn't blocking the road. Still, they didn't want to stick around for too long. They had to get a move on, especially since what Tony had told them confirmed Cal's initial thought.

"Those two guys, are they still in the truck?"

Tony nodded. Cal knew they couldn't proceed to the house in the truck. They'd have to get in Uncle Judd's vehicle and head for the house.

"Alright, let's go."

They ran to the car, Cal deciding he'd be the one to drive. He shoved the airbag out of the way, started the ignition, and drove off of the grass patch and sidewalk and back on California. His heart hammered as they made their way toward his childhood home. He hoped they weren't too late. Cal asked Tony rapid-fire questions as they drove. How long had they kept her there? Were they planning on taking her somewhere else? How often did Alfredo stop by? What kind of guard detail was there? Tony answered the questions as best as he could, but he didn't know much, since they'd pummeled his face before he could get a good look at the place.

They turned onto Talman and headed south. Cal's mouth went agape as soon as he looked at his former home. Tony let out a squeal of agony. Uncle Judd couldn't help but swear.

"Holy shit."

The house was in flames. Curious neighbors had

ventured from their homes to catch the blaze. Sirens could be heard in the distance.

"Tina!"

Tony exited the vehicle and started running for the house. Cal raced out, grabbed the boy, and held him close.

"She's not in there, Tony. There's no way she can be in there."

Tears poured down Tony's face. Cal could only hope he was right.

A dark figure walked toward them, looking as if they had risen from the ash that had once represented the home's foundation. It was the last person Cal expected to see, and he'd already had more surprises that day than at any other point in his life.

Staring back at him was Detective Brittany Wilson.

45

Brittany's soft eyes fell upon him like those of a porcelain doll staring off in the distance in a young girl's bedroom. Cal's eyes hardened in response. He was determined not to give Brittany any sort of edge. He'd had enough of her manipulative games. The only things he wanted now were answers.

"She wasn't in the house. It was a trap, just like everything else."

Brittany looked first at Tony's swollen face and blinked. Her gaze then settled on Cal. Even through the haze of smoke surrounding the area, Cal could see tears misting in her eyes. He still wasn't buying her act.

"What happened, then? You wanna explain why this house got blown up?"

Brittany put a hand on her hip and pouted. Cal kept his gaze firm, not caring that he was being an irritant. He let go of Tony and was surprised to see the boy remain still. The sound of roaring fire and the sudden collapse of the wooden home caused Cal to cringe. While there had been plenty of unhappy memories in his twelve years in the house, there had been enough good times that he was sad to see them all go up in smoke.

"It was an ambush, just like I said. We sent a team, and so did the FBI. Both units canvassed the house when the first explosion happened. Shortly thereafter there was a second explosion. They did what they were intended to do."

"So you admit that you're with the Chicago PD now? Not the FBI?"

Brittany rolled her eyes. "Yes, I played you, Cal. Is that what you want to hear? Can't you see what's happening here?"

The realization of the damage done finally hit Cal. It wasn't just his childhood home that had been destroyed but also the lives of law enforcement officials, who were just doing their job. Cal felt that if Brittany hadn't had him arrested he would've been able to prevent this, that they would've recovered Tina Fregosi already.

"Were you the only one to make it?" Cal couldn't believe she'd been so lucky.

"No. My boss ran after someone. Maybe the mafia had a presence here to make sure everything went smoothly."

"Who'd he run after?"

Brittany sighed. "My boss brought his kid with him. I thought it was a stupid idea, but hey, boss's orders. The kid ran toward the house after the first blast. Childhood curiosity, I guess. The guy I saw grabbed the boy. My boss is trying to save him."

Cal's heart dropped further in his chest. Alfredo's evil wasn't limited to ruining the former hit man's life or the lives of the Fregosi family. It was starting to extend deeper, into the core and fabric of the city as a whole. Taking the kid of a Chicago police detective was a desperate move and one that would give the mob boss more leverage.

"This is getting real," Cal said. "But that still doesn't explain why you had me arrested."

As hot as the neighborhood was from the flames that surrounded the house, Cal felt cooler than a cherry popsicle as he spoke to Brittany. He knew he was a criminal—there was no denying his past. Yet he couldn't believe Brittany would put her own career ahead of saving Tina Fregosi. Cal knew they would've found her had she not wasted her time in having him jailed. Tony had been to the property and confirmed that Tina had been here only hours ago, which would've been enough time for Cal and Brittany to save her together, without lives lost.

"You know I did what I had to do. This is one of the biggest cases this city has seen in a long time. I was getting nowhere, Cal. I had to bring you in."

"Bullshit. You lied to me. I never should've believed you were with the FBI and after Alfredo for a federal crime. I still could've given you enough info to bring him down. Did you arrest me just so you could make yourself look good? I thought you were above all of that. I thought you were on the side of justice, and for helping this young man find his sister. Their family has been through more than enough, and yet you want to score some Brownie points by throwing me in jail?"

"Cal, that's not true, and you know it. There's nothing more that I want than to find the girl and make sure justice is served."

"Oh, I see. So you care more about justice being served by locking me up than letting me save this girl? I could've done it, Brittany. You know I could've. You could've let this keep going. We were working together just fine. How many detectives spend a night with a dangerous suspect?"

Tony gave Cal a look of surprise. Brittany folded her

arms and tensed her body, the softness leaving her eyes. She was doing her best to match Cal emotion for emotion.

"You leave our personal affairs out of this. I was doing my job. I was making sure justice was served. You're suspected in the deaths of dozens of men. My job is to keep men like you behind bars and off the streets of Chicago. I don't care if you've learned your lesson and promise to make things right again. I did what I had to do, and I have no regrets. But since you've somehow managed to escape and you're still hell-bent on saving this girl, I guess I could use your help. What do you say we work together? For old times' sake?"

Cal saw the softness return to Brittany's eyes once again. She reached out her hand, ready to let bygones be bygones. Cal was sure he could never trust her again. There was no way she'd let him get away for good now that they had him for all those murders. He'd spend the rest of his life behind bars. What was to stop her from cuffing him upon shaking her hand?

He turned to face Uncle Judd and Tony and saw the tired looks on their faces. They had to know that Cal was in a tough spot. Anything he did to help Detective Wilson would bring them one step closer to saving Tina. Yet he also brought himself closer to life in the slammer. It was a trade-off of immense proportions. Partner with Brittany again, and he was closer to giving someone life. Yet if he did so, he was closer to ensuring his own death.

Cal glanced at the smoldering house and picked up a whiff of the unmistakable smell of burning flesh. It wasn't pleasant. The whole world was crumbling around him, and he felt like he was the only person who could make it right. He heard Maria's voice echoing in his head once again, her dying words pounding in his brain. As much as he couldn't stand Brittany, he knew helping her was for the best.

"You know I have no reason to do anything less than to hate your guts, right?"

Brittany frowned, then nodded and straightened her face into a more relaxed expression. Cal could tell she wouldn't let pride interfere.

"I know. I'd do the same if I was you."

Cal cleared his throat.

"Great. I'm glad we have that settled."

Cal looked at Tony and saw the immense amount of pain etched in the boy's face. Beyond the bruises and physical scars, he envisioned the mental anguish Tony felt inside. Knowing that the boy had been on the run for months since the Caruso murder, coupled with the fact his sister had been taken from the family that had already dealt with so much loss, had to be drawing him down into depths that Cal only knew as a youth. He couldn't let the boy suffer a similar fate if he could help it. He had to step in and do something about this.

If he didn't, who would?

"I'll help you," Cal said, his glare still firm, locked on Brittany's eyes like a tiger zeroed in on its prey. "But I know what we're dealing with. If we get an inkling of where Tina is now, you can bet Alfredo's going to be all over it. You can have as many officers as you want there, but you let me call the shots."

Cal took another glance around him, sensing the spirits of Tony and Uncle Judd lifting as he spoke. "I'll get Tina back, no question about it. Just let me do what I have to do."

Brittany uncrossed her arms, ran her hands back through her hair, and nodded. "Alright, hotshot. I guess it's your lucky day."

A loud chirping noise sounded. Fire trucks and an ambulance announced their entry with blaring sirens and blinding lights. Brittany reached into her pocket and grabbed her phone, ending the source of the chirping. She listened for a second, her eyes tense, and turned her back to Cal.

Cal watched, irritated, as the emergency personnel got to work on calming the maddening flames in front of him. Why had Brittany turned her back to him? Was she calling for backup? Was she telling them exactly where to pick up Cal? Who knew? Maybe she'd find a way to tie Cal to the smoldering ruins of a house before them.

Before his mind could ruminate further, Brittany turned around. Her eyes no longer seemed tired. The corners of her mouth began teasing a smile. Cal felt his heart drumming even faster, his shoulders becoming tense. Uncle Judd moved alongside Cal and scratched his head. Tony crossed his arms and shifted his gaze upward. Whatever Brittany had to tell them, Cal hoped she would spit it out.

"We got a tip from someone in Edgewater. Apparently, there's a vacant storefront with a lot of sudden activity. A few tough-looking guys with stocking caps were there, and the woman with the tip said it appeared they had dragged a child-sized object in with them."

"Could be another trap," Uncle Judd said. "You see all these firemen and EMTs running here and having nothing to show for it? No bodies left to save? That's exactly what could happen up there."

Brittany nodded, her temperament unchanged by Uncle Judd's interruption. "The informant passed along one more piece of information. She said an older gentleman had been seen walking in. He had dark-brown hair with specks of gray. Does that sound like anyone familiar?"

Uncle Judd opened his mouth and turned toward Cal. Cal stared at Brittany, wanting to believe that he would finally face off against Alfredo this time, and that he'd also be able to save the girl. He'd wanted to put a bullet through his adoptive father's brain at the cemetery, but without knowing where the girl was, it wouldn't have been right.

If what Brittany had been informed of was true, Cal knew he'd have a shot at both killing Alfredo and reuniting the Fregosi family. He had to trust Brittany's information. He had to believe.

"It could be Alfredo, but it could also be anyone. Where's this place in Edgewater?"

Brittany told him. Cal wasn't intimately familiar with the area, but the outline of a plan began building in his head. He'd need more weapons and ammo than what he had available in the police duty belt. Plus he'd have to find a way for Uncle Judd and Tony to get out of harm's way. He didn't want to drag them into this.

"You should go," Brittany said. "I'll need to stay here and debrief everyone on what happened. You can bet I'll be up there, though. That is if the team that's heading up there isn't able to save her first."

Cal's heart pounded even more. As much as he wanted Tina Fregosi to be rescued, he didn't want the Chicago PD to do it. He wanted to be there; he wanted to be the one to make it right. Cal had to get there first. There was no way Alfredo was walking out of the storefront in handcuffs; Cal would be sure to pump a few rounds in his chest before he had a chance to be taken into custody.

"Time to save my sister, Cal," Tony said weakly. "Time to take out some more scumbags."

46

Alfredo crossed the street, paid a few Benjamins to the old woman who'd called in the tip to the Chicago PD, and walked back toward the storefront. The Christmas season was truly in the air, and Alfredo felt the joy of the holidays radiate through his body, warming him beneath his black peacoat.

He entered the storefront and walked to the back, where "Flesh" Moran had joined the two punks carrying the television from earlier in the day. The man with the facial hair and stocking cap held the girl against his chest, a bag tied over her head, making it seem like they were doing nothing more than carrying a heavy sack of potatoes to the car.

Melissa Ranieri had left the shop, but only after recruiting a handful of soldiers to keep watch while the police made their move. Just like before, Alfredo knew they'd eat up the possibility of recovering Tina Fregosi. Fortunately for them, Alfredo had no more bombs in store, and he even told Melissa to order the men to stay calm and to only fire if fired upon.

The plan would play to perfection.

"Let's move out. This time to the last spot."

"Last spot?" Moran asked.

"Yes, the last spot." Alfredo looked at the two soldiers, nudged his head toward the back door, and watched as they led Tina outside, still kicking and screaming beneath her restraints. Alfredo hoped it was the last he would hear of the child's whining.

"It's time for all of the games to come to an end," Alfredo began. "Christmas is coming a little early this year, my friend. And the girl will deliver me my final present."

Moran nodded. "I see, sir. You sure this is a good idea? The more we move this girl, the more the authorities will catch on. We're not exactly a kidnapping operation, boss."

Alfredo looked at his last living capo and felt the temperature of the room soar. Sweat bubbled up to the back of his neck, and he felt his forehead becoming damp. He imagined his hands flying to Moran's neck and crushing his larynx.

As much as he wanted to assert himself, he couldn't lose another valued member of his regime. He was in control of his plan, not his recently designated capo. Alfredo wasn't about to let Moran have the satisfaction of making him angry.

"It's the best idea I've had yet, Moran. This time I'm finally gonna kill this girl. It was never about her. It was always about one man. Once I make this call, I'm going to get my Christmas present on a silver platter."

"Boyle? You've got my word, sir. I'll do whatever it takes to help you bring him down."

Alfredo laughed and flicked his brows upward. He didn't doubt Moran's loyalty but knew he was nowhere near as capable as Vinnie and Captain Joe Blutarski, the men he'd been surrounded by the last time he'd tried to take Cal down in person.

"Good. As long as you know I'm gonna be the one to kill him. If you'll excuse me, Fernando, I've got a call to make."

Moran shook his head and ventured outside into the cold night air to join the other soldiers. Alfredo didn't want anyone else from the mafia to overhear his phone call. He figured Cal's phone had been taken from him when he was jailed earlier that day, but he had Tony Fregosi's number saved thanks to his niece's due diligence in securing the information. It was time to make contact with Boyle again, and he expected the Fregosi boy to find Cal sooner rather than later once Cal escaped from jail.

He wasn't disappointed.

"Hello," croaked a voice on the other end of the line.

"Tony, put this call on speaker. I have a feeling Cal will want to hear this."

Alfredo waited as the call transitioned to speakerphone. He paused with bated breath to hear the voice of the man he despised so greatly. His eyes and neck twinged with hate at the thought of Callahan Boyle. He saw his son's body collapsing to the ground, feeling helpless at his inability to stop Cal from killing his lone living child. He knew it would only be a matter of hours before he could satisfy Vinnie's last request. Alfredo would kill Cal if it was the last thing he did.

"Alfredo?"

There it was. The voice Alfredo had so much authority and control over. Cal had only grown as strong as he had because of Alfredo's tutelage. He could just as easily kill what he allowed to rise up.

"Cal, I'll save the pleasantries. You may have heard from your lady police friend that we're keeping Tina up in Edgewater. Well, I want you to know that was a lie. We're taking her somewhere you know all too well. Somewhere that's been empty for a good three months. I haven't been in the unit since he died. You know where we're going, don't you?"

A long silence filled the air. Alfredo felt his heart race, waiting for an answer.

"Yeah, I know where to be. We've both got a good shot at getting there at the same time."

Alfredo laughed. Cal was one of the best killers he'd ever seen, but sometimes he was still as naive as a soldier fresh to the mafia life.

"You can come as soon as you want, Cal. But we've got the girl, and you don't. I'd love to see you make it out of this one alive."

Alfredo hung up, not wanting Cal to get another word in. He'd made the point he needed to make. He headed out the back door of the storefront and was pleased that the getaway car was nice and toasty as he slid into the front seat. There was no more time for talk; it was all about action.

47

Cal sped away from his old home for the last time, trying not to think of how upset his mother would've been seeing the home she worked so hard to maintain crumbling down. Uncle Judd sat in the front seat, Tony in the back. They'd just received the call that none of them had been expecting. Alfredo Petrocelli told them there was no use in traveling to the storefront in Edgewater where Brittany had been told the girl was being kept. Rather, Alfredo was taking the girl to Vinnie's old apartment, just a few floors beneath Alfredo's own penthouse in the Gold Coast.

It was the opening Cal was looking for. He didn't need the Chicago PD poking around in his business. Even without the full arsenal of weapons he was used to, Cal knew he had more than enough skill to get Tina Fregosi back and take Alfredo down once and for all. He wanted to leave Tony and Uncle Judd behind, to ensure they weren't caught up in this mess. The last thing Cal wanted was anyone else getting hurt, especially after Tony fell into the mafia's hands and suffered injuries that put him nearly beyond recognition.

Both men proved more stubborn than Cal expected and insisted they tag along. Cal only acquiesced after they promised to stay outside of the building to serve as Cal's eyes and ears on the ground. He didn't want to be caught in another trap if Alfredo planned to send more men after him once he was inside. If he was lucky, he'd get to the building ahead of Alfredo, and he'd have a chance to stake out Vinnie's old floor. There was a fat chance of that, though, especially with the building security not likely to let him up without Alfredo already being home.

"How much further?" Uncle Judd asked.

It was unlike the wise and patient Judd to pipe up with a hint of impatience. Cal scratched the back of his head as they inched toward Lake Shore Drive. He wasn't thrilled that traffic was moving slower than expected, even on Christmas Eve. At this rate, Alfredo would have everything set up with minutes to spare before Cal could enact his plan.

"It really depends on how fast this traffic gets moving. As long as the police don't know what Alfredo is up to, I'll have more than enough time."

Mercifully, once they got past Soldier Field and the Museum Campus, traffic moved nice and easy. Cal floored it as fast as he reasonably could without drawing too much attention to himself, which wasn't much more than sixty miles per hour. Uncle Judd even cracked a window, enjoying the frigid breeze slapping against his mangy hair and beard for a few seconds before Tony started bawling about the cold.

Cal took the exit onto LaSalle and entered the Gold Coast neighborhood, home of many of Chicago's elite. Cal had always felt out of place whenever venturing into the area for meetings with his adoptive father and brother. Growing up poor in Brighton Park to an alcoholic father and a struggling-to-make-ends-meet mother made him feel like he couldn't even wipe his feet on the doormat of Alfredo's second home. The riches of the mafia had their appeal, but the life of luxury never had a hold on Cal.

Once Cal turned onto Burton, he scanned the area for a nearby parking space. He couldn't venture too close to the building, as he didn't want any of the mafia soldiers to see him waltzing through the front door, but he also had to find a vantage point where Uncle Judd and Tony could alert him to any danger.

"What's that?" Tony asked.

A van passed their car on the narrow street like it was in the Indianapolis 500, blowing through a stop sign on Astor. The car swerved right and made the turn toward Alfredo's building. Cal's heart hammered in his chest like that of a blacksmith pounding on an important piece of metalwork.

"That them, champ?" Uncle Judd asked.

Cal shook his head. Alfredo and his crew wouldn't be coming the way Cal and company had driven, as they would be approaching from the north. This was something different. Why was another car speeding toward the building? Something seemed off.

"You wanna find out? My eyes may be puffier than Floyd Mayweather's after a boxing match, but I'm still a pretty damned good driver. Let Uncle Judd and I worry about the car. You take care of business. We'll be out here if you need us."

The former hit man turned toward Tony. Seeing the kid's face nearly caused Cal to wrench his jaw in sympathy. What would make Alfredo and his goons do such a thing? Was this what it was all about? Kidnapping Tina Fregosi and nearly beating Tony to a pulp? And for what?

Was Alfredo's whole plan simply to torment Cal into submission? To get Cal to show up on Alfredo's doorstep for easy pickings? Cal didn't have to think about it anymore; he already had his answer.

"I meant it when I asked you guys to stay put. Don't try anything with these guys, or they'll shoot you on the spot. Got it?"

Both men nodded. Cal opened the door and began his walk to the building.

The more he thought about it, the more he realized Alfredo wasn't the only one manipulating his way to a showdown with his greatest enemy to end his existence. That was exactly what Cal was after, too, despite his thinking that he was only in this to save Tina Fregosi. Of course he wanted to save the girl, but if he could blow Alfredo's brains out all over Vinnie's floor, that would be fine by him too.

Before he could chide himself for thinking that way, the tall skyscraper rose above him, a great concrete mountain aiming to puncture the wintry gray sky that was beginning to cloak itself in black. He scanned for the van that had just driven past, but was unable to see it. It couldn't have veered that far away.

Cal coughed, his lungs filled with a sudden tickle in the chill December air. He still couldn't believe all of this was happening during the thick of the Christmas season. Cal had never been one for presents, which probably stemmed from his poor childhood. Even living with the Petrocellis as a teenager, he never cared for the lavish gifts Alfredo and Susan bestowed on him.

The only gift he wanted was to give Tina Fregosi back to her family. His footsteps clomped along the concrete as he made his way past the circle drive and toward the building's entrance. He spotted the doorman behind the front desk in the lobby and didn't care that he'd have to schmooze his way past him. Cal reached for the policeman's gun tucked in the back of his slacks and silently wished he didn't have to use any of the few remaining bullets.

"Can I help you?"

The doorman was in his midsixties, much like Uncle Judd. He stood behind his desk, poised and confident to prevent any riffraff from entering the luxurious condominiums of the city's most prestigious residents. Cal suddenly appreciated his uncle's outfit for the occasion.

Though Cal had seen the doorman and had ventured into the spacious lobby many times before, he couldn't help but be taken aback by the white marble walls and floors that filled the entryway. His shoes made the sounds he imagined belonging to only royalty, nice clomping echoes that signified power and importance. Everything he hated about Alfredo.

"I said, can I help you?"

Cal had been so caught up in the scenery that he had forgotten his purpose. *Think, goddamn it.* So much for any hope of the man recognizing him and letting him up easy.

"Uh, yes. I believe you can help me."

Cal moved closer to the desk, until he was less than ten feet away from the man. He felt himself bringing the gun out of the back of his pants. There was a kindness in the doorman's eyes across from him, shielded behind gold-rimmed glasses. The man's gray mustache was neatly trimmed, and his suit was freshly pressed. Probably just a regular guy trying to get through another night of work, wanting to get home to be with his family for Christmas.

Perhaps he had grandkids and he was missing out on sharing *The Night Before Christmas* with them. Maybe his family was gathered around the television watching a classic like *It's a Wonderful Life* or *Christmas Vacation.* Cal wondered if he could hurt the old man if the situation called for it.

"Fuck!"

Cal heard the curse at the same time as he saw a disturbance out of the corner of his eye. Two men in the elevator bay to his right were dragging something that appeared to be a large trash bag toward the nearest elevator. He wasn't sure how they'd gotten in. In all of his past visits to Alfredo's and Vinnie's apartments, he never recalled a secret side entrance.

Both Cal and the doorman turned in the direction of the bay, and Cal's eyes locked immediately on the man not dragging the bulky bag toward the elevator. The man's eyes grew large, and his hand inched toward his waist.

With the ding of the elevator bell, Cal didn't hesitate. His hit man instincts kicked in once again. He removed the gun from his waistband, pointed toward Large Eyes, and fired into his chest. The man dropped without protest. Cal aimed at the second man, but he quickly disappeared into the elevator.

"Oh my God, that was murder right there! Nothing but murder!"

Cal looked back at the doorman, who was moving his hands toward a landline phone. Cal placed his hands over the older man's and looked at him with an icy glare that was colder than anything the Chicago winter could muster.

"That guy was going to shoot and kill both of us, plain and simple. You'll stay down here and act like nothing happened. There's some bad stuff going on in this place, mister, and I'm gonna be the one to clean it up."

Cal didn't give the man a chance to reply before running off toward the elevators. The man with the trash bag may have had a head start, but there was no stopping Callahan Boyle, especially not this time.

48

Cal made his way to the twentieth floor, not quite the top of the building but high enough to have a view of Lake Michigan beyond the traffic-infested sliver of concrete that was Lake Shore Drive. Alfredo's penthouse was only three floors above Vinnie's apartment.

As the elevator ascended, Cal felt his body coming alive. Sweat danced down his body, grooving from his shoulder to his elbow and down his forearm. His heart hopped up and down like an overeager puppy. Even his right eye twitched as if he'd consumed too much caffeine. In only a matter of moments he would come face-to-face with Alfredo, though he expected he'd have to take down a horde of men first.

Grabbing the gun of the soldier he had slain in the lobby had been a smart choice. He held Large Eyes's 40-caliber Beretta APX in his hand, pleased to discover there were ten rounds in the magazine after first detaching it from the weapon. Coupled with the remaining five in the police officer's gun in the back of his pants, Cal felt he'd have enough ammo to get through whatever forces Alfredo placed in his way.

The elevator dinged, and Cal stepped out into the hallway, holding his new pistol. The walls were covered in a green-and-white-striped wallpaper that still managed to look classy despite the fact that it was, in fact, wallpaper. A wooden table with a lamp and Keurig machine was before him, and Cal thought for a moment about grabbing a cup of coffee, before realizing not only were there no cups but that he also saw the man from the lobby dragging the heavy bag across the floor and around the corner of the hallway to his left, exactly where Vinnie's condo was located. The bag quivered against the floor as it was dragged, making Cal think there was something alive inside.

Cal pumped his legs, going as fast as he could without making too much noise with his feet—he didn't want to alert the man to his presence—until he heard the clomping of running footsteps behind him. Cal turned and saw a man hot on his heels with a weapon extended. The new Beretta felt like magic in Cal's hand, a lost toy he was more than happy to have found. He fired the Beretta, its first bullet launching with precision, heading directly for his opponent's head.

The man turned away at the last instant and screamed as the bullet clipped his shoulder. He got off two quick bursts of gunfire in Cal's direction, and Cal hurtled toward the table, knocking the Keurig machine to the floor and cursing as his ribs collided with the lip of the table.

Being out of the gunman's view for a split second afforded Cal an advantage he was determined to exploit. Two quick bullets of his own raced toward his pursuer, clipping the man once again in the arm. A shout of pain followed, and a flash of light beamed toward Cal's face, causing him to join the gunman in collapsing to the ground.

The man wheezed and grunted as he reached toward his

dropped gun. Cal could see the man's blood dripping toward him just inches from his face. Even if he lay there and did nothing, he doubted the man would be able to fight back given the successive shots to the same place.

Put him out of his misery.

Cal fired another round, this time hitting his target square in the chest. The former hit man took a deep breath, pushed off the floor, and began the walk toward Vinnie's apartment.

The instant Cal turned the corner, he lifted his leg high, ready to throw all of his might against Vinnie's door to force entry. He knew the risk of injury he'd sustain if it was fortified, but Cal knew that Alfredo wanted him there. He wanted Cal to waltz right on in and not expect a thing.

Cal wasn't surprised when the door flew open and slammed hard into the wall behind it, potentially puncturing a hole in the Rembrandt painting that was only visible when the entryway was closed and clear. The apartment had a stuffy aura, and dust floated through the soft-white moonlight that streamed through its windows.

Cal entered the dimly lit space and glanced to his left at the foyer wall, to the right down the hallway leading to a bathroom and some of the guest bedrooms, and straight in front of him to the great room. There wasn't a sound.

Where was everyone? Had Alfredo shown up with Tina Fregosi? Or had only the man with the bag shown up? How could he have disappeared so fast? Why was it so quiet?

The silence of the place began closing down on Cal like a garage door making its slow descent to the concrete below. Only instead of a faint droning sound, the emptiness that filled his ears seemed to expand further and deeper into his brain. He had to investigate and move closer to where he imagined the action was.

First, he needed to reload the Beretta. The man he'd slain in the lobby had only had one extra magazine, and even though Cal hadn't fired all of his rounds in the hallway, he preferred a full load to taking a chance with a partially dispensed magazine of ammo.

His eyes had become so engrossed in the new weapon that he failed to notice the movement of two figures, one in front of him and another who had staggered out of a bedroom to his right.

Once Cal finished reconfiguring the weapon, he turned to his right, down the hallway with the bedrooms. He froze when he was confronted by the sight of a man he hadn't expected.

Cal raised his weapon with the precision of a Western marksman and pumped two bullets into the man's chest. His latest victim crumpled to the floor. Cal wondered just how many more victims there would be tonight, how many more of Alfredo's goons were hiding behind doors one, two, and three.

Two pops caused Cal's already trembling eardrums to throb in protest. The sharp, hot sting he felt at his side was far more jolting. He couldn't help but fall to his knees, the pain was so sharp. He felt like his ribs had been sliced clean through. All it took was a head turn to his left to see that there had been someone hiding in the great room. Behind the couch, no doubt.

Cal felt the weight of his torso pulling him to the ground. Only below him this time wasn't the soft plushness of newly installed carpet but rather the polished pristine blackness of marble. The ground was spotless, immaculate, despite the fact the condo's owner had been dead for over three months.

Thinking about Vinnie's death and seeing his reflection

in the floor made Cal want to anchor himself in place. He couldn't fall now, couldn't be defeated, couldn't join Vinnie in the depths of evil that so many in the mafia life found themselves succumbing to.

He had far too much to fight for. The girl. Himself. Maria.

The heat in his side felt like an ember of hot coal. It was worse than any pain he had ever felt, and he'd been shot many times. But he would not fall, he would not give in. His head moved toward the ground, but it would not collide with the floor. His instincts told him he should fight back, but the pain in his body told him he was growing colder, told him he was dying.

Footsteps pattered toward him, and the room grew darker. Had the moon moved beyond a cloud, or were the lights going out?

Feet collided with the floor, moving closer to him. He saw a hand reach out for him and felt it on his shoulder. The effort the person made to push him down was sending him deeper into the state he did not want to go into. He couldn't give up. He couldn't fall.

Cal's torso sank further, falling from a dignified perch to a cratering abyss. He'd seen his father fall in a similar fashion many times as a child. He vowed never to be like his father.

The pain in his side was only magnified as his entire being collapsed to the floor. More footsteps were audible throughout the house. But were they footsteps? Not only had Cal's vision reduced to nothing, but his hearing was tuning out as well.

It was the last thing he thought he saw, two pairs of tiny feet in the distance of his peripheral vision, that made him realize precisely why he'd come to Vinnie's apartment.

"It wasn't Alfredo. It was never about Alfredo."

There was no mistaking that voice. It was Maria's voice calling him to the great beyond, wherever she was now.

Cal just hoped someone else would be able to save those two kids. He knew he'd never get the chance.

49

There were times in a man's life where it was expected he would give up, where it would've been perfectly acceptable to throw in the towel. He hated towels, except for this one. The one that was being wrapped around his side. And for what purpose exactly? Was this what they did at a morgue? Preparing a dead body for the afterlife?

Cal looked up at the vaulted ceiling and saw shadows dancing in the light. The unconsciousness that had overcome his body manifested most prominently in his frozen eyes, eyes filled with death.

Though he still couldn't place where he was, he definitely wasn't at a morgue. In fact, Cal wasn't sure he'd died at all. But that couldn't be, right?

He'd heard Maria's voice. He was confident he'd seen her walking toward him down the hall, stepping over the body of the last man he would ever kill. It was funny, Cal thought, that he'd wondered precisely at that moment how many more victims there would be that night. As it turned out, he'd be the only one.

"He's definitely gone, boss. I swear it."

"You nincompoop bastard. I fucking told you not to kill him!"

"I promise I didn't intend to. The trap worked to perfection, sir. Too much perfection."

"Oh yeah? Well, now not only is Carlo Dingbat over there dead, but so is Cal! I fucking told you he was mine to kill. I fucking told you!"

The click of a weapon caused Cal to blink. Twice.

"Wait!"

More footsteps sounded, this time coming closer. Cal wanted to look in their direction, to see what was approaching from the corner of his eye. He felt the brush of the body of the person who had wrapped the towel around his side being shoved away and heard the voice of "Flesh" Moran above him, a man he vaguely remembered from his mafia days as one of Al Meransky's cronies.

"I think it's your lucky day, boss."

"What makes you say that?" The vitriol in the voice was unmistakeable. Cal had never heard Alfredo this angry. To think the predator had come so close to securing its prey, only to have it snatched away by a rival carnivore had to have enraged him to the same degree as losing Vinnie had. There was no sound of hope in what Moran had said.

"Because he's still alive."

"How do you know that? Let me see."

More footsteps. If he wasn't dead yet, Cal knew he wouldn't be living for much longer. The pain coursed throughout his entire left side and was finding other ways to wreak havoc on his body. His legs and arms felt numb, and his head was rooted to the floor. An invisible string tied to his eyelids forced his gaze upward toward the ceiling. Even if he wanted to fight back, he didn't see a way he'd be able to.

"He looks dead to me, Moran. What are you talking about?"

"His eyes, sir. They blinked. Roman, didn't you see it?"

"I don't know what you're talking about. I just wrapped the towel around him in case he had any hope. I know how important it was for the boss to kill him."

Cal tuned out the arguing between the mobsters and felt a burning sensation in his throat. He had to force himself to stay in place, resist the urge to scream and let out all of his frustration. There was no way to tell where this sensation had come from, but it was overwhelming him, even more so than the gunshot wound he'd just sustained.

Was it knowing that if he did nothing, he would actually be killed? Was it the feeling of hopelessness at the paralysis resting numbly in his body? Or was it something more primal, like the desire to save an innocent girl from inevitable death? His throat burned and his legs started tingling. Something was happening within him that he couldn't comprehend. He felt an awakening stirring within him. He couldn't be a victim ready for slaughter at Alfredo's hands.

Cal's eyes were unblinking, and he forced them to stay that way as he looked at the human he loathed the most standing above him. Alfredo's jowls quivered as he stared down at Cal. A huffing and puffing of short, angry breaths blew over him like a windy Chicago evening readying for a torrential thunderstorm. Two other faces joined the mob boss's, but unlike Alfredo, their expressions weren't mired in hate. Rather, they were scared. Scared at the possibility that Cal was still alive. The itching sensation in his throat grew larger, and Cal felt his body come alive, ready to spring into action.

Muffled voices and the shuffling of feet were audible

beyond him, and he knew Tina Fregosi and the Fisher kid were only feet away. If he could summon the energy to take down Alfredo and his goons, Cal felt like he had a chance to save the children. But as much as he wanted to help them, he couldn't find the strength. Blood poured into the towel like the tears of a widow at a funeral, and any movement would only be met with certain death at the hands of Alfredo.

"Hold it. I think you're right," Alfredo growled. "Cal, are you alive and trying to play dead on me?"

Alfredo bent toward Cal, until their faces were only inches apart. Cal felt his temperature rising, felt the urge for his own jaw to quiver and his eyes to fix themselves into slants of disdain as he looked up at Alfredo. The sudden smack across his face forced him out of his trance and sent the two children behind them into a screaming frenzy under their gags.

"Goddamn it, Moran, you were right! You thought you could die on me, Cal? Drag his ass into the living room!"

Cal felt the henchmen's grubby hands pulling his arms, dragging him across the hard floor. He heard Alfredo run toward the sounds that were presumably coming from the children. Feet scurried across the floor, and Cal heard two doors shutting before Alfredo's booming steps rejoined Cal and the other men in the living room.

"Oh, Cal, I've been waiting so long for this moment. You thought you could barge your way in here and try to take me out again. Well, that's not happening this time. You should've taken me out while you had the chance back at the cemetery. My physical wounds will heal, and maybe yours would, too, if I let you live. But that would be such a waste, just like the rest of your pathetic life. You're a good-for-nothing, Callahan. You're here lying on the floor, unable to defend yourself. All you've been is a degenerate killer. As soon as I grab my gun and pull the trigger, I'll send you straight to hell, where you belong. Now, I've said all I need to—"

The condo door flew open. This time there was no chance for the mafia goons to hide and catch the entrant by surprise. A slew of bullets, at least three in all, boomed in Cal's direction, sending him into a frenzy and causing him to curl up in the fetal position on the ground.

Roman screamed and fell behind Cal with a thud. Cal turned over and tried to survey the scene. Was the entrant on his side or not? Moran returned fire to the front door, while Alfredo ran toward the office just off the living room.

The gunshots continued until Cal heard the sound of Moran's gun running out of ammo. The capo cursed, and Cal struggled to turn to his good side to see what his next move would be. As his body willed him the energy he needed to chase down Alfredo and save the kids, Cal saw a sight he hadn't expected. Running toward Moran in the living room was Brittany, her hair flowing wildly as she raced toward him.

Neither of them were shooting now, with Brittany engaging Moran in hand-to-hand combat. Cal hadn't seen Brittany fight before and was immediately impressed with her ability to deliver a roundhouse kick that Moran had to jump out of his skin to avoid. Brittany kept her charge, firing a series of jabs in Moran's direction. The capo was much more skilled than Cal expected, and he was quick to counter. He brought forth a heavy right-handed hook that connected square with Brittany's cheekbone.

"That's what you get, you bitch."

Cal struggled to a seated position, the stickiness from the blood pouring out from under his towel just another attempt to keep him glued to the floor. He placed his fingertips against his tender side, wondering just how much blood he had lost. The pain burned with a renewed ferocity as he struggled to move his legs, which tingled with sleepiness. Brittany and Moran continued to engage in a struggle, with Moran now locking his meaty paws around Brittany's neck.

The detective was undoubtedly strong, but Moran was nearly twice her size. If Cal didn't find a way to get to his feet and rush to her aid, he wasn't sure she would make it. Moran groaned, and Brittany struggled to keep her breath, trying desperately not to give in. The fact that she'd left the scene of the fire and raced to the condo showed just how much she cared, how much she was willing to put her life on the line to save Tina Fregosi and her boss's kid. Cal shook his old thoughts of frustration away, ashamed that he doubted Brittany's commitment.

Cal's fingers graced the nearest thing he could find, a coffee table, and he forced himself to his feet. He watched Brittany struggle and somehow found his strength in her moment of weakness. He steadied himself and stood before finding the urge to move forward. Brittany moved at the last instant, thrusting her leg upward and connecting with Moran's groin.

"Argh!"

Moran's hands left Brittany's neck, moving to protect his wounded groin, and the detective struggled for air as Cal lumbered toward his former partner. He used the opportunity to throw a hard right into the side of Moran's face, knocking him out cold.

Cal felt his body tremor as his strength returned to him. His hand reached for Brittany's and he pulled her from the ground. Their eyes met, and Cal felt a warm pounding in his heart. He felt no hate, no desire for vengeance this time. The only thing he wanted to do was kiss Brittany, just like he had in the street days ago. The feeling of her body in his arms was the only sensation he craved as they glanced at each other. With Moran lying on the floor, nothing could get in their way. Even the kidnapped children could wait.

Their lips moved closer together, and the vision of Alfredo's quivering face disappeared from his memory, permanently erased. They were so close now that Cal could feel their heartbeats colliding. He hadn't felt this close to anyone since Maria died in his arms three months ago. He didn't think he'd ever feel that close to someone again.

A door opened behind Brittany. Cal's eyes were closed as he felt his slightly chapped lips brush against Brittany's lush kissers, but his mind registered the movement. A sharp bang rang out, and he did the only thing he could do. He spun Brittany around like the ballerina princess that she was. Another stinging sensation rocked his shoulder blade, and he felt himself falling.

50

Cal wasn't sure how much longer he could stand. His head felt woozy, and his lungs struggled to filter air. The softness of Brittany's breasts beneath him couldn't keep him upright. He saw Brittany's face become consumed with panic. Tears started to form.

She kept her hold on him, her hands doing their best to keep Cal from falling. He was too far gone. His legs gave way first, the rest of his body anchoring him down to the ground, where he'd been only moments before. Cal slunk down Brittany's front like a stack of weights suddenly being dropped after intense exertion.

Footsteps resounded once again as Brittany reached for her gun. Cal wasn't sure if she'd spent all of her bullets on Moran, but he was hoping for her sake that she hadn't as he slipped further into unconsciousness.

"At last, I brought down the great Callahan Boyle. See that, kids? That's how you kill a man!"

"He's not dead," Brittany said with venom. "You'll never be able to kill him."

Alfredo laughed. "Is that so? True, his wound may not be fatal yet, but by the time I'm through with you it will be."

Silence filled the room for several seconds. If Cal could've done anything to help Brittany, he would've. As skilled as she was, he knew she'd have a hard time getting out of this with Moran also struggling to his feet. If Cal couldn't be of much help, he'd at least try to see what was going on. He was partially hidden from Alfredo by the overstuffed chair in the living room, and he hoped Alfredo wouldn't be able to see his movement. Cal rolled onto his back and noticed Moran rise above the chair over him. The capo made his move toward Brittany, determined to engage with her again.

Brittany turned toward him, aimed, and fired. A crimson jet burst from Moran's chest, and he fell back behind the couch. *She had bullets left in the chamber after all.*

Another explosion sounded, and Cal saw a similar splash of blood stream down Brittany's white shirt. He wanted to scream.

No, no, no. This can't be happening again.

Brittany remained standing and raised her gun once more, only to be blown back by another explosion of gunfire. Cal heard the children's deafening screams even beneath their gags. Cal's eyes met Brittany's as she joined him on the ground. She was falling, falling backward into the night.

As soon as her body hit the floor, Cal struggled to crawl to her. He couldn't let her die, not like this. He remembered the agony in Maria's voice as she died in his arms. Though he wanted nothing more than to save Brittany, he could already tell from where she'd been shot, in the stomach and just above the heart, it would be a miracle if she made it.

Cal reached out for her, his hands searching for the

towel that had been wrapped around his side, doing its best to keep him alive long enough so Alfredo could deliver the final blow. Could he find it and give Brittany any semblance of hope before Alfredo came to finish him off? Would he be able to find a way to keep either of them going, to give Tina Fregosi and Lieutenant Fisher's son a chance at life, to pry them away from Alfredo's evil?

Alfredo hovered above him as he searched for the towel, his glare menacing. Cal didn't even want to kill Alfredo just for the sake of killing. He realized now that he had to kill him not for revenge's sake but in order to save the screaming, helpless children just beyond him.

"Let those kids go," Cal said.

Each word crushed his chest like an anvil. If Alfredo so much as tapped his midsection right now, he felt like he would collapse, that he would finally cave under the weight of his wounds and his career of sin, and there would be nothing he could do.

"Face it, Cal. You don't give a damn about those kids. You want nothing more than to kill me, just like I want nothing more than to kill you. That's what it's always been about."

Cal wanted to spit at the man he used to call his father. He almost felt pity for him. He'd turned to kidnapping in order to exact his revenge on Cal. He turned to a more extreme form of evil than any of the mafia had over the years. Cal still felt a burning sensation inside as his wounds continued to ooze blood. He knew the longer he lay on the floor, the sooner he would succumb to the pain, and the less of a chance he'd have to do what he came to the condo to do.

"You're wrong, Alfredo. I'd love to kill you for what you did to Maria. But I'm not going to let that define the rest of my life."

Alfredo laughed again. "You won't have to. You don't have much of a life left."

The mob boss pointed his gun at Brittany, watching as her chest slowly rose and fell. Cal wondered if he was going to shoot her again, despite her body already descending into death. He moved his gun over to Cal, a big smile plastered on his face.

"Say hello to Maria for me, Cal. And your awful parents too."

Cal heard the cocking of the hammer and more wailing from the children. He had to delay Alfredo and find a way to keep him talking.

"Wait," Cal said. "After you kill me, what will happen to them?"

"Them? You mean those brat kids?"

Cal didn't change his expression. He didn't want to acknowledge Alfredo's use of the term "brat kids."

Alfredo moved closer to Cal, bent down, and whispered, "What do you think I'm gonna do? I'm not a kidnapper. I'm going to kill them and toss them in the river, just like I'm gonna do with you."

The mob boss moved his gun closer to Cal's temple. As if a miracle, Cal felt the pain of his bullet wounds recede. His heart drummed loudly in his chest, and his jaw clenched in anger. He simply couldn't die without saving those kids. He wouldn't allow himself to give in to the pain, no matter how much it hurt.

He balled his left hand into a fist and shoved it upward into Alfredo's right arm. Alfredo yelled as his gun clattered across the living room floor. Cal punched the first thing he could reach and was pleased that his right fist connected with Alfredo's eye.

"Fuck!"

Cal was lucky that he'd managed to surprise his adoptive father, but he knew he wouldn't be able to maintain the advantage for long, especially lying prone on his back. He grabbed Alfredo by the neck of his shirt and used all the strength he could muster to flip him on his back, screaming as his side and shoulder blade ripped in pain.

Alfredo did his best to fire back as Cal moved him, but the blows had no effect on Cal. Alfredo was the textbook definition of evil, greed, and destruction. As Cal fired right hand after right hand into Alfredo, he didn't see Alfredo for what he had done to Maria. He saw him as a sadistic bastard who had to achieve his goals by kidnapping two innocent children. If it was the last thing Cal did, he would save them from this man's evil.

Alfredo eventually caught on to Cal's strategy and blocked Cal's attack with his forearm. With his other hand, he reached into his pants and pulled out a knife. He swiped at Cal with surprising swiftness, forcing Cal to separate from the old man and move to his feet.

"I'm not going down that easy. There's a reason I'm the boss. It's because I don't take no shit from anyone."

Cal and Alfredo stared each other down as they stood toe-to-toe. Cal needed to end this as soon as he could. He saw Brittany's body grow paler on the floor and the scared-stiff bodies of the children beyond him.

Cal knew that if he got Alfredo to charge at him, he could foil the mobster. Alfredo was so blinded by his rage, so fueled by hate, that Cal figured he could easily stop him, even in his weakened state.

Alfredo charged before Cal was ready and slashed at Cal's arm, slicing through his shirt and just nicking the skin as Cal ducked away. Alfredo's momentum nearly sent him running to the door. By the time he was able to root his feet to the floor, his back was already turned.

Cal grabbed hold of Alfredo, his neck firmly nestled in the crux of his biceps. One movement of Alfredo's eyes told Cal all he needed to know. The mob boss realized he was trapped. Alfredo brought the knife backward, doing his best to get a piece of Cal.

Cal held on tight and looked at the kidnapped children and Brittany dying on the floor. She had likely given her life to protect the kids he was trying to save, giving him no pleasure in what he had to do. No surge of victory coursed through his veins at justice done for what had happened to Maria. He didn't even have any last words for the eldest Petrocelli.

Alfredo made one last thrust, and Cal groaned in pain as the blade caught him in the leg. He couldn't delay anymore and grabbed beneath Alfredo's jaw and behind his head, twisting up and to the right with all the strength he had left. Alfredo's body remained still as his head and neck pivoted sideways.

Cal let go and raced to Brittany's side. He found the towel that had been wrapped around him earlier and pressed it against her stomach. Even if he plugged that wound, the hole in her chest left a gaping, bloody injury that he'd never be able to heal on his own. Her eyes were cloudy and the movement of her chest was so minimal that he didn't know if she was breathing at all.

"No, Brittany, no."

Her hand reached out and touched his arm. She looked to the kids, who had managed to walk over to the scene. Cal could see the sadness written on their faces as Brittany, the hero who had risked everything to save all of them, gave her last breath.

Cal wanted to cry. He wanted to bury his face into Brittany's chest and sob until his own life energy escaped him, but he knew he couldn't. His leg wound was searing to an even more unbearable level than his prior injuries, but he had to keep going. He took one last look at Brittany, then at the children, and got up from the floor.

He'd done it after all. He'd managed to kill Alfredo and save Tina and the Fisher boy. He'd used his talents for good, just like Maria had urged him to.

He grabbed the children's hands and led them out of Vinnie's apartment, down the hall, and to the elevator. By the time he walked through the lobby, past the fallen goon he'd slain earlier in the evening and the still-shocked security guard, there was a line of FBI agents and Chicago PD officers in front of the building.

Cal's head spun as the sirens rang and lights flashed before his eyes. He could barely walk. His side felt like it had been torn open by a saber-tooth tiger, and his back burned. Only when the Fisher boy ran toward the man Cal presumed was his father did Cal know it was over.

He let go of Tina Fregosi's hand and saw Tony and Uncle Judd beyond, the smile evident on Tony's face despite the bruises. Everything was going to be alright.

That was when Cal allowed himself to fall again, the grateful eyes of Brittany's boss the last thing he saw.

51

Cal couldn't say what felt worse: the feeling of immense pain following two gunshot wounds and a knife injury that had wreaked havoc on his body, or the overwhelming nausea from the drug that pumped through his system to ease his suffering.

He glanced at the tubes that emptied the pain-killing fluid into his veins. He wasn't even sure if codeine was the drug he was being fed. He didn't care. Whatever it was, it wasn't doing a good enough job. He'd never felt as close to death as he felt right now, despite falling victim to many gunshot wounds over the years, far more than any human being should be subjected to.

Cal thought he'd put that part of his life behind him. He never intended to go down the killing path again after committing to leave the mafia behind three months ago. He hadn't wanted to pick up a gun ever again. But he had, and he'd gotten his revenge while saving two kidnapped children in the process. Right now it felt anything but sweet.

Cal tried to lull himself back to sleep, but the pain-killing drugs were keeping him awake. Cal kept tossing and turning despite his lack of energy, on the precipice of wakefulness and sleep. He finally managed to doze off for a good twenty minutes.

As he slept, Cal dreamt that some of Brittany's pals at the Chicago Police Department rushed in to question him. He saw Benson Forbes, Detective Bassitt, and the fat officer that Joey Bartellini had slain, each with handcuffs dangling from their hands like overly long bracelets. Their gazes signaled their shame, and Cal knew they wouldn't rest until he was sent to prison forever.

A gentle tapping on the door woke him.

"Mr. Boyle, there's someone here to see you."

Cal shifted his eyes toward the door, the lids too heavy for him to get a full picture of who was speaking to him. Based on the voice, he figured it was Nurse Culpepper. He tried squinting to get a clearer view of the speaker. Her hair was dyed brown and in a perm. Definitely Nurse Culpepper.

"Mr. Boyle, are you awake?" Culpepper asked. "I said there's someone here to see you."

"*Whoisit*?" The drugs were doing wonders for Cal's speech.

"It's your mother."

Mother? It couldn't be. His mother was dead.

"Sheese de—"

"Here she is, dear."

Nurse Culpepper's shoes pounded against the squeaky linoleum floor as she left the room. Cal's gaze was fixed on the door. He lifted his torso off of the bed and sat up tall. If the visitor really was his mother, as the nurse claimed, he wanted to be ready to see her.

From the moment his mother walked into the room, Cal knew the nurse hadn't been lying. Everything about her was consistent with his memories of her, memories that hadn't faded one bit after seventeen years.

She stood at about five feet five inches, which was the height Cal had achieved just at the start of puberty, right before her supposed death. Her face looked smooth, with only the slightest of wrinkles. Her skin was pale, just as it had always been, only changing color when she was hit with too much sun. The last thing Cal noticed was her long, dark hair, with the small white streak running down her left shoulder.

How could this be? I saw her in the coffin. I was at her funeral.

"Oh, Cal. I hate to see you like this. I never liked to see you in pain."

The heaviness that weighed down his eyelids suddenly vanished. Cal found it easier to open his eyes so he could drink in the entirety of his mother's presence. The voice sounded just like his mother's had, to the point where he had no question that it was her.

Cal wanted to say something, but he wasn't sure what. What do you say to a person who you thought had been dead for the last seventeen years? Why hadn't she told him she was alive sooner? It didn't make sense.

His mother walked around the foot of the bed and sat on it just to Cal's right. She reached out to rub his arm, her silky-smooth hands causing electrical sensations to run all over his body. It was good to feel her touch again, good to feel love after those he had most loved had perished.

"Don't you want to talk to me, Cal? I heard what happened and know it must feel awful, but I need to hear your voice again. It's been so long."

Cal swallowed hard and readied himself to speak. There was so much he wanted to say.

"Mom? I . . . I can't . . . I can't . . ."

"I know, sweetie," Mary Boyle said, rubbing his right arm faster. "I'm sure you have millions of questions for me, and we can get to all of that in time. How are you feeling, honey? That's the important thing."

Cal sighed. He was still in a lot of pain—just as much agony as he was in before he dozed off.

"It . . . it hurts. I've been shot before. Nothing like this."

"Oh, honey. What on earth has happened to you that you've been shot so many times?"

Cal wanted to explain everything that transpired following his mother's death. His adoption by the Petrocellis, growing up as best friends with Vinnie, struggling through community college, working as a bouncer and security guard, then doing odd jobs for Alfredo until he became a hit man and a destroyer of lives. But he couldn't; it wasn't the right time.

"I never hoped you'd become like your father, Callahan. He was always so nasty and mean to me. Even after he died, I knew I wouldn't be safe. So I had to make it seem like I died in that accident. His friends, they would have come for me. Oh, I'm so sorry, Callahan."

His mother leaned forward and wrapped her thin arms around Cal's neck in a tight embrace. The scent of peach blossoms in her hair remained unchanged from how she smelled when Cal was a boy.

Cal did his best to return the gesture, lifting his weak right arm up and wrapping it around his mother's back. He buried his face in her hair and remembered the horrible photograph Mayor Caruso's goon Bernie had shown him. Her dark hair had been the only part of her body visible beneath the white sheet covering her corpse. He remembered seeing the photo and only being able to identify her by the long white streak running down her hair above her right shoulder.

Her *right* shoulder.

There was no doubt from what Cal was seeing buried beneath his embrace that the white streak running down his mother's hair was above her *left* shoulder.

Cal and his mother pulled apart and she smiled at him, her soothing murmurs complete, and a radiant glow appearing on her pale face. Now that Cal wasn't squinting, he saw that the pale white on his mother's face was due to makeup, the foundation fading a bit at her temple.

"What's the matter, Cal? Is something wrong?"

The way the woman phrased the question sounded familiar to Cal. He tried to see past the facade the woman was portraying.

"Cal, remember that little yellow blankie you used to carry around the house with you when you were small? God, you must have been six years old, and whenever you would get scared, you always had that blanket."

Cal nodded. He did remember the blankie. If some strange woman was pretending to be his mother, how would she have known such an intimate detail about his childhood? There was no way. He found himself looking harder at his mother, reconsidering whether the woman was actually who she claimed to be. After all, Bernie could've doctored the photo for his benefit back when he showed it to him. He couldn't recall now what side of his mother's hair the white streak was actually on.

"I know you're not a little boy anymore," his mother continued. "But I thought I'd bring it just in case. It looks like you could use all the comfort you can get right now, so I brought it with me in my purse."

Cal felt his heart warming at the gesture. Now he was

sure that the woman he was speaking to was his mother. So what if her foundation was sloppy and the streak in her hair may have been on a different part of her hair than he remembered? Everything else about her seemed so right.

Mary Boyle turned her back to him and rummaged through her purse, looking for the little yellow blanket Cal remembered so fondly as a boy.

"You know, Cal, I'm sure you're hurting so badly. But at least I'm back by your side, honey. I'm sure there's other people out there who would love to have their whole family together."

Cal was surprised by his mother's comment. Mary Boyle had found the yellow blankie. She removed it carefully from her purse and clutched it against her lap as her eyes settled on Cal.

"What do you mean?" It was all Cal could think to mutter.

"What do I mean?" His mother's voice was shrill now, something he'd never heard before.

"I mean, think of all of the people you've hurt, Callahan. All of the people you've killed! Some of them don't have any family left because of you!"

Almost on instinct, Cal's right hand clutched at the sheets that covered him. This woman, whoever she was, had made him feel like a child, vulnerable and afraid. If it really was his mother, how had she known about his life? How had she found out he was a killer?

His mother rose to her feet, the blanket still clutched in her hand. Her eyes were wide and her nostrils flared; the rest of her body was trembling as if ready to burst from her anger. She slowly lifted her arm and pointed her long index finger at Cal.

"You killed them, Callahan. You killed my boy, and then

you killed the only person left in my life that I cared about. You ruined us, Callahan! And for that, it's time to meet your maker."

In a flash, the woman threw the blanket to the foot of the bed and unveiled a large hunting knife. She gripped it firmly in her hand and came down with the blade only inches from Cal's chest. He may have been woozy from the medication, but adrenaline filled his veins at the realization he'd be fighting for his life. He turned away from the attack just as the knife tore into the mattress beneath him.

His attacker screamed at missing Cal's body and shrieked with each new lunge. Cal twisted and turned to avoid her stabs. Her fourth attempt caught him in the left shoulder, and Cal yelled in pain.

"Does that hurt, Cal? Does it? Just imagine how much Vinnie and Alfredo hurt when you murdered them, you fucking killer!"

There was no doubt now. Susan Petrocelli, the woman who had loved him like a mother, was determined to exact the revenge against Cal that Alfredo had been unable to.

Susan thrust the knife down again; this time the blade landed within inches of Cal's neck. He caught her bony wrist just as she was determined to drive the blade deeper. Cal struggled to hold her arm at bay. He knew if he got the knife out of Susan's hands he had a chance of fighting her off, but until then he was inches from death.

"Aggh! Just die!"

Susan's determination and Cal's lack of strength from the drugs had his grip slipping. He wasn't sure he was going to be able to hold her off or stop the stabbing motion toward his neck.

As he held her wrist with his right hand, Cal used his left to pull Susan's hair, yanking her body hard. Cal rolled over, avoiding Susan's jab and positioning himself firmly behind her. He quickly reached for the knife, still buried in the mattress.

Susan glared at Cal as he fought to take the knife from her. He pulled and pulled at the hilt of the weapon before bringing the side of his hand down in a hard chop on Susan's wrist. Seizing control of the blade, he took the base of the knife and hit Susan over the head with it, not wanting to kill his adoptive mother but simply to keep her at bay until the authorities arrived.

Where the hell are they?

Susan was dazed but managed to roll over in the bed. She continued to come at Cal, clubbing his legs and chest with her tiny fists. Cal held the knife, but he felt his grip weakening. The drugs were having their desired effect, leaving him in a world of trouble. He had to end this soon.

Susan reached for the knife, determined to regain control of her prized weapon. Cal stabbed at her. She moved her hand back and cowered lower against the bed. She punched him in the groin, and Cal screamed even louder.

Why isn't someone coming to help me?

She reached for the knife again, but Cal was ready. He came down with the knife just as she was reaching for it, the blade slicing her palm. Cal dropped the knife and gripped her around the neck. He hadn't wanted to hurt her, but she'd left him with no choice.

Susan struggled beneath Cal's grip. Just one twist and her neck would be broken, exactly like Alfredo's. Cal wanted to give her a second chance. He hoped hospital security or the police or someone would come in and take her away. But no one was coming.

"What are you waiting for, Cal? An invitation just like the others? Go ahead and finish me, killer!"

Before he could twist her neck, Susan emitted a grunting noise and slipped from his grip, and Cal felt the urge to pass out.

Only a tall man in a white coat was visible before his eyelids became heavy and closed.

52

When he finally came to, Cal realized he was being pushed through a hallway in a wheelchair. He had no clue who was pushing him, nor why he had a thick bundle of blankets piled on top of him. It may have been cold outside, but the heat of the hospital was stifling.

Cal reached under the blanket, his head still woozy, wondering exactly what was going on. He felt his shoulder and was surprised to discover his hospital gown had been stripped from him. He was only left with a heavy cloth bandage taped to his left shoulder. Once he touched the bandage and felt the squishiness of blood flowing under his fingers, he recalled what had happened in the hospital room. Susan Petrocelli had tricked him into thinking his mother had returned and had come back to kill him. She nearly succeeded.

Since it was Christmas morning, Cal was surprised to see nurses and doctors scurrying between rooms. He wanted to turn his face down, to hide himself from view. While he wasn't completely sure how he'd gotten to the hospital from Vinnie's apartment building, he imagined it was under the close scrutiny of the FBI and Chicago Police Department. They wouldn't take kindly to a rogue doctor or nurse wheeling him from his room and out of sight.

The person pushing Cal took a hard left down another hallway and wheeled him into the first empty room on his left. It wasn't a room for patients but rather seemed like a small closet. Boxes of supplies were stacked from floor to ceiling, and a locker with scrubs of all sizes and white coats hung inside. The smell of hand sanitizer and rubbing alcohol was overpowering, sending a wave of fire up Cal's nose and into his drugged brain. The fluorescent lighting and reflection off yet another linoleum floor made him cringe.

Once the door had closed, Cal shook off the blankets, desperate for relief from the sweat bath that had started as soon as the thick covers were thrown on him. He was wheeled around to face the door, where the person who had saved him walked into view.

It was Doc Parker.

"Doc?"

"Yeah, Cal. It's me."

"What are you doing here? I thought you were retired."

Why would Doc Parker take Susan out and help him? It didn't make sense.

"I guess you could say I'm mostly retired. I cover a few shifts from time to time. There's always a need for help in good old emergency medicine."

That didn't explain it, though. Doc Parker had been loyal to the Petrocellis since Alfredo's father began his reign as mafia boss. Why would he come to Cal's aid after all he had done? Al Meransky, Joey Bartellini, Vinnie, Alfredo, and so many lower-level soldiers had all died at Cal's hands. These were men Doc Parker had befriended and treated at some point. Sure, the doc had treated Cal, too, but what made him so special?

"But I . . . I killed Alfredo," Cal finally stammered. "You stopped Susan from killing me. Why?"

Doc Parker shook his head and removed his spectacles. He stuck them in the front pocket of his white coat and patted it, as if he was pleased for the services the glasses had provided.

"Alfredo and I were friends for a long time, yes. I warned him that seeking revenge against you would do no good. I never approved of what Alfredo and the family did for a living, but I'm a businessman myself. I know that sometimes there's gonna be a little dirty work here and there. But kidnapping children and dragging them into a revenge ploy? Well, I didn't want to end my career picking that side."

Cal swallowed. He'd give anything for a glass of water. "So you're really retiring now?"

"Yep. Now that Alfredo's dead, there's no one I give two shits about that's still around. I think I'll finally take my wife up on the chance to move somewhere warmer. We're looking at Ecuador, but I've heard from a certain uncle that San Diego is nice."

Doc Parker winked at Cal and walked closer to him. His eyes shifted to the floor before struggling to find their way to Cal's face. Cal could see in the doc's eyes that something was going on. He was sure the doc had given a lot of tough news in his career and that his look of concern was a practiced look of empathy. Cal's heart pounded as he wondered what was to come.

"But before I head out of town, I'm afraid you're going to have to say goodbye to Chicago as well. Your uncle filled me in on what's going to happen after you're well enough to walk out of here. Even though you helped reunite a family and got a Chicago PD lieutenant's kid back, you're still wanted for several murders. These cops are demanding blood. There's a reason I took the Christmas shift besides the pay. There's a reason I pulled you out of that room, Cal. Plenty of patients don't make it in the confines of the ER or ICU. Lucky for you there's this rich young bastard that came in, coked out of his mind, with a few bullet wounds too. Must have been some drug bust gone bad. It won't be too long until he overdoses or dies from his injuries. There's enough of a resemblance there that I think we can make it work. If we just knife him up like Susan tried to do to you, I'm sure we can fool the fuzz long enough to get you out of here."

Cal remained motionless in his chair, not believing what he was hearing. Was the doc trying to help him escape? Why would he put himself on the line like this? Now that he had a real chance to retire, why risk it all to help Cal? After all, Cal knew he deserved every bit of punishment due to him.

"Let me get this straight. You want me to assume another man's identity? And you're gonna make it seem like Susan killed me?"

The doc nodded again. "Sure. I locked the door to your room on the way out. With the drug I gave Susan, she'll be asleep for a while. I'll just mix up the charts, come back with the other guy's body, plop him in your bed, make it seem like he was stabbed, and turn Susan over to the police."

The plan sounded less than foolproof. If Cal was going to go along with this, how did he know he'd be able to escape successfully? The cops weren't stupid. Eventually, they'd see that the doc's patient died from other circumstances and not from the stabbing of a crazed widow. They'd see that Susan had drugs in her system and that even if she stabbed someone it likely wasn't the patient in the room.

But all of that would take time—time that Cal desperately needed if he wanted a way out. Who cared what happened after that as long as he was home free?

"So what do I need to do? Just leave? Never come back?"

"That's the general idea. The guy you'll be trading places with, so to speak, is some fancy stockbroker in New York City. Or at least that's what Google says. Nurse tried to call an emergency contact or next of kin, but we haven't found anyone yet. Hopefully, there aren't too many people looking for him. If you wanna take a new ID once you get out of Dodge, be my guest. But that's what we've got to work with for now."

Cal knew that if he went through with Doc Parker's plan, his life would never be the same. He'd have to live an entirely different life, one on the run. He didn't know where he'd go, wasn't sure what he would do.

He thought back to the promise he'd made to Maria to live a life of good. Saving Tina Fregosi and Max Fisher from Alfredo's evil was one part of that. But was there more he could do? Maybe that was what he could focus on once he escaped.

Cal cleared his throat, still craving a glass of water. "It's not like you can just wheel me out of here."

"You're right about that. Grab some scrubs, put on your best Dr. McDreamy look, and get to the parking garage. Your uncle will take it from there."

Cal looked at the wheelchair and back up at the doc.

"Don't think for a second you can't walk. Sure, you're in pain, but you're a tough guy. Waltz your ass on out of here, Boyle, before I decide I don't want to go through with this."

53

Over a week after the last snows of Christmas had fallen upon the beautiful city of Chicago, Cal found himself in a place he wouldn't mind spending more time. He was surrounded by magnolia trees, not yet filling the air with their sweet fragrance, as well as sad, drooping willows, bowing toward the many inhabitants living permanently beneath the ground at Magnolia Cemetery in Charleston, South Carolina.

Even from his position on the road next to Uncle Judd's rented car, far enough away from Brittany Wilson's funeral procession to avoid the gaze of her Chicago police comrades that had made the trip to Brittany's hometown, Cal realized he was surrounded by history. Many Civil War soldiers and generals had been buried here. Taking a look around at the memorials, Confederate flags, and even a pyramid gave Cal an uneasy feeling. He wasn't sure why Brittany had wanted to be buried here, despite being from Charleston, but knew there was plenty of room for a real hero like her. His name would never be engraved on a tombstone in a grand place like this—that much he didn't deserve.

Uncle Judd stood quietly next to Cal. Like Cal, he donned a pair of shades to shield his eyes from the attention of the police. Even in the fifty-degree weather, Judd favored an outfit far more appropriate for Southern California, with a beige short-sleeved button-up and olive shorts. A pair of sand-colored flip-flops completed the look.

As the reverend read a barely audible chapter from his leather-bound Bible to the crowd, Judd finally turned to Cal.

"You loved her, didn't you?"

Cal twitched his jaw, the only movement he'd made since they arrived.

"What makes you think that? She put me in jail, remember."

"C'mon, I'm sure there were plenty of sparks that flew when she went in that apartment to help out."

Cal sighed. He wondered how the events of that night would've played out had Brittany never shown up. He knew he wouldn't be standing where he was today and that he'd likely be facing a burial much like Brittany was now. Alfredo and his cronies would've succeeded in killing him and probably would've killed Tina Fregosi and Max Fisher along with him. Two more families would be broken, and the Chicago mafia would continue to reign supreme over the city.

While Cal was pleased his former family was now broken and the Fregosi and Fisher families were happily reunited, he shed a tear that Brittany and her family had to suffer in the process. She'd been everything he wished he had the courage to be.

"She saved those kids' lives. That's what was important. I only wish I could've saved hers."

Uncle Judd said no more. Cal had already described the damage he sustained in the apartment, and Uncle Judd had seen Cal's wounds as part of helping Cal tend to his injuries. Cal had been warned by his uncle that he shouldn't make the trip to Brittany's funeral, that it was too risky, but Cal had insisted.

"Check your twelve," Uncle Judd said after some silence.

Cal watched as Mick Fisher, Brittany's boss, separated from the crowd of mourners and walked toward them. Uncle Judd slipped away like a thief in the night, leaving Cal alone to face a man who undoubtedly still wanted to bring him down.

Fisher walked with the swiftness of someone who knew they were in charge. His night-black suit jacket was unbuttoned and flapped in the gentle cool breeze as he walked. He, too, wore sunglasses, and Cal wondered if it was due to the sadness he felt at losing a promising detective like Brittany, or if it was simply to complete his tough-guy image.

He stopped once he reached Cal and put his hands on his hips. Cal knew he was taking a chance being here, but he wanted to pay his respects to Brittany, to honor the sacrifice she made.

The men stared at each other, seeing who would make the first move. When neither of them spoke, Fisher removed his hands from his hips and raised his head.

"Cal Boyle, we meet at last."

"I think you've got the wrong guy."

If Cal was going to hold firm with his new identity, he knew he'd have to play the part.

"Oh yeah? Who are you now? I was there, Cal, at the coroner's office, though I might've been the only one there that wasn't on the take. The guy they put in the ground wasn't you, it was someone else. How convenient, then, to make everyone else think you'd died just like Brittany. You really thought you could get away with it?"

Cal's heart leapt into his throat. He'd had a feeling Doc Parker's gimmick wouldn't work. He imagined a horde of police officers breaking away from Brittany's funeral and circling him, ready to haul him in for one of his countless crimes.

"My name is Chase Lyons. I'm a childhood friend of Brittany's. Now how can I help you, sir?"

Fisher laughed and turned back toward the crowd. The reverend was wrapping up, and members of Brittany's family were laying flowers on her casket. A man he believed to be Brittany's father laid down a colorful bouquet and kissed the top her casket, where Brittany's beautiful forehead would be. A tall woman with an Afro and amazingly long legs followed her father. It must have been Brittany's sister. Tears poured down her face.

"Look, let's cut the bullshit. I know goddamned well who you are. But none of my colleagues over there have a clue. They think you're as good as dead and that the case is closed. Hell, with so many of your mafia brethren dead, we may never be able to bring you to justice. Normally, that wouldn't sit too well with a man like me. I live for justice. I've spent my whole career fighting for it. There's nothing more I'd love than to close a few of those cold cases and put you behind bars so I can move on to the next big thing."

Fisher rubbed his chin and looked back at Cal. He removed his sunglasses, and Cal could see the softness in his eyes. This wasn't the expression of a man who was hell-bent on locking him up. It was the expression of a man who was tired, who had experienced too much pain.

"But I'm not gonna do that. When I saw you walk out of that apartment building holding my boy's hand and finally helping us save that little girl, I knew I'd be forever in your debt. I've seen a lot of kidnappings in my career. Had you not acted when you did, I'm not sure if I'd have gotten to see my little boy again. So I wanted to thank you, Cal. Thank you for saving my boy's life."

Cal felt his heartbeat slow, relief spreading through his chest as Fisher's somber eyes poured through him. He removed his sunglasses too. Would he actually be able to trust him? Was Fisher going to let him leave just like that?

"It was my honor. There was nothing more that I wanted than to save those kids."

Fisher patted Cal on the arm and turned back toward the crowd gathered around Brittany's casket. The group was starting to disperse, and Cal knew he needed to find a way to get out of there before he was discovered.

"Yeah, well. You also helped us oust Alfredo Petrocelli. Between that and bringing my boy back, I'll let your little charade slide. Just between you and me. You seem like a reformed man, Mr. Lyons. Keep fighting the good fight. I don't want to hear any more about you, you hear?"

Cal nodded and forced a smile. He'd be able to fight the good fight. The fight Maria and Brittany would want him to wage. He wasn't sure where his journey would take him next, but he was pleased he had Fisher in his corner.

He watched the lieutenant walk back toward the crowd and felt Uncle Judd place his hand on his shoulder.

"You still a free man?"

Cal turned to his uncle and smiled. He was glad to have someone by his side this time, someone who understood what he was going through. Someone who would make sure he wasn't consumed by the flames of revenge. If there was a man that could keep Cal steered in the right direction, it was Uncle Judd.

"I'm here, aren't I?"

Cal stopped, realizing he wasn't as definitive as he

wanted to be. Uncle Judd faced him, his wise eyes twinkling with the hint of acknowledgment.

"But? There's something you're not telling me."

"I may be free, Uncle, but the rest of the world isn't. Chicago may be free from Alfredo Petrocelli, and those children may be free from the mob, but there's a lot of people out there who aren't. Maria said it, Brittany hinted at it. Fisher made the same point. I've got to keep fighting the good fight."

Uncle Judd shook his head. "You don't have to do this, you don't have to be a martyr. Hell, you're a completely different person now. Why not just live your life?"

"Because I've made so many lives miserable. I've done more harm than good in my time on this earth. Every day from now on I'm going to work against that."

Uncle Judd squinted and tugged at his untrimmed goatee. "What type of work? How would you start?"

"I'm not sure yet. But if I've learned one thing, it's that trouble will find me. That's just the way it works."

GET YOUR FREE BOOK!

A HIT MAN IS BORN IN THIS RIVETING PREQUEL THRILLER

The wrong man is killed in a hit gone bad. A burgeoning drug war between the mafia and a rival gang has reached a tipping point. There's only one way this can end.

Callahan Boyle is new to his role as top hit man in the Chicago mafia and has a tough target in front of him. After following his mark for weeks, it turns out that when the deed is done that Cal has killed the wrong man. His victim? The seventeen year old brother of a rival gang leader battling with the mafia over drug territory in Chicago's South Side. On his quest to become a "made" man as a mafia outsider, Cal is caught between a power hungry mafia leadership and a warmongering drug gang. When the mafia and rival gang collide, all bets are off and all lives are at stake. Will Cal get his wish to become made and help the mafia win the drug territory they feel is rightfully theirs? Or does Cal fall victim to the most personal revenge ploy Chicago has ever seen?

Marked For Murder is a prequel novella that showcases Callahan Boyle early in his hit man career. If you like explosive shootouts, high speed car chases, and a never ending set of enemies, you've gotta grab Spenser Warren's latest Cal Boyle thriller.

Claim your FREE copy of the Cal Boyle prequel novella, *Marked For Murder*, by joining Spenser Warren's "hit list" today!

Visit the link below to get your free book and join the list.

spenserwarren.com/freebook

Enjoy this book? Make a difference with your review.

Reviews are a powerful tool in helping readers like you discover their new favorite reads. Your honest review of *Era of Evil* can make a huge difference in my career as a new author and introduce other readers that will love this book to my work.

If you've enjoyed this book, would you please take five minutes and leave a short review of *Era of Evil* on the book's Amazon page?

Thank you for your support. It means everything.

Spenser

ACKNOWLEDGMENTS

There's so much more to writing a book than meets the eye. For as much love, blood, sweat, and tears that I poured into writing this book, I haven't been alone in my dedication to the project. Deepest thanks to my amazing cover designer, Matt, for yet another amazing cover. I wondered how you would top the *Marked For Murder* cover, but you've managed to pull it off. I'd also like to thank my editor, Marcus, for his superb efforts in making my words sing on the page. My proofreader, Beth, was a lifesaver in catching items I would've otherwise missed, not to mention a great "sanity check" for some of my wilder bits of prose.

Even though it's only been a few months since I published my first novel, *One Last Kill,* it would be wrong to not give another huge shout-out to my family and friends that cheered me on as I wrote this book. Mom, Dad, Alex, Diane, Nannie, and an ever-growing army of family, friends, and readers have been there with me every step of the way, asking me what was new with the book and when it was coming out. You pushed me to make it my best, and for that I thank you.

Lastly, a huge thanks to you, adventurous reader. There are many great authors and books to read these days and it means the world to me that you've chosen my book for your latest reading adventure. Thank you, and I hope we meet again.

ABOUT THE AUTHOR

Spenser Warren is the author of *One Last Kill* and *Era of Evil,* the first two novels in the Callahan Boyle series. When he isn't busy at work on his next novel, Spenser is often reading, catching a comedy or improv show, and desperately rooting for a doomed Chicago White Sox rebuild. You can get in touch with Spenser at his website, spenserwarren.com, or by connecting with him on social media. Spenser lives in Chicago.

BOOKS BY SPENSER WARREN

Marked For Murder

One Last Kill

Era of Evil

www.ingramcontent.com/pod-product-compliance
Lightning Source LLC
Chambersburg PA
CBHW020328030826
48979CB00021B/479
* 9 7 8 1 7 3 2 9 9 0 1 7 3 *